RUSSIAN
AND SOVIET Story

L.Tolstoy

FATHER SERGIUS AND OTHER STORIES

Raduga Publishers Moscow

Translated from the Russian
Designed by *Alexander Valdman*

ЛЕВ ТОЛСТОЙ
Повести. Рассказы

На английском языке

Printed in the Union of Soviet Socialist Republics

ISBN 5—05—002048—4

CONTENTS

THE RAID

A VOLUNTEER'S STORY

I

On 12 July Captain Khlopov appeared at the low door of my hut. He was wearing epaulettes and a sword—a uniform in which I had never seen him since I came to the Caucasus.

"I've come straight from the colonel," he said in reply to my questioning look. "Our battalion is to set out tomorrow."

"Where to?" I asked.

"To N. The troops are to assemble there."

"And from there I suppose there will be some sort of offensive?"

"I expect so."

"In which direction, do you think?"

"Think? All I can tell you is what I know. Last night a Tatar brought orders from the general for the battalion to set out and to take enough rusks to last two days. But as for where to, or why, or for how long?—that's not for us to ask. The order is to march, and that's that."

"But if they've to take rations for only two days, presumably that's as long as the troops will be out."

"No, that means nothing..."

"How can that be?" I asked in surprise.

"It can! When we went to Dargo we took rations for a week and ended up nearly a month there!"

"May I come with you?" I asked after a short silence.

"You may come if you like, but my advice would be not to. Why run the risk?"

"If you don't mind, I shan't take your advice: I've been waiting here a whole month just for a chance to see some action, and you want me to miss it!"

"Well, suit yourself, but you'd really do better to stay behind. You could wait for us here, do some hunting—and we'd get on with it! That would be splendid!" he said so convincingly that for a moment I also felt it would be "splendid". Nonetheless, I said that nothing would induce me to stay.

"But what do you expect to see there?" the captain continued trying to dissuade me. "If you want to know what battles are like, read Mikhailovsky-Danilevsky's *Description of the War**. It's a marvellous book—all the details are described: where each corps was

* Or more precisely, *Description of the Patriotic War of 1812*, about the war against Napoleon's *Grande Armée*.– Tr.

positioned, how the battles developed."

"But that's exactly what I'm *not* interested in," I replied.

"What do you want, then? Just to see people being killed? In 1832 there was another civilian here, a Spaniard, I think he was. He went on two expeditions with us, wearing a sort of blue cloak. Well, he got killed, of course. That sort of thing cuts no ice here, old chap."

However shamed I was by the captain's misjudgment of my intentions, I did not try to deny it.

"Was he brave?" I asked.

"God knows; he used to ride out ahead all the time: wherever there was firing, there you'd find him."

"So he must have been brave, then?"

"No, it doesn't mean a man's brave because he pushes in where he's not wanted."

"What would you call brave?"

"Brave? Brave?" the captain repeated with the air of someone considering a question for the first time. "*A brave man*," he said after some thought, "*is one who behaves as he ought to do*."

I recalled that Plato defined bravery as *the knowledge of what should and what should not be feared*, and despite the generality and vagueness of the captain's definition, it occurred to me that the two definitions were basically not as different as they might seem to be, and that the captain's was even truer than Plato's because, had he been able to express himself as well as the Greek philosopher, the captain might have said that a brave man is one who fears *only what ought to be feared*, and not *what should not be feared*.

I wanted to explain this thought to the captain.

"Yes," I said, "I think that in every dangerous situation there is a choice to be made, and a choice determined by, say, a sense of duty, is bravery, whereas a choice determined by a base feeling is cowardice. Therefore a man who risks his life out of vanity, or curiosity, or avarice, cannot be called brave; and on the other hand a man who avoids a dangerous situation because of an honest sense of family obligation, or simply out of conviction, cannot be called a coward."

While I spoke, the captain regarded me with a rather strange expression.

"Well, that I cannot dispute with you," he said, filling his pipe, "but we have a cadet here who's fond of philosophising. Have a talk with him. He writes poetry too."

I had only got to know the captain in the Caucasus, though I had heard of him back in Russia. His mother, Maria Ivanovna Khlopova, owns a small estate less than two miles from mine. I visited her before I left for the Caucasus; the old woman was overjoyed that I would see her Pashenka (as she endearingly called the elderly and grey-haired captain) and that I could tell him all about her and deliver a small parcel. Having treated me to delicious pie and smoked duck, Maria Ivanovna went into her bedroom and returned with a fairly large black pouch containing an amulet and tied with a silk ribbon, also black.

"This is Our Lady of the Burning Bush," she said. She crossed herself, kissed the icon and gave it to me. "Please give it to him, sir. When he went to the Caucasus, you see, I prayed for him in church and vowed that if he remained alive and well I would have this icon of the Mother of God made for him. For eighteen years now the Holy Mother and the Saints have protected him: what battles he has been in, but he has not been wounded once! Believe me, from what Mikhailo, who was with him, told me—it's enough to make your hair stand on end. You see, all I know about him is what I hear from others: he never writes me anything about his campaigns, the dear boy, for fear of frightening me."

(Later in the Caucasus I learnt, though not from the captain himself, that he had been seriously wounded four times but, needless to say, had never written to his mother either about his wounds or his campaigns.)

"So tell him to wear this holy image now," his mother continued, "which I send him with my blessing. The Holy Mother will keep him! Especially in battles, that's when he must wear it. Tell him so, my good sir, tell him his mother wishes it."

I promised to carry out her instructions to the letter.

"I know you will like my Pashenka," continued the old woman. "He's such a dear! Do you know, there's never a year goes by but that he sends me money. He helps my daughter, Annushka, a lot too. And all he has is his pay, mind you. Yes," she concluded with tears in her eyes, "I thank the Lord with all my heart for giving me such a son."

"Does he write to you often?" I asked.

"Seldom, sir. Once a year, when he sends money, he writes a word or two, but not otherwise. He says if he doesn't write that means he's alive and well; and if—God forbid—something happens they'll let me know soon enough."

When I gave Captain Khlopov the present from his mother (it was in my own quarters), he asked for some paper, carefully wrapped it up, and put it away. I told him all the details I knew of his mother's life. He said nothing, and when I had finished, he went over to a corner of the room and spent a long time filling his pipe.

"Yes, she's a fine old lady," he said in a rather muffled voice, still standing there. "I wonder if God will let me see her again."

These simple words expressed a great deal of love and sadness.

"Why do you serve here?" I asked.

"One has to serve," he answered with conviction. "And the double pay here means a lot to the likes of us poor folk."

Captain Khlopov lived economically: he didn't play cards, rarely went carousing, and smoked the cheapest tobacco. I had always liked the captain: he had one of those simple, calm Russian faces with eyes it is easy and pleasant to look into. And after this conversation I felt real respect for him.

II

At four o'clock the next morning the captain came for me. He was wearing an old threadbare coat without epaulettes, wide Caucasian trousers and a sheepskin hat, once white but now yellowed and shabby, and he had an inferior Asiatic sabre strapped across his shoulder. The little white horse he rode ambled along, dipping its head and constantly swinging its scraggy tail. Although the good captain's aspect was neither very martial nor handsome, it expressed such equanimity towards everything around him that it involuntarily inspired respect.

I did not keep him waiting, but mounted my horse at once, and we rode out of the fortress gates together.

The battalion, already some five hundred yards ahead of us, looked like a dense, heaving, black mass. One could tell that they were infantry only by their bayonets, which looked like a forest of needles, and by the snatches of drumming and singing that reached us, including the magnificent voice of the Sixth Company's second tenor, which I'd often admired back at the fortress. The road ran through a deep, wide ravine, following the bank of a small river which was then in spate. Flocks of wild doves whirled overhead, sometimes settling on the rocky riverbank, sometimes wheeling and turning through the air and vanishing from sight. The sun was not yet visible, but the crest of the right slope of the ravine was beginning to brighten. The grey and whitish stones, the yellow-green moss, the dew-covered bushes of brambleberry, dogwood and elm were all picked out with great clarity in the transparent golden light of the dawn. The other slope, however, and the valley which was full of floating smoky layers of thick fog, were dank and gloomy and presented an elusive mixture of hues: pale lilacs, shades of black, dark green and white. Straight ahead of us, strikingly sharp against the dark azure of the horizon, rose the brilliant white masses of the snow-covered mountains, their shadows and outlines whimsical but exquisite in every detail. Crickets, grasshoppers and thousands of other insects awoke in the tall grasses and filled the air with their clear and ceaseless sounds, as though countless tiny bells were ringing in our ears. The air smelled of water, grass and fog—the scent of a beautiful summer morning. The captain struck a flint and lit his pipe; the smell of his cheap tobacco and tinder seemed to me extraordinarily pleasant.

We rode to one side of the track in order to catch up quickly with the infantry. Captain Khlopov seemed more pensive than usual, never taking his Daghestan pipe from his mouth and prodding his horse with his heels at every step. The horse, swaying from side to side, left a barely perceptible dark green track in the tall wet grass. From under its hooves, with the cry and the whirr of wings that makes a huntsman start, a pheasant flew out and slowly rose into the sky. The captain paid not the slightest heed to it.

We had almost reached the battalion when we heard a horse galloping behind us, and then a dashing young chap in an officer's uniform and a tall white sheepskin cap overtook us. As he passed us, he smiled, nodded to the captain and flourished his whip. I only had time to notice the peculiar grace in the way he sat in the saddle and held the reins, his wonderful dark eyes, his fine nose and bare beginnings of a moustache. What I liked most about him was that he could not help smiling when he noticed our admiration. From this smile alone one could tell that he was still very young.

"Where's he racing to?" muttered the captain with a disgruntled air, his pipe still in his mouth.

"Who is he?" I asked.

"Ensign Alanin, a subaltern in my

company. He only arrived last month from the cadet corps."

"So this is his first taste of action?" I asked.

"That's why he's so pleased!" answered the captain with a thoughtful shake of the head. "Youth!"

"But how can he help being pleased? I imagine it must be very interesting for a young officer."

The captain remained silent for a minute or so.

"That's just what I mean: youth!" he continued in a deep voice. "It's all very well being pleased when you haven't seen anything, but after you've seen it a few times you're not so pleased. Take today, for instance—of the twenty officers going into action you can be sure at least one of us will be killed or wounded. Me today, him tomorrow, someone else the next day. What's there to be pleased about?"

III

As soon as the bright sun appeared above the hill and began to light up the valley along which the troops were marching, the wavy clouds of fog lifted and it grew hot. The soldiers, laden with rifles and knapsacks, trudged slowly along the dusty road. Laughter and Ukrainian speech could be heard from

time to time. Several old soldiers in white
tunics—most of them were non-commissioned
officers—walked by the roadside smoking
pipes and conversing gravely. Heavily laden
wagons, each drawn by a team of three
horses, moved steadily on, raising clouds of
dust that hung in the air. The officers rode
out ahead: some were parading their horses,
whipping them to make them leap a few
times, then bringing them to an abrupt halt
with a jerk of the head; others were busy with
the singers, who sang song after song despite
the sultry heat.

A couple of hundred yards ahead of the
infantry rode some Tatar horsemen, and with
them, on a large white stallion, a tall
handsome officer in Caucasian costume, who
was known in the regiment for his reckless
courage and sharp tongue, regardless of whom
he was talking to. He was dressed in a black
beshmet trimmed with gold lace, leggings to
match, new close-fitting soft Caucasian boots,
also trimmed with gold, and a yellow Circassian
caftan. His tall sheepskin hat was tilted back
from his forehead. Over his chest and back
were silver straps to which were attached
a powder flask and a pistol. A second pistol
and a silver-mounted dagger hung from his
belt. At his side he wore a sword in a red
morocco sheath, and over his shoulder was
slung a rifle in a black case. His clothes, his
posture, his bearing and all his movements
indicated that he was trying to resemble

a Tatar. He even said something in a language I did not know to the Tatars with whom he was riding; but the perplexed, mocking glances which these Tatars exchanged suggested that they did not understand him either.

He was one of our young dare-devil officers who model themselves on the romantic heroes of Marlinsky and Lermontov. These men see the Caucasus only through the prism of the "Mullah-Nurs" and the other "heroes of our time"*, and in all their actions are guided not by their own inclinations but by the examples of their models.

This lieutenant, for example, probably enjoyed the company of well-bred women and important men such as colonels and aides-de-camps—indeed I am certain that he liked such company very much, for he was conceited in the extreme—but he considered it his imperative duty to be rude to all important men (though quite moderately so), and when any lady appeared at the fortress he felt obliged to parade under her windows with his Tatar cronies, wearing only a red shirt and slippers without leggings, and shouting and swearing loudly; all this was done not so much with a desire to offend her as to show her what wonderful white legs he had, and how easy it would be for her to fall in love with him if he should so desire. He also

* Cf. the romantic novels *Mullah-Nur* by A. Bestuzhev-Marlinsky and *A Hero of Our Time* by Mikhail Lermontov.

often went out into the hills at night with two or three friendly Tatars to ambush and kill some passing unfriendly Tatars; and though his heart told him that there was nothing heroic about it, he felt he had to cause suffering to people who had disappointed him in some way or whom he professed to despise or hate.

He always had two things with him: a large icon hanging round his neck, and a dagger which he wore above his shirt, even in bed. He sincerely believed that he had enemies, and to convince himself that he had to take vengeance upon somebody and wash away some insult with blood was sheer pleasure for him. He was sure that hatred, vengeance and contempt for the human race were the highest and most poetic of emotions.

But his mistress—a Circassian girl, of course—whom I happened to meet later, said that he was an extremely kind, meek person, and that every evening he would collect his gloomy thoughts in a diary, draw up his accounts on ruled paper, then get down on his knees and pray to God. And what torments he went through just to appear in his own eyes as he wished to be—for his fellow officers and the soldiers would never see him as he wanted to be seen.

On one of his nocturnal expeditions with his Tatar fellows, he chanced to wound an unfriendly Chechen in the leg with a bullet, and take him captive. For seven weeks he nursed and looked after his victim as though he were a close friend, and when he was well again he gave him gifts and set him free. Some time later, while retreating after an army raid, and firing back at the enemy, the lieutenant suddenly heard a voice calling his name from the enemy side, and then saw the man he had wounded riding forward and signing to him to do the same. The lieutenant rode out to meet his old friend and shook his hand. The other Chechens stood some way off and did not shoot; but as soon as the lieutenant turned his horse around, several of them fired at him, and one bullet grazed the small of his back.

Another time, a fire broke out in the fortress and two companies of soldiers tried to put it out. Among the crowd, lit up in the red glow of the fire, I suddenly saw the tall figure of a man on a black horse. Pushing the crowd aside, he rode right up to the fire, leapt from his horse and ran into the burning house. Five minutes later the lieutenant re-appeared with singed hair and a badly burnt arm, clutching to his bosom two pigeons which he had rescued from the flames.

His name was Rosenkranz. But he often spoke of his ancestry, tracing it back to the Varangians, and thus clearly demonstrated that he and his forbears were pure Russians.

IV

The sun had completed half its journey and was beating down through the burning air on the dry earth. The dark-blue sky was perfectly clear; only around the base of the snowy mountains were pale lilac clouds appearing. The motionless air seemed full of a kind of transparent dust. It was growing unbearably hot.

Upon reaching a small river about half way to our destination, we halted. The soldiers stacked their muskets and rushed to the water. The battalion commander sat down on a drum in the shade, and, expressing the greatness of his rank on his fat face, prepared to have a snack with some other officers. The captain lay down on the grass under his company's wagon. The brave lieutenant Rosenkranz and some other young officers settled themselves on their outspread cloaks, intending to have a good time, judging by the bottles and flasks arranged around them, and by the animation of the singers standing in a semi-circle before them, who whistled and sang a Caucasian dance-song:

Shamil* thought he could rebel,
In years gone by,

* Shamil was the ruler of Daghestan and Chechnia (North-Eastern Caucasus) from 1834. For 25 years he led the Caucasian hillsmen in their war against Russia. Finally defeated in 1859, Shamil was taken prisoner and exiled to Russia.

Tra-ra, ra-ta-ta,
In years gone by...

Among these officers was the young ensign who had overtaken us in the morning. He was very amusing: his eyes sparkled, he was a little tongue-tied—he felt like kissing everyone and declaring how much he liked them... The poor lad! He did not yet realise that this might make him look ridiculous, that the openness and tenderness with which he thrust himself upon everyone predisposed them not to affection but to derision; nor did he know how fetching he looked when he passionately flung himself down at last on his cloak and rested on his elbow, tossing back his thick black hair.

Two officers were sitting by a wagon playing cards, using a provisions box as a table.

I listened curiously to the soldiers' and officers' conversations and closely studied their expressions. But in none of them could I observe the slightest trace of the unease which I myself felt; their jokes, laughter and tittle-tattle suggested a complete indifference to the impending danger. That some of them were fated never to return by this road, appeared not even to cross their minds.

V

After six that evening, dusty and tired, we entered the wide gate of the fortress at N. The sun was setting, throwing its slanting rose-coloured rays over the tall Lombardy poplars in the gardens surrounding the fortress, over the yellow cornfields and on the white clouds, low in the sky, no less fantastic and beautiful than the snowy mountains which they seemed to be trying to imitate. The new moon hung over the horizon like a translucent cloudlet. In the nearby Tatar village, a Mohammedan was calling the faithful to prayer from a rooftop. Our singers raised their voices with renewed vigour and enthusiasm.

I rested and tidied myself up a bit, then went to call on an aide-de-camp of my acquaintance to ask him to inform the general of my intention. On the way from the suburb where I was billeted I noticed in the fortress things I did not at all expect to see. I was passed by a smart two-seater carriage, in which I apprehended a fashionable bonnet and the sound of French being spoken. From the open window of the commandant's house came the strains of a polka, played on a piano that needed tuning. As I passed a tavern I saw some clerks with cigarettes in their hands, drinking wine, and heard one of them remark, "No, when it comes to politics, old chap, Maria Grigorievna is foremost among our ladies." A Jew in a threadbare coat, with a bent back and a sickly countenance, was dragging a whining barrel-organ, and the whole suburb resounded to the finale of *Lucia*. Two women in rustling dresses, with silk kerchiefs on their heads and brightly coloured parasols in their hands, floated by along the wooden pavement. Two girls, one in a pink dress, the other in blue, stood bareheaded outside a low-roofed house, giggling in an affected manner, evidently to attract the attention of passing officers. The officers, in turn, were strutting up and down the street and the boulevard, dressed in new uniforms with white gloves and shining epaulettes.

I found my acquaintance on the ground floor of the general's house. I had barely time to explain my wish to him and to hear that it could easily be arranged, before the smart carriage I had seen earlier rattled past the window and stopped at the porch. A tall, well-built man in the uniform of an infantry major got out and entered the house.

"Oh, excuse me, please," said the aide, rising. "I must announce them to the general."

"Who is it that's come?" I asked.

"The countess," he said, and rushed upstairs, buttoning his uniform.

A few minutes later a smallish, but very handsome man in a frock-coat without epaulettes and with a white cross in his buttonhole, went out into the porch, accompanied by the major, the aide and two other officers. The general's gait, his voice, and all his movements betrayed a man with a high opinion of his own worth.

"*Bonsoir, madame la comtesse,*" he said, offering his hand through the carriage window.

A hand in a kid glove pressed his, and a pretty, smiling face in a yellow bonnet appeared at the window.

Of their conversation, which lasted several minutes, I only overheard the smiling general say as I passed, "*Vous savez, que j'ai fait voeu de combattre les infidèles; prenez donc garde de la devenir.*"

There was laughter in the carriage.

"*Adieu donc, cher général.*"

"*Non, au revoir,*" said the general as he climbed the steps of the porch. "*N'oubliez pas, que je m'invite pour la soirée de demain.*"

The carriage rattled off down the street.

"There is a man," I thought on my way home, "who possesses all that Russians strive after: rank, wealth, station. And this man, on the eve of a battle which could end God knows how, jokes with a pretty woman and promises to take tea with her, just as if he had met her at a ball!"

Later, at the house of the same aide-de-camp, I met somebody who surprised me even more. He was a young lieutenant of the K. regiment, a man of almost feminine meekness and timidity, who had called on the aide to pour out his vexation and indignation regard-

ing certain people whom he alleged were
intriguing to keep him out of the forthcoming
operation. He said it was caddish to behave
in such a way, that it let the side down, that
he wouldn't forget it, and so forth. The
more I studied his expression and listened to
the tone of his voice, the more convinced
I was that he was not putting on an act
but was genuinely outraged and grieved that
he was not to be allowed to go and shoot at
the Circassians and expose himself in turn to
their fire. He was as indignant as a child who
has been unjustly spanked... It made no sense
whatsoever to me.

VI

The troops were to move out at ten in the
evening. At half past eight I mounted and
rode to the general's. Assuming that he and
his aide would be busy, I did not go in but
tied my horse to await him.

The heat and glare of the sun had already
given place to the coolness of the night and
the pale shimmer of the new moon that was
just beginning to set against the dark starry
sky. Lights appeared in the windows of the
houses and shone through cracks in the
shutters of the earth huts. Beyond these
whitewashed, moonlit huts with their rush-
thatched roofs, the slender poplars on the
horizon seemed taller and blacker than ever.

The houses, trees and fences cast long and attractive shadows over the dusty roadway... From the river came the ringing call of frogs.* In the streets there was the sound of hurried steps and voices, then the gallop of a horse. And from the suburb drifted the strains of the barrel-organ, playing *The Winds Are Blowing*, and then some waltz.

I will not say what my thoughts were, first, because I am ashamed of the gloom that filled my heart, while all around me I saw nothing but gaiety and joy, and secondly because they are irrelevant to my story. I was so lost in thought that I did not even notice the bell striking eleven and the general with his officers riding past me.

Hastily mounting my horse, I hurried to catch up with the detachment.

The rearguard was still inside the fort, and I had great difficulty in making my way across the bridge among the guns, ammunition-wagons, supply carts, and officers shouting their orders. Once I was through the gates, I trotted past the troops, who were silently moving through the darkness, stretched out in a line nearly a mile long, and eventually I reached the general. As I passed the guns, drawn out in single file with the officers riding between them, I heard a grating German voice, discordant amid the quiet,

---

* Frogs in the Caucasus make a noise quite different from the croaking of Russian frogs.—*L. T.*

solemn harmony of the occasion, shouting,
"Herr Gott, give me a linstock!" followed by
the eager voice of a soldier: "Shevchenko, the
lieutenant wants a light."

The greater part of the sky was covered
with long, dark-grey clouds, with only a few
dim stars twinkling here and there among
them. The moon was now hidden behind the
black mountains on the near horizon to our
right, outlining their peaks in a faint, trembling
light that contrasted sharply with the impenetrable darkness enveloping the foothills.
The air was warm, and it was so still that it
seemed as if not a blade of grass, not a single
cloudlet, was moving. It was so dark that even
objects close at hand could not be made out:
by the sides of the road I felt I could see
rocks, or animals, or strange human figures,
and it was only when I heard them rustle, or
felt the freshness of the dew with which they
were sprinkled, that I realised they were
bushes.

Before me I saw a dense quivering wall,
followed by several dark spots; this was the
cavalry vanguard and the general with his
officers. Behind us moved another dark mass,
lower than the cavalry: this was the infantry.

The whole detachment was so silent that
all the mingling, mysterious sounds of the
night could clearly be heard: the mournful
howling of faraway jackals, sounding now like
sobbing, now like laughter; the sonorous,
repetitive songs of crickets, frogs, quails;

a rumbling noise, drawing closer, the cause of
which I could not fathom. These sounds, and
all the other nocturnal sounds of nature,
barely audible and impossible to understand
or define, merged into that beautiful harmony
which we call the stillness of night. This stillness was disturbed by—or rather, harmonised
with—the dull thud of hoofs and the swishing
of the tall grass as the detachment slowly
advanced.

Only very occasionally did one hear the
clang of a heavy gun, the ring of bayonets
clashing, restrained voices, or the snorting of
a horse.

Nature seemed to breathe nothing but
pacifying beauty and power.

Could it be that there was not room for
all men to live in this wonderful world, under
this fathomless starry sky? Was it really possible that in the midst of such natural
splendour, feelings of hatred and vengeance,
or the passion to destroy one's fellows, could
reside in the hearts of men? All that is evil in
man should—one would think—disappear
on contact with nature, the most direct
expression of beauty and goodness.

VII

We had been riding for more than two
hours. I was beginning to shiver and feel
drowsy. In the darkness I could dimly make

out the same vague shapes as before: a little way ahead, the dark wall and the moving spots; beside me the crupper of a white horse, flicking its tail and walking with its hind legs wide apart the back of a white Circassian coat, with a rifle in a black case bouncing on it, and the butt of a pistol in an embroidered holster; the glow of a cigarette, throwing light on a fair moustache; a beaver collar, and a hand in a kid glove. Sometimes I leant forward over my horse's neck, closed my eyes and forgot myself for a few minutes; then the familiar tramping and rustling would suddenly bring me to my senses and I would glance up, feeling as though I were standing still and the black wall in front were moving towards me, or as though the wall had stopped and I were about to ride into it. On one of these occasions I became more strongly aware than ever of the rumbling noise which I had been unable to explain: it was the sound of water. We were entering a deep gorge, drawing close to a mountain river in spate.* The roar grew louder, the damp grass grew thicker and taller, there were more and more bushes about, and the horizon gradually closed in. Now and then bright lights flared up at various points in the dark mountains, and vanished instantly.

"Do you know what those lights are?" I whispered to a Tatar riding beside me.

"Don't you know?" he answered.

---

* Rivers in the Caucasus tend to flood in July.—L. T.

"No."

"It's the mountain people: they tie bundles of straw to poles, set them alight, and wave them about."

"Why do they do that?"

"To let everyone know the Russians are coming. Oh-ho," he added with a laugh, "what a hubbub there must be in the villages just now—everyone will be grabbing his belongings and going down into the gorge."

"Surely they don't know already, so far away in the mountains, that a detachment is on its way?"

"Of course they do! They always know—that's the way we Tatars are!"

"Then their leader Shamil must be preparing for action too?" I ventured.

"No," replied the Tatar, shaking his head. "Shamil won't take part himself. He'll send his aides, while he watches the action through a telescope from above."

"Does he live far away?"

"No, not far. Over there, to the left, about seven miles away."

"How do you know?" I asked. "Have you been there?"

"Yes. All our people have been there."

"Have you seen Shamil?"

"Huh! The likes of us don't see Shamil! He has guards all round him—a hundred, three hundred, maybe a thousand of them, with Shamil somewhere in the middle!" he exclaimed with an expression of servile respect.

Overhead, the sky had cleared and was beginning to brighten in the east, while in the west the Pleiades were sinking towards the horizon. But in the gorge through which we were moving, it was still damp and gloomy.

Suddenly, a little way ahead of us, several lights flashed in the darkness, and bullets whistled past. The shots rang out through the silence, together with a loud, shrill cry. This was the enemy's outlying picket; they whooped, shot again at random, and scattered.

When it became quiet again, the general summoned his interpreter. The Tatar in the white Circassian coat rode up to him and spoke with him for some time, whispering and gesticulating.

"Colonel Khasanov, tell the men to march in open order," drawled the general, quietly but distinctly.

The detachment advanced to the river, leaving the black slopes of the gorge behind. It began to grow light. The vault of the heavens, still dotted with pale stars, seemed higher. The dawn began to glow brightly in the east, while from the west blew a fresh, chilling breeze, and a silvery mist rose like steam over the rushing river.

VIII

Our guide showed us where there was a ford, and the cavalry vanguard, followed by the general and his officers, started to cross the river. The horses were up to their chests in water, which gushed with tremendous force around the white rocks that protruded above the surface here and there, and spumed and surged around the animals' legs. The horses, surprised by the noise of the water, lifted their heads and pricked their ears, but they stepped steadily and carefully forward through the strong current over the uneven riverbed. The riders pulled up their feet and their weapons. The footsoldiers, literally in nothing but their shirts, with their clothes tied in bundles to their rifles and raised high above the water, formed groups of twenty, arm in arm, and braved the current, tremendous strain evident on their faces. The mounted artillerymen let out a yell and drove their horses into the water at a trot. The water splashed over the guns and the green ammunition-wagons, and their wheels rang against the stony bottom. But the sturdy horses pulled for all their worth, and eventually emerged from the foaming water with dripping tails and manes, and clambered up onto the opposite bank.

As soon as the crossing was completed, the general's face suddenly became thoughtful and serious. He turned his horse and, followed by the cavalry, trotted off through the broad forest clearing that opened out before us. A cordon of mounted Cossacks was deployed around the edges of the forest.

In the wood we espied a man on foot

dressed in a Circassian coat and a tall sheepskin hat. Another appeared, then a third.
One of the officers said, "They're Tatars."
Just then a puff of smoke appeared from
behind a tree, then came the report, then
another... The sound of our rapid fire
drowned the enemy's; only now and then
a bullet would fly past, buzzing like a bee,
as if to prove that not all the shots were ours.
The infantry ran quickly to join the cordon,
followed by the guns at a trot. I could hear
the guns booming, the metallic sound of
flying case-shot, the hissing of rockets, and
the crackle of rifle-fire. All over the wide
glade I could see cavalry, infantry and artillery.
The puffs of smoke from the cannon, rockets
and rifles mingled with the mist and the dewy
verdure. Colonel Khasanov galloped up to the
general and abruptly reined in his horse.

"Your Excellency," he said, raising his
hand to his cap, "shall I order the cavalry to
charge? The enemy colours are in sight." He
pointed with his whip towards a group of
Tatar horsemen, led by two men on white
horses, carrying long sticks adorned at the
top with a piece of red or blue cloth.

"Go on then, Ivan Mikhailich, God be
with you!" said the general.

The colonel turned his horse on the spot,
drew his sabre and cried, "Hurrah!"

"Hurrah! Hurrah! Hurrah!" echoed from
the ranks, and the cavalry charged after him.

Everyone watched in fascination: here

a banner flashed, there another, a third,
a fourth...

Without waiting for the attack the enemy
hid in the forest and opened fire from there.
Bullets were flying thicker.

"Quel charmant coup d'oeil!" said the
general, rising slightly, English fashion, in the
saddle of his slim-legged black horse.

"Charmant!" agreed the major, rolling his
r's and striking his horse as he rode up to the
general. *"C'est un vrrai plaisirr, que la guerre
dans un aussi beau pays."*

"Et surtout en bonne compagnie," added
the general with a pleasant smile.

The major bowed.

At that moment an enemy cannon-ball
flew past with an unpleasant hiss and hit
something. Behind us we heard the moan
of a wounded man. This moan had such a
strange effect on me that the battle instantly
lost all its charm for me. But nobody else
appeared to notice it: the major was laughing
with great gusto; another officer was repeating with perfect calm what he had been saying
before he was interrupted by the cannon-
ball; the general was looking in the opposite
direction and said something in French with
the calmest of smiles.

"Shall we fire back at them?" asked the
artillery commander, galloping up.

"Yes, give 'em a scare!" said the general
off-handedly as he lit a cigar.

The battery took up position and the firing

began. The earth groaned; lights kept flashing
all around; and my eyes were stung by the
smoke, through which I could barely discern
the artillerymen moving by the guns.

The village was being bombarded. Colonel
Khasanov again rode up, and at the general's
command galloped off to the village. The
war-cry was raised again and the colonel's
cavalry disappeared in its own cloud of dust.

It was a truly magnificent spectacle. The
only thing that spoiled the whole impression
for me—as an outsider, unaccustomed to it
and not really participating—was that all this
movement, and enthusiasm, and shouting,
seemed rather pointless. I could not help
thinking of a man wielding an axe and hitting
only air.

IX

By the time the general and his retinue, to
which I had attached myself, reached the
village, it was already occupied by our troops,
and not one of the enemy remained in it.

The long, clean huts of the village, with
their flat earthen roofs and picturesque chim-
neys, were scattered over hilly, stony ground
with a stream flowing through it. On one side,
green gardens with enormous pear and plum
trees in them, were flooded with sunlight;
on the other side, strange shadows were cast
by tall upright gravestones and long poles

with balls and multicoloured flags fastened to them. These were the graves of the *djigits*, the best warriors.

The troops were assembled outside the village gates.

A moment later, a stream of dragoons, Cossacks and infantrymen was pouring through the crooked lanes, and the village instantly came to life. Somewhere a roof collapsed, and an axe resounded against a sturdy wooden door. In another place, a haystack, a fence and a hut burst into flames, and a column of thick smoke rose into the clear sky. One Cossack was dragging a sack of flour and a carpet. A soldier with a joyful face emerged from a hut carrying a tin basin and some cloth. Another, with outstretched arms, was chasing two hens which were cackling and beating their wings beside a fence. A third had found a huge pot of milk somewhere, drank from it, then flung it away with a loud guffaw.

The battalion with which I had come from the fortress was also in the village. Captain Khlopov was sitting on the roof of a hut, smoking his cheap tobacco and emitting a stream of smoke with such a disinterested air that, when I caught sight of him, I forgot I was in a hostile village and felt quite at home.

"Aha, so you're here?" he said, noticing me.

The tall figure of Lieutenant Rosenkranz

was flitting around the village. He kept issuing orders and looked extremely busy. I saw him coming out of one of the huts with a triumphant look on his face; after him came two soldiers leading an old Tatar. The old man, whose only clothing consisted of a colourful but tattered shirt and a pair of much-patched trousers, was so frail that his bony arms, tightly bound behind his bent back, seemed ready to part company with his shoulders, and he could barely move his twisted, bare feet. His face, and even part of his shaven head, were furrowed with deep wrinkles. His distorted, toothless mouth, set between a close-cut grey moustache and beard, kept moving as though he were chewing something. But his red lashless eyes still gleamed with a fire, and clearly expressed his old man's indifference to life.

Rosenkranz asked him through an interpreter why he had not left with the others.

"Where could I go?" he said, quietly looking away.

"Where the others have gone," someone remarked.

"The *djigits* have gone to fight the Russians, but I am an old man."

"Aren't you afraid of the Russians?"

"What can the Russians do to me? I'm old," he said, glancing carelessly round the circle which had formed about him.

Later, when we were returning, I saw this same old man jolting along behind a Cossack's saddle, arms tied and bareheaded, and still looking round with the same impassive expression. He was needed to be exchanged for Russian captives.

I climbed onto the roof and sat beside the captain.

"It seems there weren't many of the enemy," I said, wishing to hear his opinion of the raid.

"The enemy?" he repeated with surprise. "There weren't any at all! Can you call that the enemy? You wait till the evening, when we're leaving—you'll see plenty of 'em pouring out then to see us off!" He pointed with his pipe to a neck of woodland we had passed that morning.

"What's that?" I asked anxiously, interrupting the captain and pointing at a group of Don Cossacks who had collected around something not far from us.

From that direction came the sound of something like a baby's cry and the words: "Stop, don't cut it ... they'll see... Have you got a knife, Yevstigneich?"

"They're up to no good, the bastards," said the captain calmly.

But just at that moment the good-looking ensign ran out waving his arms, his face flushed and frightened, and rushed towards the Cossacks.

"Don't touch him! Don't hurt him!" he cried in a childlike voice.

Seeing the officer, the Cossacks parted and

released a little white kid. The young ensign was overcome with confusion, muttered something, and stopped before them with an embarrassed expression. Seeing the captain and myself on the roof, he blushed even more and ran skipping towards us.

"I thought they were killing a child," he said with a bashful smile.

X

The general and the cavalry left the village first. The battalion with which I had left the fortress formed the rearguard. Captain Khlopov's and Lieutenant Rosenkranz's companies retreated together.

The captain's prediction proved quite correct. As soon as we entered the narrow neck of woodland he had mentioned, enemy hillsmen began to pop up on all sides, both mounted and on foot, and so close that I could clearly see some of them darting from tree to tree, stooping low, with rifles in their hands.

The captain took off his hat and piously crossed himself. Some of the other older soldiers did the same. From the woods the Tatars could be heard whooping and taunting us: "Hey, Russky, hey!" Short, dry rifle shots rattled out in quick succession, and bullets whizzed on every side. Our men fired back in silence; only occasionally came some remark from the ranks, such as "It's all right for *them*, in the trees" or "A gun would be just right here."

Eventually our ordnance was brought out, and after a few volleys of case-shot the enemy seemed to weaken; but presently, with every step our troops moved forward, the war-cries and firing intensified again.

We had scarcely retreated a third of a mile from the village when enemy cannon-balls began whistling overhead. I saw a soldier killed by one... But why should I go into the details of this terrible scene when I should fain forget it myself!

Lieutenant Rosenkranz kept firing his rifle, at the same time hoarsely shouting to his men and galloping at top speed from one end of the line to the other. He was rather pale, and this pallor was well suited to his martial countenance.

The young ensign was in delight: his handsome dark eyes shone with daring, a slight smile played on his lips; he kept riding up to the captain and asking permission to charge.

"We'll beat them back," he insisted, "I'm sure we will."

"No," replied the captain gently, "our task now is to retreat."

The captain's company were holding the edge of the forest, the men lying prostrate to fire at the enemy. The captain himself, in his threadbare coat and shabby cap, sat on his white horse with the reins held loose and his knees bent sharply in the short stirrups. He neither spoke nor moved: the soldiers knew their business too well to require orders from him. Only now and again did he raise his voice to shout at someone whose head was exposed.

There was nothing very martial about Captain Khlopov's figure; but there was something extraordinarily sincere and simple in it that I was greatly impressed. Something told me: "Now this is a truly brave man."

He was *exactly as I had always seen him*: the same calm movements, the same even voice, the same ingenuous expression on his plain but pleasant face. Only his eyes, which were brighter than usual, betrayed a man quietly concentrating on the task at hand. It is easy to say glibly that he was *"the same as ever"*. But how many different shades of behaviour did I notice in the others: one would try to appear calmer than usual, another more severe, a third jollier. Whereas the captain's face showed that it had never even occurred to him to appear anything but what he was.

The Frenchman who said at Waterloo, *"La garde meurt, mais ne se rend pas"*, and other heroes, particularly French heroes, who uttered such memorable sayings, were brave and did indeed coin memorable phrases; but the difference between their courage and the courage of Captain Khlopov is that even if a great phrase had ever stirred in my hero's heart, I am sure he would never have uttered it—first, because by uttering a great phrase he would be afraid of spoiling a great deed, and secondly because when a man feels he has the strength to accomplish a great feat, all words are superfluous. This, in my opinion, is a peculiar and lofty characteristic of Russian courage. How, then, can one's Russian heart help aching when one hears our young warriors using vulgar French phrases in imitation of antiquated notions of French chivalry?

Suddenly from the side where the young Ensign Alanin stood with his platoon came a rather uncoordinated and feeble "Hurrah!" Looking round in that direction, I beheld about thirty soldiers with rifles in their hands and knapsacks over their shoulders, running with great difficulty over a ploughed field. In spite of their stumbling, they managed to keep going, shouting as they ran. Galloping ahead of them, his sabre unsheathed, was the young ensign.

They all disappeared into the woods...

After some minutes of whooping and crackling a frightened horse ran out of the wood, and soldiers appeared carrying the dead and wounded; among the latter was the young ensign. Two soldiers held him under the arms. He was as white as a sheet, and his handsome face showed but a faint shadow of the enthusiasm for battle which had animated it a minute earlier. His head was horribly sunk between his shoulders and hung down on his chest. A small bloody stain showed on his white shirt beneath his un-buttoned coat.

"Ah, what a shame!" I said involuntarily, turning away from this sad sight.

"Of course, it's a shame," said an old soldier who was standing near me with a gloomy expression, leaning on his rifle. "He's not afraid of anything—how can you be like that!" he added, gazing intently at the wounded boy. "He's stupid yet, and now he's paid for it!"

"Are you afraid?" I asked him.

"What do you think!"

XI

The ensign was carried on a stretcher by four soldiers. Behind them a medical orderly was leading a thin, jaded horse with two green cases on its back containing medical supplies. While they were waiting for a doctor, various officers rode up to the stretcher with words of encouragement and comfort for the wounded lad.

"Well, Alanin, old chap, it will be some time before you can dance again," said Lieutenant Rosenkranz with a smile.

He probably supposed that these words would buck up the young lad's spirits, but as far as one could tell from the latter's cold, sad look, they did not have the desired effect.

Captain Khlopov also rode up. He took

a close look at the wounded lad, and an expression of genuine sympathy came over his normally indifferent face.

"Well, my dear Anatoly Ivanovich," he said, with a note of tender concern which I had not expected of him, "looks like it was God's will."

The young man turned his head. A sad smile flickered on his pale face.

"Yes, I disobeyed you."

"Let's just say it was God's will," repeated the captain.

The doctor arrived, took bandages, a probe and another instrument from the orderly, rolled up his sleeves, and approached the ensign with an encouraging smile.

"What's this, then?" he said in a jocular tone. "I hear you've got a little hole where there didn't use to be one! Let's have a look at it!"

The ensign obeyed, but he looked at the merry doctor with a mixture of surprise and reproach, which the latter did not notice. The doctor proceeded to probe and examine the wound, but the ensign, having taken all he could bear, let out a deep groan and pushed the doctor's hand away.

"Leave me!" he said in a scarcely audible voice. "I'll die anyway."

With these words he fell back, and five minutes later, when I went up to the group which had gathered round him and asked how he was, a soldier replied, "Passing away."

XII

It was already late when the detachment, formed into a wide column and singing songs, approached the fortress.

The sun was hidden behind the snowy mountain-ridge, casting its last pink rays on a long thin cloud which hung stationary over the clear horizon. The snow-covered mountains were becoming obscured by a lilac haze, so that only their crests remained clearly outlined against the crimson afterglow. The transparent moon, long risen, was beginning to whiten in the dark azure of the sky. The greens of the grass and trees darkened and became wet with dew. Over the luxurious meadows moved the dark masses of the troops with measured tread; here and there could be heard tambourines and drums and merry songs. The second tenor of the Sixth Company was singing with great power and feeling, and the sounds of his pure vibrant voice carried far abroad through the clear evening air.

1852

THE WOOD-FELLING

A CADET'S STORY

I

In mid-winter of 185..., a section of our battery was serving with a detachment in Great Chechnia district of the Northern Caucasus. On the evening of 14 February, learning that the platoon which I, in the absence of any officer, was commanding, had been detailed to fell wood next day, I retired to my tent earlier than usual, having received and issued all the necessary orders. Not having the bad habit of warming my tent with hot charcoals, I lay down without undressing on my bed, which was raised from the ground on stakes, pulled my fur hat over my eyes, wrapped myself up in my sheepskin coat, and fell into that peculiar deep and heavy sleep which overcomes one at times of anxiety caused by impending danger. It was the prospect of the next day that put me in this state of mind.

At three in the morning, when it was still

pitch dark, my warm sheepskin was pulled away and the reddish light of a candle glared unpleasantly in my sleepy eyes.

"Get up, sir," said a voice. I closed my eyes, unconsciously pulled the sheepskin around me again and fell asleep. "Get up, sir," said Dmitry once more, remorselessly shaking me by the shoulder. "The infantry are starting out." I suddenly came to my senses, gave a shudder, and leapt to my feet. After hastily drinking a glass of tea and washing in icy water, I slipped out of the tent and went to the artillery-park. It was cold, misty and dark. And it seemed all the darker because of the dim, ruddy light of the night fires which glowed here and there in the camp, showing up the figures of the drowsy soldiers sitting round them. Nearby could be heard quiet, regular snoring, and from farther off came the noise of the infantry bustling and chatting, and clattering their rifles as they prepared to start. There was a smell of smoke, dung, lamp-wicks and mist. The morning sent shivers down one's spine, and one's teeth chattered involuntarily.

It was only by the snorting and occasional stamping of the horses harnessed to them that one could tell where the limbers and ammunition-chests stood in the impenetrable darkness, and only the shining points of the linstocks showed where the artillery was. The first gun moved off with a clang, followed by an ammunition-wagon, and with the words

"God be with us!" our platoon started. We all took off our caps and crossed ourselves. Taking up a position between two infantry companies, the platoon halted and waited a quarter of an hour or so for the whole column to assemble and for the commander to ride out.

"One of our men is missing, Nikolai Petrovich," said a black figure coming towards me. I recognised the voice of the platoon's gun-sergeant, Maximov.

"Who is it?"

"Velenchuk, sir. He was there while they were harnessing—I saw him myself. And now he's gone."

Since it did not look as if the column was going to start at once, we decided to send Lance-Corporal Antonov to look for Velenchuk. Presently some horsemen trotted past us in the dark: it was the commander and his officers. Then the head of the column stirred and moved off, and so at last did we—but Antonov and Velenchuk were still absent. Hardly had we gone a hundred paces, however, than they both caught up.

"Where was he?" I asked Antonov.

"He was asleep in the artillery-park."

"Why, is he drunk?"

"Oh, no, sir."

"So what was he doing sleeping?"

"I don't know, sir."

For about three hours we moved slowly on in the silence and darkness, over unploughed,

snowless fields and through shrubbery that
crackled under the wheels of the gun-carriages.
Eventually, upon crossing a shallow but
extremely fast-flowing stream, a halt was
called and the abrupt reports of rifles could
be heard from the vanguard. These sounds
as usual had a most exhilarating effect on
everyone. The detachment seemed to wake
up: voices, movement and laughter could be
heard in the ranks. A couple of soldiers
wrestled with each other, another hopped
from foot to foot, while others chewed rusks
or shouldered and grounded arms to while
away the time. Meanwhile the fog was beginning to grow perceptibly whiter in the east,
the damp was becoming more noticeable,
and surrounding objects were gradually
emerging from the gloom. I could already
discern the green gun-carriages and ammunition-chests; the brass of the guns, damp with
the fog; the figures of my soldiers, which
I had involuntarily studied down to the tiniest
detail; the bay horses; and the ranks of infantrymen with their gleaming bayonets, bags,
ramrods and mess-tins on their backs.

Soon we were moved on again and were led
to a spot several hundred yards from the
track. Over on the right we could see the
steep bank of a winding stream and the tall
wooden posts of a Tatar graveyard; to the left
and in front of us a black strip was visible
through the fog. The platoon unlimbered.
The Eighth Company, which was covering us,

stacked their guns, and a battalion with guns and axes went into the forest.

Within five minutes fires were crackling and smoking on all sides. The soldiers dispersed to collect branches and logs, and fanned the fires with hands and feet. The forest filled with the unceasing din of hundreds of axes and falling timber.

The artillery laid their fire with a certain rivalry towards the infantry, and though it was already burning so furiously that one could scarcely come within two paces of it and thick black smoke was belching through the frozen branches which the soldiers were pressing into the flames, causing them to sizzle and spit, and though the wood was turning to charcoal beneath and the pale grass thawing all around the fire, still the soldiers were not satisfied: they brought enormous logs, heaped on weeds, and kept fanning the flames higher and higher.

When I went up to the fire to light a cigarette, Velenchuk, always a bustler but especially so today because of his guilty conscience, in a fit of zeal snatched a live coal from the centre of the fire with his bare hand, and, after tossing it from hand to hand a couple of times, dropped it on the ground.

"Try lighting a twig!" counselled another soldier.

"Better get him a linstock, fellows!" said another.

At length I managed to light my cigarette

without the aid of Velenchuk, who was again trying to pick out a coal. He rubbed his burnt fingers on the skirts of his sheepskin coat and, presumably, for want of anything better to do, picked up a large piece of plane-wood and swung it into the fire. When he finally felt he could rest, he went right up to the fire, flung open his coat, which he wore like a cloak, spread out his legs, held out his big black hands, and screwed up his eyes, twisting his mouth a little.

"Bother! I've gone and forgotten my pipe! Too bad, fellows!" he said after a short silence, addressing no one in particular.

II

In Russia there are three predominant types of soldier under which can be classified the men of all our forces—whether they serve in the Caucasus, line, guards, infantry, cavalry, artillery or whatever.

These main types, which have many subdivisions and combinations, are:

1. The submissive;
2. The domineering;
3. The reckless.

The submissive can be subdivided into (a) the coolly submissive and (b) the bustlingly submissive.

The domineering can be subdivided into (a) the sternly domineering and (b) the diplomatically domineering.

The reckless can be subdivided into (*a*) reckless comics and (*b*) reckless profligates.

The commonest type—more likeable than the others, and generally endowed with the best Christian virtues: meekness, piety, patience and devotion to the will of God—is the submissive type as a whole. The distinctive feature of the coolly submissive type is his unwavering calmness and his contempt for all the reverses of fate which may befall him. The distinctive trait of the submissive drunkard is his gentle, poetic disposition and his sensibility; the bustlingly submissive type is characterised by his limited mental capacity combined with aimless industry and zeal.

The domineering type in general is found chiefly in the higher ranks: lance-corporals, sergeant-majors and the like. The first subdivision, the sternly domineering, includes noble, energetic, pre-eminently military types, not devoid of high poetic impulses (to this type belonged Lance-Corporal Antonov, with whom I intend to acquaint the reader). The second subdivision, comprising the diplomatically domineering, has lately begun to grow considerably. The diplomatically domineering type is always eloquent and literate, wears pink shirts, doesn't eat out of the common pot, sometimes smokes Musatov tobacco, and considers himself incomparably superior to the common soldier. But he is rarely as good a soldier as the domineering type of the first subdivision.

Like the domineering types, the reckless are good in the first subdivision—the comics, who are distinguished by their unflagging jollity, their immense versatility, their giftedness and daring—and exceedingly bad in the second subdivision—the reckless profligates, who, however, to the honour of the Russian army, are very rare and, where they do turn up, are usually shunned by the soldiers themselves. The main traits of this group are want of faith and a flaunting of their vices.

Velenchuk was one of the bustlingly submissive. He was a Ukrainian by birth, already fifteen years in the service, and though he was an inconspicuous, rather blundering soldier, he was simple-hearted, kind, extremely zealous (though usually inopportunely so) and exceedingly honest. I say exceedingly honest because of an incident the previous year in which he demonstrated this characteristic quality of his very clearly. It should be pointed out that almost every soldier knows a trade—most commonly tailoring and bootmaking. Velenchuk taught himself the former, and, judging by the fact that even Mikhail Dorofeich, the sergeant-major, ordered clothes from him, had attained a certain degree of proficiency at it. A year ago, in camp, Velenchuk undertook to make a fine cloth coat for Mikhail Dorofeich. But the very night after he had cut out the cloth and measured the trimmings, and had placed them all under his pillow in his tent, a misfortune befell him: the cloth—which had cost *seven rubles*—disappeared in the middle of the night. With tears in his eyes and trembling, pale lips, suppressing his sobs, Velenchuk informed the sergeant-major. Mikhail Dorofeich was furious. In the first moment of anger he threatened the tailor, but then, being a reasonable man and well-off, he decided to forget it and did not require Velenchuk to pay for the cost of the material. However much the bustling Velenchuk may have bustled, however much he may have wept while telling of his ill luck, the thief was not found. Strongly suspected was a certain reckless profligate soldier named Chernov, who slept in the same tent, but there was no positive proof. The diplomatically domineering Mikhail Dorofeich as a man of means, and having certain business contacts with the quartermaster-sergeant and the caterer of the mess, the aristocrats of the battery, soon forgot all about the loss of his mufti coat. Not so Velenchuk. The soldiers said they feared at the time that he might take his own life or run away into the mountains, so great was the effect of the misfortune on him. He neither drank nor ate, could not even work, and was forever crying. Three days later he came to Mikhail Dorofeich, quite pale, and with a shaking hand withdrew a gold coin from under his cuff and gave it to him. "I swear it's all I've got, Mikhail Dorofeich," he sobbed, "and even it is borrowed from Zhdanov. But I'll give you the remaining two rubles as soon as I earn them, by heaven I shall. He (who *he* was, even Velenchuk did not know) has made me a rogue in your eyes. The loathsome snake took the very life out of a fellow soldier's soul ... after fifteen years' service..." It should be said, to the honour of Mikhail Dorofeich, that he did not take the remaining two rubles, though Velenchuk brought them to him two months later.

III

Apart from Velenchuk, five other soldiers of my platoon were warming themselves at the fire.

Sitting on a canteen in the best place, shielded from the wind, was the platoon's gun-sergeant, Maximov, who was smoking a pipe. His habit of commanding, and his awareness of his own dignity, were betrayed by his pose, his look and his movements—not to mention the canteen on which he was sitting, which was an emblem of power at a halting-place—and his nankeen-covered sheepskin coat.

When I approached he turned his head towards me, but his eyes remained fixed on the fire and only much later followed the movement of his head to face me. Maximov was of petty-landowner stock, had money, and had been given a rating at the NCO school, accumulating a fair amount of knowledge. He was awfully rich and awfully learned, as the soldiers said. I remember how once when we were practising plunging fire with a quadrant, he explained to the soldiers gathered around him that a water-level "is none other, as it occurs, than the atmospheric mercury having its motion". In fact Maximov was far from stupid and knew his work thoroughly; but he had the unfortunate quirk of sometimes purposely speaking in such a way that there was no possibility of understanding him, and, I am sure, that he did not even understand his own words. He was particularly fond of the words "occurs" and "continues", and when I heard him say either of these words I knew beforehand that I would understand nothing of what followed. The soldiers, on the other hand, as far as I could see, liked to hear his "occurs" and read a deep meaning into it, though they understood as little as I did. But they attributed their lack of understanding to their own stupidity, and respected Maximov all the more for it. In a word, Fyodor Maximich Maximov was of the diplomatically domineering type.

The second soldier at the fire, who was putting his sinewy red feet back into his boots, was Antonov—that same bombardier Antonov who in 1837, left with only two others in charge of an exposed gun, had fired back at a powerful enemy and, with two

bullets in his thigh, had kept by his gun, re-
loading it. "He should have been made a gun-
sergeant long ago," the soldiers said of him,
"if it wasn't for his temper." And indeed he
was a strange character. Sober, there was no
one more composed, gentle or punctilious;
but when he had had a few he became quite
another person: he refused to recognise
authority, brawled and fought, and turned
into a useless soldier. Only a week before the
event described above, he had got drunk on
Shrove Tuesday, and regardless of all threats,
admonishments and even being bound to
a gun, he carried on drinking and brawling
right through till the Monday. Then all of
Lent, though the whole detachment had been
ordered to eat normally, he fed on nothing but
dry rusks, and in the first week even turned
down the regulation cup of vodka. But one
had to see his stocky, irony, bandy-legged
figure and his shiny, whiskered physiognomy,
when, in a tipsy mood, he would take the
balalaika in his knotty hands and with a
supercilious glance strike the lively *Barynia*,
or when he walked down the street with his
coat thrown loosely over his shoulders, his
medals dangling, his hands in the pockets of
his blue nankeen trousers, and a look on his
face of pride in being a soldier and scorn for
all who were not—one had to see all this in
order to understand how impossible it was for
him at such moments to abstain from fighting
with any batman, Cossack, infantryman,

settler, or, indeed, any non-artilleryman, who was rude to him or even just happened to be around. He brawled and fought not so much for his own pleasure as to keep up the spirits of the soldiery at large, whose representative he felt himself to be.

The third soldier squatting near the fire, who had one earring, bristly little moustaches, a bird-like face and a porcelain pipe in his teeth, was the driver Chikin. "Old wag" Chikin, as the soldiers dubbed him, was a *comic*. No matter where he was—in a biting frost, up to his knees in mud, having gone two days without food, on the march, on parade or at drill—the old wag was always pulling faces, twisting his legs about, or cracking jokes that set the whole platoon rolling with laughter. At halting-places and in camp, there was always a circle of young soldiers gathered around Chikin, who played *filka** with them, told them stories about the cunning soldier and the English lord, impersonated a Tatar or a German, or simply made witty remarks at which they all roared with laughter. Admittedly, his reputation as a wit was so firmly established in the battery that he had only to open his mouth and wink to produce guffaws all round; but he did possess a genuine talent for the comic and unexpected. He noticed unusual aspects of things that would never even occur to others, and this ability to see

* A soldiers' card game.—*L. T.*

the funny side of everything stayed by him through every kind of ordeal.

The fourth soldier was an unattractive young lad, recruited only the previous year and in the field for the first time. He was standing in the midst of the smoke, so close to the fire that his worn sheepskin coat looked as if it might burst into flames at any moment; yet judging by his quiet, self-satisfied pose, with his coat flung open and his calves turned out, he was feeling highly contented.

The fifth and last soldier, who was sitting at some distance from the fire, whittling a stick, was "Grandpa" Zhdanov. He had been serving in the army longer than any other soldier in the battery and had known them all as recruits—hence their habit of calling him "grandpa". It was said that he never drank or smoked, never played cards, and never used bad language. He spent all his spare time making boots, went to church on holidays, where that was possible, or else lit a kopeck candle before an icon and opened the psalm-book—the only book he could read. He did not mix much with the other soldiers: towards those who were his seniors in rank but juniors in years he was coldly respectful, and not being a drinker, he had little occasion to keep the company of his equals. But he did like recruits and young soldiers: he always took them under his wing, offering both admonitions and assistance. Everyone in the battery considered him a capitalist because he had

about twenty-five rubles, which he gladly lent
to any soldier in real need. Maximov—the one
who was now gun-sergeant—told me that ten
years ago, when he was a fresh recruit and the
old hard-drinkers drank away his money with
him, Zhdanov noticed his unfortunate position and summoned him, severely reprimand-
ed him for his behaviour, even beat him,
lectured him on how to live in the army, and
sent him away with a shirt (Maximov had
none left) and a half-ruble in money. "He
made a man of me," Maximov always used to
say with respect and gratitude. He also helped
Velenchuk—whom he had patronised since
he was a recruit—when the misfortune with
the stolen coat occurred; and many, many
others, too, had received his help during his
twenty-five years of service.

One could not wish for a soldier who knew
his job better or who was braver or more
conscientious. But he was too meek and
retiring to be made a gun-sergeant, although
he had been bombardier for fifteen years.
Zhdanov's sole enjoyment, and even passion,
was singing; not that he could sing himself—
but he had certain favourite songs and would
often collect a circle of singers from among
the younger soldiers, and stand with them, his
hands in his coat pockets, screwing up his
eyes and expressing his sympathy by the
movements of his head and jaws. I don't
know why, but that regular movement of his
jawbone below his ears, which I never noticed

in anyone else, somehow seemed extremely expressive to me. His hoary head, blackened moustache and wrinkled, sunburnt face lent him at first sight a stern, severe expression; but on looking closer into his big round eyes, especially when they smiled (he never smiled with his lips), one was suddenly struck by something remarkably meek—almost childlike.

IV

"Bother! I've gone and forgotten my pipe. Too bad, fellows!" Velenchuk repeated.

"You should smoke ciga-ars, old chap!" retorted Chikin, twisting his mouth to one side and winking. "I always smoke ciga-ars at home—them's sweeter!"

Of course everyone burst out laughing.

"Forgotten your pipe, indeed!" interrupted Maximov, paying no attention to the general mirth, and knocking his pipe in the palm of his left hand with a superior air. "Why didn't you report this morning, eh, Velenchuk?"

Velenchuk half-turned to face him and was about to raise his hand to his cap, but lowered it again.

"You must have had plenty to sleep off if you were still falling asleep after you were up! You won't get thanked for that kind of thing!"

"Strike me down, Fyodor Maximich, if a single drop passed my lips! I really don't know what came over me," Velenchuk replied. "Fat lot I had to get drunk about!" he muttered.

"That's as may be, but someone has to answer to the authorities for the likes of you, and the way you carry on ... it's quite scandalous!" the eloquent Maximov concluded in a calmer tone.

"It's quite miraculous, lads," Velenchuk went on after a moment's silence, scratching the back of his head and addressing no one in particular. "Miraculous, it is! Sixteen years I've been serving, and nothing like that ever happened to me. When we were ordered to form up I was all right, but at the artillery-park I don't know what came over me... It just suddenly took hold of me, grabbed me, and pulled me down on the ground—and that was that! I just fell asleep, lads, without even knowing it! That must be what they call sleepies, lads!" he concluded.

"I barely managed to wake you," said Antonov, pulling on his boot. "You were like a log—I had to pull you and push you..."

"Well, well," said Velenchuk. "If I was drunk, now..."

"That's just like an old woman we had at home," Chikin chimed in. "She never got off the stove for two years. Once they tried to wake her up—they thought she was asleep—and in fact she was dead! She used to keep falling asleep like that—just like you, old chap!"

"I say, Chikin, tell us how you cut a figure during your leave," said Maximov, smiling and glancing at me as if to say: Don't you fancy listening to the silly man, too?

"I didn't cut no figure, Fyodor Maximich!" said Chikin, casting a quick sidelong glance at me. "Naturally, I told them what sort of a place this Corkasus is!"

"Oh come now, don't play modest... Tell us how you *instructed* them!"

"You know how I instructed them: they asked what life was like here," Chikin began rapidly, with the air of a man telling the same thing for the umpteenth time. "We live fine, I said. We get victuals in plenty—morning and night a cup of *chocolad* for every *soldier lad*, and at noon we get barley broth, fit for a lord, and instead of vodka they give us a glass of Madeira—to make us merry."

"I'll give you Madeira!" roared Velenchuk, laughing louder than anyone else. "Madeira indeed!"

"And what did you tell them about the Hasiatics?" Maximov went on to ask once the general mirth had subsided a little.

Bending over the fire, Chikin fished out a bit of coal with a stick, placed it on his pipe, and puffed at it through his tobacco for a long time, as though not noticing the silent curiosity aroused in his audience. When at last he had generated enough smoke he threw the piece of coal away, pushed his cap even further back, and gave a little twitch and a faint smile as he continued.

"Well," he said, "they were asking: what about these Circassians, or Turks, that you've got down in the Corkasus—do they fight fierce? And I says: there's Circassians and there's Circassians, they're all different. First of all there's the vagabonds, that live in the hills and eat stones instead of bread. They're big, I says, big as a tree-trunk, they've got one eye in the forehead, and they wear red caps— burning red, just like yours, laddie!" he added, turning to the young recruit, who was indeed wearing an absurd cap with a red crown.

At this unexpected aside, the recruit suddenly collapsed, slapped his knees, and laughed and coughed so much that he was barely able to wheeze out the words: "Vaga- bonds, I'll say..."

"And then, I says, there's the Gawks," Chikin continued, jerking his cap onto his forehead. "They come in pairs—little things and run about hand in hand, so fast you wouldn't catch 'em on a horse.

" 'D'you mean to say that them there Gawks is born like that, 'and in 'and?' " Chikin said this in a throaty bass, imitating a peasant.

"'That's right, old chap, I says, hand in hand since birth. And if you cut them apart, they pour with blood—just like a Chinaman does when you take off his hat!

" 'And do they fight fierce, then, these Gawks?'

"Fight? says I. Why, when they catch you they rip your belly up and twist your guts round your arm. This makes you laugh. And they go on twisting and twisting, and making you laugh until you laugh yourself to death..."

"Well, and did they believe you, Chikin?" asked Maximov with a slight smile, while the others were bursting at the seams with laughter.

"Those funny folk believe anything, Fyodor Maximich, they really do. But when I told them that on Mount Kazbek the snow doesn't melt all summer—you should have heard them laughing! 'Come off it, old chap,' they says, 'whoever heard of a big mountain where the snow don't melt! When the thaw sets in here, every little hillock thaws first, while the snow still lies in the hollows!' That's them folk!" Chikin concluded with a wink.

V

The light disk of the sun shining through the milky-white fog had already risen fairly high. The violet-grey horizon was gradually widening, but was marked—just as sharply though at a greater distance—by a deceptive white wall of fog. A fair-sized clearing now opened out in front of us, beyond the felled wood. The smoke from the fires, black or creamy or lilac, spread over the clearing from all directions, chased by strangely shaped layers of white fog. Now and then, groups of Tatars on horseback appeared in the far distance, and occasional exchanges of rifle and cannon fire could be heard.

This, as the good Captain Khlopov would say, "wasn't the real thing, but just a bit of fun".

The commander of the 9th Company of Chasseurs, who were our escort, came up to our guns, pointed to three Tatar horsemen skirting the forest nearly a mile from us, and with the fondness for artillery fire so common among infantry officers, asked me to let a ball or a shell fly at them.

"Do you see?" he said with a persuasive and kindly tone as he stretched his hand over my shoulder. "Look, in front of those two big trees, one on a white horse, in a black coat ... and there's another two behind him. Do you see? Couldn't you ... please?..."

"And there go another three at the edge of the forest," interjected Antonov, who had remarkably keen eyes, coming up to us and hiding behind his back the pipe he had been smoking. "The one in front has drawn his rifle. You can see them clear as daylight, sir!"

"Look, he's fired, lads! Do you see the white smoke?" said Velenchuk, standing in a group of soldiers a little behind us.

"At our line, too, the scoundrel!" remarked another.

"Look at how many have come out of the

3*

forest," said a third. "They must be looking for somewhere to place a gun. If a shell were to drop in their midst, it wouldn't half upset them!"

"It would just reach them, wouldn't it?" asked Chikin.

"Twelve hundred or so yards, no more," said Maximov coolly, as though speaking to himself, although it was obvious that he was as keen as the others to fire. "With an elevation of forty-five degrees, our 'unicorn' cannon could have an absolute bull's-eye."

"You know, if we fire into that crowd now we're bound to hit someone. Right now, when they're all together, please give the order to fire quickly," the company commander continued to wheedle me.

"Shall we take aim?" asked Antonov suddenly in a jerky bass voice, looking somewhat sullen and angry.

I confess I also very much wanted to fire, and I gave the order to point the second gun.

The words had hardly left my mouth when the shell was charged and rammed in, and Antonov, pressing against the cheek of the gun-carriage and holding two fat fingers to the back-plate, was already aligning the trail of the gun-carriage.

"A little to the left ... right a bit ... a fraction more ... more ... fine!" he said, stepping back from the gun.

The infantry officer, I, and Maximov one by one had a look through the sights, and expressed our various opinions.

"I'm sure it'll overshoot," remarked Velen-chuk, clicking his tongue, although he had only looked over Antonov's shoulder and therefore had not the slightest grounds for this supposition. "God be my witness, it'll overshoot, lads, it'll hit that tree."

"Fire number two!" I ordered.

The men withdrew. Antonov ran to one side to watch the flight of the shell. There was a flash and the brass rang. At that instant we were enveloped in powder-smoke, and the impressive boom of the discharge gave way to the metallic humming sound as the shell receded with the speed of lightning and died away into silence in the distance.

A cloud of white smoke appeared just behind the group of riders, and the Tatars galloped off in different directions. Then the report of the explosion reached us.

"Bravo! See how they galloped! Ha, the devils don't like that!" Chuckles and sounds of approval could be heard throughout the ranks of the artillery and infantry.

"If only we'd aimed just a shade lower," said Velenchuk, "we'd have got 'em. I said it would hit the tree, and there you are—it went to the right."

VI

Leaving the soldiers to discuss how the Tatars had galloped off when they saw the

shell, and why they were there in the first
place, and whether there were many left in
the forest, I walked away a few paces with
the company commander and sat down
beneath a tree to wait while the meatballs
he had offered me were being heated up.
The company commander, Bolkhov, was
one of the officers nicknamed *Bonjours* in
the regiment. He was wealthy, had previously served in the Guards, and spoke French.
Nonetheless, his comrades liked him. He was
clever enough, and had sufficient tact to be
able to wear a St. Petersburg frock-coat,
eat well and speak French, without unduly
offending his fellow officers. Having talked
about the weather, the military operations
and mutual acquaintances among the officers,
and having assured ourselves by means of
questions and answers of each other's views,
we involuntarily passed to more intimate
conversation. When people of the same circle
meet in the Caucasus, the question "Why
are you here?" invariably arises, even if it is
unspoken, and it was to this silent question
of mine that Bolkhov seemed to wish to
reply.

"When will this expedition end?" he said
lazily. "It's so tedious."

"I don't find it tedious," I said. "After
all, at headquarters it's even worse."

"Oh, at headquarters it's ten thousand
times worse," he said bitterly. "No, I mean,
when will the whole business end?"

"What is it you want to end?" I asked.

"Everything, and for good! Are the meat-balls ready, Nikolayev?"

"Why on earth did you come and serve here, if you so dislike the Caucasus?" I asked.

"I'll tell you why," he said with resolute candour. "Because of the bizarre belief in Russia that the Caucasus is some kind of Promised Land for unhappy people."

"Yes, that's more or less true," I said. "Most of us..."

"But the best of it," he interrupted, "is that all of us who come to the Caucasus in this belief make a dreadful mistake in our calculations: I see absolutely no reason why, as a result of an unhappy love affair or financial troubles, one should go and serve in the Caucasus rather than in, say, Kazan or Kaluga. In Russia, you see, the Caucasus is made out to be so majestic—with eternal virgin ice and rushing torrents, with daggers, and felt cloaks and Circassian maidens—and in fact there's nothing amusing in it at all. If only they knew that we never go near the virgin ice—and if we did we'd find it less than amusing—and that the Caucasus is divided administratively into gubernias—Stavropol, Tiflis, and so on."

"Yes," I laughed, "we look at the Caucasus quite differently when we are in Russia and when we are here. It's like reading poetry in a language one doesn't know very well: one imagines it is much better than it really is.

Have you ever experienced that?.."

"I don't know, really," he cut me short, "but I detest this Caucasus."

"No," I said, "I still like the place, only in a different way."

"Perhaps it is all right," he continued, rather irritably. "All I know is that I'm not all right here."

"Why is that?" I asked, in order to say something.

"Because, in the first place, it has deceived me. Everything I came to the Caucasus to be cured of—as the superstition would have it—has come with me, the only difference being that before it was all on a large scale, whereas now it is on a small, sordid one, where I find millions of petty anxieties, meannesses and insults at every step. Secondly, because I feel myself degenerating, morally, every day; and above all because I feel unsuited for the service here—I can't stand danger... In a word, I'm not brave!" He stopped and looked at me. "I'm not joking."

Although this uninvited confession highly surprised me, I did not contradict him (as he apparently wished me to do) but waited for him to go back on his words himself, as always happens in such cases.

"You know," he continued, "this expedition is my first taste of action, and you can't imagine what I felt like yesterday. When the sergeant-major brought the order that my company was to join the column I turned as white as a sheet and couldn't speak for nervousness. And what a night I had, if only you knew! If it is true that people get grey hair from fear, then mine should be completely white today, because I'm sure no man sentenced to death has suffered as much in one night as I did. Even now—though I feel a bit easier than I did at night—I'm still like this inside." And he turned his fist about in front of his chest. "And the funny thing is," he added, "that the most awful tragedy is being enacted here—while we sit eating meatballs and onions and pretending it's all great fun. Is there any wine, Nikolayev?" he concluded, yawning.

Just then we heard the alarmed voice of one of the soldiers—"Watch him, lads!"—and all eyes turned towards the edge of the distant forest.

Far away, a bluish cloud of smoke was expanding and rising in the wind. When I realised that this was an enemy cannon shot, aimed at us, all before my eyes at that moment suddenly took on a new and majestic character. The stacks of guns, the smoke from the fires, the blue sky, the green gun-carriages, Nikolayev's tanned and whiskered face—all this seemed to be telling me that the ball which had now left the muzzle and was flying at that instant through space, might well be directed straight at my breast.

"Where did you get the wine?" I asked Bolkhov lazily, while in the depths of my soul two equally distinct voices were speaking: one was saying, "Lord receive my soul in peace", the other, "I hope I shan't duck, but keep smiling, as the ball flies past", and at that moment something terribly unpleasant whistled overhead, and a cannon-ball crashed down a couple of paces behind us.

"Now if I had been Napoleon or Frederick," said Bolkhov, turning to me with complete composure, "I should certainly have paid you a compliment."

"You just have done," I replied, struggling to conceal the fear produced in me by danger.

"Well, and so what? No one will write it down."

"Yes they will—I will."

"Ah, but if you do, it will only be 'for criticism', as Mishchenkov says," he added with a smile.

"Pah, blast you! Nearly grased my legs!" cursed Antonov from behind us, spitting with vexation.

All my efforts to appear composed, and all our adroit phrases, suddenly seemed unbearably silly after this artless exclamation.

VII

The enemy had indeed placed two guns at the spot where the Tatars had been riding about, and every twenty or thirty minutes they fired a shot at our wood-fellers. My platoon was moved forward into the clearing and ordered to return fire. A puff of smoke would appear at the forest's edge, followed by a report and a whistle, and a cannon-ball would land in front of us or behind us. The enemy's shots were off target, and we sustained no losses.

The artillerymen performed splendidly, as always—they loaded quickly, painstakingly took aim at the puffs of smoke, and quietly joked among themselves. Our infantry escort lay near in silent inactivity, waiting their turn. The wood-fellers got on with their work, and the forest rang more and more with the sound of their axes. It was only when the whistle of a shell was heard that everything would suddenly grow quiet: voices, rather troubled, would call out in the deathly silence—"watch out, lads!"—and all eyes would follow the ball ricocheting off camp fires and chopped boughs.

The fog had now lifted and, turning into clouds, was gradually disappearing in the dark-blue sky. The unveiled sun shone brightly, glittering on the steel bayonets, the brass of the guns, and the thawing earth, spangled with hoar-frost.

In the air one could feel both the freshness of the morning frost and the warmth of the spring sunshine; thousands of different shades and colours mingled in the dry leaves on the forest-bed, and the tracks left by wheels and horseshoes showed up clearly on the smooth and shiny path.

The exchanges between the two forces were becoming louder and more powerful, with the bluish puffs of smoke appearing more and more often on both sides. The dragoons rode forward, the streamers of their lances flying; songs were struck up in the infantry companies; and a train of carts laden with firewood was formed in our rear-guard. A general rode up to our platoon and ordered us to prepare to retreat. The enemy had taken up a position in the bushes opposite our left flank and was harassing us with heavy gunfire. A bullet came humming out of the wood to the left and struck a gun-carriage, then came another, then a third... The soldiers who were covering us noisily got to their feet, took their rifles and formed a line. Firing intensified, and more and more bullets were flying. The retreat commenced, and with it— as usual in the Caucasus—began the serious part of the action.

It was plain to see that the artillerymen were no keener on the bullets than the infantry had been on the cannon-balls. Antonov frowned. Chikin mimicked the bullets and joked about them, but it was easy to see that he did not like them. About one he said, "What a hurry it's in!"; another he called a "little bee"; and a third, which seemed to fly over us slowly, with a plaintive howl, he called an "orphan"—which caused laughter all round.

The recruit, who was unaccustomed to all

this, also made the soldiers laugh by bending his head to the side and stretching his neck out every time a bullet passed. "Are they friends of yours, that you keep bowing to them?" they teased him. Even Velenchuk, normally quite indifferent to danger, was worried now; he seemed to be annoyed that we did not fire case-shot in the direction from which the bullets were coming. He repeated several times in a displeased voice: "Why should they get away with that? If we turned our gun on them and showered them with case-shot, they'd soon quieten down."

Indeed it was time to do this. I ordered them to fire a last shell and then load with case-shot.

"Case-shot!" Antonov called out as he strode through the smoke to clean out the gun when the shell was discharged.

Just then I heard a fast humming bullet suddenly stop with a dull thud, not far behind me. My heart stood still. "One of our men must have been hit," I thought, afraid to turn round, for I had a grave presentiment. To be sure, the thud was followed by the heavy fall of a body and the heart-rending groan of someone who had been wounded. "They've got me, chaps!" moaned a voice which I recognised. It was Velenchuk. He was lying on his back between the limbers and a piece of ordnance. The bag he had been carrying was thrown to one side. His forehead was covered in blood, and a thick red stream was running over his right eye and nose. He was wounded in the stomach but there was hardly any blood there; his forehead he had smashed against a tree-stump in falling.

All this became clear to me much later: at first all I could see was an indistinct mass and what seemed to be a great deal of blood.

None of the soldiers loading the gun said a word; only the recruit murmured something like "Ugh, look at the blood!" and Antonov frowned and gave an angry grunt. But it was evident that the thought of death had run through every man's soul. Everyone set to work with greater application. The cannon was charged in an instant, and the soldier bringing the case-shot walked a couple of paces to the side of the spot where the wounded Velenchuk still lay, groaning.

VIII

Everyone who has been in action has probably experienced that strange and illogical, though powerful, feeling of aversion for the spot on which someone was killed or injured. To begin with my men yielded perceptibly to this feeling, when they should have lifted Velenchuk and carried him over to the cart which had arrived. Zhdanov went up angrily to the wounded man and, though it made him scream even more loudly, picked him up by the armpits. "What are you stand-

ing there for? Take a hold of him!" he shouted, and Velenchuk was at once surrounded by
a dozen helpers, some of them superfluous.
But hardly had they moved him when he
began struggling and screaming terribly.

"What are you screaming like a hare for!"
said Antonov coarsely, holding his leg. "We'll
leave you here if you don't stop."

And Velenchuk did in fact become quiet,
only occasionally uttering, "Oh, I'm dying!
O-oh, fellows!"

When he was placed on the cart he even
ceased groaning, and I heard him saying
something in a quiet but clear voice to his
comrades; probably he was saying farewell
to them.

No one likes to look at a wounded man,
and instinctively hurrying to retreat from this
sight, I ordered him to be taken quickly to
the dressing station, and returned to the
guns. But a few minutes later I was told
Velenchuk was calling for me and I went over
to the cart.

The wounded man was lying on the floor
of the cart, gripping the sides with both
hands. In this short time his broad, healthy
face had changed entirely: he looked thinner
and had aged by several years; his lips were
thin and pale, and pressed together with
evident strain; the vacant, flitting expression
of his eyes was replaced by a serene, calm
radiance; and on his bloody forehead and
nose already lay the stamp of death.

Even though the least movement caused him excruciating pain, he asked for the little purse which he was wearing like a garter round his leg to be removed.

The sight of his bare, white, strong leg, as they pulled off his boot and untied the purse, produced a terribly heavy feeling in me.

"There are three and a half rubles in it," he said as I took the purse. "You look after it now."

The cart was about to move, but he stopped it.

"I was making a coat for Lieutenant Suli-movsky. H-he gave me two rubles. I bought buttons for one and a half, and there's a half-ruble with the buttons in my bag. Give them to him."

"Of course, of course," I said. "Get well, old man."

He did not answer me. The cart moved off and he again began moaning and groaning in the most terrible, heart-rending voice. It was as if, having wound up the affairs of this world, he could find no more reason for restraint and considered this source of relief now permissible.

IX

"Where d'you think you're off to? Come back here!" I shouted to the recruit, who with his spare linstock under his arm and some kind of stick in his hand was heading off with the utmost nonchalance behind the cart containing the wounded Velenchuk.

But the recruit merely looked round lazily, muttered something, and walked on, so that I had to send some soldiers to bring him back. He took off his red cap and looked at me with a stupid smile.

"Where were you going?" I asked.

"To the camp."

"Why?"

"Why?—Velenchuk's wounded," he said, smiling again.

"What's that got to do with you? You must stay here."

He looked at me with surprise, then quietly turned round, put on his cap, and went to his place.

In general things turned out happily. The Cossacks, we heard, launched a fine attack and brought back three dead Tatars; the infantry laid in a stock of firewood and had only six men wounded; in the artillery only Velenchuk and two horses were put out of action. For this small cost, a couple of miles of forest were chopped down and the area changed beyond recognition: where once a dense belt of trees had bordered the forest, a broad clearing had been opened up, now covered with smoking fires and cavalry and infantry returning to the camp.

Although the enemy continued to pursue us with artillery and rifle fire right up to the graveyard by the stream we had crossed that morning, the retreat was carried out successfully. I was already looking forward to the cabbage soup and the mutton ribs with buckwheat porridge which were awaiting me at the camp, when the news came that the general had ordered a redoubt to be built by the stream and that the 3rd Battalion of the K. Regiment and the platoon of the 4th Battery were to spend the night there. The carts loaded with firewood and the wounded, the Cossacks, the artillery, and the infantry with rifles and more firewood on their shoulders, all passed by us with much noise and singing. All their faces were animated and brightened by the consciousness of danger past and the prospect of a rest. Only we and the 3rd Battalion would have to wait until the morrow to savour these feelings.

X

While we of the artillery busied ourselves with the equipment—parking the limbers and ammunition-wagons, and tethering the horses—the infantry had already stacked arms, lit fires, built little huts of branches and maize straw, and begun to cook their porridge.

Dusk was falling. Heavy bluish clouds crept across the sky. The fog had turned into a light drizzle which soaked the earth and the soldiers' coats. The horizon drew closer, and gloomy shadows fell over the whole area. The damp, which I felt through my boots and on my neck, the ceaseless movement and talk, in which I took no part, the sticky mud in which my feet slid about, and my empty stomach—all this put me in a most unpleasant, depressed frame of mind, after a day of physical and moral exhaustion. I could not get Velenchuk out of my mind. The whole simple story of his life as a soldier haunted my imagination.

His last minutes were as clear and calm as his whole life had been. He had lived too honestly and modestly for his open-hearted faith in a future heavenly life to waver at the decisive moment.

"Your Honour," said Nikolayev, coming up to me, "the Captain asks you to take tea with him."

Picking my way among the stacks of arms and the camp-fires, I followed Nikolayev to where Bolkhov was, looking forward to a glass of hot tea and some cheerful conversation to drive away my sombre thoughts.

"Did you find him?" I heard Bolkhov's voice coming from a straw hut, in which a light was burning.

"I've brought him, Your Honour," replied Nikolayev in a bass voice.

Inside, Bolkhov was sitting on a dry felt cloak, with his coat unbuttoned and no cap. A samovar was boiling and there were some eatables arranged on a drum. A bayonet holding a candle was stuck into the ground. "What do you think of it?" he asked, proudly looking round his cosy establishment. In fact, it was so pleasant in the hut that over tea I completely forgot about the damp, the dark and Velenchuk's wound. We chatted about Moscow and about subjects that had nothing at all to do with the war and the Caucasus.

After one of those moments of silence which sometimes punctuate even the liveliest of conversations, Bolkhov looked at me with a smile. "I think you found our conversation this morning very strange," he said.

"No, why should I? I only felt that you are too frank, and that there are things which we all know but should never speak about."

"Why? No, if there were the faintest possibility of exchanging this life for even the poorest, most miserable life—but with no danger and no service—I wouldn't hesitate for a moment."

"Then why don't you go back to Russia?" I asked.

"Oh," he said, "I've been thinking about that for a long time. I cannot return to Russia until I obtain the Anna and Vladimir orders—an Anna round my neck and the rank of Major, as I intended when I came here."

"But why, if you say you feel unfit for the service here?"

"Because I feel even more unfit to return to Russia without obtaining what I came here for. That's another of the traditions in Russia, confirmed by Passek, Sleptsov and others, that one need only come to the Caucasus and one is sure to be showered with awards. And so everyone expects and demands it of us. Well, I've been here two years, I've been on two expeditions, and received nothing. But still my pride won't let me leave on any account until I'm a major with a Vladimir and an Anna round my neck. It's got to the stage that I am upset when Gnilokishkin is given an award and I am not. And then, how can I show myself in Russia, to the village elder, to the merchant Kotelnikov, whom I sell corn, to my Moscow aunt, and to all the other good people—with no award to my name after two years in the Caucasus? Certainly I have no wish to know these people, and they, I am sure, care very little about me; but such is the nature of man, that I may care nothing for them, yet ruin the best years of my life, my happiness and my future on account of them."

XI

Just then we heard the voice of the battalion commander outside: "Who is with you, Nikolai Fyodorich?"

Bolkhov gave my name, whereupon three officers entered the hut—Major Kirsanov, an adjutant of his battalion, and the company commander Trosenko.

Kirsanov was a smallish, stout man with black moustaches, ruddy cheeks and oily little eyes. These eyes were his most remarkable feature. When he laughed, all that remained of them were two moist little stars, and these stars, together with his stretched lips and outstretched neck, often gave him an extraordinarily senseless expression. In the regiment Kirsanov behaved and bore himself better than anyone else: his subordinates found no fault with him and his superiors respected him, although the general opinion was that he was none too clever. He knew the service, was punctilious and industrious, always had money, kept a carriage and a cook, and knew how to feign pride with great naturalness.

"What are you talking about, Nikolai Fyodorich?" he asked as he came in.

"Oh, just about the pleasures of the service here."

But at that moment Kirsanov noticed me, a cadet, and in order that I should feel his importance he ignored Bolkhov's reply and asked, looking at the drum, "What's up, are you tired, Nikolai Fyodorich?"

"No, we were just..." Bolkhov began.

But again, the dignity of a battalion commander seemed to require him to interrupt and ask another question: "Fine piece of action today, wasn't it?"

The battalion adjutant was a young ensign recently promoted from the cadet corps, a quiet, modest lad with a bashful, good-natured face. I had seen him with Bolkhov before. He often went to visit him; he would bow, sit in a corner and say nothing for several hours, rolling cigarettes and smoking them, then get up, bow again, and go away. He was a typical son of a poor Russian nobleman, who had chosen a military career as the only one possible for someone with his education, and who placed his officer's rank higher than all else in the world—a simple-hearted, pleasant type, despite the comic accoutrements inseparably associated with it: the tobacco-pouch, the dressing-gown, the guitar, and the little brush for smoothing his moustache. It was rumoured in the regiment that he boasted of being fair but strict with his batman, saying, "I punish him rarely, but when I have to he certainly knows about it," but that when his drunken batman robbed him and even began to abuse him, he led him to the guard-house, ordered him to be flogged, and then was so put out by the sight of the preparations for this that he could only say, "Look, you know... I can..."; then he ran off home, completely distraught, and was afraid thenceforth to look his man Chernov in the eyes. His comrades teased him unrelentingly about it, and several times I heard the ingenuous lad making excuses and, blushing terribly, assuring them that it was not true, indeed that the very opposite was true.

The third person, Captain Trosenko, was

an "old Caucasian" in the full sense of the word—that is, a man for whom the company under his command had become his family; the fortress where the headquarters were, his home; and the soldiers' songs his only pleasures. He was a man for whom everything that was not the Caucasus deserved scorn and was scarcely credible. Everything that was the Caucasus was divided into two halves—ours and theirs, the first of which he loved and the second of which he hated with all his heart. Above all, he was a man of steely, calm courage, uncommonly kind to his comrades and subordinates, and terribly direct, or even rude, to adjutants and *Bonjours*, whom for some reason he hated. Coming into the hut, he almost put his head through the roof, suddenly sank down and sat on the ground.

"Well?" he said, then suddenly stopped, as he noticed my unfamiliar face, and stared at me with a dull, fixed gaze.

"So what were you talking about, then?" asked the major, taking out his watch and looking at it, although I am quite certain he had absolutely no need to do so.

"Well, this chap was asking me why I serve here."

"Naturally, Nikolai Fyodorich wishes to distinguish himself here and then beat it back home."

"And you, Abram Ilyich, tell us why you serve in the Caucasus."

"I am here, you know, in the first place,

because we are all duty-bound to serve. What?" he added, though no one had spoken. "Yesterday I received a letter from Russia, Nikolai Fyodorich," he continued, evidently wishing to change the subject. "They write that ... they ask such strange questions."

"What kind of questions?" asked Bolkhov. The major laughed.

"Very strange questions... They ask, can there be jealousy without love? What?" he asked, glancing round us all.

"Well, well!" said Bolkhov with a smile.

"Yes, you know, it is nice in Russia," he went on, as though this flowed naturally from his previous sentence. "When I was in Tambov in 1852 I was received everywhere as if I were the Emperor's aide-de-camp, no less. Would you believe it—at the Governor's ball, when I came in, you know ... well, I was very well received. The Governor's wife herself, you know, conversed with me and asked about the Caucasus, and everyone was so... I didn't know what... They examined my gold sabre as if it were some rarity, and asked, what I had received it for; and what had I been awarded the Anna for, and the Vladimir?.. And I told them all about it... What? That's what the Caucasus is good for, Nikolai Fyodorich!" he continued without waiting for an answer. "They think very highly in Russia of us Caucasians. Young man, you know, a field-officer with an Anna and a Vladimir—that means a great deal in Russia... What?"

"I think you bragged to them a little, Abram Ilyich!" said Bolkhov.

"He, he!" the major laughed his stupid laugh. "One has to, you know! And how I ate those two months!"

"Is it nice, then, up there in Russia?" inquired Trosenko, as though asking about China or Japan.

"I'll say! And the amount of champagne we drank those two months, it was awful!"

"Come off it! You probably drank lemonade," said Trosenko. "Now I'd have shown them how Caucasians drink. I'd soon have been the talk of the town. I'd have let them see how we drink, eh, Bolkhov?"

"But you've been over ten years in the Caucasus, old man," said Bolkhov, "and you remember what Yermolov said... Whereas Abram Ilyich has been only six."

"I'll 'ten' you! It'll soon be sixteen! Let's have some sage-vodka, Bolkhov. Brrr, it's damp! Eh!" he added, smiling. "Let's have a drink, Major!"

But the major was already displeased by the old captain's remarks to him, and now he winced visibly and sought refuge in his own grandeur. He hummed something and looked again at his watch.

"No, I'll never go back there now," Trosenko continued, paying no attention to the scowling major. "I've forgotten how to walk and speak in the Russian way. They'd say: what kind of a crank have we got here? Something from Asia—that's what they'd say! Is that not so, Nikolai Fyodorich? Besides, what is there for me in Russia? I'll be shot here anyway some day. 'Where's Trosenko?' they'll ask. 'Shot.' What will you do with the 8th Company then, eh?.." he added, continually addressing himself to the major.

"Send the battalion officer on duty!" shouted Major Kirsanov, without answering the captain, though I again felt sure there was no need for him to any orders.

"And you, young man, I expect, are glad to be on double pay now?" said the major to the battalion adjutant, after some minutes' silence.

"Yes, sir, very."

"I find our salaries very high nowadays, Nikolai Fyodorich," he continued. "A young man can live jolly decently, and even afford a little luxury."

"Well, to tell the truth, Abram Ilyich," said the adjutant timidly, "although it is double, it's only just enough... I mean, one has to keep a horse..."

"What are you telling me, young man! I was an ensign myself once, and I know. Believe me, one can live very well. Look, count it up!" he added, bending back the little finger of his left hand.

"We always collect our pay in advance— that's all the counting you need," said Trosenko, emptying a glass of vodka.

"Well, that's as may be, but, I mean..."

At that moment a head with white hair and a flat nose was poked through the opening of the hut, and a shrill voice said with a German accent: "Are you here, Abram Ilyich? The officer on duty is looking for you."

"Come in, Kraft!" said Bolkhov.

A tall figure in the uniform of the General Staff ducked through the door and commenced to shake everyone's hands with great *élan*.

"Ah, dear Captain, so you are here too," he said, turning to Trosenko.

Despite the darkness, the new guest made his way over to Trosenko, and to the latter's extreme surprise and—as it seemed to me—displeasure, kissed him on the lips.

This is a German trying to be a jolly fine chap, I thought.

XII

My conjecture was at once confirmed. Captain Kraft asked for vodka, and gave a terrible croak and tossed his head back as he emptied the glass.

"Well, gentlemen, we had a jolly good jaunt around the plains of Chechnia today..." he began, but seeing the officer on duty, broke off in mid-word to allow the major to give his orders.

"Have you been round the lines?"

"Yes, sir."

"Have the look-outs been posted?"

"Yes, sir."

"Then give the company commanders orders to be on the alert."

"Yes, sir."

The major screwed up his eyes and thought deeply.

"And tell the men that they may now cook their porridge."

"They're already cooking it, sir."

"Very well, you may go... Now then," the major continued, turning to us with a condescending smile, "we were considering how much an officer needs. Let us count it. You need a full-dress coat and a pair of trousers... Correct?"

"Indeed."

"That is, say, fifty rubles for two years, which makes twenty-five per annum for clothes. Then for food, about forty kopecks a day, yes?"

"Oh yes, at the most."

"Well let's say that anyway. Then, for a horse and repairs to the saddle—thirty rubles— and that's your lot! So that's 25, plus 120, plus 30 ... comes to 175. And that leaves you about twenty rubles for luxuries—tea, sugar, tobacco... You see! It's true, Nikolai Fyodorich."

"But with respect, Abram Ilyich..." said the adjutant timidly, "nothing remains for tea and sugar, sir. You allow one uniform for two years, but with all these campaigns you go through more breeches than you can get hold of. And boots? I wear out a pair almost every month. Then there is underclothing, sir, and shirts, towels, footcloths—all that has to be bought. If you add all that up there's not a kopeck left over. It's true, Abram Ilyich."

"Yes, footcloths are fine things to wear!" Kraft remarked suddenly after a moment's silence, uttering the word "footcloths" with particular tenderness. "You know, it's so— Russian!"

"I'll tell you something," said Trosenko. "Count it up any way you like, it turns out we should all be famishing; but in fact we're all alive, drinking tea, smoking tobacco and drinking vodka. If you serve as long as me," he continued, addressing the ensign, "you'll learn how to live. Do you know, gentlemen, how he treats his batman?"

And Trosenko, choking with laughter, told us the whole story of the ensign and his batman, though we had all heard it a thousand times.

"What are you looking like a rose for, lad?" he went on, turning to the ensign, who was blushing, sweating and smiling, so that it was pitiful to look at him. "Never mind, lad, I was once like you, and now you see what a fine fellow I've turned out. You let these young tearaways from Russia come here—you know the kind I mean—and they develop spasms and rheumatisms and the like. But me—I'm sitting here, and it's my house, bed, the lot! You see..."

At this he downed another glass of vodka.
"Eh?" he added, staring straight into
Kraft's eyes.

"Now that's what I respect! A genuine old
Caucasian! May I shake your hand?"

And Kraft pushed us all aside, made his
way over to Trosenko and, grasping his hand,
shook it with deep emotion.

"Yes, we may say we have experienced
everything here," said Kraft. 'In '45 ... you
were there, were you not, Captain? Do you
remember the night of the twelfth, when we
spent the night up to our knees in mud, and
the next day we attacked the enemy
defences? I was attached to the commander-
in-chief at the time, and we captured fifteen
abatis in one day. Do you remember,
Captain?"

Trosenko nodded and stuck out his lower
lip, screwing up his eyes.

"You see..." Kraft began with great animation, addressing himself to the major and
making inappropriate gestures with his hands.

But the major had certainly heard the story
more than once before, and his eyes suddenly
took on such a glazed, dull look that Kraft
turned away from him and faced Bolkhov and
me, shifting his glance back and forth between
us. He didn't look once at Trosenko during
the whole of his story.

"You see, when we came out in the
morning, the commander-in-chief said to me,
'Kraft, take those abatis!' You know what

it's like in the army: no room for argument—
so it was just hand to cap, 'Yes, Your Excellency!' and into action. As soon as we got to
the first abatis I turned to my men and said,
'Now then, lads, look lively! If anyone falls
behind I'll make mincemeat out of him!'
With Russian soldiers, you know, you can't
beat about the bush. But just then there was
a shell... I look round—one soldier, two,
three ... then bullets—whee! whee! whee!
'Forward!' I cried, 'Follow me, men!' But
then, when we get there, I see a ... you know,
a ... what's it called?" And the raconteur
flourished his arms searching for the word.

"A ditch?" suggested Bolkhov.

"No... Ach, what is it? Good heavens,
what's it called now... A ditch," he said
quickly. "Guns at the ready! Hurrah! Ta-
ra-ta-ta-ta! But there wasn't a soul there.
We were all surprised. Well, no matter: on we
go to the second abatis. That was a different
matter altogether. Now our blood was stirred,
you know. We draw close to the second
abatis, I look, and I see we can't go on: there
is a—what d'you call it, a ... you know, a..."

"Another ditch," I offered.

"Not at all," he said, testily. "Not a ditch,
but a ... what's it called again?" And he made
an absurd gesture with his hand. "Ach, good
heavens, what is it..."

He appeared so upset that one could not
help wanting to help him.

"A river, perhaps," said Bolkhov.

"No, no, just a ditch. We were just trying to cross it when, would you believe it, they started firing on us ... it was sheer hell..."

At this point someone outside the hut asked for me. It was Maximov. And as I knew from having heard the story before that there were still thirteen abatis left, I was glad to seize the opportunity of returning to my platoon. Trosenko went out with me. "It's all lies," he said, when we were a few steps from the hut. "He was never anywhere near those abatis!" And Trosenko laughed so heartily that it made me laugh too.

XIII

It was already night, and only the fires dimly lit the camp, when I finished my duties and went to join my men. A large stump lay smouldering on the coals. Only three men were sitting round the fire: Antonov, who was turning a pot of *ryabko** on the fire; Zhdanov, who was pensively raking the embers with a long switch; and Chikin, with his pipe, as ever only half-lit. The others had already lain down to sleep, some under the ammunition-wagons, some on the hay, some by the camp-fires. In the faint light I could distinguish familiar backs, legs and heads; among those

* Soldiers' food made of soaked rusks and pork-fat.— L. T.

around the fire was the recruit, who seemed to be asleep already. Antonov made room for me and I sat down beside him and lit a cigarette. The smell of the fog and the smoke from the damp firewood spread through the air and made one's eyes smart, and still there was a fine drizzle falling from the dreary sky.

I could hear the regular sound of snoring, the carckling of branches in the fire, quiet voices, and now and again the noise of the infantry moving their rifles. All around, watch-fires were burning, lighting up or silhouetting the figures of the soldiers grouped around them. At the nearest fires I could make out the illuminated figures of naked soldiers waving their shirts above the flames. There were still many men awake, moving about and talking, within a space of about sixty square yards. But the dark, dense night gave a strange, mysterious air to all this movement, as though everyone was aware of the gloomy silence and was afraid to disturb it. When I started speaking I felt that my voice sounded out of place; on the faces of all the soldiers sitting by the fire I read the same frame of mind. I thought that before I came they had been talking about their wounded comrade, but that was not so: Chikin had been telling a story about receiving goods at Tiflis and about the schoolboys there.

I have always noticed, and especially in the Caucasus, the peculiar tact which the Russian soldier displays at times of danger, passing

over in silence everything which could have an
unfavourable effect on his comrades' morale.
The spirit of the Russian soldier is not based,
like the courage of southern peoples, on easily
inflammable but short-lived enthusiasm: it is
as hard to arouse him as it is to dispirit him.
He does not need effects, speeches, war-cries,
songs and drums; on the contrary, he needs
peace and order and a relaxed atmosphere.
In the Russian, in the true Russian soldier,
you will never observe bragging, showing off,
or the desire to fuddle his brains or to excite
himself in time of danger; on the contrary,
modesty, simplicity and the ability to see
something quite different from danger in a
dangerous situation are the distinguishing
marks of his character. I have seen a soldier
wounded in the leg, whose first thought was
of the hole in his new sheepskin coat, and
a cavalryman crawling out from under his
horse which had been killed, and unbuckling
the girths in order to salvage the saddle. Who
can forget the incident at the siege of Gerge-
bil, when the fuse of a loaded bomb caught
fire in the laboratory, and the gun-sergeant
told two soldiers to take the bomb and throw
it into a ravine; but the soldiers did not throw
it at the nearest place, beside the colonel's
tent, but ran farther afield with it, lest they
wake the gentlemen who were asleep in the
tent, and both soldiers were blown to pieces.
I also remember the time when, on the expedition of 1852, one of the young soldiers said

at one point that he thought the platoon was
done for, and the whole platoon angrily
descended upon him for saying such wicked
words, which they would not even repeat.
And now, when the thought of Velenchuk
must have been uppermost on everyone's
mind, and when the Tatars could creep up
and fire a volley at us at any moment, everyone listened to Chikin's sprightly story and
no one mentioned either today's action, or
the impending danger, or their wounded
comrade, as if it has all happened goodness
knows how long ago, or not at all. But it did
seem to me that their faces were rather
gloomier than usual; that they listened inat-
tentively to Chikin's story, and that even
Chikin felt that they were not listening, but
prattled on anyway.

Maximov came up and sat beside me at the
fire. Chikin made room for him, stopped
talking and began sucking his pipe again.

"The infantry sent some of their men to
the camp for vodka," said Maximov after a
long silence. "They've just come back." He
spat into the fire. "The sergeant says they saw
our man there."

"Is he alive?" asked Antonov, turning his pot.

"No, he's dead."

The recruit suddenly raised his head in its
little red cap and stared over the fire for a
moment at Maximov and me; then he quickly
dropped his head again and drew his coat
round him.

"You see, it wasn't for nothing that death visited him this morning, when I had to wake him in the artillery-park," said Antonov.

"Nonsense," said Zhdanov, turning a smouldering stump, and everyone fell silent.

In the silence, a shot rang out in the camp behind us. Our drummers beat the tattoo in response. When the last roll of the drums died away, Zhdanov got to his feet and took off his cap. The rest of us followed his example.

A harmonious choir of manly voices swelled out in the deep silence of the night:

"Our father, which art in Heaven, hallowed be Thy name. Thy kingdom come. Thy will be done on Earth, as it is in Heaven. Give us this day our daily bread, and forgive us our debts, as we forgive our debtors. Lead us not into temptation, but deliver us from evil..."

"One of our soldiers was hit by a shell just here, in '45," said Antonov, when we had put on our caps and sat down once more by the fire. "We carted him around with us on a gun-carriage for two days—do you remember Shevchenko, Zhdanov?—and then we had to leave him there, under a tree."

Just then an infantry soldier with enormous side-whiskers and moustaches, carrying a gun and a pouch, came up to our fire.

"May I have a light for my pipe, mates?" he said.

"Help yourself, there's fire enough," remarked Chikin.

"I take it it was Dargo you were speaking

of, was it?" the infantryman said to Antonov.

"Yes, Dargo in 1845," replied Antonov.

The infantryman shook his head, screwed up his eyes and squatted beside us.

"Yes, it was tough there," he observed.

"Why did you leave him behind?" I asked Antonov.

"His stomach wound was giving him a lot of pain. At the halting-places it was all right, but as soon as we moved on he would scream blue murder and beg us to leave him behind—but for a long time we couldn't bring ourselves to do it. And then *they* began to give us a bad time—they killed three of our men at the guns and one of the officers, and we got separated from our battery somehow. We were in trouble, and thought we might never get our guns away, it was so muddy."

"It was muddiest of all under the Andeisky Mountain," said one of the soldiers.

"Yes, that's where he got worse. Antoshenko—that was the old gun-sergeant—and me had a think about it: he doesn't have a hope of coming out of this alive, and he's begging us in God's name to be left. So maybe we should put him down here. And that's what we decided. There was a tree here, a sort of willow. We put down some soaked rusks for him—Zhdanov had some—leant him against the tree, put a clean shirt on him, and said farewell to him in the proper manner. Then we left him."

"And was he a good soldier?"

"Yes, not bad," said Zhdanov.

"What became of him, God only knows," Antonov continued. "A lot of our lads lost their lives there."

"At Dargo?" said the infantryman as he rose, scraping out his pipe and again screwing up his eyes and shaking his head. "It was tough."

And he left us.

"Are there many others in our battery who were at Dargo?" I asked.

"Certainly, there was Zhdanov here, me, Patsan who's on leave now, and another six or so—no more than that."

"What's Patsan up to staying away on leave all this time?" said Chikin, stretching out his legs and lying down with his head on a log. "I make it's nearly a year he's been away."

"What about you?" I asked Zhdanov. "Have you had your year's leave?"

"No, I haven't," he answered reluctantly.

"It's good to go, you know," said Antonov. "If you're from a rich family, or if you're fit to work yourself, then it's good to go, and they'll be glad to see you at home."

"But what if you have two brothers?" Zhdanov went on. "Who only scrape by as it is, without having to feed a soldier as well. You're not much help after twenty-five years' service. And besides, who knows if they're still alive!"

"Haven't you written?" I asked.

"Of course I have! Two letters, but I got no

answer. Either they're dead, or else they don't write because they're in dire straits themselves. So what's the use!"

"Did you write long ago?"

"I wrote the last letter when I got back from Dargo," said Zhdanov. "Sing us *The Birch-Tree*!" he added, turning to Antonov, who was sitting with his elbows on his knees, humming a tune.

Antonov started singing *The Birch-Tree*.

"This is Grandpa Zhdanov's most favourite song," whispered Chikin to me, tugging at my coat. "Sometimes when Filipp Antonich sings it, he even cries, he does."

Zhdanov sat perfectly still at first, with his eyes fixed on the glowing coals, and his face looked stern in the reddish light. Then his jaws started moving faster and faster below his ears, and finally he stood up, spread out his coat on the ground and lay down in the shadows behind the fire. Either it was his tossing and groaning as he settled to sleep, or it may have been the effect Velenchuk's death and the dismal weather had on me, but it really seemed to me that he was crying.

The bottom of the charred stump flared up now and again and illuminated the figure of Antonov with his grey moustaches, his red face, and his medals on the coat thrown over his shoulders; sometimes it lit up someone's boots, head or back.

The same dreary drizzle was falling, and the same scent of dampness and smoke was in the air; the dying camp-fires still glowed all around, and only the strains of Antonov's doleful song disturbed the silence. And whenever he paused for a moment, the tune seemed to be taken up by the faint nocturnal noises of the camp—snoring, the clanking of sentries' rifles, and low voices.

"Second watch! Makatyuk and Zhdanov!" cried Maximov.

Antonov stopped singing. Zhdanov got up with a sigh, stepped across a log, and set off quietly to the guns.

15 June 1855

TWO HUSSARS

DEDICATED TO COUNTESS M. N. TOLSTAYA

In the early years of the 19th century, at a time when there were no railways or highways, no gas or stearin lights, no low spring-cushioned sofas or unlacquered furniture, when there were no disillusioned youths with monocles in their eyes, no liberal-minded lady-philosophers, no *dames aux camélias* who have sprung up in such numbers in our day—in those innocent times when anyone travelling from Moscow to St. Petersburg loaded his cart or his carriage with a whole kitchenful of cooked victuals, drove eight days and nights over soft dusty or muddy roads and put his faith in fried cutlets, hot *bubliki*, and Valdai carriage-bells—at a time when wax candles smoked in long autumn evenings, casting their light on family circles of twenty or thirty members, and when the candelabra in ball-rooms were filled with wax and spermaceti candles and furniture was distributed symmetrically and the youth of our fathers was indicated not only by the absence of wrinkles and grey hair, but also by the duels they fought over ladies and the agility with which they leaped from one corner of a room to another to pick up the handkerchiefs dropped accidentally or otherwise; when our mothers wore high-waisted gowns with enormous sleeves and decided all household problems by the drawing of lots; when adorable *dames aux camélias* shrank from the light of day—in those innocent days of masonic lodges, Martinists, and the Tugendbund, in the days of Miloradovich, Davidov, and Pushkin—in those days there was an assembly of rich landowners in the town of K., centre of the gubernia, and final elections of representatives of the nobility had just been held.

I

"No matter, I shall put up in the public room if needs be," said a young officer in a greatcoat and hussar cap who had just climbed out of a sleigh and was now entering the finest hotel the town of K. could boast of.

"It's such a big assembly, Your Excellency, something extraordinary," said the page-boy who had already learned from the officer's servant that he was Count Tourbin and therefore addressed him as "Your Excellency".

"The mistress of the Afremovskaya estate has promised to leave with her daughters this evening, so if you wish I can put you up in room eleven," he said, stepping softly down the corridor in front of the count and continually glancing back.

In the public room, at a small table below a time-darkened full-length portrait of Tsar Alexander, sat a few men drinking champagne. They were, apparently, members of the local gentry, and near them was a group of travelling merchants in dark blue fur-lined coats.

When the count had entered the room and called Blücher, an enormous grey dog, he flung off his coat before the hoarfrost had melted on the collar, ordered vodka, sat down at the table in his blue satin tunic, and began talking to the gentlemen who, instantly attracted by his handsome figure and open countenance, offered him a glass of champagne. The count first tossed off a glass of vodka, then ordered another bottle to treat his new acquaintances to. The sleigh-driver came in at this point to ask for money for a drink.

"Sasha!" cried the count. "Give it to him!"

The driver went out with Sasha and returned presently, holding the money in his outstretched palm.

"Look at this, Y'r Excellency, after the way I put out on your account and your promising me half a ruble and he gives me a quarter!"

"Sasha! Give him a ruble!"

Sasha stared sulkily at the driver's boots.

"It's enough for him," he said in a deep bass voice. "And besides, I haven't got any more money."

The count took two five-ruble notes out of his purse (the last it contained) and gave one of them to the sleigh-driver, who kissed his hand and went out.

"A pretty pass I've come to!" said the count. "My last five rubles."

"That's a true hussar for you!" said one of the gentlemen with a smile. Judging by his moustache, his voice, and a certain energetic looseness in his legs, he was a retired cavalry officer. "Do you intend staying here long, Count?"

"I wouldn't stay at all if it weren't that I must get some money. There aren't even any rooms to be had in this accursed hotel, devil take it!"

"Allow me to share my room with you, Count," said the cavalry officer. "I'm in room seven. If you have no objections to putting up with me, you must try to spend three days here. Tonight the Marshal of Nobility is giving a ball. He will be delighted to have you."

"True enough, Count, do stay," put in another of the company, a handsome young man. "What is your hurry? After all, they only take place once in three years, the elections. You might at least have a look at our young ladies, Count."

"Sasha! Get out my linen: I'm going to the bathhouse," said the count, getting up. "After that we'll see—perhaps I really will look in at the Marshal's."

He called one of the waiters and said something to him that made the man chuckle and reply, "Everything's possible, Y'r Excellency." Then he went out.

"So I'll have them put my portmanteau in your room," the count called back from out in the corridor.

"I'll consider it a great favour," replied the cavalry officer, running over to the door. "Room seven, don't forget."

As soon as the count's footsteps had died away the cavalry officer came back to the table and, drawing his chair closer to the clerk and smiling straight into his eyes, said:

"He's the very man!"

"You don't say!"

"He is, I tell you—the hussar famous for duelling. Tourbin's his name, everyone knows him. I'll wager he recognized me—he must have. He and I were on a spree at Lebedyan that lasted three weeks that time I was sent there for remounts. A little incident took place—he and I were responsible for it; that's why he pretended not to recognize me. A fine fellow, eh?"

"A fine fellow indeed. And what nice manners! Nobody would guess he was that sort," said the handsome young man. "And we made friends so quickly. I don't suppose he's more than five-and-twenty, is he?"

"He doesn't look it, but he is. But one has to really know him to appreciate him. Who ran off with Madame Migunova? He did. And who killed Sablin? And who dropped Matnev out of the window by his legs? And who won three hundred thousand from Prince Nesterov? You cannot imagine what a reckless chap he is! A gambler, a duellist, a seducer. But he's got the soul of a hussar, a true hussar. People are fond of maligning us, but they don't appreciate what a true hussar is! Ah, those were the days!"

And the cavalry officer launched into an account of his debaucheries with the count at Lebedyan that not only never took place but never could have taken place. They could not, first of all, because he had never before set eyes on the count and had retired from the army two years before the count entered it; and in the second place because the cavalry officer never served in the cavalry; he had been for four years the humblest cadet in the Belevsky Regiment and had resigned as soon as he got his commission as ensign. But ten years before, on coming into his inheritance, he really had made a trip to Lebedyan where, in the company of some remount officers, he had squandered seven hundred rubles and ordered himself an Uhlan uniform with orange cuffs with the intention of joining the lancers. So great was his longing to enter the cavalry that the three weeks spent in the company of remount officers in Lebedyan remained the happiest days of his life, and he mentally transformed this longing into reality, then into recollection, so that he himself came to believe firmly in his cavalry career, a thing which in no way prevented his being, in respect to honesty and amiability, a truly worthy gentleman.

"Ah, yes, none but those who have served in the cavalry can appreciate our sort." He straddled his chair and thrust out his lower jaw as he went on in a deep bass voice: "Time was when I'd be riding at the head of my squadron with a horse under me that was more of a devil than a horse; there I'd be sitting, a devil myself, and up rides the squadron commander to review us. 'Ensign,' says he, 'we can't manage this without you. Be so kind as to lead the squadron on parade.' 'Very well, sir,' say I, and no sooner said than done. Round I whirl, shout a command to my moustachioed bravos, and away we go! Ah, those were the days!"

The count came back from the bathhouse with a flushed face and wet hair and went straight to room seven where the cavalry officer was sitting in his dressing-gown with a pipe between his teeth, reflecting with a delight tinged by apprehension on the good luck that had fallen to his lot—that of sharing his room with the famous Tourbin. "But what," thought he, "if he should suddenly take it into his head to strip me naked, lead me outside the town, and bury me in the snow, or smear me all over with tar, or simply ... but no, he wouldn't treat a comrade-in-arms like that," he comforted himself.

"Sasha! Feed Blücher!" shouted the count.

Sasha, who had a glass of vodka and was fairly tipsy, put in an appearance.

"Couldn't wait! Drunk already, you ruffian! Feed Blücher!"

"He won't die without it; see how sleek he is," said Sasha, patting the dog.

"No back talk if you please! Feed him!"

"All you care about is your dog; if your man takes a glass you shout at him."

"Ay, I'll strike you!" shouted the count in a voice that made the window-panes rattle and frightened the cavalry officer a little.

"You might ask whether your Sasha's had anything to eat today. Go ahead and strike me if you think more of a dog than a man," said Sasha. But at this point he got such a blow on the nose that he fell down, striking his head against the wall; the next instant he had leaped to his feet with his hand over his nose; he rushed out of the door and threw himself down on a trunk in the corridor.

"He's knocked my teeth out," he muttered, wiping his bloody nose with one hand while with the other he scratched the back of Blücher, who was licking himself. "He's knocked my teeth out, Blücher, but he's my count all the same and I'll go through fire and water for him, and that's the truth, because, you see, he's my count, Blücher. Are you hungry, Blücher?"

When he had lain there for a few minutes, he got up, fed the dog, and, almost sober, went to serve his count and offer him tea.

"I'll take it as an affront," the cavalry officer was saying meekly to the count, who lay on the officer's bed with his feet up on the bed-post. "I, too, am an old soldier and comrade, so to speak. Rather than have you take money from someone else I would gladly give you two hundred rubles myself. At present I don't have that much—only one hundred—but I will get the rest this very day. I would simply take it as an affront, Count."

"Thanks, old fellow," said the count, slapping him on the back and divining at once the relations that were sure to arise between them. "Thanks. Well, if that's how matters stand, we'll go to the ball. But what shall we do for the present? Tell me what goes on in this town: are there any pretty girls here? any rakes? any card-players?"

The cavalry officer said there would be a bevy of pretty girls at the ball, that the greatest rake in town was the newly-elected police captain Kolkov, but that he did not have the recklessness of a hussar, but was a good sort; that Ilyushka's Gypsy chorus had been singing here ever since elections began, that Stesha was the soloist, and that everyone was planning to go and hear the

Gypsies after the ball.

"And there's quite a lot of card-playing," he said. "Lukhnov, a wealthy visitor, plays all the time and Ilyin, in room eight, a cornet in an Uhlan regiment, has been losing heavily. They've begun already. They play every evening, and you wouldn't believe what a nice chap that Ilyin is, Count; nothing mean about him—why, he'd give you the shirt off his back."

"Then let's go and see him. We'll have a look at who's here," said the count.

"Let's go, let's go. They'll be awfully glad to meet you."

II

Ilyin, the cornet in the Uhlans, had only just waked up. The night before he had sat himself down at the card-table at eight o'clock and had played for fifteen hours at a stretch, until eleven o'clock in the morning. It was a great sum he had lost, but he himself could not have told exactly how great, for he had with him three thousand of his own money and fifteen thousand from the regiment treasury which he had long since mixed up with his own and was afraid to count lest he be confirmed in his fears that his losses had already encroached on the treasury money. It was almost noon before he had fallen into the heavy dreamless sleep that comes only to the young, and then only after heavy losses at cards. On waking up at six o'clock in the evening, at the very hour when Count Tourbin arrived at the hotel, and seeing the cards and the chalk scattered over the floor and the stained tables in the centre of the room, he remembered with horror the night's gaming, and especially his last card, a knave, that had brought him a loss of five hundred roubles, but, unwilling to accept the reality of his situation, he took his money out from under his pillow and set to counting it. He recognized certain bank notes that had passed from hand to hand in "corners" and "transports", and this brought to mind the whole course of his playing. His own three thousand were gone, as well as some two and a half thousand of the regiment's money.

The Uhlan had been playing for four nights running.

He was travelling from Moscow, where he had been entrusted with the regiment's money. In the town of K. he had been detained by the overseer of the posting-station on the pretext that there was no change of horses, but as a matter of fact by a secret agreement with the hotel owner that all travellers should be detained overnight in this town. The Uhlan, a gay young lad who had just been presented with three thousand rubles by his parents on the occasion of his being appointed to a regiment, was only too glad to spend a few days in the town of K.

during election festivities, for he hoped to have his fill of enjoyment here. A country gentleman of his acquaintance, a family man, lived in these parts, and just as he was making ready to drive out to see him and pay court to his daughters, the cavalry officer turned up and made his acquaintance. And that very evening, with no ill intentions, he had introduced him to his friend Lukhnov and some other card-players in the public room. From then on the Uhlan had been sitting at the card-table. He had forgotten all about his friend the country gentleman; he had even forgotten to ask for horses; he had, in fact, not so much as come out of his room for four days running.

When he had dressed himself and had his breakfast, he sauntered over to the window. A little walk, he thought, would help drive the insistent thoughts of the cards out of his mind. He put on his greatcoat and went outside. The sun had already sunk behind the red-roofed white houses; twilight had settled over the land. The air was warm. Flakes of wet snow were falling softly on the dirty streets. The thought that he had slept away this day, now drawing to a close, filled him with deep sadness.

"Never will this lost day come back," he thought. "I've squandered my youth," he said to himself, not because he really thought he had squandered his youth—indeed he harboured no thoughts at all on this subject—

but because the phrase suddenly came into his mind.

"What am I to do now?" he reflected. "Borrow money from somebody and go away?" A young woman passed him on the pavement. "What a foolish-looking lady," he thought for some odd reason. "There's no one I could borrow from. I've squandered my youth." He went on to a row of shops. A merchant in a coat lined with fox was standing in the door of one of them touting for customers. "If I hadn't got rid of that eight-spot I would have made up my losses." An old beggar-woman whimpered as she followed at his heels. "There's no one I can borrow from." A man in a bearskin coat drove past; a watchman stood on duty. "What could I do that would cause a sensation? Fire at these people? Too dull. I've squandered my youth. What a fine set of trappings hanging on display! Oh, to go dashing off in a sleigh-and-three! I'll go back to the hotel. Lukhnov will come soon and we shall begin playing."

He went back and counted his money again. No, he had made no mistake the first time: two thousand five hundred rubles were missing from the regiment money. "I'll stake twenty-five on the first card, then a 'corner' on the second, then seven times the stake, then fifteen, thirty, sixty times, up to three thousand rubles. Then I'll buy those trappings and go away. But he won't let me win, the ruffian! I've squandered my youth."

These were the thoughts that were passing through the Uhlan's mind when Lukhnov came into his room.

"Have you been up long, Mikhailo Vasilyich?" asked Lukhnov, slowly removing his gold spectacles from his bony nose and polishing them deliberately on a red silk handkerchief.

"No, I just got up. Slept beautifully."

"A hussar has just arrived. He's staying with Zavalshevsky. Have you heard?"

"No, I haven't. Where are the others?"

"They've dropped in to see Pryakhin. They'll come directly."

And, true enough, they were soon joined by the others: an officer from the local garrison who always accompanied Lukhnov; a Greek merchant with an enormous hooked nose, brown skin, and deep-set black eyes; a fat, cushiony landowner who ran a brewery by day and gambled by night, always for half-ruble points.

Everyone was anxious to begin playing, but no hint of this was given by the principal players, especially Lukhnov, who spoke with great composure on the lawlessness in Moscow.

"Just to think!" he said. "Moscow, one of our greatest towns, a citadel, and at night ruffians roam the streets with hooks in their hands, dressed up as goblins, terrifying the foolish rabble, robbing travellers, and nothing is done about it. What are the police thinking of!—that's what I should like to know."

The Uhlan listened attentively to his account of the lawlessness, but at last he got up and quietly gave orders to bring the cards. The fat landowner was the first to give voice to their desire:

"Well, gentlemen, why should we waste the golden hours? Let's get down to business!"

"I can understand your wanting to, after all the money you took home with you last night," said the Greek.

"But it really is time," said the garrison officer.

Ilyin glanced at Lukhnov, Lukhnov looked him straight in the eye and calmly went on talking about the ruffians disguised as goblins with long claws.

"Shall we deal the cards?" asked the Uhlan. "Isn't it too early?"

"Belov!" called out the Uhlan, reddening for some reason. "Bring me some dinner, I haven't had a bite to eat yet, gentlemen. Bring champagne, and give us the cards."

Just at that moment the count and Zavalshevsky came into the room. It turned out that Tourbin and Ilyin were in the same division. They quickly became friends, toasted each other in champagne, and in five minutes were talking like bosom-friends. Ilyin made the best possible impression on the count, who smiled as he watched him and teased him for being so young.

"There's an Uhlan for you!" said he. "Such whiskers! Such ferocious whiskers!"

The down on Ilyin's upper lip was perfectly white.

"Are you getting ready to play cards?" said the count. "Well, I hope you win, Ilyin. You're a first-rate player, aren't you?" he added with a smile.

"We are getting ready," replied Lukhnov as he opened a pack of cards. "Won't you join us, Count?"

"No, not this evening. I'd strip you clean if I did. Any bank cracks wide open when I play. But I have nothing to play with now. I lost everything at the posting-station near Volochok. A deuced infantryman with rings on his fingers cleaned me out. He must have been a card-sharper."

"Why, did you have to wait long at the station?" asked Ilyin.

"Twenty-two hours. I'll never forget that accursed station, but the postmaster will never forget me, either."

"How is that?"

"I drive up, out leaps the postmaster with his sly, ugly little mug. 'No horses,' says he. I must tell you I've made the following rule for myself: whenever I'm told there are no horses, I go straight to the overseer's chamber without taking off my coat—not to the public room, mind you, but to his private chamber, and order all the doors and windows opened, as if the place were full of charcoal fumes. So that's what I did in this case. Cold! Remember what frosts we had last month? Four below. The postmaster tried to argue with me, but I just gave him one in the nose. An old lady and some wenches and females began screeching, picked up their pots, and were about to run off to the village. I blocked their way and shouted. "Give me some horses and I'll go; if you don't you can freeze to death; I won't let anyone out!' "

"That's the way to treat 'em!" said the cushiony land-owner, going off into peals of laughter. "Like freezing out beetles."

"But I didn't keep my eye on them—went off somewhere—and the postmaster and his women gave me the slip. The only hostage left me was the old lady lying up on the stove-bunk, who kept sneezing, and saying her prayers. After that we opened negotiations: the postmaster came back and urged me from a distance to let the old lady go, but I just sicked Blücher on him—Blücher has a nose for postmasters. But he didn't give me horses till the next morning, the blackguard! That's how I got to know that deuced infantry officer. I went into the next room and began playing with him. Have you seen Blücher? Blücher! Come here!"

Blücher came. The gamblers paid him condescending attention, but it was clear they were anxious to be doing something else.

"But why aren't you playing, gentlemen? Don't let me keep you from your game. I am

something of a windbag, you know," said
Tourbin. " 'Love me, love me not'—a good
game."

III

Lukhnov moved over two candles, took out
an enormous brown purse stuffed full of
money, opened it with the slowness of one
performing a mystic rite, drew out two hun-
dred-ruble notes, and slipped them under the
cards.

"A bank of two hundred rubles, just as
yesterday," he said, putting his spectacles
straight and unsealing a new pack of cards.

"Very well," said Ilyin without looking at
him and continuing the conversation he was
holding with Tourbin.

The game began. Lukhnov dealt with
machine-like precision, stopping from time to
time to mark a point unhurriedly, or glancing
severely over his spectacles to say in a feeble
voice, "Your lead." The cushiony landowner
made more noise than anyone else making
calculations to himself aloud and smudging
the cards with pudgy fingers as he bent down
the corners. The garrison officer jotted down
his points in a neat hand and turned down the
edges of his cards ever so slightly under the
table. The Greek sat next to Lukhnov, who
was keeping the bank, and his deep-set black
eyes followed the game with the strained

attention of one waiting for something to happen. Zavalshevsky, standing at the table, suddenly became all movement: he took a red or blue bank-note out of his pocket, put a card on it, clapped his hand down on it, cried out for luck, "Come along, seven," bit his moustache, shifted from one foot to the other, grew red in the face, twitched all over, and kept on twitching till he got a card. Ilyin ate veal and cucumbers from a plate that was placed beside him on the horse-hair sofa, hurriedly wiped his fingers on his jacket, and threw down one card after the other. Tourbin, who from the very beginning had been sitting on the sofa, instantly saw what was happening. Lukhnov did not so much as glance at the Uhlan and said not a word to him; he would only glance through his spectacles at his hands from time to time. Most of the Uhlan's cards were losing ones.

"That's a card I should like to take," said Lukhnov, referring to the card of the cushiony landowner, who was playing for half-ruble stakes.

"You take Ilyin's cards—why bother about mine?" said the landowner.

And true enough, no one's cards seemed as ill-fated as Ilyin's. Each time he lost he nervously tore the offending card under the table and chose another with shaking hands. Tourbin got up off the sofa and asked the Greek to allow him to sit next to the player kepping the bank. The Greek changed his seat

and the count, taking his chair, fixed his eyes
on Lukhnov's hands.

"Ilyin!" he said suddenly in a voice which,
though in his ordinary tone, drowned out all
other sounds. "What makes you think that
card's lucky? You don't know how to play."

"However I play, it all comes to the same
thing."

"You're certain to lose if that's how you
feel. Here, let me take your hand."

"Oh no, thank you: I never let anyone play
for me. Play for yourself if you want to."

"I told you I didn't want to: I was just
offering for your sake. I'm sorry to see you
losing so."

"That seems to be my fate."

The count said nothing else; he merely put
his elbows on the table and once more stared
at Lukhnov's hands.

"Very bad," he suddenly drawled in a loud
voice.

Lukhnov glanced at him.

"Very, very bad," he repeated still louder,
looking Lukhnov straight in the eye.

They went on playing.

"A dirty business," said Tourbin as Lukhnov took another one of Ilyin's cards.

"Just what are you displeased with,
Count?" asked Lukhnov in a tone of polite
indifference.

"The way you take Ilyin's cards. That's
what's bad." Lukhnov made a slight movement of his shoulders and brows that seemed

to say one must accept one's fate, and went on playing.

"Blücher! Come here!" cried the count, getting up. "At him, Blücher!" he said quickly.

Blücher nearly knocked the garrison officer down as he leaped out from under the sofa, rushed over to his master, and stood beside him growling, wagging his tail, and eyeing the company in a way that said, "Which is the recreant, eh?"

Lukhnov put down his cards and pushed back his chair. "It is impossible to play under the circumstances," he said, "I can't abide dogs. How is one expected to play with a whole kennelful of dogs in the room?"

"Especially dogs like that—leeches they're called, I believe," chimed in the garrison officer.

"Well, Mikhailo Vasilyich, are we to go on with our game or not?" said Lukhnov to his host.

"Please don't interfere, Count," said Ilyin to Tourbin.

"Come here a moment," said Tourbin, taking Ilyin by the arm and drawing him out of the room.

Everything the count said could be heard distinctly, for he spoke without lowering his voice. And his voice was such that it could always be heard three rooms away.

"Have you gone quite daft? Can't you see that that gentleman in the spectacles is an accomplished card-sharper?"

"Oh, come. What are you saying?"

"Drop it, I tell you. What matters it to me? At any other time I myself would be only too glad to take your money away from you, but tonight for some reason I'm sorry to see you taken such advantage of. Are you sure it's all your own money you are playing with?"

"Yes! ... er... Why? What have you in mind?"

"I've travelled that same road myself, friend, and so I know all the tricks of these sharpers; and that fellow in the spectacles is a sharper, I tell you. Drop it, do; it's a bit of comradely advice I'm giving you."

"I'll only play one more round."

"I know what 'one more' means. Well, we'll see."

They came back. In one round Ilyin threw down so many cards and so many of them were beaten that he sustained heavy losses.

Tourbin spread out his hands on the table.

"Enough!" he cried. "Come away!"

"I can't now; be good enough to let me alone," said Ilyin in vexation, shuffling the bent cards without looking at Tourbin.

"Then the devil take you! Go on losing if you enjoy it so much, but I must be going. Zavalshevsky! Come along with me to the Marshal's!"

They went out. No one said a word, and Lukhnov did not deal until the sound of their steps and the click of Blücher's claws had died away down the corridor.

"What a fellow!" said the landowner, laughing.

"Well, he won't interfere with us now," added the garrison officer hurriedly, still speaking in a whisper.

And they went on playing.

IV

The musicians, the Marshal's house serfs, standing in the pantry that had been cleared for the occasion, had already turned back the cuffs of their coats and, at a given signal, had begun to play the old-fashioned polonaise "Alexander-Elizabeth", and in the soft bright light of the wax candles the couples had begun to step gracefully out on to the parquet floor of the large hall (first the governor, a general of Catherine's court, wearing a star on his breast and holding the arm of the Marshal's thin wife; then the Marshal holding the arm of the governor's wife; then all the others, members of the gubernia's ruling families in various groupings and combinations) when Zavalshevsky in a blue frock-coat with puffs on the shoulders and an enormous collar, in long hose and dancing shoes, diffusing the scent of jasmine which had been so generously sprinkled on his moustache, his lapels, and his handkerchief, entered the room accompanied by a handsome hussar in tight blue riding-breeches and a gold-embroidered red tunic ornamented with the Vladimir Cross and the Medal of 1812. The count, though not above average height, was extremely well built. His clear blue very bright eyes and the large ringlets of his thick chestnut hair added something particularly winning to his beauty. His appearance in the ball-room was not un-expected: the handsome young man who had seen him in the hotel had informed the Marshal of his intention to be present. The news had been variously received, but on the whole without great enthusiasm. "He may make fun of us," said the men and the elderly ladies. "What if he should elope with me?" was the thought that occurred to most of the girls and young women.

As soon as the polonaise was over and the dancing partners had bowed to each other and parted, the women to join the women, the men the men, Zavalshevsky, proud and happy, led the count to the hostess. The Marshal's wife, inwardly fearful lest the count reduce her to ridicule in front of everybody, turned her head and said with proud con-descension, "Charmed. I hope you will dance," following the words by a glance of distrust that seemed to say, "You would be a ruffian indeed if you insulted a lady after this!" But the count soon dispelled all prejudice by his courtesy, attentiveness, gaiety, and elegant appearance, so that in five minutes the expression of the hostess's face said to all, "I know how to manage such gentlemen; he instantly understood to whom he was talking. Wait and see, he will be paying me attention the whole evening." But at this point the governor, who had known the count's father, came up to him and drew him aside so that he might engage him in conversation, a thing that further served to calm the fears of the local gentry and raised the count in their estimation. A little later Zavalshevsky introduced him to his sister, a plump young widow who had not taken her large black eyes off him from the moment he had entered the room. The count invited her to dance the waltz that the orchestra was then playing, and his skill in dancing finally dispelled the last remnants of prejudice against him.

"He certainly dances marvellously," said the fat wife of a country gentleman as she followed the legs in the blue riding-breeches whirling about the room, and counted to herself, "One, two, three; one, two, three— marvellous!"

"What a tripper! What a tripper!" said another woman, a visitor in the town, who was considered rather vulgar in local society. "How is it he doesn't strike anyone with his spurs! Marvellous! So light on his feet!"

In his performance, the count eclipsed the three best dancers in the gubernia: the tall, tow-headed adjutant to the governor who was famous for the swiftness with which he

danced and the closeness with which he held
his partner; a cavalry officer, who had a particularly graceful way of swaying as he waltzed
and of tapping his heels very lightly and
rapidly; and still another gentleman, a civilian,
who everyone said was a superb dancer and
the life of any ball, even if he was not gifted
with a great mind. And indeed this gentleman
did not rest a moment from the beginning
to the end of a ball, asking all the ladies in
order as they sat, stopping only on rare
occasions to wipe his tired but beaming face
with a moist handkerchief. The count outdid
them all and danced with the three ladies of
most consequence at the ball: a large one—
rich and handsome and stupid; a middle-sized
one—thin, not very pretty, but elegantly
dressed; and a little one—very plain but very
clever. He danced with others, too; with all,
in fact, who were pretty, and there were
many pretty women at the ball. But the one
who pleased him most was Zavalshevsky's
sister, the widow. With her he danced a
quadrille, an écossaise, and a mazurka. He
began by paying her many compliments
during the quadrille, comparing her to Venus,
Diana, a rose, and some other flower. The
little widow responded to all these civilities
by bending her fair white neck and lowering
her eyes as she gazed at her white muslin
frock and shifted her fan from one hand to
the other. When she said, "Dear me, Count,
you are only jesting," and other things of the

same sort, her voice, which was rather husky, expressed such innocent candour and comic simplicity that as he gazed at her he could not help thinking that she really was more like a flower than a woman; and not a rose, but some full-blown pink-and-white wild flower without any scent, growing in a pristine snowbank, all by itself, in a far country.

Her artlessness and lack of the usual affectations, combined with her fresh beauty, made such an odd impression on the count that on several occasions during their conversation, as he gazed mutely into her eyes or at the lovely line of her arms and neck, he was seized by so strong a desire to take her in his arms and kiss her that he had difficulty in controlling himself. The little widow was pleased to note the impression she made, but there was something in the count's behaviour that began to disturb and frighten her, even though, besides being fawningly attentive, he was respectful to a fault, judging by prevailing standards. He rushed off to bring her refreshments, picked up her handkerchief, snatched her chair out of the hands of a scrofulous-looking young rival, and performed innumerable other small services.

Seeing that all his efforts to play the gallant made little impression on her, he attempted to be amusing by recounting funny stories and assuring her that at her bidding he would stand on his head, crow like a cock, throw himself out of the window or through a hole in the ice on the river. He was entirely successful in this. The little widow became very gay, breaking into peals of laughter that showed her beautiful white teeth. She was highly pleased with her cavalier. And with every passing minute the count became more infatuated, so that by the end of the quadrille he was truly in love.

When the idle eighteen-year-old son of the richest landowner in the region, who had long worshipped the widow (that same scrofulous-looking youth out of whose hands Tourbin had snatched the chair) came up to her at the end of the quadrille, she received him coldly and displayed not a tenth part of the perturbation excited in her by the count.

"A fine person, you!" she said to him, her eyes fixed on Tourbin's back as she unconsciously calculated how many yards of gold braid had gone into the making of his coat. "A fine one, you! You promised to come and take me for a sleigh-ride and to bring me some chocolates."

"But I did come, Anna Fyodorovna. You were not at home and I left a box of the very finest chocolates for you," said the youth, who, despite his tallness, spoke in a small, thrill voice.

"You always find excuses. I don't want your chocolates. Please don't think—"

"I can see how you have changed towards me, Anna Fyodorovna, and I know why. And it is very wrong of you," he added. He seemed to have something else to say, but his agitation set his lips to trembling so violently that he could not speak.

Anna Fyodorovna did not listen to him and went on watching Tourbin.

The Marshal, the host of the evening, a stout, toothless, majestic old gentleman, went over to the count and, taking him by the arm, invited him into his study to smoke and have a drink if he felt so inclined. As soon as Tourbin went out, Anna Fyodorovna, for whom the ball-room was now as good as empty, took the hand of a thin spinster with whom she was friendly and drew her into the dressing-room.

"Well, do you like him?" asked the spinster.

"But it's awful the way he makes up to me!" said Anna Fyodorovna, going over to a mirror and gazing into it.

Her face was shining, her eyes were laughing, she was even blushing, and suddenly, in imitation of the ballet-dancers she had seen perform at the elections, she pirouetted on one toe, then gave that charming deep-throated little laugh of hers and leaped into the air, kicking up her heels.

"And what do you think?—he asked me for a keepsake," she said to her friend. "But he'll not get a s-i-n-g-l-e th-i-ng!" She sang the last two words, holding up one finger sheathed in a kid-glove.

In the study to which the Marshal guided

Tourbin were various brands of vodka, liqueurs, and champagne, and plates of hors d'oeuvres. Members of the local gentry were sitting or walking about in a fog of tobacco smoke, discussing the elections.

"If the nobility of our uyezd honoured him by election," the newly-elected police captain, already quite tipsy, was saying, "he had no right to shirk his duties, he had no right to—"

The talk was interrupted by the advent of the count. Everyone was introduced to him and the police captain shook his hand with particular cordiality and begged him over and over again to join the party he was treating to supper after the ball at a new tavern where they could hear a Gypsy chorus. The count accepted the invitation and drank several glasses of champagne with him.

"But why aren't you dancing, gentlemen?" he asked as he was about to leave the study.

"We're not much when it comes to dancing," laughed the police captain. "We make a better showing with the bottle, Count. By the way, they've all grown up under my very nose, these young ladies, Count. And sometimes I do step out in an écossaise, Count—I'm still up to it, Count."

"Then let's step out now," said Tourbin. "Let's enjoy ourselves here before we go to hear the Gypsies."

"Why not, gentlemen? Let us do it to please our host."

And three red-faced noblemen, who had been sitting in the study and drinking since the very beginning of the ball, drew on their gloves, one a pair of black kid-gloves, the others—silk knitted ones, and were just about to go out into the ball-room when they were stopped by the scrofulous-looking young man who, white-lipped and scarcely able to restrain his tears, went up to Tourbin.

"You think that just because you are a count you can push people about as if you were in the market-place," he said, breathing with difficulty. "It's rude and ... and..."

Again the trembling of his lips put a stop to the rush of his words.

"What?" cried Tourbin, suddenly scowling, "What? You pup!" he cried, seizing the youth's hands and squeezing them so hard that the blood rushed to his face more from fright than insult. "Is it a duel you want to fight with me? If so I am at your service."

As soon as Tourbin let go of his hands, two gentlemen took the youth by the arms and led him away to the door in the rear.

"Are you mad? You must have taken too much to drink. We'll tell your father. What in the world is the matter with you?" they asked him.

"I am not drunk, but he pushes people about without so much as apologizing. He's a swine, that's what he is," wailed the youth, now close to tears.

But his complaints were ignored and he was taken home.

"Pay no heed to him, Count," said the police captain and Zavalshevsky, eager to mollify Tourbin. "He's a mere child; why, he still takes spankings. He's only sixteen years old. Whatever could have got into him? He must be mad. And his father is such a highly respected gentleman—our candidate."

"Well, the deuce with him if he doesn't want satisfaction."

And the count went into the ball-room, danced an écossaise as gaily as ever with the pretty little widow, laughed wholeheartedly on seeing the performance of the gentlemen who had come out of the study with him, and gave a roar that rang throughout the ball-room when the police captain slipped and fell down amidst the dancing couples.

V

While the count was in the study, Anna Fyodorovna, feeling that she ought to feign indifference to him, went up to her brother and asked nonchalantly, "Tell me, brother, who is that hussar who danced with me?" The cavalry officer did his best to explain to her what a very great hussar Tourbin was, adding that he had remained in town and come to the ball only because his money had been stolen from him on the road, and that he himself had lent the count one hundred roubles, but that that was too little and could not his sister lend him another two hundred? At the same time he asked her not to mention this to anyone, especially the count. Anna Fyodorovna promised to send her brother the money that very evening and to keep the matter a secret, but during the écossaise she was seized by an irresistible desire to offer the count any sum he needed. It took her some time to pluck up the courage to do it; she blushed and hesitated, but at last, with a great effort, broached the subject.

"My brother told me you met with misfortune on the road, Count, and that now you have no money. If you are in need of any, perhaps you would accept it from me? It would make me exceedingly happy."

No sooner were the words out of her mouth than Anna Fyodorovna grew frightened and turned red. All the joy went out of the count's face.

"Your brother's a dunce," he said curtly. "As you are aware, when a man insults another man he is challenged to a duel. But do you know what happens when a woman insults a man?"

Poor Anna Fyodorovna felt her neck and ears burning with shame. She dropped her eyes and said not a word.

"The woman is kissed in front of everybody," whispered the count, bending down to her ear. "Allow me to kiss your hand," he added softly after a long pause, taking pity on the lady for the confusion she was suffering.

"Oh, but not now," said Anna Fyodorovna with a deep sigh.

"When? I am leaving early tomorrow. And you owe it to me."

"But under the circumstances I cannot pay it," said Anna Fyodorovna with a smile.

"Give me the opportunity of seeing you tonight so that I can kiss your hand. But I shall find it myself."

"How will you?"

"That is my concern. I would do anything to see you. You don't object?"

"No."

The écossaise came to an end. They danced another mazurka, during which the count performed wonders, catching handkerchiefs, dropping on one knee and clicking his spurs together in the peculiar Warsaw manner, so that the old men left their card-tables to watch the dancing, and the cavalry officer with the reputation of being the best dancer acknowledged himself defeated. Supper was served, a final "Grandfather" was danced, and the guests began to depart. All this time the count had not taken his eyes off the little widow. It had been no exaggeration when he had said he was ready to throw himself through a hole in the ice for her sake. Whether for love, a whim, or mere obstinacy, all his faculties were concentrated on one desire that evening—to see her and make love to her.

When he saw Anna Fyodorovna taking leave of the hostess, he ran to the footman's room and from there, coatless, to the roadside where the carriages were waiting.

"The carriage of Anna Fyodorovna Zaitseva!" he called. A high carriage for four with lanterns on it moved towards the entrance.

"Stop!" he called to the coachman as he ran up, knee-deep in snow.

"What do you want?" called back the coachman.

"I want to get in," replied the count, opening the door as he ran alongside, trying to climb up. "Stop, damn you! You blockhead!"

"Stop, Vaska!" cried the coachman to the postillion, and he drew in his horses. "Why should you get into somebody else's carriage? This carriage belongs to Anna Fyodorovna, not you, Your Honour."

"Hold your tongue, idiot! Here, take this ruble and get down and close the door," said the count. But since the coachman did not stir, he himself pulled up the steps, opened the window, and managed somehow to slam the door to. The carriage, like all old carriages, especially those with gold braid ornamenting the upholstery, gave off an odour of mustiness and burnt bristles. The count's legs, which had been up to the knee in wet snow and were clad only in thin boots and riding-breeches, were badly chilled, and indeed his whole body was shivering. The

coachman was grumbling up on his box and
seemed about to climb down. But the count
heard and felt nothing. His face was burning,
his heart pounding. He seized the yellow strap
in tense fingers and thrust his head out of
the side window, his whole being concentrated on this moment of anticipation. It did not
last long. Someone at the entrance called out,
"Madame Zaitseva's carriage!" The coachman
flicked the reins, the carriage rocked on its
high springs, and the lighted windows of the
house marched past the carriage windows one
after another.

"Mind you say nothing to the footman
about my being here, you rogue," said the
count, poking his head through the front
window that communicated with the coachman. "If you do I'll give you a flogging; if
you don't—ten rubles."

Scarcely had he slammed down the window
when the carriage stopped with a lurch. He
shrank back into the corner, held his breath,
and even shut his eyes, so fearful was he that
something might thwart his passionate hopes.
The door opened, one by one the steps
slapped down, there was a rustle of a woman's
gown, into the musty carriage floated the
scent of jasmine, little feet pattered lightly
up the steps, and Anna Fyodorovna, brushing
the count's legs with the hem of her cloak,
sank silently, breathlessly, onto the seat
beside him.

Whether she had seen him or not no one

could have said, not even Anna Fyodorovna,
but when he took her arm and murmured,
"Now I shall certainly kiss your hand," she
showed very little alarm and said nothing,
and instantly the arm she surrendered to him
was covered with kisses at a spot high up
above her glove. The carriage set off.

"Say something. You're not angry, are
you?" he asked her.

She only shrank further back into her
corner, but suddenly, with no apparent
reason, she burst into tears and her head
dropped of its own accord upon his breast.

VI

The newly-elected police captain and his
party, the cavalry officer and other gentlemen, had been drinking and listening to the
Gypsies in the new tavern for some time
when the count, in a blue broadcloth cloak
lined with bearskin which had belonged to
Anna Fyodorovna's husband, joined them.

"Ah, Your Excellency, we had almost given
up hope of your coming!" said a black-haired,
cross-eyed Gypsy, who greeted the count with
a flash of white teeth as he rushed into the
entranceway to help him off with his coat.
"We haven't seen you since Lebedyan.
Stesha's pining away for you."

Stesha, too, came running out to meet
him; she was a graceful young Gypsy with

a warm flush on her swarthy cheeks and with deep-set black eyes whose brilliance was softened by the shadow of long lashes.

"Ah my dear count! How marvellous! What a joy!" she murmured, smiling happily.

Even Ilyushka ran to meet him, pretending to be glad to see him. Old women, middle-aged women, young wenches, jumped up and surrounded him. Some claimed kinship with him for his having stood godfather to their children, others for his having exchanged crosses with them.

Tourbin kissed all the young Gypsy girls on the mouth; the old Gypsy women and the men kissed him on the shoulder and hand. The noblemen, too, were delighted to see him, the more so since festivities, having reached their peak, were now on the decline. Each was beginning to feel surfeited. The wine had lost its power to stimulate the nerves and was only a strain on the stomach. Having indulged in all the hilarity of which they were capable, the guests were now tired of one another. All the songs had been sung and got mixed up inside their heads, leaving an impression of noise and dissipation. However original or daring the tricks now performed, no one found them amusing. The police captain was lying in an ugly pose on the floor at the feet of an old woman.

"Champagne!" he cried, kicking his feet. "The count's come! Champagne! He's come! Bring on the champagne! I'll fill a bath-tub with champagne and bathe in it! Gentlemen of the nobility! How I do love to be in such select society! Stesha! Sing *The Open Road*!"

The cavalry officer was quite as muzzy as he was, but he gave different expression to it. He was huddled in the corner of a sofa very close to a tall and handsome Gypsy girl named Lyubasha, blinking his eyes and tossing head to get rid of the blur of his drunkenness, and urging her over and over again, in one and the same phrase, to run away with him. Lyubasha, smiling, listened as if what he was saying was at the same time extremely amusing and slightly pathetic, and now and again she cast a glance at her husband, the cross-eyed Sasha, who was standing behind a chair opposite her. In reply to the cavalry officer's protestations of love, she bent down and whispered a request that he buy her some ribbons and some scent, provided nobody learned of it.

"Hurrah!" shouted the cavalry officer when the count came in.

The handsome young man, now wearing an anxious look, was walking back and forth with unnaturally firm steps and humming a tune from *The Revolt in Seraglio*.

An aged paterfamilias who had been lured to the Gypsies by the insistent entreaties of the gentlemen of the nobility, who assured him that their fun would be spoiled and it would be better for none of them to go if he refused to join them, lay on the sofa where he had stretched himself out as soon as he arrived, and no one was paying the slightest attention to him. A government official had taken off his frock-coat and perched himself, feet and all, on top of a table, where he sat ruffling his hair to show what an awful rake he was. As soon as the count came in he unfastened the collar of his shirt and hitched himself further back on the table. On the whole, the party became more lively with the arrival of the count. The Gypsies who had been sauntering about the room sat down again in a ring. The count put Stesha, the soloist, on his knee and ordered more champagne.

Ilyushka seated himself with his guitar in front of the soloist and made a sign to begin the "plyaska", which is the singing of Gypsy songs such as *Whenever I Walk Down the Street, Eh, You Hussars!* and *Hear and Understand* in a given order. Stesha sang beautifully. Her rich and flexible contralto voice that came from deep down in her chest, her winning smile, her laughing passionate glance, the little foot that involuntarily tapped in time to the song, the wild little cries she gave at the beginning of every chorus—all of these things set some resonant but rarely touched string to vibrating. She threw her whole soul into whatever she was singing, Ilyushka accompanied her on the guitar, expressing his oneness with the song in little movements of his back and legs, in

his smile, in his whole being, and as he
nodded his head rhythmically, he fixed his
eyes upon her and listened as anxiously and
attentively as if he had never heard the song
before. When the last note died away he
suddenly straightened up, and as if feeling
himself above everyone else in the world,
proudly and deliberately gave his guitar
a little toss with his knee that sent it spinning
in the air while he tapped with his heels on
the floor, tossed back his hair, and swept the
Gypsy chorus with a scowling glance. And
then he began to dance with every fibre of his
body. And twenty strong and vigorous voices
rang out, each of them vying with the others
to offer the most unique and original rendi-
tion. The old ladies gave little jumps without
getting up, waved their kerchiefs, grinned, and
shouted each other down in time and tune
to the song. The men poured out their deep
bass voices as they stood behind their chairs,
their heads tilted, the cords of their necks
swelling.

Whenever Stesha took a high note Ilyushka
would bring his guitar closer as if to help her,
and the handsome young man would cry out
in ecstasy that now they would hear her
high C.

When a dance tune was sung and Dunyasha
stepped forth, shoulders and breasts quivering,
circling in front of the count and then sailing
out into the middle of the floor, Tourbin
jumped up, flung off his jacket, and joined

her, performing such feats with his legs that the Gypsies glanced at one another and exchanged smiles of approval.

The police captain sat with his legs crossed like a Turk, beat his chest with his fist, and shouted "Bravo!", then, seizing the count by the leg, confided to him that he had come here with two thousand rubles and had only five hundred left, and that he would do anything he liked provided the count gave his sanction. The old paterfamilias woke up and wanted to go home, but he was not permitted to. The handsome young man coaxed one of the Gypsy girls to waltz with him. The cavalry officer, eager to make a show of his friendship with the count, emerged from his corner and put his arms round him.

"Ah, my dear fellow," he said, "why in the world did you leave us?" The count said nothing, his mind evidently on something else. "Where did you go? You're a sly one, Count! I know where you went!"

For some reason Tourbin was displeased by this familiarity. He stared into the face of the cavalry officer without smiling and without speaking, and suddenly let out a string of such coarse and stinging abuse that the cavalry officer was taken aback and could not make up his mind whether to take it as a joke or not. At last he smiled and went back to his Gypsy, assuring her that he would certainly marry her after Easter.

The whole company sang another song, and yet another, danced some more, sang songs in one another's honour, and fancied they were having a glorious time. There was no end to the flow of champagne. The count drank a lot. His eyes grew moist but he did not stagger; he danced better than ever, spoke in a firm voice, joined in when the Gypsy chorus sang, and harmonized with Stesha when she sang *The Gentle Flutter of Love's Wings*.

In the middle of a song the proprietor of the tavern came and asked the guests to leave, as it was nearly three o'clock in the morning. The count seized him by the nape of the neck and ordered him to do a squat-dance. He refused. The count snatched up a bottle of champagne, turned the proprietor upside-down, and had the others hold him while, amidst general merriment, he poured the whole bottle over him.

It was already growing light. All but the count were pale and exhausted.

"But it's time for me to be leaving for Moscow," he said suddenly, getting up. "Come back to the hotel with me, gentlemen, and see me off. We'll have some tea."

Everyone consented except the sleeping paterfamilias, who was left behind. They all packed themselves into three sleighs standing at the door and set out for the hotel.

VII

"Harness the horses!" cried out the count as he entered the public room of the hotel with all his guests and the Gypsies. "Sasha!— not the Gypsy Sasha, but my Sasha—tell the postmaster I'll tan his hide for him if he gives me bad horses. And bring us some tea! Zaval-shevsky, you see to the tea while I drop into Ilyin's room and find out how he's getting on," added Tourbin, and he went out into the corridor and made for the Uhlan's room.

Ilyin had just finished playing. Having lost all his money down to the last kopek, he was now lying on the torn horse-hair sofa, pulling out the hairs one by one, putting them in his mouth, biting at them, and spitting them out. Two wax candles, one of which had burned right down to the paper, were stand-ing on a table littered with cards, their light struggling feebly with the light of dawn peeping in at the window. There were no thoughts at all in the Uhlan's mind; all his mental faculties were wrapped up in the dense fog of his gambling fever; he did not even feel remorse. True, at one point he had tried to think what he was to do next, how he was to leave this place without a kopek, how he was to pay back the fifteen thousand belong-ing to the regiment, what the regiment commander would say, what his mother would say, what his comrades would say—and he had instantly been seized by such fear and disgust with himself that in order to forget everything he had jumped up and paced the floor, taking pains to tread only on the cracks between the floor-boards. Once more he went over in his mind in the most minute detail all the games he had played. He recalled how he had almost won—he had picked up a nine and the king of spades, staking two thousand rubles on it: on the right—the queen; on the left—the ace; on the right—the king of diamonds, and—all was lost. If the six had been on the right and the king of diamonds on the left he would have won everything back and would have staked it all and won another fifteen thousand clear. Ah, then he would have bought a saddle horse from his regiment commander and a pair of horses besides and a phaeton! And what else? Why ... why... oh, it would have been wonderful, wonderful!

Once more he lay down on the sofa and began chewing hairs.

"Why are they singing in room seven?" he thought. "Tourbin must be entertaining. Perhaps I ought to join them and get good and drunk."

Just then the count came in.

"Well, have you been cleaned out?" he asked.

"I'll pretend to be asleep," thought Ilyin. "Otherwise I'll have to talk, and I'm too tired."

But Tourbin came over to him and stroked his hair.

"So you've been cleaned out, my good fellow, eh? Lost everything? Speak up."

Ilyin made no reply.

The count gave his sleeve a tug.

"Yes, I lost. What is it to you?" muttered Ilyin in a sleepy voice that expressed annoyed indifference; he did not so much as turn over.

"Everything?"

"Yes. What of it? Everything. What is it to you?"

"Listen, tell me the truth, as a comrade," said the count. The wine had awakened tender sentiments in him, and he went on stroking the youth's hair. "I've really come to love you. Tell me the truth: if it is regiment money you've lost, I'll come to your aid; tell me before it is too late: is it the regiment money?"

Ilyin leaped up off the sofa.

"If you really want me to tell you, then don't speak to me as if ... as if ... please don't speak to me at all. The only thing left for me to do is put a bullet through my head!" he cried in genuine despair, dropping his head in his hands and bursting into tears, although only a moment before he had been dreaming of a saddle horse.

"Come, you're behaving like a girl! We've all been through it. No particular harm is done; I think we can patch things up. Wait here for me."

The count went out.

"In what room is Lukhnov, the land-owner, staying?" he asked the page-boy.

The boy offered to show him.

Despite the valet's protests that his master had just got in and was about to disrobe, the count went in. Lukhnov was sitting at the table in a dressing-gown, counting a pile of bank-notes that lay in front of him. There was also a bottle of Rhine wine, of which he was extremely fond, standing on the table. His winnings permitted him to indulge in this luxury. Lukhnov looked at the count through his spectacles in a hard, cold way, as if he did not know who it was.

"You seem not to recognize me," said the count striding boldly up to the table.

Lukhnov recognized the count and asked:

"What can I do for you?"

"I want to play cards with you," said Tourbin, taking a seat on the sofa.

"Now?"

"Yes."

"Another time I shall be delighted, Count, but at present I am tired and about to retire. Will you have some wine? Excellent wine."

"I want to play now."

"I have no intention of playing any more tonight. Perhaps some of the other gentlemen will play with you; I will not, Count. I trust you will forgive me."

"So you will not?"

Lukhnov gave a little shrug of his shoulders

expressing his regret at being unable to comply with the count's wishes.

"Not for anything?"

Another little shrug.

"I am asking you very earnestly: will you play or not?"

Silence.

"Will you play?" repeated the count. "Mind, now!"

Still Lukhnov was silent, then he threw a quick glance over the top of his spectacles at the count's face, which was quickly clouding.

"Will you play?" shouted the count, giving the table such a blow with his hand that the bottle of Rhine wine fell over and spilled. "You know that you won by cheating. Will you play? I am asking you for the third time."

"I told you I would not. Your behaviour is very strange, Count. Respectable people do not burst in and hold a knife to a man's throat," observed Lukhnov without lifting his eyes.

There was a brief pause during which the count's face grew whiter and whiter. Suddenly Lukhnov was stunned by a terrific blow on the head. He fell on the sofa, grasping at his money, and let out a wild and piercing cry that one would hardly have expected to come from a man who was always so calm and dignified. Tourbin swept up the money, pushed away the valet who came running on hearing his master's cry, and made for the door.

"If you want satisfaction, I am at your service; I shall be in my room for another half hour," said the count on reaching it.

"Thief! Blackguard!" came from inside the room. "I'll have you taken to court!"

Ilyin, who had given no credence to the count's promise to patch things up, was still lying on the sofa, choked by tears of despair. The count's tender sympathy had penetrated the odd mixture of impressions filling his mind, awakening him to a recognition of his plight, and this was still with him. His youth so rich in hope, his honour, the respect of his fellows, his dreams of love and friend-ship—all were lost for ever. The fount of tears was beginning to run dry, a sense of despair, all too calm, was taking firmer and firmer hold of him, and thoughts of suicide, no longer inspiring a feeling of horror and repugnance, occurred to him with growing insistence. At this point the firm steps of the count were heard.

Tourbin's face still wore a trace of his wrath, his hands were trembling slightly, but his eyes shone with kindly good-humour and satisfaction.

"Here, I won it back!" he said, tossing a heap of notes onto the table. "Count it and see if it's all there. And hurry into the public room. I'm leaving," he added, pretending not to notice the joy and gratitude expressed on

the Uhlan's face. He went out of the room
whistling a Gypsy tune.

VIII

Sasha, his girdle wound tightly about his
waist, announced that the horses were ready,
but demanded that they first go and reclaim
the count's greatcoat, which, with its fur
collar, was worth all of three hundred rubles,
and give back the wretched blue cloak to the
scoundrel who had exchanged it for the greatcoat at the Marshal's. But Tourbin said there
was no need to get back the greatcoat, and
went to his room to dress.

The cavalry officer hiccuped incessantly
as he sat in silence beside his Gypsy girl. The
police captain ordered vodka and invited all
the gentlemen to go home to breakfast with
him, promising that his wife would come
down and dance with the Gypsies. The
handsome young man was earnestly trying
to convince Ilyushka that there was more
soul in the pianoforte and that the guitar
could not take an A flat. The government
official was sitting in a corner drinking tea
and, now that daylight had come, seemed
ashamed of his debauch. The Gypsies were
arguing among themselves in their own
tongue, insisting that they sing another song
in honour of the gentlemen, but Stesha
objected, saying that the *barorai* (meaning

"count" or "prince", to be more exact, "great nobleman") would be angry. In a word, the last spark of life was dying out.

"Well, one last song in parting and everyone goes home," said the count as he came into the room in his travelling clothes, looking fresher, handsomer, and gayer than ever before.

The Gypsies had just arranged themselves in a ring for the last song when Ilyin came in with a bundle of notes in his hand and called the count aside.

"I only had fifteen thousand rubles of regiment money and you have given me sixteen thousand three hundred," he said. "These others belong to you."

"Capital! Let me have them!"

Ilyin turned a shy glance on the count as he gave him the money and opened his mouth as if to say something, but instead he simply blushed till the tears came and, seizing the count's hand, squeezed it hard.

"Be off with you! Ilyushka! Listen—here's some money; see me off with songs as far as the gates of the town," and he tossed the thousand three hundred rubles Ilyin had given him on to the Gypsy's guitar. But he forgot to give the cavalry officer back the one hundred rubles he had borrowed the night before.

It was now ten o'clock in the morning. The sun was already high over the roofs, the streets were full of people, the shopkeepers

had long since opened their doors, noblemen
and government officials were riding past,
ladies were sauntering from one shop to
another in the arcade, when the flock of
Gypsies, the police captain, the cavalry
officer, the handsome young man, Ilyin, and
the count in the blue cloak lined with bearskin came out on the steps of the hotel. The
day was sunny, the snow was melting. Three
sleighs, each drawn by three horses with their
tails tied up short, drew up at the hotel
entrance and the whole gay party got in. The
count, Ilyin, Stesha, Ilyushka, and the count's
servant Sasha, took their places in the first
sleigh. Blücher, beside himself with excitement, wagged his tail and barked at the shaft
horse. The rest of the gentlemen and the
Gypsies got into the other sleighs. As soon as
they had left the hotel the sleighs came
abreast of one another and the Gypsies began
singing in chorus.

And in this manner, with songs and the
jingling of little bells, they rode the length of
the town, out to the very gates, driving all the
vehicles they met up onto the pavement.

What was the wonder of the shopkeepers
and pedestrians, especially those who knew
them, on seeing these respectable gentlemen
riding in broad daylight through the streets of
the town, accompanied by singing, by Gypsy
girls, and drunken Gypsy men!

When they had passed through the town
gates the sleighs came to a halt and everyone

took leave of the count.

Ilyin, who had had quite a lot to drink before starting out and had driven the horses himself, suddenly grew sad and tried to persuade the count to stay for another day. When he was convinced that this was impossible, he unexpectedly threw himself upon his new friend with tears in his eyes and swore that as soon as he got back to his regiment he would put in an application to be transferred to the hussar regiment in which Tourbin served. The count was in particularly high spirits. He pushed the cavalry officer, who had been very familiar with him all morning, into a snowbank, he set Blücher onto the police captain, he snatched Stesha up in his arms and threatened to carry her off to Moscow, and at last he leaped into the sleigh and sat Blücher down beside him, though the dog would have preferred standing up in the middle. Sasha, having once more urged the cavalry officer to find the count's great-coat and send it on to them, leaped up into the driver's seat. The count shouted, "We're off!", snatched off his cap, waved it over his head, whistled at the horses in the manner of a sleigh-driver, and the three sleighs moved off in different directions.

Far away into the distance stretched the monotonous snowy plain with the dirty yellow ribbon of the road winding across it.

The bright sun, dancing and sparkling on the icy crust of thawing snow, brought a pleasant sensation of warmth to face and back. Steam rose from the sweating flanks of the horses. The sleigh-bells jingled. A peasant who was running beside his overloaded sledge pulled hastily on the ropes serving as reins to make way for the count, wetting his bast shoes in the slush of the roadside. A fat, red-faced peasant woman with a baby thrust inside the breast of her sheepskin coat was sitting on another sledge slapping the back of her white nag with the ends of the reins. Suddenly the count remembered Anna Fyodorovna.

"Turn round!" he shouted.

The driver did not understand.

"Turn round! Back to town! Quick!"

The sleigh passed back through the gates and drove swiftly up to the wooden entrance of Madame Zaitseva's house. The count ran up the steps and strode through the entrance-hall and drawing-room. Finding the little widow still in bed, he put his arms round her, lifted her up, kissed her on her sleepy eyes, and ran out. In her drowsy state Anna Fyodorovna could only lick her lips and murmur, "What has happened?"

The count leaped into the sleigh, shouted to the driver, and with no further delay and without giving another thought to Lukhnov or the little widow or Stesha, thinking only of what was awaiting him in Moscow, he left the town of K. for ever.

IX

Twenty years have passed. Much water has flowed under the bridge, many people have died, many others have been born, still others have grown up or grown old, even more ideas than people have been born and have died. Much of the good and much of the bad of the old days has vanished away; many good new things have come to maturity, even more bad new things have put in an appearance.

Count Fyodor Tourbin has been dead these many years, killed in a duel with a foreigner whom he struck with his riding-crop in the street. His son, the image of his father, is now a charming youth of three-and-twenty, and officer in the Guards. But in disposition young Count Tourbin does not resemble his father in the least. He has not a shadow of the reckless, passionate, and, to put it bluntly, dissolute propensities characteristic of the last generation. In addition to intelligence, good breeding, and the gifted nature he inherited, his most outstanding qualities are a love of respectability and comfort, a practical way of judging people and circumstances, and a cautious and sensible approach to life. The young count has advanced swiftly in the service; at twenty-three he is already a lieutenant.

When military operations began, he decided his chances of promotion would be greater if he entered active service, so he had himself

transferred to a regiment of hussars in which
he served as captain, and was soon entrusted
with a squadron.

In May, 1848, the S. Regiment of Hussars
passed through the K. Gubernia, and the
squadron under the command of young
Count Tourbin was to spend the night in Morozovka, the village belonging to Anna Fyodorovna. Anna Fyodorovna was still alive, but
so advanced in years that even she had ceased
to look upon herself as young, which is going
very far for a woman. She had grown
extremely stout, and that is said to make
a woman look younger. But deep wrinkles
had made inroads into her soft white
corpulence. She no longer rode into town,
indeed she could hardly climb into her
carriage, but she was as good-natured as ever,
and as silly, as we may admit now that there
is no longer any beauty to blind us to the
fact. Her daughter Liza, a Russian village
beauty of three-and-twenty, lived with her,
as did her brother, the cavalry officer of our
acquaintance, who, due to his easy-going
nature, had squandered all his inheritance
and depended on his sister in his old age. His
hair was completely white; his upper lip was
caved in, but the moustache growing on it was
carefully dyed black. Wrinkles covered not
only his cheeks and forehead, but even his
nose and neck; his back was bent, and yet
there was still something of the old cavalry
officer in his weak and crooked legs.

On the evening in question Anna Fyodorovna with all her family and domestics was seated in the little drawing-room of the old house, whose verandah door and windows opened upon an old-fashioned star-shaped garden shaded by lime trees. Anna Fyodorovna, grey-haired, in a lavender quilted jacket, was sitting on the sofa at a round mahogany table on which she was playing solitaire. Her old brother, in clean white pantaloons and a blue coat, had seated himself at the window and was crocheting something of white cotton thread, an occupation which his niece had taught him and which he had grown extremely fond of, since he was incapable of doing work of any importance and his eyes were too weak to allow him to indulge in his favourite pastime—the reading of the newspaper. Pimochka, a little girl Anna Fyodorovna had adopted, was sitting next to him and doing her lessons under Liza's supervision, the latter at the same time knitting her uncle a pair of socks of goat's wool. As always at that time of day, the last rays of the setting sun were falling obliquely through the lime trees, lighting up the furthermost window and the *étagère* that stood next to it. It was so quiet in the room and the garden that they could distinctly hear the quick flutter of a swallow's wings outside the window, Anna Fyodorovna's gentle sighing inside the room, and the grunting of the old man as he crossed his legs.

"Where should this card go? Please show me, Liza; I keep forgetting," said Anna Fyodorovna, pausing in her game.

Without interrupting her knitting, Liza went over to her mother and glanced at the cards.

"Oh, you've mixed everything up, dear mama," she said rearranging the cards. "This is how it should be. Still, it will come out—your guess was right," she added, slipping off one of the cards when her mother was not looking.

"You're always fooling me, always saying it will come out."

"But it really will. See? It has."

"Very well, very well, you little vixen. Isn't it time for us to be having tea?"

"I've already told them to heat the samovar. I'll go and see. Shall I have it brought in here? Hurry and finish your lessons, Pimochka, and we'll go out for a walk."

And Liza disappeared through the door.

"Liza! Lizochka!" called her uncle, his eyes fixed on his crocheting. "I seem to have dropped a stitch again. Pick it up for me, that's a dear girl."

"In a minute, in a minute! I'll just give them this head of sugar to break up."

And sure enough, in three minutes she ran back into the room, went up to her uncle, and took him by the ear.

"That's what you get for dropping your stitches," she said with a laugh. "You haven't

even done what was given you for today's
lesson."

"Come, come; do put it right—there seems
to be a knot somewhere."

Liza took the crochet hook, pulled the pin
out of her kerchief, which was then blown
open a little by the breeze coming through
the window, caught the stitch with the pin,
looped it up two or three times, and handed it
back to her uncle.

"Here, a kiss for my labours," she said,
offering him a rosy cheek as she pinned her
kerchief back in place. "You shall have rum
with your tea today. Today is Friday, you
know."

And again she went back to the tea-room.

"Come and see, Uncle! The hussars are
coming!" she cried in a clear, high voice.

Anna Fyodorovna and her brother went
into the tea-room, whose windows faced the
village, to see the hussars passing. Very little
could be seen through the windows; they
could only make out a crowd moving in a
cloud of dust.

"What a pity, sister," observed Liza's uncle
to Anna Fyodorovna, "that our house is so
small and the new wing is not finished yet.
Otherwise we would ask for some officers.
Officers of the hussars are always such fine
gay youths; I should like to have a look at
them."

"And I would rejoice with all my heart to
have them; but you yourself know, brother,

that we have nowhere to put them. There's only my bedroom, Liza's little room, the drawing-room, and your room. Where could we put them? Judge for yourself. Mikhailo Matveyev has made the elder's hut ready for them. He says it is properly clean."

"We would choose you a husband, a brave hussar, from among them, Lizochka," said her uncle.

"I don't want a hussar, I want an Uhlan; wasn't it in the Uhlans that you served, Uncle? I'll have nothing to do with those hussars; they are said to be such reckless fellows."

A faint blush dyed Liza's cheeks, but again she laughed her ringing laugh. "Here comes Ustyushka running; we must ask her what she has seen," she said.

Anna Fyodorovna sent for Ustyushka.

"As if there was not enough work to keep you busy! But no, you must go running to have a look at the soldiers!" said Anna Fyodorovna. "Well, where are the officers to be put up?"

"At Yeremkin's cottage, madam. There are two of them, and so handsome! One is a count, they say!"

"What is his name?"

"Kazarov or Tourbin or something of the sort—I don't quite remember, begging your pardon."

"You *are* a simpleton—can't tell us anything. You might at least have found out his name."

"I'll run back and ask if you like."

"Oh, you're very good at that, don't I know! No, let Danilo go; tell him to go, brother, and ask whether the officers are in need of anything; we must show them every civility; and have him say that he was sent by his mistress."

The old people sat down in the tea-room again and Liza went into the maids' room to put the sugar away. There she found Ustyushka talking about the hussars.

"My dear mistress, if you ever saw how handsome that count is!" she said. "A very cherub. If you found a husband like that for yourself, wouldn't you make a handsome couple, just!"

The other servants smiled approvingly. The old nursemaid, sitting at the window knitting a stocking, gave a deep sigh and murmured a prayer on an indrawn breath.

"So that's the impression the hussars made on you!" said Liza. "You like nothing better than to talk about such things. Bring us a fruit drink, Ustyushka—something sourish to treat the hussars to."

And, laughing, Liza went out with her sugar-bowl.

"I would like to have a look at that hussar," she thought. "Is he fair or dark? And I do not doubt but that he would be glad to make our acquaintance. But perhaps he will pass by without ever knowing that I was here and gave him a thought. And how many like him have passed me by! No one ever sees me but uncle and Ustyushka. What matters it how I do my hair, or what sort of sleeves I wear? There is no one to admire me," she thought with a sigh, gazing at her plump white arm. "I suppose he is tall, with big eyes and probably a little black moustache. Just to think, three-and-twenty already and nobody has ever fallen in love with me, except that pock-marked Ivan Ipatich. And four years ago I was even prettier than I am now. My girlhood is almost over, and nobody has had any joy of it. Oh, how unfortunate I am! A poor country girl!"

The country girl was roused from her ruminations by the voice of her mother calling her to pour out the tea. She gave a little toss of her head and went into the tea-room.

The best things are those that happen by chance; the more one tries, the worse things turn out. In the country, little attention is paid to child education, and so in most cases the education turns out to be excellent. So it was in Liza's case. Anna Fyodorovna had too limited a mind and too lazy-going a disposition to give Liza any education at all: she had not taught her music, nor the indispensable French, but quite by chance she had presented her late husband with a very pretty and healthy child—a daughter, whom she placed in the hands of a wet-nurse and a nursemaid. She fed her, clothed her in cotton frocks and goatskin shoes, sent her out to play and to gather berries and mushrooms, hired a young student to teach her reading, writing and arithmetic, and in sixteen years' time, quite by chance, she found that Liza was a good friend and a cheery, kind-hearted, industrious little house-keeper. Anna Fyodorovna herself was so kind-hearted that she was always adopting some serf child or foundling. Liza, from the age of ten, took care of her mother's wards: she taught them their letters, dressed them, took them to church, and reproved them when they became too mischievous. Then came her feeble, good-natured old uncle, who had to be tended like a baby. Then there were the house servants as well as the serfs from the village who brought all their aches and pains to the young mistress; she treated them with elder-flower water, peppermint, and spirits of camphor. And then there was the care of the house that, quite by chance, had fallen entirely upon her shoulders. And then there was the thwarted yearning for love that found an outlet in her love of nature and in religion. And so, quite by chance, Liza turned out to be a busy, cheery, amiable, independent, pure, and deeply religious woman. True, she suffered little pangs of envy on seeing her neighbours at church wearing modish hats brought from the town of K.; she was driven almost to tears by the whims of her querulous old mother; she had dreams of love that took incongruous, even crude forms—but all of these were driven away by the useful work which had become indispensable to her, and at three-and-twenty there was not a blot, not a regret to mar the bright and serene soul of this developing woman, so rich in physical and moral beauty. Liza was of middle height, more round than angular; her eyes were brown and not very large, slightly shadowed under the lower lids; her hair was long and fair; she walked with a wide, easy swing. The expression of her face when she was busy and had nothing on her mind to worry her said to all who saw it: life is good, life is a joy, for those whose consciences are clear and who have someone to love. Even in moments of vexation, indignation, alarm, or grief, when, as if in defiance of her wishes, tears filled her eyes, her lips became set, her left eyebrow scowled—even then the light of a kind and candid heart, unspoiled by sophistication, could be glimpsed in the dimples of her cheeks, the corners of her lips, and in her shining eyes.

X

It was still hot, though the sun had set, when the squadron entered Morozovka. Up ahead, in the dusty village road ran a spotted cow that had strayed away from the herd; it kept casting frightened looks behind it, and from time to time it stopped and mooed, unable to guess that all it had to do was to step out of the path of the horses. Old peasants, village wives, children, and house servants, crowded on either side of the road to gape at the hussars, who advanced in a thick cloud of dust, mounted on short-bridled, snorting black horses. To the right of the squadron rode the two officers, sitting loosely in the saddle. One of them was Count Tourbin, the commander; the other was Polozov, a young man who had but recently received his commission.

Out of the finest hut in the village stepped a hussar in a white tunic, who, taking off his forage cap, went up to the officers.

"What accommodations have been made for us?" the count asked him.

"For Your Excellency?" replied the quartermaster, his whole body stiffening. "We've cleaned this hut for you—the elder's. We asked for a room at the manor-house but were turned down. The mistress is a mean one."

"Very well," said the count, dismounting and stretching his legs as he went toward the elder's hut. "Has my carriage arrived?"

"It has, Your Excellency," replied the quartermaster, pointing with his cap at the carriage standing at the gates, then running ahead to the entrance of the hut where a peasant family had gathered to stare at the officers. He almost knocked over one old woman as he flung open the door of the recently vacated hut and stood aside to let the count pass.

The hut was large and roomy, but not entirely clean. A German valet, dressed like a gentleman, had put up an iron bedstead and was now taking bed linen out of a travelling-bag.

"Ugh, what beastly quarters!" said the count in vexation. "Dyadenko! Is it really impossible to stow us away somewhere in the manor-house?"

"If Your Excellency so orders, I shall dispatch someone there," replied Dyadenko. "But it is a poor sort of manor-house—little better than this hut."

"It is too late now. Leave me."

And the count lay down with his hands clasped under his head.

"Johann!" he called to his valet. "You've made a lump in the middle again! How is it you can't make a bed properly?"

Johann was about to remove the lump.

"No, it's too late now. Where is my dressing-gown?" the count went on peevishly.

The valet gave him his dressing-gown.

Before putting it on, the count examined the hem.

"I thought so; you haven't taken out that spot. I don't know how anyone could serve worse than you do," he added, snatching the gown out of the man's hands and putting it on. "Is it intentionally or what? Is tea ready?"

"I haven't had time," said Johann.

"Dolt!"

The count took up a French novel he had brought for the occasion and read it in silence for some time; Johann went out into the entranceway to heat the samovar. It was clear that the count was in a bad mood—due, no doubt, to his weariness, his dirty face, his tight clothing, and his empty stomach.

"Johann!" he cried again. "Account for that ten rubles I gave you. What did you buy in town?"

The count glanced over the account handed to him and made a few dissatisfied remarks as to the dearness of the articles purchased.

"I shall take rum with my tea."

"I didn't buy any rum," said Johann.

"Marvellous! How many times have I told you to keep rum on hand?"

"I hadn't enough money."

"Why didn't Polozov buy it? You might have taken it from his man."

"Cornet Polozov? I don't know. He only bought tea and sugar."

"Wretch! Get out! No one tries my patience as you do. You know very well that I always take rum with my tea when on the march."

"Here are two letters for you from Staff Headquarters," said the valet.

The count, lying on his bed, tore open the letters and began to read them. Just then the cornet, who had been seeing the men to their quarters, entered with a cheerful face.

"Well, Tourbin? Not a bad place at all, it seems. But I must admit I'm deucedly tired. It was a hot day."

"Not bad! A filthy, stinking hut and no rum for my tea, thanks to you. That fool of yours forgot to buy it, and so did mine. You might have told yours to."

He went back to his letters. When he had finished reading the first one he crumpled it up and threw it on the floor.

Meanwhile, out in the entranceway, the cornet was whispering to his servant, "Why didn't you buy some rum? You had the money, didn't you?"

"Why should we do all the buying? I stand all the expenses as it is; that German of his does nothing but smoke a pipe."

The second letter was evidently not disagreeable, for the count smiled as he read it.

"Who is it from?" asked Polozov, who had come back into the room and was making a bed for himself on some boards next to the stove.

"From Minna," replied the count gaily, holding the letter out to him. "Would you like to read it? What a charming woman! Much better than our girls. Just see how much wit and feeling there is in this letter! There's only one bad thing—she asks for money."

"Yes, that is bad," observed the cornet.

"To be sure, I promised her some; but

then we set out on this march, and ... well ...
but if I am in command of the squadron
another three months I'll send it to her.
I certainly don't grudge it; charming, isn't
she?" he asked with a smile, watching the
expression of Polozov's face as he read the
letter.

"Awfully illiterate, but rather sweet, and
she seems to be really in love with you,"
said the cornet.

"Indeed she is! It's only women of her sort
who truly love, if they love at all."

"And who is that other letter from?"
asked the cornet, handing back the letter he
had finished reading.

"That? Oh, there's a certain gentleman,
a filthy sort, to whom I lost money at cards;
this is the third time he has reminded me of
it. I can't pay him back at present. A stupid
letter," said the count, evidently annoyed by
the remembrance.

The two officers said nothing for some
time after this. Influenced by the count's
mood, the cornet drank his tea in silence,
afraid to begin a conversation, for Tourbin,
at whose handsome face he glanced from
time to time, was staring steadfastly out of
the window, deep in thought.

"Oh, well, everything may turn out all
right," said the count suddenly, turning to
Polozov and giving his head a little toss.
"If there are promotions all along the line
in our regiment this year, and if we move

into action besides, I may get ahead of my friends who are captains in the Guards."

The conversation was following this course over a second glass of tea when old Danilo came in, bringing Anna Fyodorovna's message.

"And Her Honour bade me ask if Your Honour was not the son of Count Fyodor Ivanovich Tourbin?" added Danilo of his own accord, having heard the officer's name and remembering the visit of the late count in the town of K. "Our lady Anna Fyodorovna knew him very well indeed."

"He was my father; tell your mistress that we are very grateful to her for her thoughtfulness and are in need of nothing, but say that we should be very much obliged if a cleaner room might be found for us somewhere, at the manor-house or elsewhere."

"Why did you say that?" asked Polozov when Danilo had gone. "What difference does it make? We'll only be here for one night so why should we put them to all that inconvenience?"

"You and your scruples! Haven't we had enough of sleeping in hovels? It's clear that you are not a practical man. Why should we not take advantage of the opportunity of sleeping in comfort if only for one night? They, on their part, will be very much flattered. There's only one thing I don't like: her having known my father," went on the count, exposing his brilliant white teeth in a slow smile. "I always blush at the memory of that papa of mine—always some scandal or some debt. That's why I can't bear to run into former acquaintances of his. But then, the times were like that," he added seriously.

"I forgot to tell you," said Polozov, "I once met the commander of an Uhlan brigade named Ilyin. He was anxious to meet you and was devoted to your father."

"He seems to have been a worthless fellow, that Ilyin. And the thing is that all those gentlemen who claim to have known my father so as to make up to me, tell me tales about him I am ashamed to listen to, though they give them out as charming anecdotes. I cannot deny—I always try to take a cool, objective view of things—that he was too hot-tempered and sometimes did things he shouldn't have. But it was all because of the times. In our day he might have turned out to be very successful, for to do him justice, he was extremely talented."

A quarter of an hour later Danilo returned and brought them an invitation from his mistress to spend the night at her house.

XI

On learning that the young hussar officer was the son of Count Fyodor Tourbin, Anna Fyodorovna was all aflutter.

"Goodness gracious! Bless you, Danilo!

Hurry back there and say that the mistress invites them here," she said, jumping up and scurrying off to the maids' room. "Lizochka! Ustyushka! We must make your room ready, Liza. You will move into your uncle's room, and you, brother ... you, brother, will have to spend the night in the drawing-room. It won't hurt you for one night."

"Indeed it won't, sister; I will lie on the floor."

"He must be handsome indeed if he resembles his father. Oh, to have a look at him, the darling! Just you wait and see, Liza! What a good-looking man his father was! Where are you taking that table? Leave it here," cried Anna Fyodorovna as she bustled about. "Bring two beds—fetch one from the bailiff's—and take the crystal candle-stick that brother presented me with on my birthday and put a stearin candle in it."

At last everything was ready. Despite her mother's interference, Liza arranged her room for the two officers according to her own taste. She brought fresh bed linen scented with mignonette and made the beds herself; she had a decanter of water and a candle placed on the tables next to the beds, she burned some perfumed paper in the maids' room and made up her own bed in her uncle's room. When Anna Fyodorovna had become more composed she sat down in her usual place and took up her cards, but before she dealt them out she put a puffy elbow on the table and fell to dreaming. "How time flies! How it does!" she whispered to herself. "It seems like yesterday... I can see him now... Oh, what a reckless fellow he was!" And tears came to her eyes. "Now it is Lizochka's turn—but she is not what I was at her age—a pretty child, but ... not what I was..."

"Lizochka, you had better put on your *mousseline de laine* this evening."

"Do you intend to entertain them, mama? Oh, I don't think you ought," said Liza, unable to suppress her agitation at the thought of meeting the officers. "I really don't think you ought, mama."

In actual fact, she more feared than desired to meet them, for she sensed that some great and perturbing happiness lay in store for her.

"Perhaps they themselves will want to make our acquaintance, Lizochka," said Anna Fyodorovna, stroking her daughter's hair and thinking to herself: "It isn't what my hair was at her age... Oh, Lizochka, I could wish for you..." and she did indeed wish something for her, but she could not hope for her marriage with the young count, and she could hardly want Liza to enter upon relations with the young count such as she herself had had with the elder. And yet she wished for something, and that very ardently. Perhaps she hoped to revive, through her daughter, the emotions she had felt with the late count.

The old cavalry officer, too, was somewhat

excited by the count's arrival. He went into his own room and locked the door. A quarter of an hour later he came out in a military tunic and blue riding-breeches. Wearing the look of pleased self-consciousness with which a young girl dons her first ball gown, he went into the room prepared for the guests.

"We shall see what the new generation of hussars is like, sister. The late count was a true hussar if there ever was one. We shall see, we shall see!"

The officers went to the room assigned them through the back entrance.

"What did I tell you?" said the count, lying down just as he was, in his dusty boots, on the freshly-made bed. "Isn't this better than that hut full of beetles?"

"Of course it is better, but we have put ourselves under obligation to our hosts..."

"Tut-tut! One must always take a practical view of things. You can be sure they are dreadfully pleased. I say!" he shouted. "Ask them to hang something over that window to keep out the draught at night!"

At this point the old man came in to make the acquaintance of the officers. Naturally he could not resist saying, though he blushed a little in doing so, that he had been a comrade of the late count, that he had enjoyed his kind regards, and was even indebted to him for certain kindly services rendered on his account. Whether under "kindly services" he had in mind the count's neglecting to return the hundred rubles he had borrowed, or his pushing him into a snowbank, or his showering him with abuse, it is hard to say--the old man offered no explanations. The young count was extremely courteous to the old cavalry officer and thanked him for putting them up.

"You must excuse its not being very luxurious, Count," (he almost said "Your Excellency", so unused had he become to addressing people of rank) "my sister's house is very small. We'll have something hung over that window, and everything will be fine," he added, and under the pretence of going for a curtain, but really so that he could give an account of the officers, he shuffled away.

The pretty little Ustyushka came in with her mistress's shawl to hang over the window. Her mistress had also told her to ask the gentlemen if they would not care to have tea.

Decent quarters evidently had a brightening effect upon the count's spirits: he smiled and joked with Ustyushka so gaily that she called him a naughty man; he questioned her as to whether her young mistress was pretty, and when she asked whether he cared to have tea, he said he supposed they might as well bring it in, but that it was more important, since his man had not yet got supper ready, to have some vodka if they could spare it, and something to eat, and also some sherry, if there was any on hand.

Liza's uncle went into raptures over the young count's manners and praised the young generation of officers to the sky, saying that they were incomparably superior to their fathers.

Anna Fyodorovna disagreed—no one could have been superior to Count Fyodor Ivanovich. In the end she even became tetchy, remarking coldly, "For you, brother, the last person who is kind to you is the best. Everyone knows, of course, that people have grown more clever, but Count Fyodor Ivanovich was so polite and danced an écossaise so beautifully that everybody, you might say, lost their heads; and yet he paid no attention to anyone but me. And so you see there were good people in the old times, too."

Just then word was brought of the request for vodka, food, and sherry.

"Now just see, brother! You never do the right thing! You ought to have ordered supper," said Anna Fyodorovna. "Liza! Do take things in hand, my dear!"

Liza ran into the storeroom for mushrooms and fresh butter and ordered the cook to broil some steak.

"Have you any sherry left, brother?"

"No, sister. I never had any."

"How is that? You take something with your tea, don't you?"

"Rum, Anna Fyodorovna."

"What difference does it make? Give them

that ... er ... rum; it doesn't matter. But hadn't we better invite them in here, brother? You know what is right. They won't take offence, will they?"

The cavalry officer said he was certain the count was much too generous to decline their invitation and he would bring them without fail. Anna Fyodorovna went to put on her grosgrain dress and a new cap, but Liza was so busy that she had no time to take off the wide-sleeved pink linen dress she was wearing. And she was dreadfully nervous: she felt that something stupendous was about to happen. She took the count, the handsome hussar, to be a glorious creature, new and incomprehensible. His ways and manners and speech—everything about him must be such as she had never known before. All that he thought and said must be clever and true; all that he did must be upright; every detail of his appearance must be beautiful. She had no doubt of it. Had he demanded not only food and sherry, but a perfumed bath as well, she would not have been surprised and would not have blamed him, but would have been firmly convinced that it was only right and proper.

The count accepted Anna Fyodorovna's invitation the minute it was communicated to him by the cavalry officer. He combed his hair, put on his coat, and took his cigar case.

"Come along," he said to Polozov.

"I don't think we ought to," replied the cornet. *"Ils feront des frais pour nous recevoir."*

"Nonsense. It will give them pleasure. I've already made inquiries—it seems the lady has a pretty daughter. Come along," said the count in French.

"Je vous en prie, messieurs!" said the cavalry officer just to let them know he understood French and had caught what they said.

XII

Liza, with blushing face and downcast eyes, pretended to be all absorbed in filling the teapot, for she was afraid to look at the officers when they came into the room. Anna Fyodorovna, on the contrary, jumped to her feet and made a little curtsey, and without taking her eyes off the count's face, spoke incessantly, telling him how like his father he was, introducing her daughter, offering him tea, jam, and country fruit-paste. The cornet was so modest in appearance that no one paid the least attention to him, for which he was duly grateful since it gave him an opportunity to study, as far as that was decent, every detail of Liza's beauty, which he was evidently quite struck by. The uncle sat waiting for his sister to finish speaking to the count, hardly able to restrain himself, so anxious was he to give his reminiscences of life in the cavalry. The count lighted a cigar that was so strong that Liza could hardly keep from coughing. He was very loquacious and courteous, at first inserting a word now and then in the stream of Anna Fyodorovna's talk, later holding forth all by himself. One thing struck his listeners as being rather strange: his use of words which, if considered inoffensive in the society to which he was accustomed, were shocking here. Anna Fyodorovna was a bit frightened by them, and Liza blushed to the tips of her ears. But the count did not notice this and remained his serene and courteous self. Liza filled the glasses in silence and instead of putting them in the hands of her guests, she set them down within easy reach. Still greatly excited, she listened avidly to the count's every word. The triteness of his stories and his faltering manner of speech helped to restore her composure. She did not hear the wise utterances she had expected him to make, nor did she discover that elegance in all things which she had vaguely hoped he would display. During the third glass of tea, when she shyly lifted her eyes to his and he held them with his glance, going on talking quite unperturbed, smiling the faintest of smiles as he gazed at her, she felt a certain hostility rising up within her and soon realized that not only was there nothing extraordinary about him, but he was in no way distinguishable from all the people she knew, and therefore there was no reason to fear him; true, his nails were long and carefully tended, but he was not even particularly handsome. And suddenly, having discovered with a pang of regret that her dreams were unfounded, Liza grew calm; the only thing which disturbed her now was the glance of the silent cornet which she felt fixed upon her. "Perhaps not he, but he is the one!" she thought.

XIII

After tea the old lady invited the guests into the other room, where she sat down in her accustomed place.

"Perhaps you would like to rest, Count?" she asked. "How shall I amuse you, my dear guests," she added on receiving a reply in the negative. "Do you play cards, Count? You might see to that, brother—arrange a hand of something."

"But you yourself play 'preference'," replied her brother. "Shall we have a game? Would you like to, Count? And you?"

The officers declared they were ready to do anything their hosts found agreeable.

Liza brought the old pack of cards with which she was used to telling fortunes, to divine whether Anna Fyodorovna's toothache would soon pass, when her uncle would arrive home from a journey to town, whether the neighbour would pay them a call, and such things. These cards, although they had been in use for two months, were cleaner than the ones with which Anna Fyodorovna told fortunes.

"But perhaps you do not care to play for small stakes?" asked the uncle. "Anna Fyodorovna and I play for half a kopek a point. Even so, she ruins us all."

"Oh, for anything you wish, I shall be only too glad," said the count.

"Then let it be for one kopek—paper-money. Anything for such exceptional guests—let them drive an old lady like me to the poorhouse," said Anna Fyodorovna, settling comfortably in her armchair and patting down her lace shawl. To herself she said, "Perhaps I shall win a ruble from them." She had, it seemed, developed a slight gambling fever in her old age.

"If you like I shall teach you to play 'with honours'," said the count. "And 'with misery'. Very amusing."

Everyone was delighted with the new St. Petersburg manner of playing. The uncle declared he had once known it, that it was the same as playing Boston, but he had forgotten it a little. Anna Fyodorovna understood nothing, and understood nothing for so long that she found it advisable to smile and nod and declare that now she understood and everything was clear. There was a great deal of laughter in the middle of the game when,

with the ace and the king in her hand, Anna
Fyodorovna called 'misery' and was left with
the six. She was quite nonplussed, smiled
weakly, and hastened to assert that she had
not quite got used to the new way of playing.
But it was scored against her nevertheless,
and scored heavily, especially since the count,
due to his habit of playing for big stakes, was
cautious, kept exact accounts, and failed to
grasp the meaning of the cornet's kicks under
the table and the glaring blunders the latter
made in playing.

Liza brought in more fruit-paste, three
sorts of jam, and a special sort of preserved
apples. From her position behind her
mother's chair she followed the game, glancing
up at the officers from time to time, especially at the pink nails and white hands of the
count as he threw down the cards and picked
up the tricks with such skill, grace, and
confidence.

Again Anna Fyodorovna grew fluttered
and completely lost her head as she recklessly
tried to outdo the others, bidding as high as
seven, taking only four, and, on the demand
of her brother, scribbling some unintelligible
figures on the score-sheet.

"Cheer up, mama, you will win it all back,"
said Liza with a smile, trying to rescue her
mother from the ridiculous position she had
fallen into. "You'll take Uncle's cards and
then he'll be in a hole."

"You might come to my aid, Lizochka,"

said Anna Fyodorovna, casting a frightened glance at her. "I don't know how..."

"I don't know how to play according to these rules either," said Liza, quickly calculating her mother's losses in her mind. "But you will lose everything at this rate, mama. There won't even be enough left to buy Pimochka a frock," she added in jest.

"Indeed you can easily lose at least ten silver rubles in this way," said the cornet, gazing at Liza and longing to start a conversation with her.

"Why, aren't we playing with paper-money?" asked Anna Fyodorovna, glancing round at the players.

"Perhaps," said the count, "but I for my part do not know how to calculate paper-money. How do you ... that is, what is this paper-money?"

"Nobody plays with paper-money nowadays," put in the uncle, who was winning.

The old lady had some fruit drinks brought in, she herself drank two glasses, grew red in the face, and seemed, so to speak, to have thrown up her hands in despair. She even neglected to tuck in a lock of grey hair that had escaped from under her cap. No doubt she felt that she had lost millions and was a ruined woman. Again and again the cornet kicked the count under the table. The count regularly wrote down all the old lady's losses.

At last the game was over. Despite all

Anna Fyodorovna's efforts, at the expense of her conscience, to add something to her accounts, to pretend that she had made a mistake in her calculations, and that in general she could not calculate, and despite her horror at the enormity of her losses, in the end the calculations showed that she had lost nine hundred and twenty points. "Is that not nine rubles in paper-money?" she asked several times, and she was quite incapable of grasping the full extent of her losses until her brother, to her horror, explained that she had lost thirty-two rubles and a half in paper-money and that it must be paid without fail.

When the game was over the count got up without bothering to estimate his winnings and went to the window near which Liza was laying out refreshments and putting mushrooms on a plate for supper. Directly, and with perfect ease, he did what the cornet had been wanting to do all evening and had been unable to: he began a conversation with Liza about the weather.

The cornet at that moment found himself in a most disconcerting position. When the count, and especially, when Liza, who had kept up Anna Fyodorovna's spirits, went away, the old lady could no longer control her feelings.

"I am very sorry that we should have won your money," said Polozov for the sake of saying something. "It was not very polite of us."

"And to have thought up those 'honours' and 'miseries' of yours! I don't know how to play that way. How much did you say it amounted to in paper-money?" she asked.

"Thirty-two rubles; thirty-two and a half," said the old cavalry officer, whose own winnings had put him in a jolly mood. "Give us the money, sister; come, give it to us."

"It's the last time I shall ever be able to give you any. I shall have none to give. I can never hope to win back so much."

And Anna Fyodorovna hurried away with her rocking walk and came back with nine paper rubles. It was only on the insistence of the old man that she paid up in full.

Polozov nurtured a faint fear that Anna Fyodorovna might launch a tirade against him if he spoke to her. And so he quietly slipped away and joined the count and Liza, who were standing and talking at the open window.

On the table laid for supper stood two wax candles. Now and again their flames flickered in the fresh warm breeze of the May night. It was light at the window that opened into the garden, but the light was entirely different from that inside the room. An almost full moon, which by this time had lost its golden tinge, was sailing over the high tips of the lime trees, pouring more and more light upon the diaphanous white clouds that kept flowing across it. Frogs were croaking in chorus down at the pond; through the trees could be glimpsed a bit of water, shimmering silver in the moonlight. Some little birds could be heard hopping about and ruffling their feathers in the fragrant lilac bush whose moist clusters of blossom nodded beside the window.

"What divine weather!" said the count, going over to Liza and sitting down on the low windowsill. "I suppose you often go for walks?"

"Yes," said Liza, for some reason feeling not the least discomfiture in talking with the count. "At seven in the morning I walk out to attend to my household duties, and I also take walks with Pimochka, the little girl mama has adopted."

"It is such a pleasure to live in the country!" said the count, screwing his monocle into his eye and glancing now into the garden, now at Liza. "Do you ever go out to walk in the moonlight?"

"Not now. Three years ago Uncle and I used to go for walks every moonlit night, but then he was taken by a strange ailment— could not sleep; he could never fall asleep when there was a full moon. His room—that one over there—opens directly into the garden and the window is low; the moon shines full on him."

"Strange," observed the count. "I thought that was your room?"

"I am sleeping there only for tonight. My room is the one you are sleeping in."

"Really? Dear me! I shall never forgive

myself for inconveniencing you!" And the count dropped the monocle out of his eye as an indication of his sincerity. "Had I known our presence would cause you such inconvenience—"

"No inconvenience at all. On the contrary, I'm very glad. Uncle's room is charming—very light and cheerful, and with a low window. I shall sit at it until I fall asleep, or perhaps I shall even climb out into the garden and take a stroll before I go to bed."

"What a sweet girl!" thought the count, screwing in his monocle again to get a better look at her and trying to touch her leg with his foot as he sat down on the windowsill. "And how cunningly she has let me know that I may see her at the window if I so desire." Indeed, so easy did his conquest over her seem that she lost much of the attraction she had held for him.

"What delight it must be," said he as he gazed ruminatively into the dark alley, "to spend a night such as this in a garden with a creature you adore."

Liza was somewhat embarrassed by these words and by another touch, as if by chance, of his leg against hers. Without thinking, she hastened to say something to cover her embarrassment. "Yes," she said, "it is delightful to walk in the moonlight." Feeling uncomfortable, she quickly tied up the mushroom-jar and was about to walk away with it when the cornet came up and she had a sudden desire to find out what sort of person he was.

"What a beautiful night!" he said.

"They speak about nothing but the weather," thought Liza.

"And what a charming view!" went on the cornet. "But I suppose you have already grown weary of it," he added, due to a strange habit he had of always saying something unpleasant to people he liked very much.

"Why should you think so? One grows weary of eating the same things or wearing the same frock, but one never grows weary of a beautiful garden, especially when the moon rises even higher in the sky. From Uncle's room one gets a view of the entire pond. I shall see it tonight."

"I think there are no nightingales here, are there?" asked the count, greatly displeased that Polozov should have intruded at just this moment and kept him from making more definite arrangements for a rendezvous.

"No. There used to be, but last year a sportsman caught one, and this year—last week, in fact—I heard one singing beautifully, but the constable rode by with bells on his trap and frightened it away. The year before last Uncle and I used to sit under the trees in the alley and listen to them for hours at a stretch."

"What is this little chatterbox telling you?" said her uncle, coming up to them.

"Would you not like something to eat, gentlemen?"

After supper, during which the count, by praising the food and displaying a good appetite, managed to somewhat improve Anna Fyodorovna's temper, the officers took their leave and went to their room. The count shook the uncle's hand, and, to the astonishment of Anna Fyodorovna, shook her hand without kissing it, and even shook Liza's, gazing straight into her eyes as he did so and giving one of his faint but pleasant smiles. Again his gaze embarrassed her.

"He is good-looking," she thought, "but he thinks too much of himself."

XIV

"Aren't you ashamed?" said Polozov when the officers reached their room. "I did my best to make us lose and kept kicking you under the table. You have no conscience at all. The old woman was quite distressed."

The count burst out laughing.

"She's simply killing! How she did take it to heart!"

And he burst into another roar of laughter so catching that even Johann, who was standing in front of them, dropped his eyes and gave a furtive little smile.

"The son of the old friend of the family! Ha, ha, ha!" and the count went on laughing.

"But really it wasn't nice, I even felt sorry for her," said the cornet.

"Fiddlesticks! You're still so young! Did you expect me to lose? Why should I? I, too, lost before I learnt how to play. I can find good use for that ten rubles, my friend. A man has to take a practical view of life if he doesn't want to join the fools."

Polozov grew silent. He wanted to withdraw into himself and think about Liza, whom he found to be a remarkably pure and lovely creature. He got undressed and lay down in the soft, clean bed that had been made for him.

"What nonsense—the honour and glory of life in the army!" he thought as he gazed at the window draped with a shawl through which the pale light of the moon was shining. "This is happiness—to live in some quiet retreat with a simple, clever, charming wife. This is true and lasting happiness."

But for some reason he did not confide his thoughts to his friend and did not so much as mention the country girl to him, although he was certain that the count, too, was thinking of her.

"Why aren't you undressing?" he asked the count, who was pacing the floor.

"Somehow I have no desire to sleep. Put out the light if you wish; I do not need it."

And he went on walking back and forth.

"Has no desire to sleep," repeated Polozov. The events of the evening had made him resent the count's influence over him more than ever, and had thrown him in a mood to resist it. "It is not hard to guess," said he mentally to Tourbin, "what thoughts are brewing in that sleek head of yours! I saw how taken you were by her! But you are incapable of understanding so simple and honest a creature. It's the Minnas you want, and a colonel's epaulettes. But here, let me ask him how he liked her."

But just as Polozov was about to turn over and address the count, he changed his mind. He felt that he would not only be unable to protest if the count's opinion of Liza turned out to be what he supposed, but that he would even find himself acquiescing, so used was he to giving in to his influence, although with every passing day this was becoming more unjust and unbearable.

"Where are you going?" he asked when the count put on his cap and went to the door.

"Out to the stables. I want to make sure that everything is all right."

"Strange," thought the cornet, but he put out the candle and turned over, making an effort to drive away the absurdly jealous and antagonistic thoughts that his former friend inspired.

Meanwhile Anna Fyodorovna, having tenderly kissed and made the sign of the cross over her brother, her daughter, and her ward, as was her custom, had also withdrawn to her room. Long had it been since she

had experienced so many keen sensations
in a single day. She could not even say her
prayers calmly, so disturbed was she by sad
and vivid memories of the late count and of
this young dandy who had so shamefully
taken her money away from her. And yet she
climbed into bed as usual after she had
undressed and drunk the half a glass of kvass
which was always left for her on the little
table next to her bed. Her favourite cat crept
softly into the room. Anna Fyodorovna called
it over and began stroking it, listening to its
purring, unable to fall asleep.

"It's the cat that keeps me awake," she
thought, and pushed it away. The cat dropped
softly on the floor, then, curling up its fluffy
tail, jumped up on the stovebunk. At this
point the serving maid who slept on the floor
in her mistress's room brought her felt mat,
spread it out, put out the candle, and lighted
the icon-lamp. Soon she was snoring away,
but sleep refused to bring peace to Anna
Fyodorovna's troubled soul. As soon as she
closed her eyes the face of the hussar rose
before her, and when she opened them all
the objects in the room—the commode, the
table, the white frock hanging there, dimly
lighted by the icon-lamp—all of them seemed
to represent him in strange forms. One minute
she felt suffocated by the down quilt, the
next she was annoyed by the striking of the
clock or the snoring of the maid. She woke
the girl up and ordered her to stop snoring.

Thoughts of her daughter, of the old count and the young one, of the game of "preference" mingled oddly in her mind. Now she saw herself waltzing with the late count, saw her plump white shoulders, felt someone's lips pressed against them, then she saw her daughter in the arms of the young count. Once more Ustyushka began to snore...

"Oh, no; people are not what they used to be. He was ready to go through fire and water for my sake. And there was good reason for it. But that one, you may be sure, is sleeping like the dolt he is, gloating over his winnings, unwilling to bestir himself for love-making. But the professions his father made to me on bended knee! 'What would you have me do? Kill myself? I would gladly do it for your sake.' And he would have, too, if I had wanted it."

Suddenly there was a patter of bare feet out in the hall, and Liza, pale and trembling, with a shawl thrown over her shoulders, ran into the room and almost fell on her mother's bed...

After saying good-night to her mother, Liza had gone alone to her uncle's room. Having put on a white dressing-jacket and tied up her long hair in a kerchief, she put out the candle, opened the window, and sat on a chair with her legs tucked up under her, gazing pensively at the pond, whose whole surface was now shimmering with silvery light.

All her usual interests and occupations

suddenly appeared to her in an entirely
new light: her old, capricious mother, unquestioning love for whom had become part
of her very being, her kind but feeble uncle,
the house servants who adored their young
mistress, the milch-cows and the calves—all
of them, and all of her natural surroundings,
which had known the decline of so many
autumns and the renewal of so many springs,
and in the midst of which, loving and being
loved she had been reared—all of this now
seemed to be *nothing*; seemed wearisome and
unwanted. It was as if someone had whispered
to her, "You little fool! You little fool!
For twenty years you've been wasting your
time waiting on others without knowing what
real life and happiness are!" Now, as she sat
gazing into the depths of the bright, still
garden, these thoughts broke upon her
forcefully, more forcefully than ever before.
What had prompted them? Not at all a sudden
love for the count, as one might suppose.
On the contrary, she did not like him. She
could more easily have fallen in love with
the cornet, but he was plain, poor and taciturn.
She had already forgotten him. But it was
with anger and resentment that she
remembered the count. "No, he is not the
one," she said to herself. Her ideal was someone wholly beautiful, someone who, on
a night like this, in a setting like this, could
be loved without violating the beauty all
around—an ideal that had never been cut

down to fit coarse reality.

At first her life of solitude and the absence of people who could interest her had preserved whole and undisturbed in her heart that great force of love that Providence has implanted equally in the heart of each of us; now, however, she had lived too long with the rueful joy of sensing within herself the existence of this something (sometimes stealing glimpses into the mysterious coffer of her heart to rapturously contemplate the treasure it contained)—too long to lavish it heedlessly now on the first chance comer. God grant that she might enjoy this meagre happiness to the end of her days! Who could say but that it was the best and the greatest joy? That it, alone, was the only true and possible joy?

"O Lord!" she murmured. "Is it possible that youth and happiness have passed me by ... that I shall never know them? Can it be true?" And she raised her eyes to the high bright sky where fluffy white clouds were blotting out the stars as they moved towards the moon. "If that top cloud touches the moon it is true," she said to herself. A foggy, smoky strip ran across the lower half of the bright disc, and little by little the light shining on the grass, the crowns of the lime trees, and the pond, grew dim, and the black shadows of the trees grew indistinct. And as if in the wake of the melancholy shadows darkening nature, a light breeze passed over the leaves, wafting to the window the fragrance of dewy leaves, moist earth, and lilac blossom.

"No, it is not true," she consoled herself. "And if a nightingale sings tonight, then all these sad thoughts are foolish and there is no reason to despair," she thought. And for a long time she sat on in silence, waiting for someone, while the moon now came out of the clouds, making the scene bright again, now went behind them, throwing the earth in shadow. She was just about to fall asleep when she heard a nightingale singing clearly down by the pond. The country girl opened her eyes. Once more, with new rapture, her soul was revived by a mysterious union with nature, which lay so bright and serene all about her. She leaned on both elbows. A sweet sadness pressed upon her heart and tears of a vast and pure love which yearned for fulfilment—good, comforting tears—filled her eyes. She folded her arms on the windowsill and laid her head upon them. Her favourite prayer rose of itself in her heart, and she drowsed off just as she was, her eyes still wet with tears.

She was roused by the touch of a hand. She woke up. The touch was light and pleasant. The clasp tightened upon her arm. Suddenly she realized where she was, gave a little cry, jumped up and telling herself that it could not be the count who was standing there by the window, radiant in the moonlight, she ran out of the room.

XV

But it was the count. On hearing the girl's cry and the coughing of the night watchman as he came down the other side of the fence in response to it, he instantly ran through the dew-wet grass into the depths of the garden, feeling like a thief caught in the act. "What a fool I am!" he said to himself. "I frightened her. I should have been more cautious, and waked her up by speaking to her. What a clumsy beast I am!" He stopped and listened: the watchman had entered the garden through the gate and was dragging his stick along the sandy path. He must hide. He ran down to the pond. The frogs startled him by leaping up in alarm from under his very feet and flopping into the water. In spite of his wet feet he squatted down and went over in his mind all that he had done: how he had climbed over the fence, sought her window, and at last caught sight of her white shadow; how, fearful of the slightest rustle, he had approached her several times, only to withdraw; how at one minute he had been certain that she was waiting for him, that she was even vexed with him for keeping her waiting so long, and at the next he was sure she could not possibly have given such ready consent to this rendez-vous; and how at last, assuming that the bash-fulness of a provincial girl had led her to pretend to be asleep, he had gone up to her and seen clearly that she really was asleep;

for some reason he had instantly run away, but a feeling of shame for his cowardice had made him come back and boldly put his hand upon her arm. The night watchman coughed again and the gate creaked as he went out of the garden. The window of the young girl's room was banged shut and inside shutters were fastened over it. The count found this very annoying. He would have given anything for the chance to begin all over again. Oh, he would not have behaved so foolishly a second time! "A charming girl! So fresh! Simply adorable! And I let her slip through my fingers! What a dunderhead I am!" By this time he had lost all desire to sleep, and with the firm step of one who has been sorely vexed, he set off down the alley of lime trees.

But even to him this night brought as its peace offering a tranquillizing sadness and longing for love. The clay path with bits of grass or dry stalks sprouting out of it here and there was mottled by pale moonlight that fell in direct rays through the thick foliage of the limes. Sometimes a twisted branch, lighted on one side only, gave the impression of being overgrown with white moss. The silvered leaves whispered together from time to time. The lights were put out in the house; all sounds died away; only the nightingale filled with song all this bright, silent, unencompassable space. "What a night! What a glorious night!" thought the count, drawing deep into his lungs the fresh and fragrant air of the garden. "But there's something amiss. I seem to be dissatisfied with myself and others, dissatisfied with life itself. What a dear sweet girl she is! Perhaps she really was offended..." Here his musings took a new turn; now he saw himself in the garden with the country girl in the most odd and varied situations; then the country girl was supplanted by Minna. "What a fool I was! I ought to have simply seized her round the waist and kissed her!" And with this regret in mind, the count went back to his room.

The cornet had not yet fallen asleep. He immediately turned over in bed to face the count.

"Aren't you asleep?" asked the count.

"No."

"Shall I tell you what happened?"

"Well?"

"Perhaps I oughtn't to—but I shall. Here, move over."

And, shrugging off thoughts of his bungled opportunity, he sat down on his friend's bed with a lively smile on his face.

"Would you believe it? That young lady agreed to a rendezvous with me!"

"What are you saying!" cried Polozov, jumping up.

"Well, listen."

"How? When? I don't believe it!"

"While you were calculating your winnings at 'preference' she told me she would be waiting for me at the window, and that I could climb through it into her room. There's the advantage of being practical-minded! While you were making your calculations with the old lady, I was arranging my affairs. Why, you yourself heard her say she intended sitting at the window and gazing out at the pond tonight."

"But she meant nothing by it."

"That's it; I can't make up my mind whether she said it by chance or not. Perhaps she really did not have that in mind, but appearances are against her. The whole thing had an odd ending. I acted like a perfect fool," he added with a contemptuous smile.

"But how? Where have you been?"

The count told him what had happened, omitting nothing except his vacillations before going up to the window.

"I spoiled everything myself. I ought to have been bolder. She cried out and ran away."

"So she cried out and ran away," repeated the cornet, smiling awkwardly in response to the smile of this count whose influence over him had been so strong and had lasted so long.

"Yes. Well, now it's time to go to bed."

The cornet turned his back to the door again and lay in silence for ten minutes or so. It is hard to say what went on in his innermost soul during that time, but when he turned back again his face wore a look of pain and determination.

"Count Tourbin," he burst out.

"Are you delirious?" said the count serenely. "What is it, Cornet Polozov?"

"Count Tourbin, you're a cad!" cried Polozov, jumping out of bed.

XVI

The squadron left the next day. The officers did not see their hosts and did not seek them out to say good-bye. Nor did they speak to each other. They had agreed to hold a duel at their first halt, but Captain Shultz, a good comrade, an excellent horseman, a favourite among the hussars, and the man whom the count had chosen as his second, was able to arrange matters in such a way that not only was the duel averted, but not a soul in the regiment got wind of it. Tourbin and Polozov, while never resuming the close friendship that had been theirs, continued to use the intimate form of address when speaking to each other and sometimes met at dinners and parties.

1856

YARDSTICK

(A Story About a Horse)

Dedicated to the Memory of M. A. Stakhovich

I

The light rose higher and higher, the sunrise spread wider, the opaque silvery dew glistened whiter, the sickle of the moon grew fainter, the forest—noisier, people began to stir, and in the horse-yard of the manor-house the snorting and shuffling in the straw became more insistent and there were even shrill whinnyings as the horses pushed each other angrily about and bickered over something.

"Whoa, there! Plenty of time! Ye ain't starved yet!" said the old herdsman as he opened the creaking gate. "Back!" he shouted, waving his arm, as a mare made a lunge for the gate.

Herdsman Nester was wearing a Cossack jacket held in by a leather belt decorated with ornate silvery studs; his whip was thrown across his shoulder, and his bread, wrapped in a linen towel, was thrust into his belt. He was carrying a saddle and a bridle.

The horses were neither frightened nor offended by the herdsman's mocking tone, they pretended not to care and turned unconcernedly away from the gate—all but an old bay mare with a shaggy mane, who folded back her ears and swiftly turned her back on him. At that a young mare standing behind her, who really ought not to have taken any notice, gave a whinny and kicked up her hind legs at the first horse that came near her.

"Whoa!" cried the herdsman in a louder and more menacing tone as he made for a far corner of the yard.

Of all the horses in the enclosure (there were about a hundred of them), the one who showed the least impatience was a piebald gelding standing alone under an overhanging roof and gazing about with half-closed eyes as he licked the oak post of the shed. It is hard to say just what the taste of this post was, but the piebald gelding looked very grave and pensive as he licked it.

"Up to mischief, eh?" said the herdsman in the same tone as he came up to him and put down the saddle and well used saddle-cloth on a manure pile.

The piebald gelding stopped licking and stood staring at Nester without moving a muscle. The horse did not laugh, did not frown, did not lose his temper, but in a few seconds a shudder passed over his belly, he gave a deep sigh, and turned away. The herdsman encircled his neck with his arm and put on the bridle.

"What are you sighing for?" asked Nester.

The gelding gave a whisk of his tail, as much as to say, "Oh, nothing in particular, Nester." The herdsman put on the saddle and saddle-cloth, the gelding laid back his ears to show his disapproval, but he was only called a fool for it. When the girth was tightened, the gelding blew himself up to stop it, but a finger thrust into his mouth and a knee-kick in the belly knocked the breath out of him. And yet when Nester pulled on the strap with his teeth, the gelding dared to lay back his ears again and even glance round at him. He knew it would do no good, but he wanted Nester to know he disapproved and had no intention of hiding his disapproval. Once saddled, he relaxed his swollen right leg and set to chewing on his bit, although he ought to have known by this time that nothing could be more tasteless than a bit.

When Nester had put his foot in the short stirrup and mounted, he unwound his whip, pulled his coat out from under his knees, struck the pose in the saddle peculiar to coachmen, fox-hunters, and herdsmen, and pulled on the reins. The gelding lifted his head as a mark of readiness to go wherever he was told, but did not stir. He knew that before they set out his rider would bellow a string of orders to Vaska, the other herdsman, and to the horses as well. And sure enough, Nester began to shout.

"Vaska!" he called. "Hi, Vaska! Have you let out the mares? Where are you, rascal? Asleep? Open the gates! Let the mares out first!" and other things of the same nature.

The gates creaked. Vaska, cross and sleepy, was standing at the gatepost holding one horse by the bridle as he let the others out. The horses passed through one after another, stepping cautiously over the straw and sniffing at it: fillies, yearlings, colts, mares heavy with young, who, solicitous of their great bellies, went through the gates in single file. The young mares pushed ahead in twos and threes, thrusting their heads over another's backs and tripping over their feet in their hurry, for which they were sworn at by the herdsmen. The suckling colts darted between the legs of even strange mares, and whinnied shrilly in response to the neighing of their elders.

A frisky young mare turned her head down and to one side as soon as she was out of the gates, kicked up her hind legs, and let out little cries, but she did not dare to rush ahead of old dappled Zhuldyba, who, as always, walked at the head of the other horses with a slow, heavy, dignified tread, her big belly swinging from side to side.

A few minutes later the enclosure, that had just been so lively and crowded, was empty. The posts holding up the roof-shelters looked sad and lonely and there was nothing else to be seen but crumpled, dung-covered straw. The piebald gelding was used to this scene, and yet it seemed to have a depressing effect on him. He swung his head slowly up and down as if nodding to someone, sighed as deeply as the girth permitted, and dragged his stiff and crooked legs in the wake of the herd, carrying old Nester on his bony back.

"As soon as we reach the road he is sure to strike a light and smoke that old pipe of his with the brass trimmings and the chain," he thought to himself. "And very glad I am, for it is pleasant to catch the fragrance of his pipe early in the morning, while the dew is still on the grass; the smell of it reminds me of many pleasant things. The only objection I have is that as soon as the old man has a pipe between his teeth he puts on airs, fancies himself a great person, and sits sidewise—and always on the side that hurts me. But the devil with him! It's not the first time I have had to sacrifice myself for the sake of another's enjoyment. Horse that I am, I've even come to take a certain satisfaction in it. Let him put on airs, poor fellow; he only does it when he's alone and nobody sees him. Let him sit side-wise if it gives him pleasure," reflected the gelding as he walked down the middle of the road, stepping cautiously on his shaky legs.

II

Having driven the herd to the river-bank where the horses were to graze, Nester climbed down and unsaddled the gelding. Slowly the horses made their way towards the fresh water-meadows that were drenched in dew and veiled in the mist rising from the earth and the encircling arm of the river.

As soon as the bridle was removed Nester scratched the gelding under the chin, at which the horse closed his eyes to express pleasure and gratitude. "He loves it, the old ninny," muttered Nester. But the gelding did not love it at all; it was only a delicacy of feeling that made him pretend to, and to nod his head in acquiescence. But suddenly, without warning or reason (unless, perhaps, Nester felt that too much familiarity might lower his importance in the gelding's eyes), the old man pushed the horse's head away and swung out with the bridle, striking the gelding painfully on his skinny leg with the buckle, and then without a word he walked over to a stump on a knoll where he usually sat.

Such behaviour could not but vex the gelding, but he gave no sign of it. He merely turned and made his way down to the river, slowly swinging his stringy tail, sniffing the air, and browsing for the sake of appearances. The young mares, yearlings, and sucklings, rejoicing in the fine morning, were cutting capers all around him, but he paid no attention to them. Knowing that the best thing for one's health, especially at his age, was to have a good drink on an empty stomach and only then to take one's breakfast, he selected the most sloping and expansive spot on the river-bank, wet his hoofs and fetlocks, poked his muzzle into the water, and began to suck it up with his ragged lips, expanding his sides and switching his streaked and scanty tail that had gone bald where it joined the spine.

A mischievous bay mare who was always teasing the old gelding and causing him annoyance, came through the water towards him as if on some business, but really to stir up the water where he was drinking. But by this time the gelding had drunk his fill, and, as if unaware of the mare's ill intentions, he calmly drew one foot out of the mud after another, shook his head, withdrew to a safe distance from the young folk, and began his breakfast. He ate for three hours on end, scarcely lifting his head, flinging out his legs in odd postures so as to trample down as little grass as possible. When he had eaten so much that his belly hung from his sharp protruding ribs like a stuffed sack, he balanced himself on his four aching legs in a way that would cause as little pain as possible, especially in his right foreleg, the weakest of all, and fell asleep.

Sometimes old age is majestic, sometimes repulsive, sometimes pathetic. Sometimes it is both majestic and repulsive. The piebald gelding's old age was of that sort.

The gelding was a big horse—least five and a half feet tall. He was almost black with cream-coloured spots. That is, he had been once, but now the spots had become a dirty brown. He had three colour spots on him in all: one slanting up one side of his nose, covering the top of his head and half his neck. His long mane, matted with burrs, was white in some places, brown in others. The second spot extended along his right side and took in half his belly. The third was on his crupper and spread over the upper part of his tail and half his flanks. The rest of his tail was streaked and whitish. His big bony head, with deep hollows around the eye sockets and a dark and pendant lower lip that had been torn some time in the past, hung low and heavy at the end of a scrawny neck that seemed carved of wood. His pendant lower lip gave glimpses of a blackish tongue lolling in the side of his mouth, and some stumps of yellow teeth. His ears, one of which had a rip in it, flopped over most of the time, but occasionally he would twitch them to scare off a too persistent fly. A remnant of forelock hung down behind one ear; his bare forehead was sunken and furrowed, and his dewlaps hung like empty bags. The knotted veins on his head and neck shook and trembled at every touch of a fly. The expression of his face was sternly patient, profound, and long-suffering. His forelegs were bowed at the knee, both hoofs were swollen, and there was a lump the size of a fist near the knee of his spotted right foreleg. His hind legs were in better shape, but the nap had once got scrubbed off his flanks and had never grown back. His legs looked too long for his skinny body. His ribs, though well rounded, were so exposed and protruding that the skin seemed to have grown fast to the hollows between them. His withers and back bore the scars of many a beating and there was a fresh sore, swollen and festering, on his hind quarters. The black tail-stump, ridged with vertebrae, hung down long and almost bald. On the bay crupper near his tail there was a sore or a horse bite the size of a hand with white hairs growing out of it and on his shoulder-blade there was the scar of another sore. His hocks and tail were stained by chronic diarrhea. The short hair of his hide stood up like bristles. Yet, despite the repulsive senility of this gelding, one could not help thinking, and an expert was sure to say, that he had been a fine horse in his day.

Indeed, an expert would say there was only one stock in Russia that could produce such broad bones, such large knee-pans, such fine hoofs, such slender legs, such a graceful neck, and, most important of all, such a fine head, with its large, black, radiant eyes, its aristocratic knotting of veins on face and neck, its refinement of hide and hair. There really was something majestic about the horse, even in the terrible combination of repulsive decrepitude (enhanced by the piebald colouring) and serene self-confidence of look and manner, characteristic of those who are aware of their strength and beauty.

Like a living ruin the horse stood alone in the dewdrenched meadow, while not far away could be heard the stamping and snorting, the neighing and youthful whinnying of the scattered herd.

III

The sun had already climbed above the forest and was shining brightly on the meadow and the curve of the river. The dew had shrunk into drops as it dried; here and there above the swamp and forest the dissolving mist hovered like thin smoke. Clouds came billowing up, but there was still no wind. In the fields across the river the rye stood in short green bristles, and the air was fragrant with verdure and blossom. A cuckoo called hoarsely from out of the forest, and Nester, sprawled on his back, was counting the number of years of life left to him. Larks soared over the rye fields and water-meadows. A belated hare found itself caught among the herd; it scurried to a safe distance and sat down under a bush, alert to danger. Vaska drowsed off with his head buried in the grass; the mares circled widely round him and scattered over the lower half of the slope. The older ones, snorting, left a bright trail in the dew as they sought grazing spots where no one would disturb them, and having found them, nibbled at the succulent grass. The whole herd moved imperceptibly in the same direction. And again dignified old Zhuldyba, taking the lead, showed the others the way. Young Mushka, who had foaled for the first time, lifted her tail, giggled and snorted at her little mauve colt who, with trembling knees, kept sidling up to her. Brown Swallow, still single, with a hide as smooth and glossy as satin, dropped her head until her silky black forelock covered her brow and eyes as she played with the grass, biting it off, throwing it up into the air, and striking it with her dew-wet fetlock as it came down. One of the older colts, waving its tail like a plume, no doubt imagining it was playing a game, had already run twenty-six times round its mother, while she, used to the ways of her son by now, went on calmly cropping grass, merely darting a glance at him every once in a while with her big black eyes. One of the smallest of the colts, a black one with a large head and a forelock that lent it a look of surprise by standing straight up between its ears, and with a tail that was still twisted to one side as it had been in the womb, stood stock-still with its ears cocked and its eyes fixed on the playful colt, whether in envy or disapproval it would be hard to say. Some of the young were poking their mothers' bellies impatiently with their muzzles, seeking the nipple, others went loping away at a quick, ungainly gait in defiance of their mothers' calls and in exactly the opposite direction, as if they were looking for something, and then, still for no good reason, stopping suddenly and giving piercing cries; still others were sprawling on the ground, or learning to crop grass, or scratching behind their ears with their hind legs. Two mares who had not yet foaled had withdrawn from the others and were browsing together walking with difficulty. The others clearly had respect for their state and none of the colts dared to go near and disturb them. If some frisky young thing ventured near them a twitch of the ear or the tail was sufficient to point out to him the impropriety of his conduct.

The yearlings and fillies put on the airs of grown-ups; rarely did they allow themselves to leap into the air or join the gay youngsters. With great dignity they munched the grass, curving down their clipped swan-like necks and waving their little whisk-brooms as if they, too, had tails. Like their elders, they would sometimes lie down and roll over or scratch one another's backs. Gayest of all were the two- and three-year-old fillies and the virgin mares. They almost always formed a separate group of spirited maidens who were forever stamping their feet, snorting, whinnying, and neighing. They would come together, put their heads on each other's shoulders, sniff each other, leap into the air, and sometimes, with a snort and a flourish of their tails, parade in front of each other coquettishly, in a half-trot, half-amble.

The most beautiful and impish of these gay maidens was the bay mare. Whatever she did, the other did too. Wherever she went the whole flock of pretty maidens followed. She was in particularly high spirits this morning. Her gay mood had come upon her just as it comes upon humans. After playing her prank on the old gelding at the river, she had rushed along the water's edge, pretended to be frightened by something, let out a snort, and dashed at top speed into the meadow, so that Vaska had to gallop after her and the others who had followed her. When she had eaten a little, she rolled over on the ground, then set to teasing the old mares by racing under their very noses; then she chased one of the colts away from its mother and ran after it as if to bite it. The mother was terrified and the colt whinnied plaintively, but the bay mare did not so much as touch it, she only gave it a fright for the entertainment of her girl-friends, who watched with delight. Then she had the bright idea of turning the head of a grey plough-horse that was being driven by a muzhik in a rye field on the far side of the river. She stopped, threw up her head proudly, shook herself, and gave a sweetly tender, long-drawn whinny. There was spirit and feeling and a certain sadness in this whinny. And there was also desire, and the promise of love, and the longing for it.

A corncrake deep in the reeds was hopping about and calling passionately for a mate; a cuckoo and a quail were singing of love; even the flowers were sending sweet-smelling dust down the wind to each other.

"I am young and beautiful and strong," whinnied the mare. "And yet I have not yet been allowed to taste the sweetness of love; more than that, no lover, not a single one, has yet set eyes on me."

And this meaningful whinny spread sadly and youthfully, down the slope and over the fields and reached the ears of the distant grey horse. He pricked up his ears and came to a standstill. The peasant kicked him with his bast shoe, but the grey horse was so enchanted by the silvery sound that he stood still and whinnied in response. The peasant grew angry, pulled on the reins, and gave him another kick in the belly, so hard this time that he broke off in the middle of his call and moved on. But a sweet sadness had come over the grey horse, and the sound of his passionate whinnies and of the peasant's angry protests were carried from the distant rye field to the herd of horses on the other bank.

If the mere sound of the mare's voice could so enchant the grey horse that he forgot his duty, what would he have felt had he seen all the beauty of her, as she called to him, standing with ears pricked up, nostrils dilated, sucking in the air and straining forward, trembling in every limb of her young and beautiful body.

But the mare did not give herself up to her feelings for long. When the answering voice died away she whinnied once more, then, dropping her head, pawed the ground and rushed off to tease and annoy the piebald gelding. He was the constant brunt of the young horses' jesting and joking, and suffered more from them than from humans.

Yet he had never done harm to either. Human beings still had need of him, but why should the colts torture him so?

IV

He was old, they were young; he was skinny, they were sleek; he was sad, they were gay. In a word, he was a strange, alien, utterly different being, and so not to be pitied. Horses pity only themselves, with rare exceptions for those of their kind whom they imagine to be like themselves. But surely the piebald gelding could not be blamed for being old and skinny and ugly? One would not suppose so. But according to the other horses he was to blame, and only those were blameless who were young and strong and happy, those who had everything before them, those whose muscles quivered and tails stood upright at the slightest provocation. Perhaps the piebald gelding realized this and in his more rational moments admitted that he was to blame for having lived out his life, and was willing to pay the penalty. But he was a mere horse after all, and as he looked at these young folk who tortured him for nothing but what each of them would have to face as their lives came to an end, he could not help feeling sad, indignant, and offended. There was an aristocratic sentiment behind the heartlessness of the horses. Each of them had a pedigree tracing back to the famous Smetanka, whereas nobody knew from whom the old piebald descended. He was a nobody who had been bought three years before at the horse-market for eighty rubles.

The bay mare walked up to him in the most nonchalant way and gave him a push. He expected nothing better, and without so much as opening his eyes he put down his ears and bared his teeth. The mare turned her back on him and made as if to kick him. He opened his eyes and walked away. No longer sleepy, he took to browsing. Again the mare and her friends sauntered over to him. A silly bald-headed two-year-old filly, who always aped everything the bay mare did, walked beside her and, like all imitators, overdid what the mare was initiating. The bay mare usually approached him as if she were going about her own affairs, passing under his very nose without so much as looking at him, so that he could never tell whether he had a right to get angry or not, and that was most amusing. She did this now, but her bald-headed friend, who was feeling very playful, struck the gelding full force with her chest. Again he bared his teeth, let out a cry, and with an asperity hardly to be expected from him, set out after her and bit her in the flank. The bald-headed filly struck him with her hind quarters, hitting him painfully on his bare ribs. The old horse snorted and was about to set out after her, but thought better of it and, sighing deeply, walked away.

Apparently all the young folk in the herd resolved to get revenge for the daring attack the gelding had made on the bald-headed filly, for they did not even give him a chance to eat for the rest of the day, so persistently did they plague him. Several times the herdsman drove them away from him and was quite at a loss to explain their behaviour. The gelding was so frightfully offended that he himself went up to Nester when it was time to drive the herd home, and he felt much happier and more secure when he was saddled and the herdsman was on his back.

Who can say what thoughts came into his mind as he carried the old herdsman home? Perhaps he brooded sadly over the heartlessness of youth, or perhaps, in the way of the old, he forgave his offenders, holding them in proud and silent contempt. Whatever his ruminations, he kept them to himself until they reached the horse-yard.

That evening some neighbours paid Nester a call. As he drove the herd past the huts belonging to the manor-house servants he noticed a horse and cart tied to the post of his hut. He was in such a hurry to reach home that as soon as the herd was in the enclosure he let the gelding go, shouting to Vaska that he was to unsaddle him. Then he locked the gate and went to join his friends.

An extraordinary event took place in the enclosure that night, due perhaps to the insult meted out to the bald filly, Smetanka's great-granddaughter (and therefore to the aristocratic feelings of the entire herd) by the "mangy nag" bought at the horse-market and knowing neither father nor mother; or perhaps to the fantastic appearance the gelding presented to the other horses in his high saddle without any rider. All the horses, young and old alike, ran with bared teeth after the gelding, chasing him to and fro, thumping his hollow sides with their hoofs, forcing loud groans from him. When the gelding could stand it no longer he came to a halt in the middle of the enclosure, his face expressing the feeble fury of impotent old age, an expression supplanted by one of despair. He dropped his ears and suddenly did something that made all the horses stop dead in their tracks. Vyazopurikha, the eldest mare, sniffed the gelding and drew a deep sigh. The gelding, too, drew a deep sigh...

V

In the middle of the moonlit enclosure stood the tall figure of the gelding with the high saddle on his back. The other horses stood silent and motionless around him as if amazed by something he had just told them. And indeed they were.

This is what it was.

THE FIRST NIGHT

"I am the son of Gracious-the-First and Baba. According to my pedigree my name is Muzhik-the-First. But, though my pedigree name is Muzhik-the-First, I have always been called Yardstick, a name people gave me because of my long stride, the like of which was not to be found in all Russia. No horse in the world has more thoroughbred blood flowing through his veins than mine. I would never have told you this—why should I?—you would not have recognized me any more than Vyazopurikha did, who lived with me in Khrenovo in my youth and has just discovered who I am; you would not believe me now if it were not for the witness of Vyazopurikha,

and I would never have told you—I have no
need to be pitied by a set of horses—but you
made me. Yes, I am that Yardstick whom the
connoisseurs of horseflesh are searching for
everywhere and cannot find, that same
Yardstick whom the count himself knew and
banished from the stud because I outran his
beloved Swan."

"I was born without knowing what *piebald*
meant. I thought I was just a horse. I remember that the first remarks made on my
colouring deeply shocked my mother and me.
I was born at night, it seems, and by morning,
after my mother had licked me clean, I could
stand on my legs. I remember wanting something, and everything seemed very astonishing
and yet very simple. Our stalls were in a long
warm corridor with grating on the doors
through which we could see everything.
Mother offered me her teats, but I was
still so innocent that I poked my muzzle
now into her foreleg, now into her breast.
Suddenly mother glanced through the grating,
put a leg over me, and drew back. The groom
for that day was staring at us through the
grating.

" 'Just see, Baba has foaled,' he said, and
pushed back the bolt. He walked over the
fresh straw and put his arms about me.

" 'Come and look, Taras,' he called. 'He's
as piebald as a magpie.'

"I darted away from him and fell on my knees.

" 'Hi! you little devil!' he said.

"Mother was uneasy but made no effort to protect me; she merely heaved a deep sigh and turned away. The other grooms came in and looked at me. One of them went to tell the keeper of the stables. All of them laughed at my colouring and gave me all sorts of funny names. Neither my mother nor I understood the meaning of them. Up to this time there had never been a piebald horse among us or our relatives. We had no idea that there could be anything blameworthy in a horse's colouring. Even then everyone praised me for my strength and handsome form.

" 'Just see what a lively little fellow he is!' said the groom. 'There's no holding him.'

"In a little while the keeper came in; he showed astonishment and even seemed distressed.

" 'Where did such a little monster come from?' he said. 'The general won't keep him in the stud. Damn it all, Baba, you've done me a fine turn!' he said, turning to my mother. 'You might better have given us a bald colt than this piebald clown!'

"My mother said nothing; she only heaved another sigh, as was her habit in such circumstances.

" 'Who the devil does he take after? Just like a muzhik,' he went on. 'He can't be left

in the stud, he'll disgrace us, and yet he's
a fine horse—very fine,' he said, and everyone
who looked at me said the same.

"A few days later the general himself came
to see me, and he, too, was horrified, and upbraided me and my mother for the colour of
my hide.

"'And yet he's a fine horse—very fine,' said
everyone who laid eyes on me.

"We lived in the mare stables until spring,
each to himself, the colts with their mothers;
but when the snow on the shed roofs began
to melt in the heat of the sun we were
occasionally allowed to go out with our
mothers into the large enclosure strewn with
fresh straw. Here for the first time I made
the acquaintance of my relatives, near and
distant. I saw all the most famous mares of
that time come out of separate doors with
their colts. Among them were old Golanka;
and Mushka, Smetanka's daughter; and
Krasnukha; and Dobrokhotikha, the saddle-
horse—all the celebrities of the day. They
gathered there with their offspring, walked
about in the sun, rolled in the straw, and
sniffed each other, just as common horses
do. To this day I remember the sight of that
enclosure filled with beauties. You must
find it strange and hard to believe that I,
too, was once young and frisky, but I was.
It was there I met Vyazopurikha, then a year-
ling—a very kind, gay, and spirited horse.
And yet I must say, meaning no offence,

that although you look upon her as a rare thoroughbred, in those days she was considered one of the least of the herd. She herself will confirm this.

"My piebaldness, so detested by humans, was found very pleasing by the horses. They all surrounded me, admired me, and played with me. I began to forget what people said about my colouring and felt happy. But soon I was to experience my first sorrow, and it was caused by my mother.

"When the thaw set in and the sparrows twittered under the roofs and the air was filled with the scents of spring, my mother's attitude towards me changed. Indeed, everything about her changed: she raced and capered about the enclosure in a manner unbecoming to one of her age; or she fell into a brown study and began to whinny; or she bit and kicked the other mares; or she sniffed me and snorted contemptuously, or she stood in the sun with her head over the shoulder of her cousin Kupchikha and scratched her back long and pensively, pushing me unceremoniously away from her teats.

"One day the keeper came and had them put a bridle on her and lead her away. She neighed, I answered and ran after her. But she did not so much as look at me. Groom Taras seized me in his arms and held me as the door was locked behind her. I struggled and threw the groom down in the straw, but the door was locked and I could only hear my mother's whinnying growing fainter and fainter. And in her whinnying I heard not a call to me, but something quite different. As I learned later, another voice, a deep and powerful voice, answered her; it was the voice of Dobry, who was being led by two grooms to a rendezvous with my mother. I was so heartbroken I didn't even notice Taras leave our stall. I felt that I had lost the love of my mother for ever. 'And all because I am piebald,' I thought as I recalled the remarks people had made about my colouring, and such anger rose within me that I began to beat the walls of the stall with my head and knees, and went on beating them until I broke out in a sweat and stood still exhausted.

"In a short while my mother came back. I heard her come trotting at an unusual pace down the corridor. The door was opened to her and I scarcely recognized her, so young and pretty had she become. She sniffed me, snorted, and began to guffaw. Everything about her indicated she no longer loved me. She told me how handsome Dobry was and how deeply she loved him. Again and again she was taken to meet him, and the relations between her and myself grew colder and colder.

"Soon we were let out to grass. This brought me new joys that somewhat compensated for the loss of my mother's love. I acquired friends and comrades, and together we learned to crop grass, to neigh like grown-up horses, and to gallop in circles round our mothers. Those were happy days. Everything was forgiven me, everyone loved me, admired me, and was indulgent with me.

"But this did not last long. Soon a terrible thing happened." The gelding drew a deep sigh and walked away.

Dawn had come. The gates creaked and Nester came in. The horses dispersed. The herdsman tightened the saddle on the gelding and drove the herd to pasture.

VI

THE SECOND NIGHT

As soon as the horses were driven home in the evening they again gathered about the piebald gelding.

"In August I was taken away from my mother," he went on. "I suffered no particular grief. I saw that my mother was about to give birth to my younger brother (the famous Usan) and I no longer meant to her what I once had. I was not jealous. I felt my love for her cooling. Furthermore, I knew that on leaving my mother I would be put in the colt stables where we would live together in twos and threes, and every day we would all be taken out for an airing. I was put in a stall with Darling. Darling was a saddle-horse who later became the Emperor's mount and was painted by artists and modelled by sculptors. At that time he was an ordinary colt with a soft, glossy hide, a swanlike neck, and legs as thin and straight as harp strings. He was always jolly, good-natured, and gracious, and he loved to frisk, lick his comrades, and play tricks on horses and men. He and I became great friends, and our friendship lasted all through our youth. At that time he was gay and frivolous. He had already begun to fall in love and flirt with the fillies, and he laughed at my innocence. To my grief, my sense of self-respect led me to copy his ways. Very soon I was in love. This early infatuation was the cause of an enormous change in my life.

"Yes, I fell in love. Vyazopurikha was one year older than I was and she and I were fast friends. But towards the end of autumn I noticed that she began to be shy of me... I shall not attempt to tell the whole sad story of my first love; she herself remembers the mad passion I had for her which ended in the most important change in my life. The herdsmen drove her away from me and beat me mercilessly. One evening they took me into a special stall. I cried all night long, as if I foresaw what was to happen on the next day.

"In the morning the general, the stable keeper, the grooms, the herdsmen came down the corridor to my stall and a dreadful row began. The general shouted at the keeper, the keeper defended himself by saying he had given orders not to let me out but the grooms had disobeyed him. The general said he would give everyone a thrashing and the colt must be castrated. The keeper said all his orders would be carried out. Everything quieted down and they went away. I understood nothing but could see they intended doing something to me.

"On the next day I stopped whinnying for ever; I became what I am now. The whole world changed for me. I no longer took any joy in anything, I withdrew into myself and gave myself up to reflection. At first nothing could rouse me. I even refused to eat and drink and walk, let alone play with my comrades. Later on I sometimes felt an urge to leap up, to canter and whinny, but then I would ask myself the dreadful question: 'Why? What for?' and all the life would go out of me.

"One evening I was taken out for a walk as the herd was driven back from the fields. In the distance I saw a cloud of dust enveloping the vague forms of our mares. I heard their gay snorting and stamping. Despite the cutting of the rope into my neck as the groom pulled on it, I halted and gazed at the approaching herd as one gazes at a happiness that is irrevocably lost. As they drew near I recognized one after another—all my old friends, so handsome, majestic, sleek, and healthy. A few of them glanced in my direction. The groom kept jerking on the rope, but the pain was as nothing. Forgetting myself, I neighed in the old way and cantered towards them. But my neighing sounded sad, comical, incongruous. None of my old friends laughed, but I noticed that many of them turned their backs on me for the sake of propriety. Evidently they found the sight of me repulsive, pathetic, shameful, and above all—ridiculous. My thin, stringy neck must have looked comical, and my big head too (I had lost a lot of weight), and my long, awkward legs, and the silly trotting gait with which I circled round the groom as I had done in the old days. No one answered my neighing, everyone turned away from me. And suddenly I understood everything, I saw that I had become a stranger to them for ever. How I got back to the stable I don't know, so great was my grief.

"Even before this I had shown an inclination to be grave and reflective; now I became wholly so. My piebaldness, exciting in people such an incomprehensible contempt, my strange and unexpected misfortune, the peculiar position I found myself in on the stud-farm, a position I was aware of but could in no way account for forced me to withdraw into myself. I brooded over the injustice of human beings, who blamed me for being piebald; I brooded over the fickleness of maternal love, and the love of women in general, depending as it does on purely physical factors; most of all I brooded over the whims of that particular variety of animal called man, who plays such an important role in our lives—whims giving rise to that peculiar position of mine on the farm that I was aware of but could not explain. The following incident was a complete revelation to me of the human qualities from which it sprang.

"It happened during the winter holidays. I had been given no food or drink all day long. As I learned later, this was because the groom was drunk. On that day the keeper looked into my stall, and on seeing I had not been fed he addressed a string of abuse to the absent groom and went away. When the groom and his friend brought hay to our stall on the next day I noticed he was particularly pale and depressed, and there was something about his long back that attracted my attention and roused my sympathy. He tossed the hay through the grating angrily. I poked my head out and wanted to lay it on his shoulder, but he gave me a punch in the nose that sent me flying back. This was followed by a kick in the belly.

"'Nothing would have happened if it hadn't been for this mangy devil!' he said.

"'Why?' asked another groom.

"'He don't go round checking up on the count's colts, but he looks in on *his own* twice a day.'

"'Why, have they given piebald to him?' asked another.

" 'The devil knows whether they gave it to him or sold it to him. The count's colts can die of starvation for all he cares, but how did I dare starve his property! "Lie down!" says he, and he lays on the switch. A fine Christian, him! Thinks more of beasts than humans. Anyone can see he's a godless man. Counted the strikes himself, the brute. The general never gave a man such a flogging—ploughed up my whole back, he did. No soul on him.'

"I understood very well what he said about Christianity, and floggings, but at that time I had not the slightest conception of what the words *his own, his property* meant. I could see they implied some sort of connection between me and the keeper. At that time I had no idea what this connection was. It was not until some time later, when I had been separated from the other horses, that I understood. At that time I could not possibly understand how I could be called the property of a man. The words *my horse*, referring to me, a living horse, sounded as strange as if he had said *my earth, my air, my water*.

"And yet these words made an enormous impression on me. I pondered them all the time, and it was only after experiencing the most varied relations with human beings that I at last comprehended the meaning people attach to these odd words. The meaning is as follows: people are guided in life not by deeds, but by words. It is not the chance to do or not to do something that they enjoy, it is the chance to apply certain conventional words to objects. Among the words to which they attach most importance are my and mine, which they apply to all sorts of creatures and objects, even to land, people, and horses. They have agreed among themselves that only one person shall have the right to apply the word *my* to a given object. And the one who wins the right to apply this word to the largest number of objects in this game they play is considered the happiest of men. Why this should be I cannot imagine, but so it is. For a long time I tried to discover some direct advantage in it, but I could not.

"For instance, many of the people who called me their property did not ride me; I was ridden by quite different people. And it was not they who fed me, but quite different people. And it was not they who did me kind services, but quite different people— coachmen, grooms, and the like. And so, as a result of wide observation, I came to the conclusion that in respect to all things, not only to us horses, the conception of *my*, and *mine*, is founded on nothing but the low and bestial human instinct which they themselves call the instinct (or the right) of private property. A man says '*my* house', although he does not live in it, he only builds it and keeps it up. A tradesman says '*my* cloth shop', although he does not wear clothes of the finest cloth in his own shop. There are people who call a certain piece of land theirs, and yet they have never seen or put foot on that land. There are even people who call other people theirs, and yet they have never even seen those people, and the only connection they have with them is that they do them harm. There are men who call certain women *their* women, *their* wives, although these women live with other men. And people's aim in life is not to do as much good as they can, but to call as many things *theirs* as they can. Herein, I am convinced, lies the main difference between us and human beings. Human activities, at least the activities of all those humans with whom I have had any contact, are guided by words, while ours are guided by deeds, and this alone, to say nothing of all the other advantages we have over human beings, is sufficient to allow us to say that we stand one rung higher in the ladder of living creatures than human beings.

"Well, this right to call me *my* horse was given to the keeper of the stables, and for that reason he flogged the groom. I was overwhelmed by this discovery, as well as by the thoughts and attitudes my colouring evoked in people. All this, added to the melancholy resulting from my mother's unfaithfulness, made of me the grave and reflecting gelding I now am.

"I was thrice unfortunate: I was piebald, I was a gelding, and instead of belonging only to God and myself, as is natural for every living creature, people imagined that I belonged to the stable keeper.

"There were many consequences of their imagining such a thing about me. The first of them was that I was kept apart from the other horses, was fed better, was exercised more often, and was broken in earlier. It was in my third year that a bridle was put on me for the first time. Well do I remember the day when that very keeper who imagined I was his property came with a crowd of grooms to hitch me up, supposing that I would resist and become unmanageable. They cut my lip; they tied me with ropes as they forced me between the shafts; they put a wide cross of leather straps on my back and fastened it to the shafts to keep me from kicking; and all the while I was filled with the single desire to show my love for and longing to work.

"They were amazed on seeing me step out like an old horse. They began to drive me and I began practising trotting. I made such excellent progress that at the end of three months the general and many others praised my gait. But strange as it may seem, precisely because they imagined I belonged to the keeper rather than to myself, my gait had an entirely different meaning for them.

"My brother colts were taken to races, had their records kept, people came to see them, they were hitched to gilded sulkies and had expensive horse-cloths thrown over their backs. I was hitched to the keeper's common cart and driven on his business to Chesmenka and other villages. And this was all because I was piebald, and because in their opinion I belonged to the keeper rather than to the count.

"Tomorrow, if we are still alive, I shall tell you what grave consequences the keeper's assumption that I was his property held for me."

All the next day the horses treated Yardstick with the greatest deference. But Nester was as rough with him as ever. The peasant's grey plough horse made its way to the herd and whinnied, and again the bay mare flirted with him.

VII

THE THIRD NIGHT

A new moon was born and the light of its slender crescent fell on Yardstick standing in the middle of the enclosure with the other horses crowding round him.

"The most surprising result of my belonging not to the count or to God, but to the keeper," went on the piebald gelding, "was that my fast gait, a horse's greatest virtue, became the cause of my banishment.

"One day as Swan was being exercised, the keeper, who was returning from Chesmenka, drove me up to the track. Swan passed us by.

He was going well, but showing off, and lacked the technique I had developed of lifting one hoof the instant the other touched the ground, so that not a single movement should be wasted and every effort should serve to impel the body forward. Swan, as I have said, passed us by. I made for the track and the keeper did not stop me. 'Why not let the piebald have a try?' he cried, and when Swan came up to us the next time he let me go. Swan had already got up speed and so I was left behind on the first round, but on the second I began to gain ground, I caught the sulky up, came abreast, held my own, outstripped him. I was given a second try. The same thing happened. I was faster. And that terrified everybody. It was decided I must be sold in some distant place where no one would get wind of me. 'There will be a fine row if the count hears of it!' was what they said.

"And so I was sold to a horse-dealer as a wheel horse. The dealer did not keep me long. I was bought by a hussar who had been sent for remounts. All this was so cruel and unjust that I was glad when I was taken away from Khrenovo, taken away for ever from all that had been so near and dear to me. Too painful was it for me to remain among my former comrades. For them—love, honour, freedom; for me—work and humiliation, humiliation and work to the end of my days. Why, oh why? Simply because I was piebald,

and for that reason had been made somebody else's property."

Yardstick had no chance to go on with
his story that night. Something happened
that caused great excitement among the
horses. Kupchikha, the mare who had not
yet foaled, had been listening attentively to
the story, but all of a sudden she turned and
went slowly off to the shed, where she began
to groan so loudly that all the horses turned
their heads. They saw her lie down, scramble
to her feet, lie down again. The old mares
understood what was the matter with her, but
the young colts were so alarmed that they
abandoned the gelding and gathered round
her.

By morning there was another colt standing
shakily on its legs. Nester called to the groom,
who led the mare and her colt into the stable,
and he drove the herd away without her.

VIII

THE FOURTH NIGHT

That evening, when the gates were closed
and everything was still, the piebald gelding
resumed his story.

"I saw a great deal of men and horses as
I passed from hand to hand. I was held
longest by two masters: one was a prince, an
officer in the hussars; the other was an old

woman who lived near the church of St. Nicholas the Miracle-Worker.

"The best days of my life were spent with the hussar. Even though he was the cause of my ruin, even though he never in his life loved anybody or anything, I loved him, and loved him just because of this. I loved him because he was handsome, rich, and happy, and therefore loved nobody. You can understand this; it is the most exalted feeling we horses have. His coldness, his cruelty, my utter dependence upon him, lent particular strength to my love for him. 'Beat me, drive me to death,' I used to think in those good old days, 'I will only be the happier for it.'

"He bought me for eight hundred rubles from the horse-dealer to whom the keeper had sold me. He bought me because nobody had any piebald horses. Those were the best days of my life. He had a mistress. I knew this because I took him to her every day and sometimes took them riding together. His mistress was handsome, and so was he, and so was his coachman, and I loved them for it. I was supremely happy.

"This is how my days passed: in the morning the groom came to tend to me—not the coachman, but the groom. The groom was a lively young lad of peasant stock. He would open the door to let out the steam from our bodies and throw out the dung, then he would take off our horse-cloths and begin to scrape me with a curry-comb, letting the

scrapings fall in whitish rows on the floor-
boards, all scratched and indented by my
hoofs. I would bite at his arm playfully and
stamp my feet. When my turn came he would
lead me to a tub of cold water and gaze
admiringly at his work, at my legs, straight
as arrows and ending in broad hoofs, and at
my glossy back and crupper, smooth enough
to slide on. Then some hay would be thrown
over the high grating and oats poured into
the oaken manger. At last Feofan, the head
coachman, would come in.

"The coachman resembled his master.
Neither one feared or loved anyone but himself, and for that reason both were loved by
all. Feofan wore a red blouse, plush trousers,
and a sleeveless coat. I used to enjoy having
him come into the stable on holidays in his
sleeveless coat, his hair and whiskers shining
with oil, and cry out, 'Forgotten me, you
beast?' and give me a poke in the flank with
the handle of a pitchfork, not painfully, just
in fun. I knew it was just in fun and would
flatten my ears and gnash my teeth.

"We had a black colt who worked in a pair.
At night I was hitched up with him. This
Polkan had no sense of humour and was a
spiteful devil. His stall was next to mine, and
sometimes we would bite each other through
the bars, not the least in fun. Feofan was not
afraid of him. He would walk straight up to
him and roar as if he meant to kill him, but
no—he would just walk past and come back

with the halter. Once Polkan and I broke into
a gallop along Kuznestky Street. Neither the
master nor the coachman were frightened,
they just laughed and shouted at the people
and held us in and guided us so skilfully that
not a soul was hurt.

"I gave half my life and all my best
qualities to them. They allowed me to drink
too much and ruin my legs, but even so, those
were the best days of my life.

"At twelve o'clock they came to harness
me, grease my hoofs, wet my mane and forelock, and put me between the shafts.

"Ours was a wicker sleigh lined with velvet,
the harness had little silver buckles on it, and
the reins were of silk, as was the netting.
The harness was such that when all the belts
and straps were in place and fastened you
could not tell where the harness stopped and
the horse began. I was usually hitched up in
the shed. Feofan would come in such thick
coat that his backside was broader than his
shoulders, and his red girdle was up under
his armpits, he would put his foot in the
stirrup, make some jest, hang up the whip
just for the looks of it, for he never used it
on me, and say, 'Off we go!' And I would go
prancing out of the gates, and the cook who
had come out with a bucket of slops would
stop in the doorway, and the peasants bringing firewood into the yard would stand
agape.

"Outside the gates we would drive on

a little way before we came to a halt. Then the lackeys and the other coachmen would gather about us and fall to gossiping. There at the entrance we would wait, all of us, sometimes for as long as three hours, occasionally taking a little run, only to come back and go on waiting.

"At last there would be a noise in the entranceway and grey-haired pot-bellied Tikhon would run out in a frock-coat crying, 'Drive up!' In those days they did not have the foolish habit of crying, 'Forward!' as if I didn't know whether to go forward or backward. Feofan would click his tongue. We would drive up, and the prince, in cap and greatcoat, with a grey beaver collar hiding his handsome, ruddy, black-browed face that never should have been hidden, would hurry out with a casual air, as if there were nothing extraordinary about the sleigh, the horse, and Feofan, who arched his back and held his arms outstretched in an attitude one would think he could not possibly hold for long— the prince, I say, would come out with a clatter of spurs and sabre and brass heels, stepping over the carpet as if he were in too great a hurry to notice me and Feofan and all the things that everyone but he were staring at in awe and admiration. Feofan clicked his tongue, I pulled at the traces and moved forward at a decent pace, and stopped. I cast a sidelong glance at the prince and tossed my thoroughbred head with its silky forelock.

If the prince was in a good humour he would
make some witty remark to Feofan, Feofan
would turn his handsome head ever so slightly
as he answered him, and, without lowering his
arms, would make a scarcely perceptible
movement of the reins that I alone understood,
and off I would go, clop, clop, clop widening
my pace with every step, trembling in every
muscle of my body, kicking the snow and
mud back onto the dashboard. In those days
there was not that other foolish habit of
calling out, 'Ekh!' as if the coachman had
a pain in his belly; in those days they called
out, 'Watch out!' and Feofan called out,
'Watch out' and the people scattered, cleared
the way and stood craning their necks to see
the handsome gelding and the handsome
coachman and the handsome prince go by.

"I loved to outstrip a trotter. If Feofan
and I caught sight of a harness worthy our
effort we would fly after it swift as the wind,
gradually coming closer and closer until I was
splashing mud on the back of the other sleigh,
then running abreast of the passenger and
snorting over his head, then running abreast
of the horse's yoke, then running so far ahead
that I could not see my rival and could only
hear the sound of him growing fainter and
fainter behind me. The prince and Feofan and
I did not utter a sound, pretending to be so
intent on our own business that we took no
notice of the second-rate horses drawing those
we passed on the way. I loved to outstrip

other horses, but I also loved to catch sight of a good trotter coming towards me: a single instant, a swish, a glance, and it was past, and again we were flying on alone, each in its own direction."

The gates creaked and the voices of Nester and Vaska were heard.

THE FIFTH NIGHT

The weather was changing. The sky had been sullen since morning and there had been no dew, but the air was warm and the mosquitoes were pestering. As soon as the herd was back in the enclosure the horses gathered round the piebald gelding and he concluded his story.

"Soon my happy life came to an end. It had lasted only two years. At the end of the second winter I experienced the greatest joy I had ever known, and soon after that, the greatest sorrow.

"During Shrovetide I took the prince to the races. Atlasny and Bychok were racing. I do not know what my master talked about in the betting-booth, but when he came out he ordered Feofan to drive me on to the track. I remember being driven on and made to race with Atlasny. Atlasny was drawing a sulky, I, a town sleigh. At the turn I passed him and was met by a roar of laughter and cheers.

"A whole crowd surged after me when I was walked around the paddock. Some five horse-lovers offered the prince thousands for me. He only laughed, displaying his fine white teeth.

"'Oh, no,' he said, 'he is not a horse but a friend; I wouldn't sell him for a mountain of gold. Good-day, gentlemen,' and he pulled aside the fur cover and got into the sleigh.

"'To Ostozhenka Street!' That was the address of his mistress. Off we went.

"And that was the last happy day I knew. "We reached her house. He called her 'his', but she loved another and had gone off with him. This he was told on reaching her flat. It was five o'clock, and without taking me out of the harness he set off after her. And a thing was done to me that had never been done before: I was lashed with the whip and made to gallop. For the first time I made a misstep; I was ashamed and wished to redeem myself, but suddenly I heard the prince shout at the top of his lungs, 'Run, damn you!' and the whip whistled through the air and struck me and I galloped ahead, striking my legs against the metal dashboard. When we had gone twenty-five versts we caught her up.

"I brought him home, but I could not stop trembling all night long and could eat nothing. In the morning they gave me some water. I drank it, but from then on I was a different horse. I fell ill, they tortured and mutilated me—'gave me treatments', as people call it. My hoofs came off, I broke out in sores, my legs went crooked, my chest caved in, I became languid in spirit and weak in body.

"They sold me to a horse-dealer. He fed me carrots and something else and made me out to be something I no longer was, so as to fool the ignorant. I no longer had strength or a fast gait. The horse-dealer further tortured me by coming into my stall whenever a customer appeared and thrashing me with the whip and frightening me out of my wits. Then he would wipe off the marks of the whip and lead me out.

"An old woman bought me. She was always driving me to the church of St. Nicholas the Miracle-Worker, and she flogged her coachman. The coachman used to come to my stall and cry. That is how I discovered that tears have a pleasant salty taste. Then the old woman died. Her steward sold me to a village shopkeeper, and while with him I ate too much wheat and my ailments increased. He sold me to a peasant. I pulled his plough and ate almost nothing at all. One day my leg was cut with a ploughshare and again I fell ill.

"I was bartered to a Gypsy. He treated me abominably and at last sold me to the bailiff here. And here I am."

No one made a sound. It began to rain.

IX

As the herd was being driven home the following evening, they came upon the master, who had a visitor with him. Zhuldyba had seen them first as she approached the house—two male figures: one of them was the young master in a straw hat, the other was a tall, fat man in military uniform. The old mare looked askance at them and sidled past. The others, being young, felt shy and uneasy, especially when the master and his guest walked straight into the midst of them and began pointing out things to each other and talking.

"I bought that one, the dappled gray, from Voyeikov," said the master.

"Whose is that young black with the white socks? She's a beauty," said the guest.

They looked over a number of the horses, running after them and making them stand still. They noticed the bay mare.

"She's of the Khrenovo saddle-horse stock," said the master.

They could not examine all the horses on the go. The master called Nester and the old man drove his spurs into the sides of the piebald gelding and came trotting up. The gelding put forth an effort, though he limped on one leg, and it was clear he would not have murmured had he been ordered to run at top speed to the end of the earth. He would have liked to have galloped, and made an attempt to with his good leg.

"You'll not find a better mare than her in the whole of Russia, take my word for it," said the master, pointing to one of the horses. The guest said something complimentary. The master ran here and there excitedly, showing off the animals and giving the history and pedigree of each of them. The guest seemed to be bored, but he invented questions to give the appearance of being interested.

"Yes? Ah," he said absent-mindedly.

"Just look at this," said the master, unconscious of his guest's boredom. "Look at these legs. She cost me a pretty sum, but her three-year-old son is trotting already."

"A good trotter?" asked the guest.

They talked about one horse after another until they had discussed them all and there was nothing else to say. There was a pause.

"Well, shall we go?"

"Let's."

They went through the gate. The guest was glad the demonstration was over and they could go home, where they could eat and drink and smoke. He seemed to be in better spirits. As they passed Nester on his piebald mount waiting for further orders, the guest struck the gelding on the crupper with his big fleshy hand.

"Here's a beauty for you!" he said, "I had a piebald horse once myself, remember my telling you?"

Since the remark did not concern his own

horses, the master did not listen, he just went on gazing at his herd.

Suddenly he was startled by a weak, senile, absurd attempt at a neigh in his very ear. It was the gelding neighing, but he broke off in confusion without finishing. Neither the guest nor the master paid any attention to him and went on home.

Yardstick had recognized the fat man as his beloved master, the once rich and handsome Prince Serpukhovskoi.

X

The rain kept on coming in a drizzle. It was dismal in the enclosure, but not in the big house. A luxurious tea was being served in a luxurious drawing-room. At the table sat the host, the hostess, and their guest.

The hostess was pregnant, as could be seen from her swollen belly, the erectness with which she sat behind the samovar, her plumpness, and especially from her large eyes, which had a meek and solemn expression and seemed to be turned inward upon herself.

The host was holding a box of extra-quality ten-year-old cigars that nobody but he owned, or so he boasted to his guest. The host was a handsome man of about five-and-twenty—fresh-looking, well-brushed, well-groomed. At home he wore a loose woollen suit tailored in London. Massive gold trinkets hung from his watch-chain. His cuff-links, too, were of massive gold set with turquoise. His beard was clipped à la Napoleon III, with little mouse tails sticking out on either side of his upper lip, waxed and twisted as neatly as if done in Paris. The hostess was wearing a gauzy silk gown patterned with bunches of flowers, and there were big twisted gold pins in her thick brown hair—very beautiful hair, even if it was not all her own. She had many expensive rings and bracelets on her arms and hands. The samovar was of silver, the tea service of the finest china. A footman, magnificent in tails, white waistcoat, and neckerchief, was standing at the door like a statue, waiting for orders. The furniture was ornate, full of twists and carvings, the wallpaper dark and floral. Near the table lay the most purebred of greyhounds with a silver chain round its neck that clinked from time to time. The dog had been given an extraordinary English name which neither its master nor mistress could pronounce since neither of them knew English. An inlaid grand piano stood among plants in one corner. All the furnishings had the air of being new, rare, and expensive. That would have been all very well if they had not also borne the stamp of luxury, ostentation, and the absence of intellectual interests.

The host was mad on race-horses. He was a strong and healthy man of sanguine disposition, a type of person that never dies out, one who rides about in sable coats, tosses expensive bouquets to actresses, drinks the most expensive wines of the newest brands in the most expensive hotels, offers prizes in his own name, and keeps the most expensive mistresses.

His guest, Nikita Serpukhovskoi, was a man over forty—tall, fat, and bald, with a large moustache and side whiskers. He must have been very handsome in his youth; now he had the appearance of one who has gone to pieces physically, morally, and financially.

He was so deeply in debt that he had had to go into the government service to keep out of jail. At present he was on his way to a provincial town where he had been put in charge of horse-breeding. It was only through the efforts of influential relatives that he had got even this post. He was wearing a military tunic and blue trousers. The tunic and trousers were such as only the rich wear, so was his linen, and his watch had been made in England. His boots had extraordinary soles almost an inch thick.

Nikita Serpukhovskoi had gone through a fortune of two million rubles, and was now a hundred and twenty thousand rubles in debt. A fortune of such a size gives a man a reputation that enables him to get money on credit and go on living almost in luxury for another ten years. These ten years had expired and the reputation had evaporated, and now Nikita's life had become a burden. He began to drink—that is, wine had begun to make him drunk, a thing that had never happened to him before. As for drinking, he had never really begun or ended. His fallen state was evident most of all from the uneasiness of his glance (his eyes had begun to wander) and the hesitancy in his voice and movements. This uneasiness was the more striking in that one could easily see it was new to him, that never before had he feared anyone or anything, and that it was only his recent vicissitudes that had thrown him into a state of apprehension quite incompatible with his nature. The host and hostess both noticed this and exchanged glances indicating that they understood each other's thoughts and would put off a discussion of the man until they were in bed; for the present they would put up with poor Nikita and even be nice to him. Nikita felt humiliated by the happiness of his host; it forced upon him recollections of his irretrievable past and made him envious.

"Do you mind our smoking, Mary?" he asked, addressing the lady in that peculiar, that elusive tone that comes of great experience—a polite and friendly tone, but not entirely respectful—the tone in which the sophisticated address their friends' mistresses in distinction to their wives. Not that he wished to offend her—on the contrary, he wished to enter into the good graces of her and the host, even though he himself would hardly have admitted it. It was just that he was used to adopting this tone with such women. He knew that she herself would have been surprised, even offended, if he had treated her as a lady. And besides, he had to keep in reserve the accepted tone of esteem for use when speaking to the real wife of his equal. He always addressed kept women with respect, not because he shared the so-called convictions expressed in the magazines (he never read such trash) as to the worth of every human being regardless of his station, the falseness of marriage, and all the rest, but because all decent people treated them in that way and he was eminently decent, even if fallen.

He took a cigar. The host tactlessly picked up a handful of cigars and offered them to him.

"Here, take these, you'll see how good they are."

Nikita pushed away the cigars and an expression of insult and injury flashed into his eyes.

"Thank you," he took out his cigar-case. "Try mine."

The hostess was more sensitive. Noticing what had happened, she hastened to say, "I'm terribly fond of cigars. I think I would be tempted to smoke myself if everybody about me were not always smoking." And she gave one of her pretty, kindly smiles. He half smiled in response; two of his teeth were missing.

"No, take this," insisted the unfeeling

host. "Those others are weaker. Fritz, *bringen Sie noch eine Kasten*," he said, *"dort zwei."*

The German footman brought in a fresh box.

"Which do you like better? Strong ones? These are capital. Take them all," he went on insisting. His delight at being able to show off his rare possessions made him oblivious of everything else. Serpukhovskoi lighted up and hastened to resume the conversation they had begun.

"What were you saying you paid for Atlasny?" he asked.

"A lot. At least five thousand, but the horse was worth it. You ought to see his offspring!"

"Racers?"

"Every one. This year his son took three prizes: in Tula, Moscow, and St. Petersburg, running against Voyeikov's Voronoi. If that rascal of a jockey had not made four blunders he would have left him behind the flag."

"He's a little raw yet. Too much Dutch blood in him if you want my opinion," said Serpukhovskoi.

"And what about the mares? I'll show them to you tomorrow. I paid three thousand for Dobrinya and two for Laskovaya."

And again the host began boasting of his riches. The hostess could see that this was painful for Serpukhovskoi and that he was only pretending to listen.

"Will you have some more tea?" she asked.

"No," said the host, and went on talking. She got up, but the host stopped her, put his arms round her and kissed her.

Serpukhovskoi was about to smile as he watched them—smile in an unnatural way for their benefit, but when the host got up, put his arm about her waist and saw her to the door, his expression suddenly changed. He gave a deep sigh and a look of despair came over his puffy face. There was even a shade of angry resentment in it.

XI

The host came back smiling and sat down opposite Nikita. They did not speak for a while.

"You were saying you bought him from Voyeikov?" Serpukhovskoi remarked in an offhand way.

"Yes, Atlasny. I wanted to buy some mares from Dubovitsky but there was nothing worth having."

"He's ruined," said Serpukhovskoi, then suddenly stopped and glanced about him. He remembered that he owed this "ruined" gentleman twenty thousand rubles. If people spoke of Dubovitsky as ruined, what must they say about him? He was silent.

Again there was a long pause. The host went over in his mind all the things he might boast about to his guest. Serpukhovskoi wondered what he could say to show he did not consider himself ruined. But the minds of them worked sluggishly, in spite of the bracing cigars.

"When is he going to offer me a drink?" thought Serpukhovskoi.

"We'd better be having a drink, otherwise I'll die of boredom," thought the host.

"Do you intend staying here long?" asked Serpukhovskoi.

"Another month. What about a little supper, eh? Is it ready, Fritz?"

They went into the dining-room. Under a chandelier stood a table with candelabra on it and laid with all sorts of fine things: siphons, bottles with dolls stuck into the corks, vodka, decanters filled with remarkable wines, plates filled with remarkable food. They drank, ate, drank again, ate again, and at last began to talk. Serpukhovskoi grew red in the face and spoke without reserve.

They talked about women. They talked about the women they had lived with—Gypsy women, French women, dancers.

"And so you left Matier?" asked the host. Matier was the woman who had brought about Serpukhovskoi's ruin.

"Not I; she left me. Ah, when I think of the wealth I've squandered! Nowadays I'm happy to get my hands on a thousand rubles and I count it a pleasure to be going away from everybody. I can't bear living in Moscow any more. Oh, when I think of it!"

The host was bored with Serpukhovskoi's
talk. He wanted to talk about himself, he
wanted to boast. And Serpukhovskoi wanted
to talk about himself, about his brilliant past.
The host poured him out a glass of wine and
waited for him to finish so that he could tell
him how he had arranged his stud-farm in
a way nobody had ever thought of before,
and that Mary loved him not just for his
money, but with her whole heart.

"I was just going to tell you that on my
farm—" he began, but Serpukhovskoi interrupted.

"I can truly say that there was a time when
I loved life and really knew how to live," he
said. "You were just talking about riding; tell
me this, what was the fastest horse you ever
drove?"

The host jumped at the chance to talk
about his stud-farm, but before he had scarcely
begun Serpukhovskoi interrupted him again.

"Oh, yes," he said, "you owners of farms
are interested only in becoming famous, not
in enjoying yourselves, not in having a good
time. I was never like that. Remember my
telling you today that I once had a piebald
trotter, spotted just like that horse your
herdsman was riding? There was a horse for
you! You wouldn't believe it. That was way
back in '42, I had just come to Moscow. I go
to the horse-dealer and see a piebald gelding.
Good points. Price? One thousand. I liked
him, bought him, began driving him. Neither

you nor I, nor anybody else has ever had or
ever will have a horse his equal! Couldn't be
matched for speed or strength or beauty!
You were just a boy then, you wouldn't
have known him, but you must have heard
of him. All Moscow had."

"Yes, I seem to have heard of him," said
the host reluctantly. "But I wanted to tell
you about my—"

"Of course you did. I bought him just
like that, without any papers or pedigree or
recommendation. Voyeikov and I traced his
line. He was Yardstick, son of Gracious-the-
First. A stride this long. The Khrenovo stud-
farm sold him to the stable keeper because he
was piebald, and the keeper castrated him and
sold him to a horse-dealer. There never was
a horse his like! Ah, those were the days!
Youth, my lost youth!" he sighed, quoting
a Gypsy song. He was getting drunk. "Yes,
those were the days. I was five-and-twenty,
I had eighty thousand a year, not a single grey
hair, all my teeth, and each like a pearl. I was
successful in everything I turned my hand to,
and now—everything is over."

"In those days horses didn't have the speed
they have now," said the host, taking
advantage of the pause. "If you'd like to
know, my first horses began to run without—"

"Your horses! Why, they were a lot faster
in those days."

"What do you mean, faster?"

"Just that—faster. I remember once driving

Yardstick out to the races in Moscow. I didn't enter any horses of my own. I never liked race-horses, only kept thoroughbreds: General, Cholet, Mohammed. I drove the piebald out. I had a capital coachman, too. Loved the fellow. Drank himself to death. Well, I got to the racing grounds. 'When are you going to go in for race-horses, Serpukhovskoi?' they asked me. 'What do I want with race-horses? This piebald nag of mine will outrun your blessed race-horses,' I said. 'Not on your life, he won't,' they said. 'A thousand rubles on it,' I said. We shook hands on it. Raced them. Mine came in first by five seconds and I won the thousand rubles. But that was nothing. Once I did a hundred versts in three hours with a troika of thoroughbreds. It was the talk of Moscow."

Serpukhovskoi lied so steadily and skilfully that the host could not get a word in edgewise and sat opposite him with a crestfallen expression on his face, finding his only diversion in pouring out wine for himself and his guest.

It began to get light. Still they sat on. The host was unspeakably bored. He got up.

"Well, time to turn in," said Serpukhovskoi and, struggling to his feet and puffing out his cheeks, he staggered off to his room.

The host was lying beside his mistress. "He's simply impossible. He got drunk and told nothing but lies."

"And he tried to flirt with me."

"I'm afraid he'll ask me for a loan."

Serpukhovskoi lay puffing away, fully dressed, on top of the bed.

"I seem to have been telling lies," he thought. "What of it? Good wine, but he's a pig. Like a merchant. And I'm a pig," he said to himself and burst out laughing. "First I kept them, now they are keeping me. The Winkler woman's keeping me—I take money from her. Serves him right, he deserves it. But I'd better get undressed. Can't get these boots off."

"Hey!" he shouted, but the man who served him had gone to bed long before.

He sat up, took off his tunic and waistcoat and managed to kick off his trousers, but he could not take off his boots—his soft paunch was in the way. One of the boots was off at last, but no puffing and pulling could get the other off. And so he flopped down with this boot still on and began to snore, filling the room with the smell of tobacco, wine, and nasty old age.

XII

There were many things Yardstick could have recalled that night, but he was distracted by Vaska, who threw a horse-cloth over him and galloped away and kept him tied all night outside of a public-house next to a horse belonging to a peasant. The two horses licked each other. In the morning they rode back to the herd and Yardstick began scratching himself.

"Why should I itch so?" he thought to himself.

Five days passed. They called the veterinary surgeon.

"He's got scab," said the surgeon gleefully. "Sell him to the Gypsies."

"What for? Cut his throat or anything you like so long as he's out of the way this very day."

The morning was clear and quiet. The herd had gone to pasture. Yardstick had been left behind. A strange-looking man came up to him—thin, dark, dirty, with stains all over his coat. He was the flayer. He took hold of the halter without glancing at Yardstick and led him away. Yardstick went quietly, without glancing back, dragging his legs as usual, stumbling in the straw with his hind ones. When they were out the gate he turned in the direction of the well, but the flayer pulled him back, saying,

"What's the use?"

The flayer and Vaska, who was walking behind, took him to a ravine behind the brick shed and stopped as if there were something extraordinary about this most ordinary of spots, and there the flayer, after handing the halter to Vaska, took off his coat, rolled up his sleeves, took a knife and

whetstone out of his boot top, and began
sharpening the blade. The gelding reached for
the halter rope so that he could while the
time away by chewing on it, but it was too
far away, and so he just heaved a sigh and
closed his eyes. His lip hung down, revealing
his stumps of yellow teeth, and he began to
drowse to the sound of the whetting of the
knife. The only thing that annoyed him was
the twitching of his relaxed sore leg with
the swelling on it. Suddenly he felt someone
take him by the jaw and jerk his head up.
He opened his eyes. He saw two dogs standing
in front of him. One was sniffing the air in
the direction of the flayer, the other was
sitting and staring at the gelding as if expecting
something of him. The gelding looked at them
and began to rub his cheek against the arm
that was holding him.

"They are going to give me a cure," he
thought. "Well, let them."

And sure enough, he felt them doing
something to his throat. There was a stab of
pain; he started, kicked out with his legs, then
checked himself and waited to see what
would happen next. A warm liquid began to
stream down over his neck and breast. He
drew in so deep a breath that his sides swelled
out, and instantly he felt much better. The
whole burden of his life fell away from him.
He closed his eyes and let his head drop.
Nobody held it up. He dropped his neck, his
legs began to tremble, and his body tottered.

He was less frightened than surprised. Everything was so different. In his surprise he tried to dart forward, to leap upward, but his legs got twisted and he began to fall over on his side. In trying to catch himself he plunged forward on his left side. The flayer waited and held off the dogs until the convulsions were over, and then, coming closer, he took hold of one leg and turned the horse over on his back, asking Vaska to hold him while he flayed him.

"A good horse in its day," said Vaska.

"And a fine hide if it had a little more flesh on it," said the flayer.

The herd came back up the hill in the evening, and those on the left side could see some dogs busy at a red object lying on the ground, and some crows and kites flying above it. One dog dug its two paws into the object and tore at it with its teeth, shaking its head until a piece came off with a crunching sound.

The bay mare stood still, stretched out her neck, and sniffed the air for a long time. The others could hardly make her come away.

At dawn some wolf cubs whimpered playfully in the thick underbrush of the ravine cutting through the old forest. There were five of them, four almost of a size, and a

smaller one with a head bigger than its body.
A thin and scrawny mother wolf came out of
the bushes, dragging her bursting belly with
the teats hanging down to the ground, and sat
down opposite the cubs, who formed into
a semicircle. She went up to the smallest one,
bent her forelegs, lowered her head, opened
her jaws, made a few convulsive movements
of her belly, and threw up a big piece of horse
flesh. The bigger cubs rushed at it, but the
mother chased them back and gave the whole
piece to the little one. The little one growled
as if in rage, seized on the piece, held it
between its paws, and began to tear it apart.
In the same way the mother threw up a second
piece, a third piece, and so on until all five
had food; only then did she lie down near
them and rest.

Within a week's time nothing remained
near the brick shed but a big skull and two
femurs; everything else had disappeared. In
summer a peasant collecting bones took away
even the skull and femurs and ground them
up for his needs.

The dead body of Serpukhovskoi that went
about eating and drinking was committed to
earth much later. Of no use to anyone was his
skin, flesh, and bones. And just as his dead
body walking about on the earth had been
a burden for twenty years, so the committing
of this body to earth was nothing but a

bother to those to whom the task fell.

For a long time nobody had any need of him, had found him only a nuisance, and yet the dead who bury the dead considered it necessary to clothe his bloated, decaying body in a fine uniform and good boots and lay it in a fine new coffin with new tassels at all four corners and put this new coffin in another lead coffin and take it to Moscow, where other older human bones were dug up so that in precisely that spot his decaying, worm-ridden body in its new uniform and polished boots could be buried in earth.

1885

THE DEATH OF IVAN ILYICH

I

In the large building of the Law Courts, during an intermission in the hearing of the Melvinsky case, members of the court gathered with the public prosecutor in the office of Ivan Yegorovich Shebek, and the talk centred on the Krasovsky case. Fyodor Vasilyevich hotly denied that it was within the jurisdiction of the courts, but Ivan Yegorovich was not to be moved. Pyotr Ivanovich, who had taken no part in the argument from the very beginning, was reading the newspaper that had just been delivered.

"Gentlemen!" he said. "Ivan Ilyich is dead."

"Not really!"

"Here, read this," he said to Fyodor Vasilyevich, handing him the fresh issue, still smelling of printer's ink.

Inside a black border was written: "Prasko-vya Fyodorovna Golovina is grieved to inform relatives and friends that her beloved husband,

Ivan Ilyich Golovin, Member of the Judicial Council, passed away on the 4th of February, 1882. The funeral will be held on Friday at one o'clock."

Ivan Ilyich had been a colleague of the gentlemen gathered there, and all of them had liked him. He had been ill for many weeks and it was said that his disease was incurable. His post had been reserved for him, but it was rumoured that in the event of his death Alexeyev might be appointed in his place, and either Vinnikov or Shtabel would succeed to Alexeyev. And so on learning of the death of Ivan Ilyich the first thought that entered the mind of each of the gentlemen in the office was the changes and promotions affecting their own positions or those of their friends that would result.

"I am sure to be appointed in place of Shtabel or Vinnikov," thought Fyodor Vasilyevich. "The post was promised to me long ago, and the promotion will mean a salary increase of 800 rubles in addition to grants for office expenses."

"I must put in an application to have my brother-in-law transferred from Kaluga," thought Pyotr Ivanovich. "My wife will be happy. Now she won't be able to accuse me of never doing anything for her family."

"I was sure he would never get over it," said Pyotr Ivanovich out loud. "What a pity."

"Just what was the matter with him?"

"The doctors could not decide. That is,

they did decide, but each for himself. The last time I saw him I thought he looked better."

"I haven't been there since the holidays. I kept meaning to go."

"Do you think he was a man of means?"

"His wife had a little something, but nothing to speak of, it seems."

"Well, now we can't get out of calling. They live so deucedly far away."

"From you. Everything's far away from you."

"He just can't forgive me for living over the river," said Pyotr Ivanovich, smiling at Shebek. This led to a discussion of relative distances in the town, and then they went back into the court-room.

In addition to speculations as to possible changes and promotions which the news of this death gave rise to, the very fact of the death of one they had known so well made each of them rejoice that it was his friend rather than himself who had died.

"Fancy that: he is dead, but I am not," was the thought or the feeling of each one of them. The more intimate acquaintances, the so-called friends of Ivan Ilyich, involuntarily added to themselves that now they had to carry out the wearisome duty imposed by decorum of attending the funeral and then paying the widow a call of condolence.

None had been such close friends as Fyodor Vasilyevich and Pyotr Ivanovich. Pyotr Ivanovich had been a fellow-student of Ivan

Ilyich's, and besides this he considered himself to be under certain obligations to him. At dinner that evening he told his wife the news of the death of Ivan Ilyich and informed her of the chances of having her brother transferred to their circuit now, and then, without lying down for his usual rest, he put on his frock-coat and set out for the house of Ivan Ilyich.

A carriage and two cabs were standing at the entrance when he got there. Downstairs in the entry, next to the hat-stand, a coffin lid decorated with tassels and highly polished gilt braid stood propped against the wall. Two women dressed in black were taking off their coats. He knew one of them, the sister of Ivan Ilyich; the other was a stranger. Schwartz, a friend of Pyotr Ivanovich's, had just started down the stairs, but on catching sight of him he stopped and gave him a wink, as if to say, "Ivan Ilyich has certainly bungled things; it's quite different with you and me."

As always, there was a certain elegant solemnity about Schwartz, with his English side whiskers and his lean figure in a frock-coat; and this solemnity, always in such striking contrast with the playfulness of his character, had on the present occasion a peculiar piquancy. That, at least, is what Pyotr Ivanovich thought.

Pyotr Ivanovich stepped aside to let the ladies go first, and then slowly followed them up the stairs. Schwartz checked his steps and waited for him at the top. Pyotr Ivanovich guessed why: he no doubt wanted to settle where they should meet to play cards that evening. The ladies went in to see the widow, and Schwartz, his lips set in a serious line and his eyes glinting playfully, made a movement of his brows to point out to Pyotr Ivanovich the room in which the deceased lay.

Pyotr Ivanovich went in wondering, as one always does wonder, what he was expected to do. He knew it never did any harm to cross oneself on such occasions. He was not quite sure whether he ought to bow or not, and so he did something halfway in between: on entering the room he crossed himself and made a little movement that might be taken for a bow. To whatever extent this was possible, he simultaneously glanced about the room. Two young men, probably nephews, one of them a schoolboy, were crossing themselves as they went out. An old woman was standing motionless. A woman with her eyebrows raised in an odd way was whispering something to her. A deacon in a frock-coat—a spirited, resolute man—was reading something in a loud voice and in a tone that brooked no contradiction; Gerasim, the pantry-boy, passed in front of Pyotr Ivanovich with a light step as he sprinkled something on the floor. On seeing this, Pyotr Ivanovich instantly became conscious of a faint odour of decay. The last time he had called on Ivan Ilyich he had seen this man in his room; he had been

watching at the sick man's bedside, and Ivan
Ilyich had been particularly attached to him.
Pyotr Ivanovich kept crossing himself and
bowing slightly in a direction between the
coffin and the deacon, facing the icons on
the table in the corner. When he felt he was
in danger of overdoing the crossing, he
stopped and gazed at the dead man.

The body, like all dead bodies, gave the
appearance of being particularly heavy as it
lay, in the manner of the dead, with its stif-
fened limbs sunk among the cushions of the
coffin and its head now permanently bent
forward on the pillow, displaying, as dead
bodies always do, its yellow wax-like forehead,
the shiny spots on its sunken temples, and the
protruding nose that seemed to be pressing
down on the upper lip. Ivan Ilyich had
changed greatly. He had grown much thinner
since Pyotr Ivanovich had last seen him, and
yet, like all dead men, his face had assumed
an expression of greater beauty—or rather,
of greater significance—than it had worn in
life. The expression seemed to say that what
had to be done was done, and done properly.
Furthermore, the expression seemed to be
a reproach, or a reminder to the living.
Pyotr Ivanovich found this reminder uncalled
for; at any rate it had nothing to do with
him. He began to feel uncomfortable, and so
he crossed himself hurriedly—hardly within
the bounds of decency, he felt—and went out.

In the next room he found Schwartz waiting for him, his feet planted wide apart, his hands playing with the top-hat he held behind his back. One glance at this playful, well-groomed, elegant figure was enough to revive Pyotr Ivanovich's spirits. Pyotr Ivanovich realized that he, Schwartz, stood above all this and refused to become a prey to mournful influences. His whole appearance seemed to say: "The incident of the funeral of Ivan Ilyich can in no wise be considered sufficient grounds for calling off our usual gathering, i. e., nothing is to interfere with our meeting this evening and opening up a new pack of cards as the footman sets up four new candles. In general there is no reason to suppose that this incident can keep us from enjoying ourselves this evening." And he really whispered all this into Pyotr Ivanovich's ear as he passed through the room.

But Pyotr Ivanovich was not destined to play cards that evening. Praskovya Fyodorovna, a fat, shortish woman, much wider towards the base than at the shoulders despite all her efforts to achieve the opposite, dressed all in black with a lace scarf over her head and with eyebrows raised in the same odd manner as the woman standing at the coffin, came out of her room in the company of some other ladies whom she showed to the door of the room where the body lay and said, "A service is about to begin; come in."

Schwartz, with a vague sort of bow, stopped without accepting or rejecting the invitation. On recognizing Pyotr Ivanovich, Praskovya Fyodorovna gave a sigh and came straight up to him, taking his hand and saying, "I know you were a true friend of Ivan Ilyich's..." Then she looked at him in expectation of a fitting response. Just as Pyotr Ivanovich had known he was expected to cross himself in there, he knew he was expected to press her hand, sigh, and say, "I assure you..." That is just what he did, and having done it felt he had achieved the desired effect. He was touched and so was she.

"Come here before it begins, I want to speak to you," said the widow. "Give me your arm."

Pyotr Ivanovich gave her his arm and they withdrew into the inner rooms, passing Schwartz, who gave Pyotr Ivanovich a rueful wink which seemed to say:

"There's your card-game for you! Don't mind if we find someone else to take your place. And when you are free you can make a fifth."

Pyotr Ivanovich sighed more deeply and sorrowfully, and Praskovya Fyodorovna squeezed his fingers gratefully. On entering her drawing-room done in pink cretonne and lighted by a dim lamp, they sat down at a table—she on the sofa, Pyotr Ivanovich on a low ottoman with broken springs that careened when he sat on it. Praskovya Fyodorovna wanted to warn him against using it but she felt it would not be in keeping with the present situation. As he sat down on the ottoman Pyotr Ivanovich recalled how, when Ivan Ilyich had been decorating this drawing-room, he had consulted him as to the pink cretonne with green leaves. In passing the table to sit on the sofa (the room was crowded with furniture and brick-à-brac) the widow caught the lace of her black scarf on the elaborate carving of the table. Pyotr Ivanovich half rose to detach it, and as he did so the released springs gave him a little push. The widow disentangled the lace herself and Pyotr Ivanovich resumed his seat, thus suppressing the recalcitrant springs. But the widow had not quite disentangled the lace, and Pyotr Ivanovich again half rose, and again the ottoman upsurged and even gave a little click. When this was over she took out a white batiste handkerchief and began to weep. But Pyotr Ivanovich's spirits had been chilled by the episode with the lace and the struggle with the ottoman, and so he just sat and scowled. The strain of the situation was broken by the entrance of Sokolov, Ivan Ilyich's man-servant, who announced that the place in the cemetery selected by Praskovya Fyodorovna would cost 200 rubles. She stopped weeping to cast upon Pyotr Ivanovich a martyr's glance and tell him in French how hard this was for her. Pyotr Ivanovich gave a sigh expressing his sympathy.

"Smoke if you wish," she said in a magnanimous, yet stricken tone, and turned to discuss with Sokolov the price of the grave. As he lighted up, Pyotr Ivanovich noticed that she made detailed inquiries into the cost of various grave plots and made an astute choice. When this matter was settled she discussed the question of hiring choristers. Then Sokolov went out.

"I see to everything myself," she added to Pyotr Ivanovich, pushing aside the albums lying on the table. Noticing that the ashes of his cigarette were in danger of falling upon the table, she quickly handed him an ashtray, saying, "It would be mere pretence if I said I was unable in my grief to attend to practical affairs. On the contrary, if anything is able to ... er ... not console, but distract me, it is the doing of things for his sake." Again she took out her handkerchief as if about to weep, but, with a sudden effort, she took herself in hand, gave a little toss of her head, and spoke calmly.

"There is a business matter I wish to consult you about."

Pyotr Ivanovich bowed without allowing the springs, which gave new signs of revolt, to have their way.

"The last few days he suffered horribly."

"Did he?" asked Pyotr Ivanovich.

"Simply horribly! He screamed incessantly, not for minutes, but for hours. He screamed for three days running, without stopping for breath. It was unspeakable. I don't know how

I ever endured it; he could be heard three
rooms away. If you ever knew what I went
through!''

"Do you mean he was conscious right up to
the last?" asked Pyotr Ivanovich.

"Yes," she whispered. "To the very last.
He took leave of us only fifteen minutes
before he died, and asked us to take Volodya
away."

Despite a disagreeable awareness of his own
and this woman's hypocrisy, Pyotr Ivanovich
was deeply shaken by the thought of the sufferings of one he had known so well, first
as a gay and carefree schoolboy, then as a
grown man, his colleague. Once more he saw
that forehead, and that nose pressing down
on the upper lip, and fear for himself took
possession of him.

"Three days of horrible suffering and
death. Why, at any moment the same thing
might happen to me," he thought, and for
a brief second he was gripped by fear. But
instantly, he himself could not have said why,
the usual thought came to his aid that death
had visited not him, but Ivan Ilyich, and that
such a thing could not and should not happen
to him. Such thoughts would only lead him
into a state of depression, a thing that was to
be avoided, as the face of Schwartz had so
eloquently told him. By following this line
of reasoning, Pyotr Ivanovich recovered his
composure and even displayed genuine
interest as he enquired into the details of

the death of Ivan Ilyich, as if death were a mishap that could happen only to Ivan Ilyich—never to himself.

It was only after a detailed account of the truly horrible physical suffering of Ivan Ilyich (Pyotr Ivanovich learned of the tortures of Ivan Ilyich in the light of their effect on the nerves of Praskovya Fyodorovna) that the widow found it possible to proceed to matters of business.

"Ah, Pyotr Ivanovich, how hard it is for me, how terribly, terribly hard!" and again she fell to weeping.

Pyotr Ivanovich gave another sigh and waited for her to blow her nose. When she had blown her nose he said, "I assure you..." and again she began to speak and now got down to the business she had wanted to consult him about. She asked him how, in connection with her husband's death, she could get a grant of money from the government. She made out to be asking him about a pension, but he could see that she knew of matters that even he was ignorant of, and knew them down to the last detail; she knew exactly the amount of money this death entitled her to, but she wanted to find out if there were not any means by which she could wheedle out some more. Pyotr Ivanovich tried to think of how this might be done, but after considering the matter for some minutes and showing his sympathy by upbraiding the government for its stinginess, he said he was afraid it was impossible to get more. At this she drew a deep sigh and apparently gave herself up to thoughts of how she could bring the interview to a close. He divined this, put out his cigarette, got up, shook her hand, and went out into the hall.

In the dining-room where the clock hung that Ivan Ilyich had been so happy to have bought in a curio shop, Pyotr Ivanovich found the priest and a few other acquaintances who had come to the funeral, and he also saw the pretty daughter of Ivan Ilyich. She was dressed all in black, which made her slender waist seem slenderer than ever. She wore a gloomy, determined, almost angry look. She bowed to Pyotr Ivanovich as if he were to blame for something. Behind her stood a young man who looked just as disgruntled as she did. Pyotr Ivanovich knew him—he was a rich young man, an examining magistrate, who was said to be the young lady's fiancé. Pyotr Ivanovich gave a melancholy bow and was about to return to the room where the body lay when Ivan Ilyich's son, a schoolboy who greatly resembled his father, appeared from under the staircase. The lad might have been the young Ivan Ilyich whom Pyotr Ivanovich had known as a law student. His eyes were red from crying and were like the eyes of most scrubby little boys of thirteen or fourteen. On catching sight of Pyotr Ivanovich he frowned shamefacedly. Pyotr Ivanovich nodded to him and went into the room where the body was lying. The service began. Candles, groans, incense, tears, sobs. Pyotr Ivanovich stood with drawn brows, staring down at his feet. Not once did he glance at the body or at anything that might cause him to fall prey to depressing influences, and he was one of the first to leave the room. There was nobody out in the hall. Gerasim, the pantry-boy, ran quickly down the stairs and rummaged with strong hands through the mountain of wraps until he found Pyotr Ivanovich's coat and held it for him.

"Well, Gerasim," said Pyotr Ivanovich in order to say something, "are you sorry?"

"It's the Lord's will, sir. We'll all die some day," said Gerasim, revealing an unbroken line of strong white peasant teeth; then, like a man in a rush of extra work, he opened the door, shouted to the coachman, helped Pyotr Ivanovich into the carriage, and leaped back up the steps as if impatient to find something else to do.

Pyotr Ivanovich found it particularly pleasant to breathe in the fresh air after the smell of incense, the corpse, and carbolic acid.

"Where to?" asked the coachman.

"It isn't late yet. I'll drop in to see Fyodor Vasilyevich."

And off he went. He found them just finishing the first rubber, so that it was convenient for him to make a fifth for the next.

II

The story of the life of Ivan Ilyich is simple, ordinary, and appalling.

Ivan Ilyich died at the age of 45, a member of the Judicial Council. He was the son of an official who, in various ministries and departments in St. Petersburg, made for himself the sort of career which brings men at last to a post from which, even though it is clear they are incapable of doing anything of true importance, it is impossible to dismiss them because of their long term of service and high rank, and therefore they hold fictitious offices and receive by no means fictitious salaries of from six to ten thousand on which they live to a ripe old age.

Such was Privy Councillor Ilya Yefimovich Golovin, superfluous member of various superfluous institutions.

He had three sons, of whom Ivan Ilyich was the second. The eldest made for himself a career similar to his father's only in a different ministry, and soon he would reach the age of service at which salaries are paid by inertia. The third son was a failure. He had made a bad reputation for himself in various positions and was now working for the Railway Department. His father and brothers, and especially their wives, avoided meeting him and even forgot about his existence whenever possible. Their sister was married to Baron Greff, the same sort of St. Petersburg official as his father-in-law. Ivan Ilyich was *le phénix de la famille*, as they were fond of saying. He was not so cold and punctilious as his elder brother and not so reckless as his younger. He was something in between—a clever, lively, attractive man. Both he and his younger brother had attended the school of jurisprudence. The younger never finished for he was expelled when he reached the fifth course. Ivan Ilyich finished very creditably. As a law student he had been exactly what he continued to be all his life: capable, cheerful, sociable, good-natured, and strict in carrying out whatever he considered his duty, and he considered all things his duty that were designated as such by men in high position. Neither as a child nor as a grown man had he been a toady, but from earliest youth he had been drawn to those who stood above him, as a moth is drawn to the flame; he had adopted their manners and views, and had established friendly relations with them. All the enthusiasm of childhood and youth passed away without leaving a trace; he had at one time indulged his vanity and sensuality, and, in the last years of his student days, he had played with liberalism, but all within the judicious limits dictated by his instincts.

During his student days he had done things which, at the time, he had looked upon as loathsome and had made him disgusted with himself, but later, seeing that the same things were done by men of high standing without any scruples, he forgot all about them. While not regarding them as good, he was not haunted by memories of his sins.

On completing the law course and receiving money from his father for his outfit, Ivan Ilyich ordered some suits made at Sharmer's, hung a medallion bearing the inscription *respice finem* on his watch-chain, took leave of the head of the school, dined in state with his friends at Donon's, and then, with fashionable new bags, suits, linen, shaving and toilet articles, all ordered and purchased at the finest shops, left for a provincial town to occupy the post his father had secured for him as Secretary on Special Commissions for the governor of the province.

In the provincial town Ivan Ilyich immediately made his life as easy and pleasant as it had been during his student days. He worked, he saw to his career, and at the same time indulged in pleasant and well-bred forms of recreation. Occasionally he travelled into the countryside on assignments for his chief, on which occasions he preserved his dignity when dealing with those below as well as above him, and he fulfilled the duties entrusted to him (having to do mostly with Old Belivers) with an accuracy and incorruptibility of which he was justly proud. When engaged in official duties he was, in spite of his youth and love of amusement, exceedingly reserved, official in his manner, and even strict. But in society he was jovial and witty, always good-humoured, courteous, and, as his chief and his chief's wife, whose house he frequented, said, a *bon enfant*.

Here in the provinces he formed a connection with one of the ladies who threw herself at the stylish young advocate; there was also a milliner; there were drinking parties when high-ranking officers visited the town, and after-supper calls at a house on a distant street. There were services rendered to his chief and even to the wife of his chief. But all of this was done in a tone of such elevated good breeding that it could hardly be called by a bad name; it was all excused by the French saying: *il faut que jeunesse se passe*: it was done with clean hands, in a clean shirt, with French words, and, what was most important, in high society, which meant with the approval of those in high position.

Ivan Ilyich held this position for five years, and at the end of this time there came a change in the law. New courts were instituted and new men were needed.

Ivan Ilyich was one of those new men.

He was offered a post as examining magistrate and he accepted the offer, even though it meant going to a different gubernia, breaking his present connections, and making new ones. Ivan Ilyich was given a farewell party, his friends had a group photograph made for him, they presented him with a silver cigarette-case, and off he went to his new appointment.

As an examining magistrate Ivan Ilyich
was just as *comme il faut* and well-bred, displayed just as great a talent for separating
his public duties from his private ones and for
inspiring general respect as he had when
carrying out special commissions for the
governor. He found the post of magistrate
much more interesting and pleasant than
his former one. It had, of course, been very
gratifying in his former post to stride with
an easy swing in his trim uniform from
Sharmer's, straight past the anxious clients
and clerks sitting in the waiting-room and
throwing him envious glances, and go into
the office of his chief to sit with him over
a glass of tea and a cigarette. But there had
been few people directly under him—only
the district police superintendents and the
Old Believers he met when sent into the
countryside on commissions. And he enjoyed
nothing better than to treat such people with
civility, to discuss matter in an almost comradely way with them, making them feel that he,
who had it in his power to crush them, actually dealt with them in a friendly, unpretentious
manner. But there had been few such people.
Now, as examining magistrate, he felt that
all, all without exception, including the most
important and self-satisfied—all were in his
power, and he had but to write down certain
words on a sheet of paper with an official
heading and even the most important and
self-satisfied would be brought before him as

witnesses or even as the accused, and if Ivan
Ilyich did not deign to invite them to sit
down, they would have to stand before him
as they answered his questions. Ivan Ilyich
never took advantage of his power; on the
contrary, he tried to use it graciously. But
the awareness of this power and his right to
be gracious constituted for him the main
interest and attraction of his new post. In
the actual fulfilment of his duties, that is,
when examining, Ivan Ilyich quickly mastered
the art of eliminating all circumstances for
which he, as examining magistrate, was not
directly responsible, and of devising written
forms of expression for even the most complicated cases that registered only their
external aspects, completely diverting them
of his personal opinion and yet observing,
above everything else, all the formalities.
This work was new, and he was one of the
first to give practical application to the
reforms in judicial procedure introduced
in 1864.

On arriving in the new town as examining
magistrate, Ivan Ilyich formed new contacts,
made new acquaintances, assumed a new line
of conduct, and adopted a new tone. This
time he held himself dignifiedly aloof from
the local authorities, choosing his friends
from among the best law circles and the
wealthy gentry, and he adopted a tone of
moderate liberalism and social-mindedness,
allowing himself to mildly criticize the

government. And while taking as many pains with his clothes as ever, he stopped shaving his chin and allowed his beard to grow as it liked.

Here in the new town Ivan Ilyich's life became just as pleasant as it had been in the old. The group that set itself against the governor's circle proved to be very friendly and interesting; his income was bigger, and a new diversion was added by Ivan Ilyich's learning to play whist. In general he had a knack for playing cards good-humouredly and making quick and subtle decisions, so that as a general rule he won.

When he had been living in this town for two years Ivan Ilyich met his future wife. Praskovya Fyodorovna Mikhel was the brightest, cleverest, most brilliant and attractive young lady of the set in which Ivan Ilyich moved. To the amusements and diversions bringing him relief from his duties as examining magistrate, Ivan Ilyich now added a light flirtation with Praskovya Fyodorovna.

As Secretary on Special Commissions, Ivan Ilyich had danced as a rule; as Examining Magistrate, he danced as an exception. He danced to show that, although he was an executor of the new legal code and a lawyer of the fifth rank, in matters of dancing, too, he was above the average. And so he occasionally danced at the end of an evening with Praskovya Fyodorovna, and it was mostly during these dances that he conquered her. She fell in love with him. Ivan Ilyich had no clear, definite intention of getting married, but when this girl fell in love with him he faced the question. "Why," said he to himself, "should I not get married?"

Praskovya Fyodorovna came of an aristocratic family and was attractive; she also had a little money. Ivan Ilyich could have counted on making a better match, but this was not a bad one. He had his salary; she—her income, which he hoped would amount to as much again. He would acquire worthwhile in-laws. She was a sweet, pretty, well-bred young woman. To have said that Ivan Ilyich married her because he loved her and she sympathized with all his views of life would have been just as erroneous as to have said that he married her because the people of his set approved of the match, Ivan Ilyich married her because of both of these considerations: in acquiring this particular wife he did what brought him pleasure as well as doing what those in high position considered it proper for him to do.

Ivan Ilyich got married.

The actual process of getting married and the first period of married life, with its conjugal caresses, new furniture, new dishes, new linen—the period up to his wife's first pregnancy—passed very well; so well, in fact, that Ivan Ilyich began to think that marriage was in no way a hindrance to the pleasant, easy-going, diverting, well-bred life approved

of by society; that it even intensified this
life. But during the first months of his wife's
pregnancy he was confronted by something
new, unexpected, disagreeable, unseemly,
and hard to bear; something he could not
possibly have foreseen and could do nothing
about.

For no reason at all, simply *de gaité de
coeur* as he said to himself, she began to spoil
the pleasantness and the decorum of their
living: for no reason at all she began to be
jealous of him and demand that he pay her
more attention, to find fault with everything
he did and make coarse, indecent scenes.

At first Ivan Ilyich hoped to free himself
from the unpleasantness of the situation by
preserving the same well-bred and easy-going
attitude that had brought him his early
success. He tried ignoring his wife's fits of bad
temper and went on living in a pleasant, easy-
going way: he invited his friends for cards and
he himself went to the club or to his friends'
houses. But on one occasion his wife upbraided
him in such coarse language and thereafter
upbraided him so furiously every time he
failed to do what she told him to (having
apparently firmly resolved not to let up until
he succumbed to her rule, which meant until
he sat home and moped as she did) that Ivan
Ilyich was appalled. He realized that being
married—at least to his wife—did not necessar-
ily augment the pleasures and proprieties
of life, but, on the contrary, threatened them,

and that therefore he must guard himself against these threats. And Ivan Ilyich set about finding a means of doing this. Since his work was the only thing that impressed Praskovya Fyodorovna, Ivan Ilyich began to use his work and the obligations it entailed as a means of combating his wife and preserving his independence.

With the birth of the baby, bringing troubles with feeding, and real and fancied illnesses of baby and mother (which Ivan Ilyich was expected to sympathize with, but which he had no understanding of), the necessity of fencing off for himself a world outside of the family grew more urgent. The more irritable and exacting his wife became, the more deliberately he transferred the centre of gravity of his life to his office. He grew more attached to his work and more ambitious than ever.

Very soon, only one year after his marriage, Ivan Ilyich realized that conjugal life, while offering certain conveniences, was actually a very complicated and difficult matter, and that in order to perform one's duty in this respect, which meant putting up a decent front to win the approbation of society, one must work out definite principles, just as one must do in respect to one's profession.

And Ivan Ilyich worked out these principles. Of married life he demanded only the conveniences of dinners at home, of wife, and bed, and, most important, the preserving of

good form, for upon this depended social
approbation. He wanted to find pleasure in
family life. If he got it, he was grateful; if
he was rebuffed and heard nothing but
grumbling and complaints, he instantly retired
to his fenced-off world of business and found
his pleasure there.

Ivan Ilyich won approval by his diligent
service, and in three years he was promoted
to assistant public prosecutor. His new duties,
the importance of them, his right to bring
people to trial and put them in prison, his
public speaking and the success it brought
him—all of these things increased the
attraction his work held for him.

Other children were born. His wife grew
more querulous and ill-tempered, but the
principles of family life that Ivan Ilyich
had adopted made him almost immune to
her grumbling.

After serving for seven years in this town
Ivan Ilyich was made public prosecutor of
a different gubernia. They moved, they
were short of money, and his wife disliked
the new town. Though his salary was bigger,
the cost of living was higher. In addition, two
of their children died, making family life
more disagreeable than ever for Ivan Ilyich.

Praskovya Fyodorovna blamed her husband
for every misfortune that befell them in the
new town. Almost every subject of conversation between husband and wife, especially
the education of their children, brought up

questions on which they had quarrelled at one time or another, and these past quarrels always threatened to break out afresh. There were rare periods of being in love, but they never lasted for long. They were mere islands on which the couple rested briefly before setting out again upon the sea of secret hostility expressed in complete aloofness. This aloofness would have distressed Ivan Ilyich if he had supposed it should not exist, but he had by this time come to look upon it as not only normal but desirable, a relationship he consciously sought to achieve. He aimed to free himself more and more from all the upsets of family life and to keep them from becoming harmful or indecorous. He achieved this by spending less and less time at home, and by securing the peace when he had to be thereby inviting outsiders. The most important thing in his life was his work. The world of his official duties formed the one real interest of his life, and this interest absorbed him completely. The consciousness of his power, his right to ruin anyone he desired to ruin, the weightiness of even his appearance as he entered the court and spoke to his subordinates, his popularity with those above and below him, the skill with which he handled his cases, and his own appreciation of this skill—all these things brought him joy, and, together with his talks with his colleagues, the dinners he attended, and the whist he played, made his life a full one.

And so, on the whole, Ivan Ilyich's life was just what he considered it ought to be—pleasant and decorous.

This continued for another seven years. His daughter was now sixteen years old, one more child had died, one son remained—a schoolboy who was the cause of much dissension. Ivan Ilyich wanted him to be sent to the school of jurisprudence, and just for spite Praskovya Fyodorovna had insisted on his going to the gymnasium. The girl studied at home and was making good progress; the boy, too, was rather a good student.

III

In this way Ivan Ilyich spent seventeen years of his married life. He was already an experienced public prosecutor who had declined several good offers in expectation of a better one, when something occurred that upset the even tenor of his life. Ivan Ilyich had set his heart on being appointed presiding judge in a university town, but in some way Goppe managed to step in ahead of him and get the appointment. Ivan Ilyich was greatly upset, made accusations, quarrelled with Goppe and his immediate superiors. Their attitude chilled towards him, and when the next appointments were made he was again passed over.

This happened in 1880. It turned out to be

the most unpleasant year of Ivan Ilyich's life. On the one hand, his income was insufficient to support his family; on the other, he was being slighted, and what seemed to him to be the most flagrant and heartless injustice was accepted by others as quite ordinary. Even his father did not consider it his duty to help him. Ivan Ilyich felt that everyone had abandoned him, whereas they felt it was quite normal, and even fortunate, that he should be drawing a salary of 3,500 rubles. He alone knew that, what with the snubs he had received, the incessant nagging of his wife, and the debts he had accumulated by living beyond his means, things for him were far from normal.

That summer, with the purpose of cutting expenses, he and his wife went to live in the country with his wife's brother during his holiday. There in the country with nothing to do for the first time in his life, Ivan Ilyich was more than bored; he was so unspeakably miserable that he decided he must do something, must take decisive measures.

After a sleepless night, which he spent walking back and forth on the verandah, he resolved to go to St. Petersburg and try to get himself transferred to a different ministry, thereby punishing those who had failed to appreciate him.

On the next day, despite the protests of his wife and brother-in-law, he set out for St. Petersburg. He had only one purpose in going:

to secure himself a post that would pay five thousand rubles. He did not care in what ministry or department it might be or what sort of work it required. He only wanted a post paying five thousand in any administrative organization, any bank, any railway office, one of the Empress Maria's institutions, even in the customs. The only essential was that it pay five thousand and enable him to stop working for a ministry that did not appreciate him.

And this trip was crowned by amazing and unexpected success. When his train arrived at Kursk, a friend of his by the name of F. S. Ilyin got into his first-class carriage and told him of a telegram that had just been received by the governor of Kursk saying that an important change was about to take place in the ministry: Ivan Semyonovich was to be appointed in place of Pyotr Ivanovich.

The proposed change, in addition to the significance it had for Russia, was of particular significance for Ivan Ilyich, since in advancing a new man, Pyotr Petrovich, and apparently, his friend Zakhar Ivanovich, circumstances were made propitious for Ivan Ilyich. Zakhar Ivanovich was a good friend of Ivan Ilyich's.

In Moscow the news was confirmed, and on reaching St. Petersburg Ivan Ilyich looked up Zakhar Ivanovich, who promised to procure him a post without fail in the same Ministry of Law in which he served.

A week later he sent the following wire to his wife:

Zakhar appointed Miller's place stop I get appointment after first report.

Thanks to this change Ivan Ilyich unexpectedly received an appointment in his ministry that raised him two ranks above his colleagues, gave him a salary of five thousand, with three thousand five hundred to cover the expenses attending his change of residence. He forgot the resentment he had harboured against his opponents and the ministry, and was entirely happy.

Ivan Ilyich returned to the country more cheerful and content than he had been for many a day. Praskovya Fyodorovna's spirits rose too, and peace reigned for the time being. Ivan Ilyich described how cordially he had been received in St. Petersburg, and how all those who had been his enemies were disgraced and now fawned upon him, and envied him his new position and especially the favour in which he was held in St. Petersburg.

Praskovya Fyodorovna listened attentively, pretended to believe everything he said, and opposed him in nothing, giving herself up wholly to making plans of how they would live in the new town to which they were to move. And Ivan Ilyich was happy to see that her plans coincided with his, that they were in agreement, and that after this little upset his life was once more to become pleasant and decorous, which he felt was in the natural course of things.

Ivan Ilyich had come back for only a brief stay. On the 10th of September he had to take over his duties, and furthermore he had to settle himself in the new place, move all his possessions from the provincial town, buy many new things and order many others. In a word, he had to set himself up in the manner he had resolved upon in his mind, and Praskovya Fyodorovna had resolved upon in her soul.

Now that everything was settled so favourably and he and his wife were in agreement, and, moreover, saw little of each other, they became more friendly than they had been since the first days of their married life. Ivan Ilyich had at first thought of taking his family with him at once, but on the insistence of his sister-in-law and brother-in-law, who suddenly became very solicitous and amiable towards Ivan Ilyich and his family, he set out alone.

Ivan Ilyich set out alone, and the happy frame of mind evoked by his success and the harmonious relations with his wife, the one augmenting the other, remained with him all the time. He found a charming flat, exactly what he and his wife had dreamed of. Large, high-ceilinged drawing-rooms in the old style, an enormous and convenient study, rooms for his wife and daughter, a room for his son to be tutored in—all as if purposely planned for them. Ivan Ilyich himself undertook the furnishing and decorating, selecting wall-paper and upholstery and buying furniture, mostly old pieces, which seemed to him to be particularly *comme il faut*, and everything grew and grew until his future home approached the ideal he had set for himself. When the work was only half done the result exceeded his expectations. He could see in his mind's eye how handsome and correct, without a shade of vulgarity, the flat would look when ready. He fell asleep at night with a vision in his mind of the finished reception-room. As he glanced into the unfinished drawing-room he could see the fireplace, the screen, the *étagère*, the chairs placed at random here and there, the walls hung with fine china plates, the bronzes in their places. He found pleasure in thinking of how he would delight his wife and daughter, who also had a taste for such things. They could not dream of what was in store for them. He was particularly fortunate in making cheap purchases of old furniture, which added elegance to the general impression. In his letters he intentionally described things as being worse than they were so as to heighten the final effect. He was so taken up by these activities that even his new official duties, which were of the sort he most enjoyed, absorbed him less than he had expected. During court sessions he would sometimes become abstracted, his mind

wandering to a consideration of whether the
cross-piece at the top of the hangings should
be plain or draped. So taken up was he by all
this that he himself often lent the workmen
a hand, moving furniture here and there and
hanging *portières*. One day, when he had
climbed a ladder to show a workman how he
wanted the draperies hung, he slipped and
almost fell, but so strong and agile was he that
he saved himself, escaping with nothing but
a bad bruise from striking his side against the
handle of the window-frame. He had a pain in
his side for a little while, but it soon went
away. All this time Ivan Ilyich felt particularly
well and cheerful. He wrote: "I feel fifteen
years younger." He expected to finish everything in September, but the work dragged on
until the middle of October. The results,
however, were ravishing. He was not the only
one who thought so; everyone who saw the
flat agreed.

As a matter of fact it was just what is
achieved by all people who are not really rich,
but who wish to resemble the rich, and end
up by only resembling one another: hangings,
ebony, flowers, carpets, and bronzes, everything dark and highly polished—precisely
what a certain class of people create so as to
make themselves like all other people of this
particular class. And his flat was so very like
other people's that it made no impression.
But he felt it to be very exceptional. When
he went to the station to meet his family and

brought them back to the brightly-lighted flat, and a footman wearing a white necktie opened the door into the flower-bedecked entrance-hall, from which they went into the drawing-room, then into his study, and when they gasped with delight—when all this happened he was extremely happy, he showed them over the whole place, doted on their praises, and beamed with satisfaction. During tea that evening, when Praskovya Fyodorovna asked him how he had fallen, he laughed and gave an amusing demonstration of how he had slipped, and how he had given the workman a fright.

"It's a good thing I'm a good gymnast. Another man would have had a bad fall, but I got off with just a little bump here on my side; it still hurts when I touch it, but it's going away. Nothing but a bruise."

And they began to live in their new place, which, as is always the case when a house gets lived in, lacked but one room to make it perfect; and on their new income, which, as is always true, needed but the least little bit more—five hundred rubles—to make it sufficient for all their needs. But on the whole, everything was fine. Everything was especially fine at the beginning, before the flat was quite complete, when there were still things that had to be bought or ordered or mended or shifted from one place to another. True, little misunderstandings did occasionally crop up, but both husband and wife were so pleased and there was so much to keep them occupied, that these misunderstandings were always straightened out before they developed into real quarrels. When the flat was complete, life became rather dull and something seemed to be missing, but by this time they were making acquaintances and developing habits that kept them busy.

Ivan Ilyich spent his mornings in court and returned home to dinner; at first he was in the best of spirits, although he suffered a little because of the house (every spot on the table-cloth or the upholstery, every loose cord on the hangings, was a cause of irritation to him—after all, he had spent too much effort in arranging things that the least sign of destruction caused him pain). But on the whole the life of Ivan Ilyich became just what he believed it ought to be: easy, pleasant, and decorous. He got up at nine, had his coffee, read the paper, then put on his official uniform and went to court. There the yoke that was his daily work had been made ready for him and he easily slipped into it. Petitioners, enquiries sent to the office, the office itself, sittings—public and preliminary. One had to be able to delete from these matters all that, being fresh and vital, would impede official business; one must have no relations with people except official ones; the very cause of these relations must be official, and the relations themselves must be purely official. For instance, a man comes in to make enquiries about something. Ivan Ilyich could not possibly have any dealings with such a man outside of his official position, but if this man bears some relation to him as a member of the court (a relation that can be expressed on a sheet of paper bearing an official heading) then within the limits of this relationship Ivan Ilyich will do everything for him, absolutely everything within his power, and will even treat him with respect— that semblance of human, even friendly, relations. But the minute official relations end, all others end likewise. Ivan Ilyich had an extraordinary gift for isolating official relations, keeping them quite separate from real life, and so highly had he developed it, thanks to his talent and experience, that he had reached a stage of virtuosity at which he could allow himself to occasionally mix human and official relations, as if in fun. He could allow himself to do this because he had the strength of will to again isolate the official and discard the human if necessity demanded. Ivan Ilyich did this not only easily, pleasantly, and with decorum; he did it with virtuosity. In between times he smoked, had tea, talked a little about politics, a little about professional matters, a little about cards, and a lot about appointments. At last, tired, but with the satisfaction of a virtuoso who had given a superb performance, in his case as one of the first violins of the orchestra, he would return home. At home his wife and daughter would be either going out for the evening or entertaining; his son would be at school or preparing his lessons with a tutor, diligently studying all that is taught at the gymnasium. Everything was fine. After dinner, if there were no guests, Ivan Ilyich would sometimes read a book that was the talk of the day, then he would sit down to work examining documents, looking up laws, studying testimony and bringing it in line with the law. He found this neither dull nor entertaining. It was dull if it meant giving up a card-game, but if there was no game on, it was better than sitting alone or with his wife. Ivan Ilyich's greatest pleasure was to give little dinner parties to which he invited ladies and gentlemen of good social position, and the manner in which they spent the evening together was as much like the manner in which these people were used to spending their evenings as his drawing-room was like their drawing-rooms.

Once they even held an evening party with dancing. Ivan Ilyich was in the gayest of spirits and everything went off capitally except that he had a nasty row with his wife over the bon-bons and pastries. Praskovya Fyodorovna had made up her mind about the refreshments, but Ivan Ilyich insisted that they be ordered from the most expensive confectioner; he ordered a great many pastries and the quarrel arose because many of them were left over and the bill came to forty-five rubles. How serious and unpleasant the quarrel was may be judged by the fact that Praskovya Fyodorovna called him "a fool" and "spineless" and he clutched his head and made angry utterances about getting a divorce. But the party itself was jolly. All the best people came and Ivan Ilyich danced with Princess Trufonova, sister to the Trufonova who founded the charitable institution called "Take My Yoke Upon Thee". The joy he derived from his official labours lay in the gratification of his ambition; the joy he derived from social life lay in the gratification of his vanity; but the most genuine joy of all was that he derived from playing cards. He confessed that no matter what happened, however great the disappointments he suffered, there was one joy that shone through all like a bright little candle, and that was the joy of sitting down with some good players, with partners who did not shout, to a quiet, sensible four-hand game of "vint" (it is too painful in a five-hand game to be the one who has to sit by and watch, even though you pretend not to mind in the least), then to have supper and drink a glass of wine. Ivan Ilyich always went to bed in a particularly good humour after a game of cards, especially if he had won a little something (big winnings made him feel uncomfortable).

And so their life went on. They moved in the best circles, their house was frequented by people of importance and by young folk.

Husband, wife, and daughter were in complete accord as to who should form their set, and without consulting each other they showed equal skill in shaking off all sorts of undesirable friends and relatives, whom they considered blots on their scutcheon, and who insisted on coming to pay their respects in the drawing-room with the Japanese plates on the walls. Soon these undesirable creatures stopped coming, and the Golovins were left with friends from only the best society. Liza was courted by promising young men, and the young examining magistrate Petrishchev, son of Dmitry Ivanovich and sole heir to his estate, courted her with such zeal that Ivan Ilyich spoke of it to Praskovya Fyodorovna and suggested having a sleighing party or getting up some theatricals for them.

That is how they lived. Everything went on without change from day to day, and everything was fine.

IV

All of them were well. Sometimes Ivan Ilyich complained of a strange taste in his mouth and something wrong with his left side, but this could hardly be called an illness.

But the something wrong grew worse, and although it was not yet real pain, it was a feeling of pressure in his side which threw him into a constant state of depression. The state of depression deepened and began to spoil the pleasure of the easy and decorous life that the Golovin family had recaptured. Husband and wife began to quarrel more often, and soon the ease and pleasure of living disappeared and the decorum was preserved with difficulty. Rows took place more frequently. Once more there were only islands, and those few, on which the husband and wife could find themselves together without an explosion occurring.

And now Praskovya Fyodorovna could say with justice that her husband had a trying disposition. With the exaggeration characteristic of her, she said he had always had such a trying disposition and that only one with her angelic disposition could have stood it for twenty years. It was true that he was now the one who began the arguments. He usually found fault just before sitting down to dinner, or when the soup was being served. Either the dishes were chipped, or the food was bad, or his son put his elbow on the table, or his daughter's hair was not combed properly. And he blamed Praskovya Fyodorovna for everything. At first Praskovya Fyodorovna fought back and said horrid things to him, but on two occasions he was thrown into such a wild fury at the very outset of dinner that she realized it was the sickness brought on by eating that accounted for his bad temper, and so she controlled herself and did not answer him back; she merely tried to get through dinner as quickly as possible. Praskovya Fyodorovna took great credit to herself for exercising such self-control. Having decided that her husband had an impossible disposition and had made her life a misery, she began to pity herself. And the more she pitied herself, the more she hated her husband. She began to hope he would die, but she could not really hope for such a thing because then there would be no income. This set her against him the more. Her sense of injury was heightened by the realization that even his death could not save her. She was irritated by this, and she concealed her irritation, and her suppressed irritation aggravated his irritation.

After a scene in which Ivan Ilyich had been particularly unjust in his accusations, so unjust, in fact, that during the reconciliation he had confessed to being irritable but had said it was due to his illness, she had told him that if he was ill he must take measures to cure his illness, and insisted on his consulting a celebrated physician.

He did. The visit was just what he had expected it to be, just what it always is: the waiting, the physician's important mien (so familiar to him, for it was the same mien he himself assumed on entering the court), the tapping, the listening, the questions requiring answers that were obviously superfluous since they were all known beforehand,

the significant look insinuating that all would
be well if he just put himself in the doctor's
hands, for the doctor unquestionably knew
just what had to be done—one and the same
approach to every patient, no matter who
he was. Everything was just as it was in court.
The doctor assumed the same air of importance
in dealing with his patients that he himself
assumed in dealing with the accused.

The doctor said: this-and-that indicates
that this-and-that is wrong with you, but if
an analysis of this-and-that does not confirm
our diagnosis, we must suspect you of having
this-and-that. If we assume you have this-
and-that, then ... and so on. There was only
one question Ivan Ilyich wanted answered:
was his condition dangerous or not? But
the doctor ignored that question as irrelevant.
From the doctor's point of view, such a
question was unworthy of consideration.
One had only to weigh possibilities: floating
kidneys, chronic catarrh, or an ailment of
the caecum. There was no question of the
life of Ivan Ilyich—nothing but a contest
between floating kidneys and the caecum.
In the presence of Ivan Ilyich the doctor
gave a brilliant solution of the problem in
favour of the caecum, with the reservation
that the analysis of his water might supply
new information necessitating a reconsidera-
tion of the case. This was exactly what Ivan
Ilyich had done a thousand times, and in just
as brilliant a manner, in the presence of the

accused. And now the doctor made a brilliant résumé, glancing triumphantly, even jovially, over his glasses at the accused. From the doctor's résumé Ivan Ilyich concluded that things were bad with him, but that it mattered nothing to the doctor, nor indeed to anyone else. Ivan Ilyich was painfully shocked by this conclusion, which roused in him a strong feeling of self-pity, and an equally strong feeling of resentment against the doctor for being so indifferent to a matter of such vast importance. But he made no protest, he simply got up, put the fee on the writing-table, and said with a sigh:

"I suppose you are used to having your patients ask you foolish questions, but, in general, would you call my illness dangerous or not?"

The doctor shot him a severe look over his glasses, as if to say to the accused, "If you do not restrict yourself to the questions allowed I shall be compelled to have you put out of court."

"I have already told you all that I considered necessary and proper," said the doctor. "Anything further will be revealed by the analysis." And the doctor bowed him out.

Ivan Ilyich went out slowly, sat down glumly in his sleigh, and rode home. All the way home he kept going over in his mind what the doctor had said, trying to translate all those vague and confusing scientific terms into plain language and find in them the answer to his question: "Bad—very bad, or not yet too bad?" And he fancied that the essence of all the doctor had said was that things were very bad. Now everything Ivan Ilyich set eyes on looked dismal: the cab-drivers looked dismal, the houses looked dismal, the passers-by, the shops—everything looked dismal. His pain—that dull, aching pain that did not let up for a second—assumed a new and graver significance in the light of the doctor's obscure remarks. And he concentrated his attention on it with a new sense of alarm.

He reached home and told his wife what had happened. She listened, but in the middle of the story his daughter came in with her hat on. She and her mother were going out. She forced herself to sit and listen to his dull account for a while, but not for long, and his wife, too, did not hear him out.

"Well, I'm very glad," said his wife. "See that you take your medicine regularly now. Give me your prescription. I'll send Gerasim to the apothecary's." And she went out to change her clothes.

He held his breath as long as she was in the room, then he gave a deep sigh.

"Oh, well," he said, "maybe things aren't really so bad after all."

He began to take medicine and to follow all the doctor's instructions, which were changed after the analysis of his water. But there was some sort of misunderstanding about the analysis, or about what should have followed from the analysis; it was impossible to appeal to the celebrity about such a trifling matter, but somehow things were not turning out as he had said they should. Either the doctor had forgotten something, or had lied to the patient, or had concealed something from him.

However, Ivan Ilyich followed his instructions explicitly, and at first the very following of them brought some relief.

After his visit to the doctor Ivan Ilyich's main occupation became the explicit following of the doctor's instructions about hygiene and the taking of medicine and the registering of any change in his pain and in the functioning of his body. Ivan Ilyich's main interest in life became human ailments and human health. Whenever anyone spoke in his presence of someone who was ill or who had died or was recuperating, especially from an illness that resembled his own, he would listen intently, trying to hide his nervousness, would ask questions and make mental comparisons with his own state.

The pain did not subside, but Ivan Ilyich forced himself to think he was feeling better. And he succeeded in deceiving himself as long as everything went well, but as soon as he had a row with his wife, or unpleasantness at the office, or bad luck at cards, he was made acutely conscious of his illness. Formerly he had bravely withstood misfortune, confident that he would overcome it, he had put up resistance, certain that he would be successful, would at last have his "grand slam." Now every mishap knocked the ground out from under his feet and threw him into a state of despair. He said to himself: here I was, just beginning to get better, the medicine was just beginning to take effect, and this accursed mishap or misfortune had to come along... And he fumed against the misfortune, or against the people who were killing him by bringing him misfortune, and he felt that his fuming was killing him, but there was nothing he could do about it. Surely he ought to have realized that the anger he vented on people and circumstances only aggravated his illness, and for that reason he ought not to have paid any attention to chance disturbances. But his reasoning took just the opposite direction: he said that what he needed was peace, and was on his guard against anything that disturbed his peace, and the slightest violation made him furious. He made things worse by reading medical books and consulting doctors. He grew worse so gradually that it was easy for him to deceive himself by comparing one day with the next—the difference was almost imperceptible. But when he sought the advice of doctors he felt that he was not only growing worse, but doing it very rapidly. And in spite of this he kept on consulting doctors.

That very month he visited another celebrated physician. This celebrity said practically the same thing as the first, although he posed the problem a bit differently. The advice of this celebrity only increased Ivan Ilyich's doubts and fears. A friend of a friend of his—an excellent doctor—gave an entirely different diagnosis, and while he promised that Ivan Ilyich would get well, his questions and suppositions only confused him the more and increased his doubts. A homeopath gave still another diagnosis and prescribed another medicine, and for one week Ivan Ilyich took this medicine without letting anyone know. When the week passed without bringing relief, destroying his faith in this as well as other means of treatment, he became more depressed than ever.

Once a woman of his acquaintance told of cures that had been worked by icons. Ivan Ilyich found himself listening attentively and believing in the possibility of such cures. This incident frightened him. "Have I really become such an imbecile?" he asked himself. "Nonsense! What I must do is to stop being so nervous, choose one doctor and keep strictly to the course of treatment he prescribes. That is what I shall do. Enough. I will stop thinking about myself and sctrictly carry out the doctor's orders until summer, and then we shall see. No more vacillating!"

It was easy to make this decision, but impossible to carry it out. The pain in his side wore him down, it seemed to be getting worse, it gave him no rest, the taste in his mouth became more peculiar, he felt that he had a disgustingly bad breath, he lost his appetite and grew weaker. There was no deceiving himself: something dreadful was happening to Ivan Ilyich, something novel, something of such great moment that nothing of greater moment had ever happened to him. And he alone was aware of this; the people about him either did not understand or did not care to understand, and went on thinking that everything in the world was just as it had always been. It was this that tortured him more than anything else. The people in his house—especially his wife and daughter, who were going through the height of the social season—saw nothing, understood nothing, and were annoyed with him for being so downcast and exacting, as if it were his fault. No matter how hard they tried to hide it, he saw that they looked upon him as a nuisance, and that his wife had adopted a certain attitude towards his illness that she clung to despite anything he said or did. This was her attitude: "You see," she said to her friends, "unlike all ordinary people, Ivan Ilyich is incapable of carrying out doctors' orders to the letter. Today he takes his drops and eats what he is told; tomorrow, if I don't keep an eye on him, he forgets to take his medicine and eats sturgeon (which is forbidden), and sits up playing cards till one o'clock in the morning."

"When have I ever done such a thing?" Ivan Ilyich once asked her in vexation. "Only once, at Pyotr Ivanovich's."

"And last night with Shebek."

"That doesn't count; I couldn't sleep for the pain."

"It doesn't matter, if you keep that up you'll never get well and just go on torturing us."

Judging by what Praskovya Fyodorovna said to her friends and to Ivan Ilyich himself, her attitude towards her husband's illness was that he himself was responsible for it, and that the whole thing was just another means of causing her trouble. Ivan Ilyich felt that this attitude was not intentional, but that did not make it any the easier for him.

At work too, Ivan Ilyich noticed, or at least thought he noticed, a strange attitude towards him; at times he felt that his colleagues were stealing glances at him as at one who was about to vacate a post; at other times his friends would chaff him amiably about his fancied illness, as if that fearful, that horrible, that unheard-of something that was growing inside of him and gnawing at his vitals night and day, irresistibly dragging him off somewhere, was a highly appropriate subject for a joke. He became especially irritated with Schwartz, whose liveliness, playfulness, and quality of being always *comme il faut* reminded Ivan Ilyich of himself ten years earlier.

His friends came to play cards with him. They sat down at the table, shuffled and dealt the new cards, he arranged his hand, putting all the diamonds together—seven in all. His partner said, "No trumps," and put down two diamonds. What else could he wish for? He ought to have felt delighted—a "grand slam".

But suddenly Ivan Ilyich is aware of that gnawing pain and that taste in his mouth, and he feels it is madness under the circumstances to take pleasure in a "grand slam". He sees how his partner, Mikhail Mikhailovich, strikes the table with a meaty hand and indulgently refuses to pick up his tracks, pushing them towards Ivan Ilyich, so that he may have the pleasure of taking them in without exerting himself by stretching out his hand very far. "Does he suppose I am too weak to stretch out my hand?" thinks Ivan Ilyich, forgetting what is trump and trumping his partner's card, thereby missing a "grand slam" by three. The worst of all is that he can see how upset Mikhail Mikhailovich is, and yet he does not care. And it is dreadful to think why he does not care.

Everyone can see how bad he feels, and they say to him, "We can stop if you're tired. Take a little rest." Rest? Why, he is not tired in the least, he will finish the rubber. They are all glum and silent. Ivan Ilyich knows that he is responsible for the gloom but is unable to disperse it. They have supper and the guests go home, leaving Ivan Ilyich alone with the knowledge that his life is poisoned and that he is poisoning the lives of others, and that instead of growing weaker, the poison is penetrating deeper and deeper into his being.

And it is with this knowledge, and the physical pain, and the sense of horror as well, that he must lie in bed, often kept awake by pain the greater part of the night. And in the morning he must get up again, dress himself, go to court, talk, and write, and if he did not go to court he would have to spend the same twenty-four hours at home, every one of them a torture. And he has to go on living like this, on the brink of doom, all by himself, without a single person to understand and pity him.

V

One month, then another went by in this way. Just before the new year his brother-in-law came to pay them a visit. Ivan Ilyich was at court when he arrived. Praskovya Fyodorovna was out shopping. On coming home Ivan Ilyich found his brother-in-law, a hale and hearty man, in his study unpacking his bag. He raised his head on hearing Ivan Ilyich's step and stared at him a moment in silence. This stare revealed everything to Ivan Ilyich. His brother-in-law opened his mouth to gasp, but checked himself. And this confirmed everything.

"Why, have I changed?"

"Y-yes, you have."

After that, try as he might, Ivan Ilyich could not get his brother-in-law to make a single comment on his appearance. Praskovya Fyodorovna arrived and his brother-in-law went into her rooms. Ivan Ilyich locked the door and examined himself in the looking-glass, first in profile, then full-face. He picked up a photograph he had taken with his wife and compared it with what he saw in the looking-glass. The difference was terrible. He bared his arm to the elbow and examined it, then he pulled down his sleeve, sank down on an ottoman, and gave himself up to thoughts blacker than night.

"I mustn't, I mustn't," he said to himself. He jumped up, went to his writing-table, opened his notes on a case, and tried to read, but could not. He opened the door and went into the reception-room. The door into the drawing-room was ajar. He tiptoed over to it and listened.

"Oh, you're exaggerating," said Praskovya Fyodorovna.

"Exaggerating? Can't you see for yourself? He's like a dead man. Look at his eyes. No life in them. What's the matter with him?"

"Nobody knows. Nikolayev" (another doctor) "said something, but I can't tell... Leshchetitsky" (the celebrated doctor) "said just the opposite."

Ivan Ilyich walked away, went to his room, lay down and fell to thinking: "Kidneys. A floating kidney." He recalled all that the doctors had told him, how the kidney had come loose and how it was floating about. And in his imagination he caught the kidney and fixed it in place. It was so easy, it seemed. "Yes, I must go and see Pyotr Ivanovich" (the friend who had a doctor friend). He rang, ordered the carriage, and made ready to go and see him.

"Where are you going, *Jean*?" asked his wife in a particularly mournful and unusually kindly tone.

The unusual kindliness of her tone annoyed him. He gave her a black look.

"I've got to go and see Pyotr Ivanovich."

He went to his friend's who had the doctor friend, and together they went to see the doctor. The doctor was at home and he had a long talk with him.

Everything became clear to Ivan Ilyich as soon as he found out all about the anatomical and physiological changes that, according to the doctor, were taking place inside of him.

There was something, the smallest of somethings, in the caecum. It could be remedied. The functioning of one organ had to be strengthened, of another had to be weakened, the something had to be absorbed, and everything would be all right.

Ivan Ilyich was a little late for dinner. After dinner he sat talking cheerfully for some time and could not make himself go and work in his study. At last he went to his study and sat down to work. He read through some cases, concentrated on his work, but in the back of his mind he was constantly aware of some pressing and private matter that he had put off, but which he would attend to as soon as he was through. When he finished he remembered what the private matter was: ruminations on his caecum. But he did not give himself up to them; instead he went into the drawing-room for tea. There were guests who were talking and playing the piano and singing. Among them was the examining magistrate, a desirable fiancé for his daughter. Praskovya Fyodorovna observed that Ivan Ilyich was the gayest of the party, but not for a minute did he forget that he had put off important ruminations on his caecum. At eleven o'clock he took leave of everyone and retired to his room. Ever since his illness he had been sleeping alone in a little room adjoining his study. He went in, undressed, and took up a novel by Zola, but instead of reading he gave himself up to his thoughts. He fancied that the longed-for cure of his caecum had been effected. Absorption, ejection, and a restoration of normal functioning. "Of course," he said to himself, "all we must do is assist nature." This reminded him of his medicine; he raised himself, took it, and lay on his back, feeling what a beneficial effect the medicine had, how it eased his pain.

"Only I must take it regularly and avoid all bad influences. I feel better already, ever so much better." He poked his side. It was not painful to the touch. "I don't feel anything at all, I am really much better." He put out the candle and lay on his side. His caecum was improving, was absorbing. Suddenly he felt the old familiar gnawing pain—quiet, serious, insistent. And the same bad taste in his mouth. His heart sank, he felt dizzy. "My god, my god!" he muttered. "Again, again, and it will never stop." And suddenly he saw things in an entirely different light. "The caecum. Kidneys," he said to himself. "It isn't a matter of caecum and kidneys, it is a matter of life ... and death. Yes, once there was life, and now it is passing away, passing away, and there is nothing I can do to stop it. Why should I deceive myself? Is it not clear to everyone except me that I am dying, that it is merely a question of weeks, days, even hours? There was light, now there is darkness. I was here, I am going there. Where?" He broke out in a cold sweat and he had difficulty in breathing. He could hear nothing but the beating of his heart.

"I will no longer exist. What will exist? Nothing. Where will I be when I cease to exist? Is this really death? Oh, I don't want to die!" He jumped up to light the candle, he felt for it with trembling hands, he dropped the candle and candlestick on the floor, and fell back on the pillow again.

"What does it matter? It's all the same," he said to himself as he stared into the darkness with wide-open eyes. "Death. Yes, death. And they don't know it and don't want to know it, and have no pity. They are playing." (He heard the distant trilling of a woman's voice and the piano accompaniment coming through the closed door). "It's all the same to them now, but soon they will die too. The fools. I shall go first, then they; it will come to them, too. Now they are rejoicing, the beasts." His resentment fairly choked him. He was horribly, unspeakably miserable. It was inconceivable that everyone, always, should be doomed to this horror. He raised himself.

"Something is wrong; I must calm myself and think it through from the beginning." And he began to think. "The beginning of my illness. I struck my side, but I was just the same then, and the following day; it only ached a little, but then it got worse, and then I started going to see doctors, and then I felt downcast, depressed, and then more doctors; and all the while I was moving closer and closer to the edge of the precipice. My strength gave out. Closer and closer. And here I am a wreck, no life in my eyes. Death. And I still think about my caecum. I think of mending my caecum, and all the time it is death. But is it, really?" And again he was seized by terror; he gasped, bent down, felt for the matches, and knocked his elbow against the bedside table. It was in the way and it hurt him and he became angry with it and struck it a second time harder and knocked it over. In desperation, gasping for breath, he fell on his back and waited for death to come that very moment.

The guests were going home. Praskovya Fyodorovna, who was seeing them off, heard the table fall and came into the room.

"What's the matter?"

"Nothing. I accidentally knocked it over."

She went out and came back with a candle. He lay there with his eyes fixed on her, breathing loudly and quickly, like a man who has had a long run.

"What is it, *Jean*?"

"N-nothing. I knocked it ... over." ("Why should I tell her? She won't understand," he thought.)

And she did not understand. She picked up and lighted the candle, and hurried away. She had to see one of her guests off.

When she came back he was still lying on his back staring at the ceiling.

"What is it, are you worse?"

"Yes."

She shook her head and sat down.

"I'm wondering, *Jean*, if we shouldn't send for Leshchetitsky?"

Sending for the celebrity meant spending a lot of money again. He gave a sardonic smile and said no. She sat down for a little while, then went over to him and kissed him on the forehead.

He hated her with his whole heart when she kissed him, and it cost him a great effort to keep from pushing her away.

"Good-night. God willing, you'll fall asleep."

"Yes."

VI

Ivan Ilyich saw that he was dying, and he was in a constant state of despair. In his heart of hearts he knew he was dying, and it was not simply that he could not get used to the idea; he could not grasp it, could not possibly grasp it.

All his life he had regarded the syllogism he had learned while studying Kiesewetter's *Logics*: "Caius is a man, men are mortal, and therefore Caius is mortal," as being true only in respect to Caius, not to himself. Caius was a man, a man in the abstract sense, and so the syllogism applied to him; but Ivan Ilyich was not Caius, and not a man in the abstract sense; he had always been quite, quite different from all other men. He had been little Vanya to his mamá and papá, to his brothers Mitya and Volodya, to the coachman and the nursemaid and to his toys, and to Katya; Vanya, who had lived through all the joys and sorrows and ecstasies of childhood, boyhood and youth. Had Caius ever known the leathery smell of a ball that Vanya had loved so dearly? Had Caius ever kissed his mother's hand with such feeling, or so loved the rustle of her silk skirts? Had Caius ever made a row over the buns at school? Or ever been so in love? Or presided so brilliantly over a court session?

Caius was indeed mortal, and it was only right and proper that he should die, but he, Vanya, Ivan Ilyich, with all his thoughts and feelings—it was quite a different matter with him. And it could not be right and proper that he should die. The thought was too horrifying.

That was what he felt.

"If I were doomed to die like Caius I would have known of it, some inner voice would have told me. But I have never been aware of anything of the sort; I have always known, and so have all of my friends, that I was not of the same stuff as Caius. And now, lo and behold!" he said to himself. "But it cannot be. It cannot be. It cannot be, and yet it is. How is it possible? How is one to understand it?"

He could not understand it and tried to drive the thought away as being false, misleading, and unwholesome, and he tried to evoke true, wholesome thoughts to take its place. But the thought was more than a thought, it was reality itself, and it kept coming back and confronting him.

One by one he summoned up other thoughts to take its place in the hope of finding support in them. He tried to recover a former way of thinking that had protected him from thoughts of death. But, strange as it may seem, the things that had once screened, hidden, obliterated the consciousness of death, were now unable to do so. Ivan Ilyich had spent most of his time of late trying to recover a former way of thinking that had screened death from him. He would, for instance, say to himself, "I must lose myself in work; after all, that was once my whole life." And he would go to court, driving all his doubts out of his mind. He would enter into conversation with his friends, and take his seat among them as he always had, casting a vague and ponderous glance over the people gathered in the court-room as he sat down, grasping the arms of his oaken chair with his thin hands, bending towards his neighbour, shifting the papers about, whispering, then suddenly straightening up and raising his eyes to pronounce the well-known words with which proceedings were opened. But in the very middle of a court sitting that pain in his side, irrespective of the stage proceedings had reached, would begin *its* gnawing proceedings. Ivan Ilyich would pay it brief attention, then try to drive it out of his mind, but *It* went right on with its work, and came and stood facing him, staring him straight in the eye, and he was confounded, and the light went out of his eyes, and once more he asked himself, "Is *It* the only truth?" And his colleagues and subordinates saw with surprise and grief that he, who had always been such a brilliant and subtle judge, was getting muddled and making mistakes. He would give a toss of his head and try to pull himself together and somehow carry proceedings through to the end, and return home, sadly aware that legal proceedings could no longer hide from him that which he wished to hide; that no legal proceedings could enable him to escape from *It*. And the worst thing of all was that *It* demanded all his attention without asking him to do anything but just stare at *It*, stare it straight in the eye, doing nothing but suffer unspeakable torment.

To escape this horrible state of mind Ivan Ilyich sought other comforts, other screens, and he found other screens, and for a while they seemed to bring relief, but very soon they collapsed, or rather grew transparent, as if *It* had the power of penetrating all things and nothing in the world could shut it out.

Sometimes in those latter days he would go into the drawing-room, that he had taken such pains to furnish, into the very drawing-room where he had fallen, and for which, as he would think with a bitter smile, he had sacrificed his life, for he was certain that his illness had begun with his fall. He went into that drawing-room and saw a deep scratch on his polished table. He looked for the cause of the damage and discovered it in the twisted clasp of an album with bronze trimmings. He

picked up the album, a costly one that he
himself had filled with loving care, and grew
indignant at the carelessness of his daughter
and her friends: there were torn pages, and
some of the photographs were upside-down.
He painstakingly put the pictures in order
and straightened the bronze trimmings.

Then he had the idea of transferring the
whole *établissement* with the album on it to
another corner of the room, where the plants
were. He called the footman. His wife or
daughter came to help him, they disagreed,
objected to the change, he argued and grew
angry. But that was all very well, because it
helped him to forget about *It*; *It* was pushed
out of sight.

But when he began to move the table himself his wife said, "Don't. Let the servants do
it, you'll hurt yourself again," and suddenly
It stepped out from behind the screen, *It*
flashed across his sight. He hoped *It* would
disappear again, but he involuntarily became
conscious of the pain in his side—the something was still there, was still gnawing, and he
could not forget *It*, and *It* was staring at him
very clearly from behind the plants. And so
what was the use of all this fuss?

"Can it be true that here, on these hangings,
as at the storming of a bastion, I lost my
life? Not really! How ghastly! How absurd!
It cannot be. It cannot be ... but it is."

He went into his study, lay down, and once
more found himself alone with *It*. Face to

face with *It*, and there was nothing he could do about it. Nothing but contemplate *It* and feel his blood running cold.

VII

It is hard to say how it came about that, in the third month of Ivan Ilyich's illness, his wife, his daughter, his son, the servants, his friends, the doctors, and especially he himself knew that the only interest he held for others any more lay in how soon he would leave his post vacant, free the living from the constraint of his presence, and himself from his sufferings. It is hard to say because it came about slowly, imperceptibly, step by step.

He slept less and less. They gave him doses of opium and began morphine injections. But this brought no relief. At first the dull misery of his half-conscious state was a relief in the sense that it was something novel, but soon it became just as great, if not greater suffering than the unalleviated pain.

Special foods were prepared for him according to the doctor's instructions, but he found all of them more and more unpalatable, more and more revolting.

And special arrangements were made for his bowel movements. This was a daily torture—a torture because of the uncleanliness, the unseemliness, and the stench, and because another person had to assist at the operation. But this disagreeable business brought Ivan Ilyich one comfort: Gerasim, the pantry-boy, always came to carry out the chamber-pot.

Gerasim was a fresh, clean peasant lad who was flourishing on town food. He was always bright and cheerful. At first it embarrassed Ivan Ilyich to see this clean lad in traditional Russian clothes performing such a disgusting task. Once, on getting up off the pot, he collapsed into an armchair, too weak to draw on his trousers, and lay back staring in horror at his naked thighs with the flaccid muscles hanging upon them.

At that moment Gerasim came in with his light, vigorous stride, emanating an odour of fresh wintry air and the tar his stout boots were rubbed with. He was wearing a clean homespun apron and a clean cotton shirt with the sleeves rolled up, baring his strong young arms. Without looking at Ivan Ilyich (afraid, perhaps, to taunt him with the joy of life radiating from his own face) he went over to the pot.

"Gerasim," said Ivan Ilyich feebly.

Gerasim gave a little start, fearing he had done something amiss, and with a quick movement turned his fresh, simple, good-natured young face, which was showing the first signs of a beard, to the sick man.

"What is it, sir?"

"You must find this very disagreeable.

Forgive me. I can't do it myself."

"What are you saying, sir!" and Gerasim's eyes and teeth flashed in a smile. "Why shouldn't I help you? You're sick."

And with strong able hands he did his usual task, walking out of the room with a light step. Five minutes later he came back with just as light a step.

Ivan Ilyich was still lying in the armchair.

"Gerasim," he said when the lad had put down the clean pot, "please help me, come here." Gerasim went up to him. "Lift me up. I can't get up myself and I've sent Dmitry out."

Gerasim bent down. With strong hands and a touch that was as light as his step, he picked him up gently, deftly, and held him with one hand while he pulled up his trousers with the other. He was about to put him in the chair again, when Ivan Ilyich asked him to help him to the sofa. Gerasim effortlessly and gently led, almost carried him to the sofa.

"Thank you. How capable you are ... how well you do everything."

Gerasim smiled again and was about to go out, but Ivan Ilyich was so glad to have him near that he did not let him go.

"Here, bring over that chair if you don't mind. No, that one, to put under my feet. I feel better when my feet are up."

Gerasim carried over the chair, dropped it with one swift movement almost to the floor, then checked the movement and set it down noiselessly and put Ivan Ilyich's feet up on it. It seemed to Ivan Ilyich that he felt better when Gerasim lifted his feet up.

"I feel better with my feet up," said Ivan Ilyich. "Bring the pillow and put it under them."

Gerasim did what he was asked. He lifted up the sick man's feet again and put the pillow under them. Again Ivan Ilyich felt better while Gerasim held his feet up. When he let them down he felt worse.

"Gerasim," he said, "are you busy at present?"

"No indeed, sir," said Gerasim, who had learnt from the townsfolk how to address his betters.

"What else have you to do?"

"Why, nothing else. I've done everything except chop some wood for tomorrow."

"Could you hold my feet up high like that for a little while?"

"Indeed I could, sir." Gerasim held his feet up high and Ivan Ilyich fancied that he felt no pain at all in that position.

"And what about the wood?"

"Don't trouble yourself about that, sir. I'll have time for that."

Ivan Ilyich had Gerasim sit down and hold his feet and talk to him. And strange as it may seem, he fancied he really did feel better while Gerasim was holding his feet.

After that Ivan Ilyich would send for Gerasim from time to time and have him put his feet up on his shoulders, and he loved to talk to the lad. Gerasim did everything willingly, easily, simply, and with such good humour that Ivan Ilyich was touched. The health, strength, and cheerfulness of everyone but Gerasim irritated Ivan Ilyich. Gerasim's health and cheerfulness, on the contrary, soothed rather than irritated him.

Ivan Ilyich suffered most of all from the lie—the lie adopted by everyone for some reason, which said that he was only ill and not dying, and that everything would be all right if he just kept quiet and did what the doctors told him to. He knew perfectly well that no matter what was done, nothing would change except that his sufferings would increase and he would die. He was tortured by this lie, tortured by no one's wanting to acknowledge the lie, by his knowing the truth and everyone else's knowing the truth, and yet pressing this lie upon him because of the horror of his position, forcing him to become a party to the lie. This lie, the lie forced upon him on the eve of his death, the lie degrading the solemn, awesome act of his dying to the level of their social calls, portières, and oysters for supper, was an unspeakable torture to Ivan Ilyich. And, strangely enough, time and again when they played their parts, he came within a hair's breadth of shouting out, "Stop your lying! You know and I know that I am about to die. You might at least stop lying!" But he never had the courage to

do it. He could see that the dread, the fear-
some act of his dying had been degraded by
those about him to the level of a chance unpleasantness, a sort of breach of etiquette
(they behaved towards him as they might
to a man who gave off a foul odour on
entering a drawing-room), a violation of that
"decorum" to which he had been a bondslave
all his life. He saw that no one felt sorry for
him because no one cared to understand his
position. The only person who understood
and who felt sorry for him was Gerasim. And
for that reason the only person Ivan Ilyich
cared to be with was Gerasim. He was quite
content when Gerasim sat with him sometimes the whole night through, holding his
feet and refusing to go to bed, saying, "Don't
trouble yourself about that, Ivan Ilyich;
I'll sleep later"; or when he would say to
him, "Why should I not serve you, now that
you are ill?" Gerasim was the only one who
did not lie; everything he did showed that he
was the only one who understood the true
state of affairs and saw no need of hiding it.
He simply felt sorry for his poor wasting
master. Once when Ivan Ilyich sent him away
he said to him quite frankly, "We'll all die
some day. Why should I not help you now?"
And in saying this he said that he did not find
waiting on Ivan Ilyich irksome because he
was doing it for a dying man, and he hoped
that someone would do the same for him
when his time came.

Next to the lie and all it entailed, the most painful thing for Ivan Ilyich was that no one felt sorry for him as he would have liked them to. There were moments when, after long suffering, the thing he most wanted, even though he was ashamed to admit it, was to be fondled pityingly, like a sick child. He wanted to be petted, kissed, cried over, as sick children are kissed and comforted. He knew that he was an important member of the law court and that his beard was turning grey and that therefore such a thing was impossible. But that was what he wanted. There was something approaching this in his relations with Gerasim, and that was why he found comfort in Gerasim. Ivan Ilyich wanted to cry, wanted to be petted and wept over, but here comes Shebek to see him, his colleague Shebek, also a member of the law court, and instead of crying and seeking comfort, Ivan Ilyich puts on a grave, profound look and, from sheer inertia, gives his opinion of the importance of the decisions of the Court of Appeal and stubbornly defends it.

Nothing did so much to poison the last days of Ivan Ilyich as this lie within him and all around him.

VIII

Morning had come. The only evidence that morning had come was that Gerasim went out and Pyotr, the footman, came in, put out the candles, drew back the hangings over one of the windows, and began to tidy up the room quietly. Morning or night, Friday or Sunday, made no difference, it was all the same—the same gnawing, racking pain that did not let up for a moment; the same consciousness that life was irrevocably passing away but was not yet gone and that abhorrent death, the only reality, was slowly and implacably creeping up on him; and then—the lie. What thought could there be of days, weeks, hours?

"Will you have tea, sir?"

("The man must have his routine: in the morning the family takes tea," thought Ivan Ilyich.

"No," he said.

"Perhaps you would like to shift to the sofa, sir?"

("He must tidy up the room and I am in the way, I am messing up the room, creating disorder," thought Ivan Ilyich.)

"No. Leave me alone," he said.

The footman busied himself a little longer. Ivan Ilyich held out his hand. Pyotr came over solicitously.

"What is it, sir?"

"My watch."

Pyotr picked up the watch that was lying within Ivan Ilyich's reach and handed it to him.

"Half past eight. Are the others up?"

"Not yet, sir. Vasily Ivanovich" (the son)

"has gone to school and Praskovya Fyodorovna left orders to call her if you asked for her. Shall I call her, sir?"

"Don't bother." ("Perhaps I should have some tea?" he thought.) "Bring me some tea."

Pyotr made for the door. Ivan Ilyich was frightened by the prospect of being left alone. ("What can I do to keep him? Ah, yes; my medicine.")

"Pyotr, give me my medicine." ("Why not? It really might help.") He took a spoonful. ("No, it cannot help. Nonsense. Self-deception," he decided as soon as he again became conscious of that familiar sweetish, hopeless taste in his mouth. "I don't believe in it any more. But why, oh why must I suffer this pain? If it would only let up for a minute!") He gave a groan. Pyotr came back.

"No, go. Bring me some tea."

Pyotr went out. Left alone, Ivan Ilyich moaned less from pain, however agonizing it was, than from misery. "The same thing on and on, the same endless days and nights. If only it would come quickly! If only what would come quickly? Death, darkness. No, no! Anything is better than death!"

When Pyotr came back with the breakfast tray Ivan Ilyich looked at him in perplexity for some time, unable to comprehend who he was and what he wanted. Pyotr was disconcerted by this look. His disconcertment brought Ivan Ilyich to his senses.

"Oh, yes," said he. "Tea. Good. Put it

down. Only help me wash myself, and give me a clean shirt."

And Ivan Ilyich began to wash himself. Resting now and again, he washed his hands and face, brushed his teeth, combed his hair, and looked at himself in the mirror. He was horrified, especially horrified to see how his limp hair clung to his pale forehead. When his shirt was being changed he knew he would be even more horrified if he looked at his body, and so he did not look at it. At last everything was done. He put on a dressing-gown, threw a rug over his legs, and sat down in an armchair to have his tea. For a single moment he had felt refreshed, but as soon as he began to drink tea he again became conscious of his pain and the taste in his mouth. He forced himself to drink it and then lay down, stretching out his legs. He lay down and told Pyotr to go away.

The same thing all over again. One moment the glimmer of a drop of hope, the next a raging sea of despair, and always this pain, this pain, this misery, on and on. The misery is unbearable when he is alone, he wishes to call someone, but he knows beforehand that it will only be worse. "If they'd only give me morphine again to stop the pain. I must tell the doctor to think of something. This is impossible, impossible."

One hour, another hour passed in this way. The bell in the entrance hall rang. Perhaps the doctor. Yes, it was the doctor—healthy, fat, energetic, cheerful, wearing an expression that said, "Come, now; something has frightened you, but we'll have it all straight in a trice." The doctor knew that this expression was inappropriate here, but he had put it on once and for all and could no more change it than he could change the frock-coat he had donned in the morning before he had set out on his round of calls.

The doctor rubbed his hands together vigorously, comfortingly.

"I'm chilled. Dreadfully cold out. Wait a minute until I warm up," he said in a tone suggesting that it was necessary only to wait a minute until he warmed up and then he would put everything right.

"Well, how are you feeling?"

Ivan Ilyich was sure the doctor would have liked to say, "How's our tummy?" but felt it would be a little too waggish and changed it to "How did you spend the night?"

Ivan Ilyich looked at the doctor in a way that said, "Will you never feel ashamed of lying?" But the doctor did not wish to understand.

"In the same ghastly way," said Ivan Ilyich. "The pain never stops and never lessens. If only you would give me something!"

"Come, come, all you patients are the same. Well, now, I seem to have warmed up. Even Praskovya Fyodorovna, strict as she is, could not find fault with my temperature now. Well, good morning," and the doctor shook hands with him.

Throwing off all his playfulness, the doctor put on a serious face and began examining his patient, taking his pulse, his temperature, sounding his chest, listening to his heart.

Ivan Ilyich knew very definitely and without question that this was all nonsense, empty deception, but when the doctor got down on his knees in front of him and leaned over, placing his ear now lower, now higher, and went through all sorts of contortions with the gravest mien in the world, Ivan Ilyich fell under his spell, just as he had fallen under the spell of lawyers' speeches, even though he knew very well they were lying and even knew why they were lying.

The doctor was still on his knees on the sofa tapping his chest when a rustle of silk came from the doorway and Praskovya Fyodorovna was heard remonstrating with Pyotr for not having told her of the doctor's arrival.

She came in and kissed her husband and instantly began to explain that she had been up for a long time and it was just because of some misunderstanding that she had not been in the sick man's room when the doctor arrived.

Ivan Ilyich looked at her, he took in every detail of her person, and he resented her whiteness, her plumpness, the cleanliness of her arms and neck, the lustre of her hair and the shine of her eyes, so full of life. He hated her with every fibre of his being. Every time she touched him he felt an upsurge of hatred.

Her attitude towards him and his illness had not changed. Just as the doctor had developed an attitude towards his patients that he could not change, so she had developed an attitude towards him—that he was doing what he ought not to do and so he himself was to blame for his condition and her only recourse was to reprove him lovingly for it—and she could not change this attitude.

"He simply will not listen! He does not take his medicine regularly. And the worst thing is that he insists on lying in a position that surely must be bad for him—with his feet up in the air."

And she told how he made Gerasim hold up his feet.

The doctor gave a fond, condescending smile: "What is to be done about it? These patients of ours are always thinking of absurd tricks, but we have to forgive them."

When he had finished his examination the doctor glanced at his watch, and then Praskovya Fyodorovna announced to Ivan Ilyich that whether he liked it or not, she had asked a great celebrity to come and see him today and he and Mikhail Danilovich (that was the name of the ordinary doctor) would examine him together and hold a consultation.

"No protesting, if you please, I am doing this for my own sake," she said ironically, letting him know that she was doing it for his sake and had just said this to deprive him of

the right to protest. He frowned and said
nothing. He was aware that he was caught
in such a web of lies that it was impossible
to distinguish the true from the false. Everything she did for him was done entirely for
her own sake, and she told him she was doing
for her own sake what she actually was doing
for her own sake, representing it as something
so incredible that he would take it as meaning
just the opposite.

True enough, at half past eleven the celebrated doctor arrived. Again there were
soundings and professional talk in his
presence and in the other room about kidneys
and caecum, and questions and answers
uttered with as grave a mien as if instead of
the real question of life and death, which was
the only one confronting Ivan Ilyich now,
there had arisen a question of kidneys and
caecum that were not behaving themselves
and were therefore being taken in hand by
Mikhail Danilovich and the celebrity and
made to toe the line.

The celebrated doctor took leave of him
with a grave but not hopeless look. And when
Ivan Ilyich raised eyes glistening with fear
and hope and timidly asked him whether
there was any chance of recovery, he replied
that he could not say for sure, but there was
a chance. So touching was the gleam of hope
in Ivan Ilyich's eyes as they followed the
doctor to the door that Praskovya Fyodorovna broke down as she went out of the study

to give the celebrity his fee.

The doctor's encouragement caused his spirits to rise, but not for long. Again the same room, the same pictures, hangings, wallpaper, phials, and the same aching, suffering body. Ivan Ilyich began to groan. They gave him an injection and he fell into a state of oblivion.

When he roused it was twilight. They brought him his dinner. He forced himself to take some broth. Again everything the same; again the coming of night.

After dinner, at seven o'clock, Praskovya Fyodorovna came into the room in evening dress, with her full bosom laced up and traces of powder on her face. In the morning she had reminded him that they were going to the theatre. Sarah Bernhardt had come to town and they had taken a box at his own insistence. He had forgotten all about it and was hurt by the sight of her elaborate toilette. But he hid his feelings on remembering that he himself had insisted on their taking the box because he felt that the aesthetic enjoyment would have educational value for the children.

Praskovya Fyodorovna came in looking pleased with herself, yet with a slightly guilty air. She sat down and asked how he was feeling, merely, as he could see, for the sake of asking and not because she wanted to find out anything, for there was nothing to find out, and then she said what it was needful to say: that she would not think of going if it were not that the box was taken for the season and that Ellen and their daughter and Petrishchev (the examining magistrate who was their daughter's fiancé) were going and she could not let them go unchaperoned, but that she would much prefer sitting at home with him, and would he please be sure to do everything the doctor had told him to while she was away.

"And Fyodor Petrovich" (the fiancé) "wants to see you. May he come in? And Liza, too."

"Let them."

His daughter came in all dressed up, with much of her young body naked, making a show of it, while his body was causing him such torture. She was strong and healthy, evidently very much in love, and annoyed that his illness and suffering and death should cast a shadow upon her happiness.

Fyodor Petrovich came in wearing evening clothes and with his hair curled *à la Capoul*, his long, sinewy neck encircled by a stiff white collar, his chest covered by an expanse of white shirt-front, his strong calves sheathed in narrow black trousers, one hand encased in a white glove, the other holding an opera hat.

Behind him Ivan Ilyich's son, the schoolboy, slipped in unnoticed, all decked out in a new uniform, poor chap, and with gloves on his hands and those dreadful dark circles under his eyes that Ivan Ilyich knew the meaning of.

He had always felt sorry for his son. And now there was something dreadful for him in the boy's frightened, pitying glance. Ivan Ilyich felt that Vasya was the only one besides Gerasim who understood and pitied him.

They all sat down and asked him again how he felt. A pause. Liza asked her mother about the opera-glasses. This brought on a little tiff between mother and daughter as to which of them had mislaid them. Very unpleasant.

Fyodor Petrovich asked Ivan Ilyich if he had ever seen Sarah Bernhardt. At first Ivan Ilyich did not understand the question, then he said:

"No. Have you?"

"Yes. In *Adrienne Lecouvreur*."

Praskovya Fyodorovna said that she was particularly enchanting in something-or-other. The daughter objected. There began a discussion of the charm and naturalness of her acting, in which they said the same things that are always said on the subject.

In the middle of the conversation Fyodor Petrovich glanced at Ivan Ilyich and stopped talking. The others also glanced at him and stopped talking. Ivan Ilyich was staring in front of him with glittering eyes, unable to hide his resentment. Something had to be done, but nothing could be done. The silence had to be broken, but nobody dared to break it. They all began to fear that something might expose the lie that was being supported for decency's sake, and things would suddenly be seen in their true light. Liza was the first to pluck up courage. She broke the silence. She did it with the intention of hiding what everyone was feeling, but instead she gave it utterance.

"Well, *if we are going*, we must go," she said, glancing at her watch, which had been a present from her father, and smiling significantly but scarcely perceptibly at her young man about something that only they two were aware of. Then she got up with a rustle of silk.

They all got up, said good-bye, and went away.

Ivan Ilyich fancied he felt better when they were gone: at least the lie was gone, too—it had departed with them.

But the pain remained. The same old pain, the same old fear that made nothing harder, nothing easier. And it kept growing worse.

Again the time dragged on, minute by minute, hour by hour, just the same, without end, yet with the horror of the certain end growing upon him.

"Yes, send up Gerasim," he said in reply to Pyotr's question.

IX

It was late when his wife returned. She tiptoed into the room but he heard her. He opened his eyes and quickly closed them again. She wanted to send Gerasim out and sit beside him herself, but he opened his eyes and said:

"No, go away."

"Are you suffering very much?"

"It doesn't matter."

"Take some opium."

He consented and drank it. She went out.

Until three in the morning he was in a semiconscious state of torture. He fancied they were torturing him by trying to push him into a narrow black sack, and that they kept pushing him in deeper and deeper but could not push him to the bottom. And this dreadful business was causing him suffering. He was afraid, yet he wanted to get into the sack, and he simultaneously resisted and tried to get in. Suddenly he broke loose and fell and woke up. Gerasim was still sitting on the foot of the bed, drowsing quietly, patiently. And Ivan Ilyich was lying with his emaciated stockinged feet on the lad's shoulders. The candle was still burning behind the shade, and the pain was still with him.

"Go to bed, Gerasim," he whispered.

"That's all right, sir, I shall stay a while."

"No, go away."

He lowered his legs and turned over on his side and began to pity himself. He waited until Gerasim had gone into the next room, and then, letting himself go, cried like a baby. He cried because of his helplessness, because of his dreadful loneliness, because of the heartlessness of people and of God, and because of the absence of God.

"Why hast Thou done all this? Why didst Thou bring me into the world? What, oh what have I done that Thou shouldst torture me so?"

He did not expect an answer, and he cried because there was not and could not be any answer. The pain began again, but he did not stir, did not call anyone. He merely said to himself, "Very well, hit me again. Harder! But what for? What have I ever done to Thee?"

Then he grew quiet and not only stopped crying, but stopped breathing as well and was all attention: he seemed to be listening not to the speaking voice, but to the voice of his soul, to the stream of thought flowing through him.

"What do you want?" was the first concept sufficiently lucid to be expressed in words. "What do you want? What do you want?" he repeated to himself. "Not to suffer. To live," he replied.

And once more he was all attention, such strained attention that even his pain could not distract him.

"Live? Live how?" asked the voice of his soul.

"Live as I lived before; a good, pleasant life."

"And was your life so good and pleasant before?" asked the voice. And he began to go over in his mind the best moments of his pleasant life. But, strange as it may seem, all the best moments of his pleasant life no longer seemed to be what he had considered them. All, except the earliest memories of his childhood. In his childhood there had been something really pleasant, something worth living for, if it could have been brought back again. But the person who had experienced this pleasantness was no more. He seemed to be calling up memories of someone else.

As soon as his memories involved the person who turned out to be the present Ivan Ilyich, all that had once seemed joyful dissolved under his fixed attention and turned into something worthless and even disgusting.

The further away he went from his childhood and the closer he came to the present, the more worthless and dubious became his joy. This began with the school of jurisprudence. He had known things that were genuinely good there: he had known gaiety, friendship, and hope. But these good things grew more rare as he reached the higher classes. Later, during his first years of service as secretary to the governor, he had again known some good things; most of them had been connected with being in love. Then his life had grown complicated and the good things had decreased. Later on there was even less of the good, and the further he went, the less there was.

His marriage—such a chance marriage, and

the disillusionment, and the odour of his wife's breath, and the sensuality, and the pretence! And that lifeless profession of his, and the worry over money—year after year, one year, two, ten, twenty, without any change. And the longer it lasted, the more lifeless everything became. "As if I had been going steadily downhill, while I fancied I was going uphill. Yes, that is how it was. In the opinion of my fellows I was going uphill, but only to the extent that life itself was crumbling away under my feet. And now here I am, dying.

"What is happening? Why? Incredible. Incredible that my life should have been so disgusting and meaningless. But even if it was so disgusting and meaningless, why must I die, and die in such agony? Something must be wrong.

"Perhaps I did not live as I ought to have?" was an idea that came into his mind. "But it cannot be that I did not live as I ought to have, for I did everything as it ought to have been done," he said to himself, and instantly drove away this one answer to the whole problem of life and death, considering it utterly impossible.

"What do you want now? To live? To live how?

"As if you were in court, and the usher was crying out, 'The Judge is coming!' The Judge is coming, the Judge is coming!" he repeated to himself. "Here he is, the Judge.

But I am not to blame!'' he cried out indig-
nantly. "What am I to blame for?" And he
stopped crying, and, turning his face to the
wall, went on thinking of the same thing over
and over: "Why, for what reason, must I go
through all this horror?"

But think as he might, he could find no
answer. And whenever the thought occurred
to him (as it often did) that all of this was
because he had not lived as he ought to have,
he instantly drove away so preposterous
a thought by recalling how correctly he had
lived.

X

Two more weeks went by. Ivan Ilyich no
longer got up off the sofa. He lay on the sofa
because he did not want to lie in bed. And as
he lay there, mostly his face to the wall, he
suffered all alone the same inexplicable suffering, and pondered all alone the same inexplicable questions: "What is it? Can it really
be death?" And the inner voice answered,
"Yes, it really is." "But why this suffering?"
and the inner voice answered, "For no reason
at all." That was as far as it went—nothing
but this.

Ever since the very beginning of his illness,
since the day he first went to the doctor,
Ivan Ilyich's life had become divided between
two opposite moods that kept alternating one

with the other: one a mood of despair and the anticipation of a dreadful and incomprehensible death; the other a mood of hope, which led him to take a lively interest in observing the functions of his body. Now he saw before him a kidney or a caecum that was temporarily refusing to perform its duty; now he saw nothing but death, dreadful and unfathomable, from which there was no escape.

These two moods had alternated from the very beginning of his illness; but the further the illness progressed, the more fantastic and unlikely appeared his speculations on his kidneys and the more actual his consciousness of approaching death.

The mere remembrance of what he had been three months earlier and what he was now, the remembrance of how steadily he had been going downhill, was sufficient to destroy all possibility of hope.

During the last days of the solitude in which he lived, lying on the sofa with his face to the wall, of his solitude in the midst of the populous town, among all his many friends and relatives, a solitude that could not possibly have been more complete at the bottom of the sea or in the bowels of the earth—during the last days of that dreadful solitude Ivan Ilyich lived only in the past. One by one pictures of bygone days passed through his mind. They always began with something from the immediate past and went back to times more remote, to his childhood, and lingered there. If he recalled the stewed prunes he had been offered in the morning, he was sure to recall the sticky, wrinkled French prunes of his childhood, their peculiar taste, and the strong flow of saliva, caused by the sucking of their stones, and this memory of a taste brought a whole train of recollections of that time in its wake: nurse-maid, his brother, his toys. "I mustn't think of them ... it is too painful," Ivan Ilyich said to himself, and switched his thoughts to the present. The button on the back of the sofa and the fold in the morocco. "Morocco is expensive and does not wear well; I quarrelled with my wife over it. That time when we ripped papa's brief-case the morocco was different, and so was the row we had, and we were punished for it and mama brought us pastries." And again his thoughts centred on his childhood, and again he found them painful and tried to drive them away by thinking of something else.

And simultaneously with this train of memories, others pressed themselves upon him—memories of how his illness had begun and developed. And he felt that the further back he went into the past, the more vital his life had been. There had been more good-ness in his life earlier, and more vitality. The one merged with the other. "Just as my sufferings are growing worse and worse, so my whole life has grown worse and worse," he thought. There was only one bright spot, and that was back at the very beginning of life. After that things grew blacker and blacker, faster and faster. "In inverse ratio to the square of the distance separating me from death," thought Ivan Ilyich. And the metaphor of a stone falling with increasing velocity flashed into his mind. Life, a series of increasing sufferings, is falling faster and faster towards its goal, which is unspeakable suffering. "I am falling..." He started, shuddered, tried to resist; but he now knew there could be no resisting. And again, weary from contemplating, but unable to turn his eyes away from that which rose up in front of them, he stared at the back of the sofa and waited—waited for that fearful fall, the final shock, the destruction. "There is no resisting," he said to himself. "If I could only understand why it should be so! But that, too, was impossible. It might make some sense if I had not lived as I ought to have. But such an admission is impossible," he said to himself, remembering all the correctness, the decorum, the propriety of his life. "I cannot admit such a thing," he said to himself, drawing his lips apart as if someone could see his smile and be deceived by it. "There is no sense to it. Agony. Death. Why?"

XI

Another fortnight passed in this way. During that time the event he and his wife had hoped for occurred. Petrishchev made a formal proposal. It happened in the evening. The next morning Praskovya Fyodorovna came to her husband's room, going over in her mind how she would announce the proposal to him, but during the night Ivan Ilyich had undergone a change for the worse. Praskovya Fyodorovna found him on the same sofa, but in a different position. He was lying on his back, groaning and staring before him with a fixed gaze.

She began to speak to him about his medicine. He turned his eyes upon her. She did not finish what she was saying, so great was the hatred—the hatred of her—that she read in his eyes.

"For God's sake, let me die in peace," he said.

She made as if to go out, but at that moment their daughter came in and went over to say good-morning to him. He looked at her just as he had looked at his wife, and when she asked him how he felt he answered dryly that they would soon be rid of him. Both of them were silent, sat down for a moment, then went out.

"Why are we to blame?" Liza asked her mother. "You might think it was our fault.

I feel sorry for papá but why should he torture us so?"

The doctor came at the usual time. Ivan Ilyich answered "Yes" and "No" without taking his glowering eyes off him, and towards the end he said:

"You know perfectly well you can't help me at all; leave me alone."

"We can lessen your suffering," said the doctor.

"No, you can't even do that; leave me alone."

The doctor went into the drawing-room and told Praskovya Fyodorovna that his condition was very bad and there was only one thing, opium, that could relieve his suffering, which must be dreadful.

The doctor said his physical suffering must be dreadful and so it was; but more dreadful than his physical suffering was his moral suffering; in this lay his real torment.

His moral suffering came from having, that night, gazed at the sleepy, good-humoured, broad face of Gerasim and thought: "What if all my life, all my mature life, really has not been what it ought to have been?"

He was struck by the thought that what had formerly seemed to him utterly impossible (that his life had been spent not as it ought to have been) might be true. He was struck by the thought that those scarcely perceptible impulses to struggle against what people in high position considered good, scarcely perceptible impulses which he had always suppressed, might be the real thing, and all the rest might be aside from the real thing. His official duties, his manner of living, his family, his social and professional interests—all of these might be aside from the real thing. He attempted a defence of these things, but suddenly he became aware of the worthlessness of what he was defending. There was nothing to defend.

"If that is the case," he said to himself, "and I am taking leave of life with the realization that I have squandered all that was given to me, and that it is too late to do anything about it—what then?" He lay on his back and began reviewing his life from an entirely different point of view.

When, in the morning, he saw first the footman, then his wife, then his daughter, and at last the doctor, their every movement, their every word, confirmed the dreadful truth revealed to him in the night. In them he saw himself, saw all that had formed his life, and saw clearly that all of this was aside from the real thing, that it was all a dreadful and enormous deception hiding the truths of life and death. This realization increased his physical sufferings, multiplied them tenfold. He moaned and tossed and clutched at his clothes. His clothes seemed to be squeezing him, suffocating him, and he hated them.

He was given a big dose of opium that

made him fall into oblivion, but at dinner-time it all began again. He drove everyone out and lay tossing on the bed.

His wife came to him and said:

"*Jean*, dear, do this for me." (For me?) "It cannot do you any harm and it often helps. It doesn't mean anything. And even well people sometimes—"

He looked at her wide-eyed.

"What? Take the sacrament? Why? I don't want to. And yet..."

She began to cry.

"Won't you, dear? I'll send for our priest, he is such a good man."

"Very well. Excellent," he said.

When the priest came and had heard his confession, the heart of Ivan Ilyich was softened, he seemed to be relieved of his doubts, and this brought him relief from his sufferings, and for a moment he had hope. Again he began to think of his caecum and the possibility of curing it. There were tears in his eyes as he took the sacrament.

When they laid him down again after the sacrament he felt better for a moment, and he was filled once more with the hope of recovery.

He thought of the operation the doctor had suggested performing. "I want to live, to live," he said to himself. His wife came in to congratulate him; she said the usual things, and then added:

"You really do feel better, don't you?"

"Yes," he said without looking at her.

Her dress, her figure, the expression of her face, the sound of her voice—everything said to him: "Aside from the real thing. Everything that has been and still is your life is a lie and a deception hiding the reality of life and death from you." And the minute this thought came to him, hatred rose within him; and with the hatred, agonizing physical suffering; and with the suffering, the realization of his imminent and inevitable end. New sensations put in an appearance: something inside of him began to twist and snap and choke the breath out of him.

The expression of his face when he pronounced that "yes" was terrible. And having pronounced it, looking her straight in the eye, he flung himself down on his face with a swiftness incredible in anyone as weak as he was, and shrieked:

"Go away! Go away! Leave me alone!"

XII

From that moment there began three days of such terrible and uninterrupted shrieking that even two rooms away one could not hear it without shuddering. The moment he had replied to his wife's question he had understood that all was over, that there was no hope, that the end, the very end, was at hand, that all his doubts remained doubts and would never be answered.

"Ah! Ah! Ah!" he shrieked in different tones. He had begun by shouting, "I don't wa-a-nt to!" and had gone on shouting that "Ah!"

Throughout those three days, which for him were timeless, he struggled in that black sack that some invisible and irresistible force was pushing him into. He struggled as one who is condemned to death and knows there is no hope of escape struggles in the arms of the executioner. And he realized that with every minute, despite the desperateness of his struggle, he was coming closer and closer to that which terrified him. He felt that his torture was caused by his being pushed into that black hole, but even more by his being unable to crawl into it himself. He was prevented from crawling into it by the belief that his life had been a good one. This defence of the life he had lived was the hindrance that kept him from moving ahead, and it caused him more torture than anything else.

Suddenly some force struck him in the chest and the side and cut off his breath; he plunged straight into the hole, and there, at the end of the hole, he found a glimmer of light. He had the sensation he had once experienced while riding in a railway carriage, when he had thought he was moving forward and was actually moving backward and suddenly became aware of the true direction.

"Yes, it is all aside from the real thing,"

he said to himself. "But that is all right. I can still make it the real thing. But what is the real thing?" he asked himself, and suddenly grew quiet.

This took place at the end of the third day, an hour before his death. Just then his son crept into his room and up to his bed. The dying man was still screaming wildly and throwing his arms about. One hand fell on the head of his son. The boy seized it, pressed it to his lips, and began to cry. It was just at this moment that Ivan Ilyich plunged into the hole and saw the light, and it was revealed to him that his life had not been what it ought to have been, but he could still mend matters. "What is the real thing?" he asked himself, and grew quiet, listening. It was then he realized that someone was kissing his hand. He opened his eyes and looked at his son. He was filled with pity for him. His wife came in. He glanced at her. She stood looking at him with her mouth hanging open, with the tears unwiped on her nose and cheeks, with an expression of despair on her face. He was filled with pity for her.

"I am torturing them," he thought. "They feel sorry for me, but things will be better for them when I am gone." He wanted to tell them this, but lacked the strength. "But what is the use of speaking? I must do something," he thought. He turned to his wife and indicated his son with his eyes.

"Take him away," he said. "Poor boy ...

and you..." He wanted to add, "Forgive", and it came out, "Forget", but he had not the strength to correct himself; he merely gave a little wave of his hand, knowing that the one who was to understand would understand.

And presently it became clear to him that all he had been tortured by and been unable to throw off, was now falling away of itself, falling away on two sides, ten sides, all sides at once. He felt sorry for them, he must do something to ease their pain. He must relieve them and himself of this suffering. "How good and how simple!" he thought. "And the pain?" he asked himself. "How am I to dispose of it? Here, where are you, pain?"

He felt for the pain.

"Ah, here it is. What of it? Let it be."

"And death? Where is death?"

He searched for his accustomed terror of death and could not find it. Where was death? What was death? There was no fear because there was no death.

There was light instead of death.

"So that is it!" he suddenly said out loud. "What happiness!"

All of this took place in an instant, but the significance of that instant was lasting. For those present his death agony continued for another two hours. Something rattled in his throat; his emaciated body twitched. But gradually the wheezing and the rattling ceased.

"All is over," someone said.

He heard these words and repeated them in his soul.

"Death is over," he said to himself. "There is no more death."

He drew in a deep breath, broke off in the middle of it, stretched out his limbs, and died.

1886

THE KREUTZER SONATA

> "...But I say unto you, That whosoever looketh on a woman to lust after her hath committed adultery with her already in his heart."
>
> Math. 5; 28.
>
> "His disciples say unto him, If the case of the man be so with his wife, it is not good to marry. But he said unto them, All men cannot receive this saying, save they to whom it is given. For there are some eunuchs, which were so born from their mother's womb: and there are some eunuchs, which were made eunuchs of men: and there be eunuchs, which have made themselves eunuchs for the kingdom of heaven's sake. He that is able to receive it, let him receive it."
>
> Math. 19; 10, 11, 12.

I

It was early spring. We had been travelling for almost two days. Passengers who were going short distances kept entering and leaving the carriage, but three, like myself, had been travelling since the train set out. One of them was an unattractive middle-aged woman with a haggard look, who smoked cigarettes and wore a mannish coat and hat; another was an acquaintance of hers, a loquacious man of about forty, with tidy new luggage; the third was a gentleman who held himself aloof. He was of middle height, his movements were impulsive, he was not yet old but his curly hair had turned prematurely grey, and his eyes had an unusual shine to them and kept darting quickly from one object to another. He was wearing an astrakhan cap and an old coat with an astrakhan collar that had evidently been made by an expensive tailor. When he unfastened his coat one caught a glimpse of a Russian jacket and a Russian blouse with an embroidered collar. A peculiarity of this gentleman lay in his making odd sounds from time to time that resembled the clearing of one's throat or the breaking out into a laugh that was instantly stifled.

Throughout the journey this gentleman painstakingly avoided all talk and contact with other passengers. He made curt, brusque answers whenever spoken to and spent his time reading, gazing out of the window, smoking, or rummaging for food in his old sack and then having tea or a snack.

Fancying that he was oppressed by his solitude I made several attempts to talk to him, but each time our eyes met (and this occurred frequently, since we were sitting opposite each other) he turned away and either picked up a book or looked out of the window.

During a prolonged stop at a big station on the evening of the second day, this nervous gentleman went out for boiling water and

made himself some tea. The man with the
tidy luggage (a lawyer, as I learned later) and
his friend, the woman who smoked and was
wearing a mannish coat, went to have tea in
the station restaurant.

During the absence of the lady and gentleman several new passengers entered our
carriage, among them a tall, clean-shaven,
wrinkled old man, apparently a merchant, in
a fur-lined coat and a cloth cap with an
enormous peak. The merchant took a seat
opposite the place where the lawyer and
the woman had been sitting and instantly
entered into conversation with a young man
who had the appearance of being a shop
assistant and had also just entered the carriage.

I was sitting obliquely opposite, and since
the train was standing still, caught snatches
of their conversation when people were not
passing to and fro. The merchant announced
that he was on his way to his estate, only one
station away, then they launched into the
usual discussion of trade and prices, which led
them to the usual observations on the Moscow
market and the Nizhni-Novgorod fair. The
shop   assistant   began   to   describe   the
debaucheries at the fair of some rich tradesman whom they both knew, but the old man
interrupted by telling him about the debaucheries in Kunavino in which he himself had
taken part.

He was evidently proud of having taken
part in them, and with a gloating look on his

face told how he and that same acquaintance had done something when they were both drunk that had to be described in a whisper; the shop assistant burst out into a roar of laughter that filled the whole carriage, and the old man laughed too, revealing two long yellow teeth.

Not expecting to hear anything of interest, I got up with the intention of taking a walk on the station platform until the train left. In the doorway I met the lawyer and the woman, who were holding an animated conversation.

"No time for a walk," the sociable lawyer said to me. "The second bell will ring any moment now."

And true enough, before I had gone the length of the train the last bell rang. I returned to find the lawyer and the woman talking as animatedly as ever. The old merchant was sitting in silence across from them, staring fixedly in front of him and showing his disapproval by giving a chew on his two teeth from time to time.

"And so she simply announced to her husband," the lawyer was saying with a smile as I walked past, "that she could not and would not live with him any more because—"

But the rest was lost. Other passengers came in after me, then the conductor, then an artisan ran past, and for some time there was so much noise and confusion that I could not hear what was being said.

When things quieted down and the lawyer's voice was carried to me again, his account of a particular case had led to a discussion of a general situation. The lawyer was saying that the question of divorce was occupying public opinion in Europe, and that cases of divorce were becoming more and more common in Russia. On noticing that his was the only voice to be heard, he turned to the old man.

"It was not like that in the old days, was it?" he said with a pleasant smile.

The old man was just about to answer when the train started up and he took off his cap, crossed himself, and began to say a prayer under his breath. The lawyer courteously turned his eyes away and waited for him to finish. When the old man had finished praying and had crossed himself three times, he put his cap on very straight, pulled it down tightly, settled himself in his seat, and began to speak.

"There were such cases in the old days, but they were fewer," he said. "But it is only to be expected these days. People are getting too much education."

The train went clattering as it gathered speed, making it hard for me to hear, and since I found the matter interesting, I took a seat closer to the speakers.

My neighbour, the nervous gentleman with the glittering eyes, also seemed to find it interesting, for, without leaving his seat, he strained forward to listen.

"Is it wrong to get an education?" the woman said with a faint smile. "Do you think it is better to get married as people used to, with the bride and bridegroom never even seeing each other before the wedding?" she went on, replying, in the manner of many women, not to what the other person had said, but to what she thought he would say. "They married whoever came along without knowing whether they loved each other or ever could love each other, and then suffered tortures for the rest of their lives. Do you think that was better?" she said, obviously appealing to me and the lawyer rather than to the old man.

"It's a great deal of education they're getting these days," repeated the merchant, looking contemptuously at the woman and letting her question go unanswered.

"And what connection do you find between education and unhappy marriages?" asked the lawyer with a faint smile.

The merchant was about to reply when the woman interrupted.

"Oh no, those times have gone for ever," she said.

"Wait, let him tell us what he thinks," put in the lawyer.

"Education brings a lot of foolishness with it," said the old man decisively.

"They make people marry who do not love each other, and then are amazed to find them unhappy together," said the woman hurriedly, glancing at me and the lawyer and even the shop assistant, who had got up and was standing leaning on the back of the seat and listening with a smile on his face. "It is only animals that can be mated at their master's will; human beings have their own tastes and preferences," she said, evidently wishing to be cutting to the old man.

"What you are saying is not right, madam," said the old man. "Animals are beasts; human beings have the law to go by."

"And how do you propose that a person is to live with one he doesn't love?" said the woman, anxious to air ideas which she seemed to consider novel.

"Formerly no such distinctions were made," said the old man weightily. "That's a new-fangled idea. You never used to hear her say, 'I'll up and leave you.' Even the peasants have caught on to the new style. 'Here,' she says, 'take your shirts and breeches; I'm going off with Vanya—his hair is curlier.' And there you are. It's fear that should rule a woman's heart."

The shop assistant looked from the lawyer to me, and from me to the woman, suppressing a smile and ready to either approve or laugh at the merchant's views, depending on how they were received.

"Fear of what?" asked the woman.

"What? Of her husband, that's what."

"Well, my good man, the time for that is past," said the woman testily.

"No, madam, that time will never be past. Eve was made out of the rib of the man, and so she will remain to the end of time," said the old man so sternly and with such a convincing shake of his head that the shop assistant instantly decided he had won the victory and gave a loud guffaw.

"It's only you men who think like that," said the woman, with a look that said she had not given in. "You've taken all the freedom for yourselves and want to keep us women in jail. You give yourselves the right to do anything you like."

"Nobody gives us the right, but there's no increase in the household from what a man does, while a woman's a weak creature," went on the old man in the same impressive tone.

This tone seemed to convince his listeners; the woman felt that her cause was damaged, but even so she did not surrender.

"But surely you must admit that a woman is a human being too and has feelings just as a man has. What is she to do if she does not love her husband?"

"Doesn't love him?" repeated the merchant grimly, drawing down his brows and lips. "But she'll come to love him!"

This unexpected answer particularly tickled the shop assistant and he let out a cry of approbation.

"No she won't," said the woman. "If she doesn't love him, she cannot be forced to."

"And what if a wife is not true to her husband?" asked the lawyer.

"That is not to be allowed," said the old man. "One has to keep a sharp eye out for that."

"But if it happens, what then? After all, it does happen."

"Perhaps it does among some people, but not among our class," said the old man.

No one said a word. The shop assistant shifted his feet, moved closer, smiled, and began to speak, as if anxious not to be left out of the conversation.

"There was a scandal in my employer's family once. And very hard it was to place the blame. The son's wife turned out to be a loose woman. She began her tricks. He was an able, respectable young man. First she had an affair with the bookkeeper. He tried to bring her round by talking to her. Did no good. She was very nasty. Began stealing his money. He beat her. Only made her worse. She had an affair with one of the unbaptized—that is, with a Jew, if you don't mind my saying so. What was he to do? He left her. Lives as a bachelor to this day, and she leads a loose life."

"He was a fool," said the old man. "If he had given her no rope from the very first and if he had drawn her up short as he ought to have, she would no doubt be living with him to this day. It's wrong to let them have their own way from the very beginning.

'Don't trust a horse in the pasture or a wife in the home!' "

Just then the conductor came to collect the tickets for the next station. The old man handed him his.

"Yes, the fair sex has to be taken in hand from the very outset, otherwise everything is lost."

"And what about the tale you told a while back about the way you married men carried on at the fair in Kunavino?" I could not resist saying.

"That's a different matter," said the merchant, and shut up like a clam.

When the whistle blew the old man got up, dragged his sack out from under the seat, folded his greatcoat round him, lifted his cap, and went out.

II

As soon as he was gone, several voices spoke simultaneously.

"A man of the old school," said the shop assistant.

"A patriarchal despot," said the woman. "What primitive ideas he has about the women and marriage!"

"Hm, we're way behind European views on marriage," said the lawyer.

"The main thing that such people fail to understand," said the woman, "is that a marriage without love is no marriage at all, that only love sanctifies marriage, and that the only true marriage is that sanctified by love."

The shop assistant smiled as he listened, trying to memorize as many of these clever observations as he could for future use.

In the middle of what the woman was saying I heard something behind me that sounded like a stifled laugh or sob, and turning round saw my neighbour, the lonely grey-haired gentleman with the glittering eyes. We had not noticed that during our conversation he had drawn closer, evidently interested in what we were saying. He was standing leaning on the back of the seat and seemed to be very much agitated. His face was red and a muscle on one of his cheeks was twitching.

"Just what is that love ... that love ... that love that sanctifies marriage?" he stuttered.

Seeing his agitation, the woman answered him gently and seriously.

"True love. If such love exists between a man and woman, then marriage is possible," she said.

"Yes, but how are we to understand what true love is?" said the gentleman with the glittering eyes hesitantly, with a self-conscious smile.

"Everyone knows what true love is," said the woman, evidently anxious to end the conversation.

"Not I," said the gentleman. "It is necessary to define what you have in mind."

"That's simple enough," said the woman, but she stopped and considered. "Love? Love is the preferring of one person to all others," she said.

"A preference lasting how long? A month? Two days? Half an hour?" said the grey-haired gentleman with a laugh.

"But wait, perhaps you are thinking of something quite different."

"No, I am thinking of the same thing."

"She means to say," put in the lawyer, "that marriage should spring, first of all, from devotion—love, if you wish—and that only if this exists can marriage be looked upon as something ... er ... sacred, so to speak. Further, that any marriage which is not founded on this mutual devotion—love, if you wish—does not carry any moral obligations. Have I understood you correctly?" he said, turning to the woman.

The woman nodded.

"And then..." said the lawyer, but he was cut short by the gentleman, whose eyes were now burning like coals and whose agitation had reached such a pitch that he could no longer restrain himself.

"That is precisely what I am talking about—the preferring of one man or woman to all others, but what I am asking is—for how long?"

"For how long? For very long, sometimes

for a whole lifetime," said the woman with a shrug of her shoulders.

"But that only happens in novels, never in life. In life this preference for one person lasts in rare cases for years, more often for a few months, sometimes for mere weeks or days or hours," he said, obviously aware that he was shocking everyone by his opinion and pleased to be doing so.

"What are you saying! Nothing of the sort. But listen—" the three of us protested in one voice. Even the shop assistant let out a grunt of disapproval.

"Oh, yes, I know," cried the grey-haired gentleman in a voice that drowned us all out. "You are speaking about what is thought to exist; I am speaking about what actually does exist! Every man experiences what you call love whenever he sees a beautiful woman."

"But it is dreadful, what you say! After all, there is a feeling between people that is called love and which lasts not months and years, but a lifetime."

"No, no, there is no such thing! If we admit the possibility of man's preferring a certain woman all his life, it is more than probable that the woman prefers someone else. That is the situation as it is and always has been," he said, taking out a cigarette-case and lighting up.

"But it is possible for the feeling to be mutual," said the lawyer.

"No, it is not," the other retorted. "It is

no more possible than for two peas, selected beforehand, to fall next to each other when a whole waggon is being loaded with peas. Besides, in the case of a man and woman it is not so much the law of probability as the fact of satiation that determines things. To love one man or one woman all one's life— why, that would be the same as to expect a single candle to burn a lifetime," he said, drawing greedily on his cigarette.

"But you are speaking only of carnal love. Do you not admit of love based on a unity of ideas, on spiritual affinity?" asked the woman.

"Spiritual affinity! Unity of ideas!" he echoed, again making the sound I had noticed. "In that case, there is no reason for sleeping together (forgive my bluntness). Who ever heard of unity of ideas leading people to sleep together?" he said with a nervous laugh.

"But wait," said the lawyer. "Facts contradict your contention. We see that conjugal relations exist, that all mankind, or at least the majority, live in this way, and that many live a faithful married life to the end of their days."

The grey-haired gentleman laughed again.

"First you say that marriage is based on love, and when I express my doubt as to the existence of any but carnal love, you prove the existence of love by pointing to the existence of marriage. These days marriage is nothing but deception!"

"Oh, no; I protest," said the lawyer. "The only thing I said was that marriages exist and have always existed."

"True. But on what basis do they exist? They exist and always have existed among people who see something holy in marriage, a holiness that involves duties for which they are answerable to God. Among such people they exist, but not among people of our class. Among us, people get married without seeing in marriage anything but copulation, and therefore their marriages turn out to be either violence or deception. Deception is the lesser of the two evils. The husband and wife deceive others into thinking they are living in monogamy, when actually they are living in polygamy. That is foul, but tolerable. But when, as is usually the case, the husband and wife take upon themselves the obligation of living together all their lives, and after the first month hate each other and long to separate and still go on living together, it results in that unspeakable torture that drives people to drink, to commit suicide, to kill and poison themselves and each other," he said with growing agitation, speaking faster and faster, as if afraid somebody might put in a word. When he finished there was an awkward silence.

"Oh, yes; unquestionably there are critical moments in married life," said the lawyer, hoping thereby to put an end to this excited, unseemly talk.

"I see you have recognized me?" said the grey-haired gentleman softly and with a semblance of composure.

"No, I have not had the pleasure of—"

"Hardly a pleasure. I am Pozdnyshev, the one who went through the critical moment you mentioned and killed his wife in doing so," he said, casting a swift glance at each of us.

Finding nothing to say, we all sat silent.

"It doesn't matter," he said, making that strange sound again. "But I must beg your pardon. I ... er ... do not wish to embarrass you."

"Come, I say..." put in the lawyer, not knowing himself what he meant by that "I say".

Ignoring him, Pozdnyshev turned quickly and went back to his seat. The lawyer and the woman whispered together. I, who sat next to Pozdnyshev, said nothing. It was too dark to read and so I closed my eyes and pretended to fall asleep. In this way we travelled in silence as far as the next station.

There the lawyer and the woman changed to another carriage, as they had arranged with the conductor to do. The shop assistant lay down on the bench and fell asleep. Pozdnyshev smoked endless cigarettes and drank the tea he had made while the train was at the previous station.

When I opened my eyes and glanced at him, he suddenly addressed himself to me in an irritated determined tone.

"Perhaps you find it disagreeable to be in my company now that you know who I am? If so, I will leave you."

"Oh, not at all."

"In that case, perhaps you will have some? But it's very strong," he said as he poured me out some tea. "Talk, talk ... and nothing but lies."

"What are you referring to?" I asked.

"The same thing: that love of theirs, and what it really is. Are you very tired?"

"Not at all."

"Then if you like I shall tell you how I was led to do what I did by that same love."

"If you don't find it too painful."

"I find it more painful to say nothing. Drink your tea. Or is it too strong?"

The tea was indeed like beer, but I drank a glass. Just then the conductor passed by. My companion followed him with burning eyes and waited until he was gone to begin his story.

III

"Well, then, I shall tell you. Are you sure you want me to?"

I repeated that I did. He waited a minute, rubbed his face with his hands, and began.

"If I am to tell it at all, I must begin from the very beginning; I must tell you why I got married and what I was like before my marriage.

"Before my marriage I lived like everyone else—everyone, that is, of our class. I am a landlord with a master's degree from the university, and I was a Marshal of Nobility. Before my marriage I lived like everyone else—which means I lived a life of profligacy, and like all the people of our class I was sure that in living such a life I was doing the right thing. I considered myself a good sort, quite a decent fellow. I was not a seducer, had no depraved tastes, and did not make this the main interest of my life as many men of my age did; I indulged my lust in a dignified, decorous way, merely for the sake of my health. I avoided women who might become an encumbrance by having babies or forming too strong an attachment. As a matter of fact there may have been babies and strong attachments, but I shut my eyes to them. And I not only looked upon this as highly moral; I was even proud of it."

He stopped and made the sound he seemed to be in the habit of making whenever a new thought occurred to him.

"And that is the most foul thing of all," he cried. "Depravity does not lie in the physical act; there is nothing depraved about the physical act; depravity—true depravity—lies in the shaking off of all moral responsibility in respect to the woman with whom you enter into physical relations. And I counted it a feather in my cap that I was able to shake off this moral responsibility. I remember the pangs of conscience I once suffered because I had forgotten to pay a woman who, having apparently fallen in love with me, gave herself to me. I regained my equanimity only when I had sent her the money, thereby releasing myself from all moral responsibility in respect to her. Do not nod your head as if you agreed with me," he suddenly shouted. "I know better. You, you, all of you—you are all the same, unless you are some rare exception. At your best you hold the same views as I held. But what of it? Forgive me," he said. "I cannot help it; it is so dreadful, dreadful, dreadful."

"What is so dreadful?" I asked.

"That abyss of error in which we live so far as women and our relations to them are concerned. No, I cannot speak calmly on this subject, and not so much because that 'critical moment' as that gentleman called it occurred in my life, as because ever since it occurred my eyes have been opened and I have seen things in an entirely different light. Everything inside out, inside out!"

He lighted a cigarette, leaned over with his elbows on his knees, and resumed. I could not see his face in the darkness, but I could hear his earnest, pleasant voice speaking above the rattle of the railway carriage.

IV

"Yes, it was only after suffering as I suffered, only because of that, that I realized wherein lie the roots of the evil, realized how things ought to be, and beheld all the horror of things as they are.

"And now allow me to tell you how and when everything began that led me to that critical moment. It began when I was in my sixteenth year. It happened when I was still a gymnasium student and my elder brother was in the first year of the university. I was still a virgin, but, like all the unfortunate children of our class, I was not innocent. For two years I had been under the demoralizing influence of other boys. I already knew the torment of woman—not some particular woman, but woman in general, as something sweetly tantalizing—every woman, and the nakedness of woman. I was not pure in my solitude. I suffered the tortures that ninety-nine per cent of our boys suffer. I was horrified, I suffered, I prayed, I succumbed. I sinned in fact and in fancy, but I had not yet taken the final step. I was ruining myself, but I had not yet laid a hand on any other creature. But one evening a friend of my brother's, a student, very jolly, one of those 'good fellows', who teach others to drink and play cards and are really rogues of the first order—this friend of my brother's suggested after a drinking-party that we go 'there'. We went. My brother was also a virgin and had his fall on that same night. I, a fifteen-year-old boy, sullied myself and was party to the sullying of a woman without comprehending what I was doing. Never had I heard from my elders that what I was doing was wrong. And no one hears it today. True, the ten commandments tell us it is wrong, but the only reason we have to know the ten commandments is so that we can give the correct answer to the priest when we take our examinations in Bible Study, and even so the knowledge is not very important, much less important than knowing the use of 'ut' in conditional clauses.

"And so not a single one of my elders whose opinion I valued had ever told me that what I was doing was wrong. On the contrary, I heard people whom I respected say it was right. I heard that my struggles and tortures would be eased after I had done it. I heard this and I read it, heard my elders say it was good for the health; I heard my companions say it was the right thing and the smart thing to do. And so on the whole I could see nothing bad in it. The danger of infection? This had all been foreseen. A solicitous government had taken measures in this respect. It saw to it that brothels were under surveillance so that schoolboys might indulge their lust in safety. It paid doctors a salary to see to this. And that was only natural. Since it assumed that profligacy was good for the health, it had to create conditions insuring a nice, clean sort of profligacy. I have known mothers who saw to these matters for their sons. Science itself sends young men to brothels."

"Science?" I said.

"Are not doctors scientists? Priests of science. Who is it that depraves our youth by asserting that their health demands it? They do. And then they set about with grave faces to cure syphilis!"

"Why shouldn't they cure syphilis?"

"Because if one-hundredth of the effort which is expended on the curing of syphilis were devoted to the wiping out of profligacy syphilis would have disappeared long ago. But our efforts are expended not on the wiping out of profligacy, but on the encouraging of it, on making it safe. But that is not the point. The point is that I, like nine-tenths (if not more) of the youth not only of my class but of all classes including the peasantry, sinned not because there was some particular woman whose charms I could not resist: No, there was no woman who seduced me, I sinned because of the society in which I lived; I sinned because some of the people around me looked upon my sin as a proper measure for insuring my health, and others looked upon it as a natural form of amusement for a young man, and found it not only pardonable, but even quite innocent. I myself did not regard it as a sin; I simply began to indulge in what was partly a pleasure, partly the satisfying of a need characteristic (or so I was told) of a certain age; I began to indulge my lust as I had earlier begun to smoke and drink. And yet there was something touching and exceptional about this first fall. I remember that at the time, before I had even gone out of the room, a great sadness came over me and I wanted to weep—to weep for my lost innocence, to weep for a relationship with women that was gone for ever. Yes, a natural, simple relationship was gone for ever. From that time on it was not and could not be pure. I became what is called a lecher. And to be a lecher means to be in a physical state corresponding to that of a drunkard, a smoker, or a dope addict. Just as a drunkard, a smoker, or a dope addict is not a normal person, so a man who has taken several women for the sake of his pleasure is not a normal person, is a person spoiled for all time, is a lecher. And just as a drunkard or a dope addict can be recognized by his face and behaviour, so a lecher can be recognized. A lecher can resist, can struggle against his vice, but never again can he know a pure, bright, simple relation to women—a brotherly relation. A lecher can instantly be recognized by the way in which he looks at a young woman. And I became a lecher and have remained one, and that is what brought about my ruin."

V

"Things went on in this way for some time, during which I took up new aspects of the same experience. Good God! The remembrance of all my bestiality fills me with horror! I remember myself as one whom my comrades laughed at for my so-called innocence. And the gilded youth! The officers! The Parisians! I remember all of these gentlemen and myself—thirty-year-old profligates, guilty of hundreds of the most dreadful and various crimes against women. I remember how we thirty-year-old profligates strutted about, well-scrubbed and clean-shaven, in spotless linen, scented, in frock-coats and uniforms, in drawing-rooms and ball-rooms—so handsome!—very symbols of purity!

"Just consider for a moment how things ought to be and how they are. When such a gentleman comes to see my sister or daughter, I, who know what sort of life he leads, ought to go up to him, draw him aside, and say quietly, 'Listen, my dear fellow, I know the sort of life you lead, where and with whom you spend your nights. This is no place for you. There are pure and innocent girls here. Go away.' That is how it ought to be. But actually when such a gentleman turns up and begins to dance with my daughter or sister, putting his arm round her waist, we rejoice if he is a gentleman with means and connections.

He may yet favour my daughter with his attentions after his night at Rigolbouche! It makes no difference even if he is tainted or diseased. Nowadays they know how to cure such things. Why, I know several girls from well-known families whose parents were delighted to give them in marriage to syphilitics! How vile! How loathsome! Surely the time will come when this vileness and deception will be exposed."

He made his odd sound several times and set to drinking tea. It was fearfully strong and there was no water with which to dilute it. I definitely felt the effects of the two glasses I had drunk. He must have felt them too, for he grew more and more excited. His voice became more expressive and sing-song. He kept shifting his position, now taking off his hat, now putting it on, and odd changes of expression crossed his face in the half-shadow in which we were sitting.

"And so that is how I lived to the age of thirty, without relinquishing for a moment my intention of marrying and setting down to the most pure and elevated family life, and with this purpose in mind I kept my eye out for a suitable girl," he went on. "At the same time that I was wallowing in the muck of fornication, I was looking for a girl whose purity would make her worthy of being my wife. I turned down many of them just because they were not pure enough for me. At last I found one whom I considered worthy. She was one of two daughters of a landlord from Penza who had once been very wealthy but had lost most of his money.

"One night as we were returning home in the moonlight after spending the day boating, and I was sitting beside her gazing with admiration at her graceful form encased in a tight woolen jersey, and at her curly hair, I suddenly decided that she was the one. That evening I fancied she understood all my thoughts and feelings, and that they were on the most elevated plane. As a matter of fact it was only that the jersey and the curls were most becoming to her and that after being so close to her all day long I wanted to be even closer.

"It is astonishing how complete can be the illusion that beauty is good. A beautiful woman may talk rot and you listen and fancy she is saying clever things instead of rot. She says and does vile things and you find them charming. And if by any chance she says pretty things instead of rot and vileness, you are instantly convinced that she is a very paragon of goodness and wisdom.

"I returned home in a state of rapture, convinced that she was moral perfection itself, and that therefore she was worthy to become my wife. On the next day I proposed to her.

"But just see the falseness of it all! Of a thousand men who get married (unfortunately men not only from our class but from the

lower classes as well), hardly one can be
found who has not been previously married
at least ten times, and perhaps a hundred or
a thousand, like Don Juan. True, I have heard
and observed that nowadays there are pure
men who know and feel that this is a great
and profound act and not a trifling matter.
May God give them His blessing! But in my
day there was not one of that sort in ten
thousand. And everybody knows this and
pretends not to know it. All the novels give
detailed descriptions of the hero's feelings,
of the flowers and pools beside which he
strolls, but in describing the great love the
handsome hero feels for some young lady,
they say nothing about how he spent his
time previously—nothing of the brothels,
the parlourmaids, the cooks, the wives of
other men. And whenever such indecent
novels are written, they are not given into the
hands of those who most need to read them
and learn about such things, that is, into the
hands of innocent young ladies. At first their
elders would have the young ladies believe
there is no such thing as the licentiousness
making up half the life of our towns and even
our villages; later they become so accustomed
to this pretence that in the end they themselves, like the English, come to believe
sincerely that they are people of high moral
principles living in a highly moral world.
And the young ladies, poor things, believe
this very seriously. My unfortunate wife was

just such a young lady. I remember showing her my diary when I was already her fiancé; from this diary she could get a glimpse of my past, she could at least learn what I most wanted her to know—about my latest affair. Others might have told her about it and that is why I felt it expedient to tell her myself. I remember her horror and despair and bewilderment when she found out and understood. I could see she wanted to break off ties with me then and there. Oh, if she only had!"

He made that sound again, stopped talking, and took a swallow of tea.

VI

"But no! Better as it was, better as it was!" he cried. "It served me right! But that is aside from the story. What I wanted to say was that the unfortunate girls are the only ones who are deceived. Their mothers know everything, especially those mothers who have learned from their own husbands. They pretend to believe in the pureness of men, but they behave just the opposite. They know what bait to use in catching men for themselves and their daughters.

"It is only we men who do not know, and we do not know because we do not wish to know; the women know very well that the most exalted and poetic so-called love is inspired not by moral virtues, but by being physically close, and besides by *coiffeurs*, by the colour and cut of a frock. Ask an experienced coquette who has set her cap for a certain gentleman, which risk she would rather take: that of being accused in his presence of cruelty, deception, even of depravity, or of appearing before him in an ugly, ill-fitting gown. She is sure to choose the first. She knows that we men are just lying when we talk of elevated feelings; what we want is the body, and therefore we will forgive her her sins, but never an ugly, ill-fitting, tasteless gown. A coquette is consciously aware of this, but any innocent young girl knows it intuitively, as an animal knows it.

"That accounts for those loathsome jerseys, those bustles on their behinds, those bare shoulders and arms and almost bare bosoms. Women, especially those who get their knowledge from men, know only too well that talk on elevated themes is mere talk, and that what a man really wants is the body and whatever adds to the seductiveness of the body, and so this is what they offer him. If we could view the life of the upper classes in its true light, not through the prism of a habitual attitude that has become second nature to us, we would see that it is a veritable brothel. You disagree? Here, I shall prove it to you," he said, not giving me a chance to speak. "You say the women of our class have other interests than the women in a brothel, but I say you are wrong and will prove that you are wrong. If people have different aims in life, if their inner lives are different, the outer forms of their lives will be different too. But look at the unfortunate women whom we despise and then at young ladies from the very highest society: the same toilettes, the same fashions, the same perfumes, the same bare arms, shoulders and bosoms, the same exaggerated behinds, the same passion for precious stones and expensive, glittering ornaments, the same amusements—dancing, music, and singing. All the same means of enticing men are used by one as by the other. No difference at all. To make a very strict distinction between them we can only say that short-term prostitutes are usually despised whereas long-term prostitutes are esteemed."

VII

"And so I was ensnared by the jerseys, curls, and bustles. It was easy to catch me because I was brought up in those special conditions that, like hothouses for cucumbers, cultivate the love-tendency in young folk. The superabundance of stimulating food and drink that we consume, combined with complete physical idleness, is nothing less than a systematic stimulation of lust. That is a fact, whether it astonishes you or not. I myself failed to realize it until lately. But now I do realize it, and that is why I become so upset on seeing that others do not understand and talk the same sort of claptrap as that woman who was here.

"This spring some peasants were working on a railway not far from me. The usual diet of a young peasant is bread, kvass, and onions: it keeps them alive, cheerful, and busy at easy field work. He goes to work on the railway, and his daily fare becomes porridge and a pound of meat. But he expends this meat on a sixteen-hour working-day wheeling a barrow weighing thirty poods. His fare is just right for him. And what about us, eating as much as two pounds of meat, poultry, and other caloric dainties and drinks—how do we expend it all? On sensual excesses. If we really expend it, everything is all right for the safety valve is open. But if it is closed, as mine was from time to time, it results in a sensual excitement that, passing through the prism of our artificial life, finds expression in an over-refined sort of love, sometimes even platonic love. And I fell in love like everyone else. And my love had all the attributes: rapture, adoration, poetry... As a matter of fact this love of mine was created on the one hand by her mother and dressmaker, and on the other by the excess food which I consumed, living as I did a life of idleness. If, on the one hand, there had been no boating, no

dressmaker emphasizing her waist-line and
other points, if my future wife had been
wearing a shapeless dressing-gown and sitting
at home, and if, on the other hand, I had
been living in the normal conditions of a man
who consumes only as much food as is
required by the work he does, and if my
safety valve had been open (it happened to
be closed at the time) I would not have
fallen in love and there would have been no
consequences."

VIII

"But it so happened that everything
coincided: my physical state, her toilette,
and the boating. Twenty times before things
had not clicked but this time they did. Like
falling into a trap. I am not joking. In our day
marriages are set beforehand, like traps. What
is the natural thing? A girl comes of age, she
must be married off. A very simple thing,
it seems, if the girl is not a monstrosity and
there are men who wish to get married. That
is how it was done in the old days. A girl
came of age and her parents found a husband
for her. That is how it was and still is done
among all peoples—Chinese, Indians, Moham-
medans, and our own peasants. That is how
it is done among at least ninety-nine per cent
of the people of the world. But one per cent
of the people, profligate creatures like us,

have decided that this is wrong and have
thought of a new system. And what is the
new system? The new system consists in
having the girls sit down while the men walk
up and down in front of them as at a fair,
making their choice. The girls sit there and
say to themselves, not daring to say it out
loud, 'Here, take me! Me! Not her, but me!
Look what fine shoulders and ... er ... other
things I have!' And we men walk up and
down and gaze at them and are very much
pleased to have this show put on for our
benefit. We gaze, and if we are not careful—
snap!—we are caught!"

"And how else could it be?" I asked.
"Would you have the women do the
proposing?"

"I don't know how else, but if there is
supposed to be equality, let there be real
equality. And if the making of matches by
parents is considered degrading, this is a
thousand times more so. In the first case the
rights and chances are at least even, whereas
in this case the woman is either a slave sold
on the market, or a bait put in a trap. But
if you dared to suggest to a girl (or her
mother) that the only thing she was occupied
with was the catching of a husband—my God,
what offence would be taken! And yet that
actually is the only thing she does, and there
is nothing else for her to do. It is an awful
thing to see young and innocent creatures
occupied in this way. And again, if it were all

done in the open, but no, it is all underhand. "Ah, the origin of the species! How very interesting! My Liza dotes on painting! And you intend going to the exhibition too? How edifying! And sleigh-rides, and the theatre, and symphony concerts? How marvellous! My Liza is mad on music. How is it you do not share these views? And boating!..' And all the while her one thought is: 'Take me, me, or my Liza! No, me! Just for a try!' Ugh! The falseness! The horror!'' and, saying this, he drank the last of the tea and set about putting away the cups and saucers.

IX

"You are perhaps aware," he began again as he put the tea and sugar in his sack, "that all of this springs from the domination of woman—a source of untold trouble in this world."

"What do you mean by the domination of woman?" I said. "The law gives the advantage to man."

"Yes, yes, that is just it," he interrupted. "That is just what I wanted to tell you; it is that that explains the extraordinary pheno-menon of woman dominating, even though she has been reduced to the lowest stage of humiliation. The one is compensation for the other, just as the Jews find compensation for the oppression they suffer in the power their money gives them. 'So, you would like us to be nothing but traders and money-lenders, would you? Very well, then as traders and money-lenders we shall wield power over you,' say the Jews. 'Ah, you would like us to be nothing but sensual creatures? Very well, as sensual creatures we shall make you our slaves,' say the women. A woman's lack of rights does not lie in her not having the right to vote or become a judge—the exercising of these functions is no right at all. It lies in her not being the equal of the man in sexual life, in not having the right to give herself to a man or refuse to give herself to him as she likes, in not having the right to choose a man as she likes instead of being chosen by him.

"You say this is an outrage. Very well. Then the man should not have this right either. At present the woman is deprived of a right which a man enjoys. And so to compensate for the loss of this right she acts on the man's sensibilities, subjugates him through acting on his sensibilities to such an extent that his choosing is a mere formality. It is she who does the real choosing. Once she has found this means of achieving her end, she takes advantage of it to wield a dreadful power over all people."

"Wherein lies this dreadful power?" I asked.

"Wherein? In everything, everywhere. Go through the shops of any large town. Millions of hands—more than can be counted—have laboured over the things displayed there, and just see! Can anything for men's use be found in nine-tenths of these shops? All the luxuries of life are demanded and consumed by women. Count the factories. The enormous majority of them are engaged in making useless ornaments, carriages, furniture, and nicknacks for women. Millions of people, generations of slaves, wear themselves out at this cruel factory labour to satisfy the whims of women. Women, like queens, have forced nine-tenths of the human race to labour for them as their slaves. And all because they have been humiliated and deprived of equal rights with man. And so they wreak vengeance by acting on our sensibilities, by catching us in their trap. Yes, it is all because of this. Women have made of themselves so effective an instrument for working on men's sensibilities that men are unable to preserve their equanimity in their presence. As soon as a man finds himself with a woman he becomes stupified, as by a narcotic. Formerly I cringed and felt uncomfortable when I saw a woman all decked out in a ball gown. Now I feel terrified, for I see in her something dangerous, something unlawful, and I have an impulse to call for help, for the police, to demand that this danger be taken away and locked up.

"Laughing?" he shouted at me. "There is nothing to laugh at. I am certain that the time will come, and perhaps soon, when people

will understand this and be amazed that
there could have existed a society permitting
anything as disturbing to the peace as the
ornamenting of the female body with the
direct intent of exciting the sensibilities. Why,
it is just the same as if we set traps along the
paths upon which men walked. Even worse!
Why is it that gambling is forbidden, but
the dressing up of women in prostitutical
finery meant to excite man's feelings is not
forbidden? That is a thousand times more
dangerous!''

X

"And so, as I say, I was caught. I was what
they call 'in love'. I not only found that she
was the acme of perfection, I found that I,
too, during my engagement, was the acme of
perfection. After all, the blackguard does not
exist who cannot find someone who in some
respect is worse than he is and therefore gives
him some reason to be proud and pleased
with himself. So it was with me: I was not
marrying for money, greed was not a motive
with me as it was with most of my acquaintances, who married either for money or
connections; I was rich and she was poor.
That was one thing. Another was that others
married with the intention of continuing to
live the same sort of polygamous lives as they
were accustomed to living, but I had made

the firm resolve to be strictly monogamous after my marriage, and this made me unspeakably proud of myself. Yes, I was a loathsome pig who fancied himself a saint.

"My engagement did not last long. I cannot recall that time without blushing with shame. We assume that it is a period of spiritual and not sensual love, but if it is spiritual love, spiritual communion, then our words, our talks, our conversations ought to reflect this spiritual communion. But this was not the case. Whenever we were left alone it was very difficult to talk at all, it required a sort of Sisyphean effort. It would take me a long time to think of something to say. I would say it, fall silent, and try to think of something else to say. There was nothing to talk about. Everything that could be said about our future lives together, about our plans and arrangements, had been said. What else was there? If we had been animals, we would have known that we were not expected to talk; but as humans we were expected to talk and there was nothing to talk about, because that which occupied our thoughts was not a fitting subject for conversation. And in addition to all this, that disgusting tradition—chocolates, the stuffing of ourselves with sweetmeats, and all those loathsome preparations for the wedding—getting ready the apartment, the bedroom, the bedding, dressing-gowns, linen, the wardrobe. Don't you see that under the patriarchal system defended by that old man, the dowry, the bedding, the feather-beds—all of these things were details attending the mystery. But nowadays, when hardly one man out of ten preparing to get married believes in the mystery, or even that what he is about to do carries with it any obligations, when hardly one man out of a hundred can be found who has not already been married before his marriage, and hardly one out of fifty who is not ready to deceive his wife at the first opportunity, when the majority of those getting married look upon the church ceremony as merely the condition laid down for the coming into ownership of a certain woman—when you think of all this, the dreadful significance of all these preparations becomes clear. It turns out that they are an end in themselves. It turns out to be a sort of sale: an innocent girl is sold to a dissolute man and the sale is attended by fitting rites."

XI

"That is how everyone gets married, and that is how I got married and set out on the much-sung honeymoon. How vulgar the very name!" he muttered viciously. "In Paris I once went to an exhibition of various monstrosities, where I saw a bearded woman and a dog that was half fish. It turned out that the bearded woman was just a man dressed up in woman's clothes and the dog had been put into a seal's hide and made to swim in a bath-tub. There was nothing of interest to be seen, but when I was going out the barker pointed to me and said to the public: 'Here, ask this gentleman whether or not it is worth seeing! Get your tickets! Get your tickets! One franc only!' I was ashamed to say the show was not worth seeing, and this was evidently what the barker counted on. I suppose that is how it is with those who have had the disgusting experience of a honeymoon; they are ashamed to disillusion others. I, too, refrained from disillusioning others, but now I see no reason for hiding the truth. I even consider it my duty to tell the truth. My honeymoon was embarrassing, shameful, loathsome, pathetic, and above all else—boring. Unspeakably boring. It was something similar to the time when I learned to smoke, when I drooled and wanted to throw up, but swallowed down my droolings and pretended to be enjoying myself. The enjoyment of smoking comes later, if it comes at all, and so it is with this: the couple must train themselves to this vice if they are to get any pleasure out of it."

"Vice, you say?" I put in. "But you are speaking of the most natural human function."

"Natural?" said he. "Natural? No, I must say that I have come to the opposite conclusion—that it is against nature, that it is highly unnatural. Ask children. Ask innocent young girls. When my sister was very young she married a dissolute man twice her age. I remember how surprised we were on the night of her wedding to have her come running out, pale and in tears, crying that she wouldn't—not for anything, not for anything! That she could not even find words to describe what he wanted of her!

"And you call it natural! There are things that are natural. There are things that are pleasant and delightful and without shame from the very beginning. But not this. This is loathsome and shameful and painful. No, it is not natural! And I am convinced that an innocent girl always hates it."

"But how," said I, "is the human race to be perpetuated?"

"How is the human race to be perpetuated?" echoed he in a voice of irony, as if he had been expecting this usual and shameful question. "It is possible to preach birth control so that English lords may have enough to gorge themselves on; it is possible to preach birth control so that one may enjoy oneself without unpleasant consequences; but the minute one opens one's mouth to preach birth control in the name of morality—oh, what a din is raised! How is the human race to be perpetuated if a dozen or two individuals resolve that they have had enough of being pigs? But I beg your pardon. That light annoys me, do you mind if I put something over it?" he said, pointing to the lamp.

I said it made no difference to me, and he climbed up on the bench in his impulsive way and pulled the curtain over the light.

"And yet," said I, "if everyone were to adopt your ideas, the human race would become extinct."

His answer was not instantly forthcoming.

"You are worried about the perpetuation of the human race?" he said, once more taking a seat opposite me, spreading his legs far apart and leaning down to put his elbows on his knees. "Why should it be perpetuated, the human race?" he asked.

"Why do you ask? Otherwise you and I would not exist."

"And why should we exist?"

"To live."

"And why should we live? If there is no aim in life, if life is an end in itself, then there is nothing to live for. And if this is true, then Schopenhauer and Hartmann and the Buddhists are perfectly right. But if there is an aim in life, then it is clear that life should come to an end when this aim is reached. That is the only conclusion," he said with agitation, evidently placing great store in this idea. "That is the only conclusion. Observe this: if the aim of human life is goodness, kindness, love; if the aim of human life is what is told us in the prophecies, that all people are to be united by love, that the sword is to be melted down for the sickle, and all the rest, then what is it that prevents us from achieving this aim? Our passions. And of all the passions, the strongest, the most vicious and persistent, is sexual, carnal love, and therefore if the passions are subdued, especially this, the most powerful of them, carnal love, then the prophecies will be fulfilled and mankind will be united into one, the aim of human life will be achieved, and there will no longer be anything to live for. As long as mankind exists it is inspired by the ideal, and certainly not the ideal of pigs and rabbits, which is to have as many offspring as possible, nor the ideal of monkeys and Parisians, which is to get the most refined enjoyment out of sexual indulgence. It is the ideal of goodness achieved through continence and purity. Man always has and always will strive to attain this. But see what comes of it.

"This is what comes of it: carnal love, it appears, is a safety valve. The present generation has not achieved the aim of mankind, and it has not achieved it only because of its passions, the strongest of which is sex. The sex passion exists, it produces a new generation, the new generation is presented with the opportunity of achieving the aim. But the new generation does not achieve the aim either, and so the opportunity is passed on to the next generation, and to the next, and to the next, until the aim is achieved, until the prophecies are fulfilled, until all mankind is united into one. How could it be otherwise? Let us imagine that God created human

beings for the achievement of a certain aim,
but created them either mortal and without
the sex instinct, or immortal. If he created
them mortal but without the sex instinct,
what would be the result? They would live
without achieving their aim and then die, and
for the achievement of the aim God would
have to create new people. If He created them
immortal, then it is possible (although it is
harder for one and the same people to correct
their errors than for new people to correct
the errors of their forebears and approach
perfection)—it is possible, I say, that after
many thousands of years they would achieve
their aim. But what would be the use of these
immortals then? What could be done with
them? No, things are better as they are. But
perhaps you object to such a statement of the
case? Perhaps you are a supporter of the
theory of evolution? The result is the same.
The highest form of animal life—human
beings—must unite like a swarm of bees in
order to survive the struggle with other
animals; they must not give themselves up to
unlimited reproduction. Like the bees, they
must develop sexless individuals, that is,
must aspire to chastity rather than to the
indulging of the sex instinct as is done in our
society." He paused a moment. "The end of
the human race? But can anyone, no matter
what his views, doubt the inevitability of
that? It is as certain as death. All sacred
teachings foretell the end of the world, and

all scientific teachings do the same. Is it, then, so strange if moral teachings point to the same end?"

For a long time after this he was silent. He drank more tea, finished smoking his cigarette, took a new supply out of his sack, and put them in his old, stained cigarette-case.

"I understand your idea," I said. "The Shakers have a similar one."

"And they are right," he said. "The sex passion, in whatever form it is presented, is an evil, a dreadful evil, which is to be combated and not encouraged as it is with us. The words of the Bible, that anyone who looks upon a woman with lust has already committed adultery with her, apply not only to other men's wives, but also and primarily, to our own wives."

XII

"In our world, everything is just the opposite. If a man practises abstinence while a bachelor, as soon as he gets married he considers abstinence no longer necessary. After all, those trips taken after the wedding, that seclusion into which the young people withdraw with the sanction of their parents—it is nothing but the sanction of profligacy. But moral laws inflict their own punishment if violated. Hard as I tried to turn our holiday into a honeymoon, I did not succeed. From beginning to end it was shameful, disgusting, and boring. But soon it became even more trying. Very soon. On the third, or perhaps the fourth day I found my wife depressed. I asked her the reason and began to pet her, thinking that must be what she wanted, but she pushed my arm away and began to cry. Why? She could not tell me. But she was unhappy, she was miserable. Probably her strained nerves told her the truth as to how loathsome our relations were, but she could not express it. I pressed her, she muttered something about missing her mother. I felt it was not the truth. I began to coax her, ignoring what she had said about her mother. I did not understand that she was simply miserable and used her mother as an excuse. But she took offence with me for having ignored her mother, as if I had not believed her. She said she was sure I did not love her. I accused her of being capricious, and suddenly her face changed completely; the expression of misery was supplanted by one of irritation, and in the most biting terms she began to accuse me of selfishness and cruelty. I looked at her. Her whole face expressed utter frigidity and hostility, almost hatred of me. I remember how shocked I was. 'How is this?' I thought. 'Instead of love, a union of souls—this. Impossible! She is not herself.' I tried to mollify her, but I found myself confronted by such an implacable wall of cold, caustic hostility, that before I knew it I myself had flown into a rage and we said a lot of nasty things to each other. That first quarrel made a dreadful impression on me. I call it a quarrel, but it was not really a quarrel; it was merely a revelation of the great gulf that lay between us. Our love was exhausted as soon as our desire was satisfied, and now we stood facing each other in our true relationship, which was of two completely alien and completely selfish individuals who only wanted to get the greatest amount of satisfaction out of each other.

"I have called what happened a quarrel, but it was not a quarrel; it was merely the exposure of our true relationship brought about by the cessation of sensual desire. I did not realize that this attitude of cold hostility was the normal relationship between us, and I did not realize it because soon this attitude of hostility was hidden from sight by a new wave of sensuality, of being in love.

"I thought we had quarrelled and made it up, and that we would never do such a thing again. But in this first month of honey-mooning we soon reached another period of surfeit when we no longer needed each other, and this brought on another quarrel. I found the second quarrel more painful than the first. 'And so our first quarrel was not an accident after all,' I thought, 'it was only what was to be expected and will surely be repeated.' I found the second quarrel particularly shocking because it arose from the most trivial of causes—something about money, of which I was never sparing and could not possibly have begrudged my wife. I only remember that she twisted something I had said into meaning that my money gave me power over her and that I alone had the right to dispose of my money, or something equally vile and stupid and unworthy of either of us. I became angry and accused her of showing a lack of tact, she answered me back, and again we were off. In her words, in the expression of her face and eyes, I again saw that cold, cruel hostility that had shocked me so the first time. I remember having quarrelled with my brother, my friends, even my father, but never had there been that peculiarly poisonous malevolence that I saw here.

"With the passage of time, however, this mutual hatred was again screened by the state of being in love, that is to say by sensuality, and again I consoled myself with the thought that these two quarrels had been mistakes that could be righted. But then there came the third and the fourth, and I realized once and for all that they were not accidents, that they could not have been avoided then and could not be avoided in the future, and the prospect horrified me. I was further tormented by the thought that it was only my marriage that had turned out so badly, so differently from my expectations, and that other marriages were successful. I was not then aware that this is everyone's fate, and that everyone thinks, just as I then thought, that his misfortune is an exception and hides this exceptional and shameful misfortune not only from others, but even from himself, refusing to admit it.

"Our hostility began as soon as we were married and went on and on, growing deeper and more relentless. From the very first week I felt in my heart that I had fallen into a trap, that this was not at all what I had expected, and that marriage, instead of being a great happiness, was a great misfortune. But I, like everyone else, did not want to admit it (I would never have admitted it if it had not been for the outcome) and I hid the truth not only from others, but from myself as well. When I think back over it I am amazed that for so long a time I could have failed to see things as they really were. The very fact that our quarrels began with matters so trivial that we could not even remember them afterwards should have made everything clear to me. Our reason was given no opportunity to invent weighty motives to support the perpetual state of hostility we found ourselves in. But even more shocking were the sham motives for our reconciliations. Sometimes there were words, explanations, even tears, but at other times—how loathsome the recollection!—after having said the most cruel things to each other, we would steal shy glances, smile, kiss, embrace. Ugh, how low! How could I possibly have failed to see the vileness of it all?"

XIII

Two passengers entered and took their places in the far end of the carriage. He stopped talking until they had settled themselves, then resumed, not for a moment having lost his train of thought.

"The most loathsome thing about it," he began, "is that love is supposed to be something ideal, something elevated, whereas actually it is something so vile and bestial that even to talk or think of it is vile and shameful. And nature had her reasons for making it vile and shameful. Once it is vile and shameful it ought to be accepted as such, but instead people pretend that what is vile and shameful is beautiful and elevated. What were the first signs of my love? My indulgence in animal excess without the least shame, with even a sense of pride in being able to indulge myself in excess, and in doing so I showed not the least regard for her spiritual or even her physical welfare. I could not understand why we were so cross with each other, but the reason is clear: this crossness was nothing other than the protest made by our human nature against being subjected to the animal nature.

"I was amazed by our hatred for each other. But nothing else could have been expected. It was the mutual hatred of two parties to a crime—to the instigation and perpetration of a crime. For was it not a crime indeed when she, poor thing, became pregnant the very first month and still our animal relations went on? Do you think this is all irrelevant to the story? You are wrong. It is all part of the story of how I killed my wife. At the trial they asked me how I killed her and what I killed her with. Fools! They thought I killed her on the 5th of October with a knife. It was not then that I killed her, it was much earlier. And I did it in just the same way as all the others are doing it—all, all!"

"What do you mean?" I asked.

"That is the amazing thing—nobody wants to admit the plain and simple truth, a truth that the doctors ought to know and preach but about which they keep silent. Men and women are made just like animals in that an indulgence in carnal love is followed by pregnancy, the feeding of the offspring, a physical state during which physical love is harmful for both mother and child. There is an equal number of men and women. What does that indicate? I think it is clear. It does not require great wisdom to draw the conclusion drawn by animals, namely—abstinence. But it is not drawn. Scientists are clever enough to have discovered a lot of useless things such as leucocytes that swim about in the blood, but they are not clever enough to have discovered this. I, at least, have not heard them mention it.

"And so there are only two ways out for

the woman: one is to mutilate herself by destroying at once or by degrees her ability to be a woman that is, a mother, so that her husband may take his pleasure whenever he likes; the other is hardly a way out, it is simply the coarse and direct violation of laws of nature that is committed by all of our so-called upright families. It means that a woman, despite her nature, must be an expectant mother and a nursing mother and her husband's mistress at one and the same time, an imposition that not a single animal will submit to. And she has not the strength for it. That is why women of our class become nervous and hysterical, and women of the peasant class become *klikushi*.* Observe that young girls, innocent young girls are never *klikushi*, only women, and women who have husbands. That is true of our people. It is just as true of Europeans. All the hospitals are filled with women who have been made hysterical by violating laws of nature. But *klikushi* and Charcot's patients are women who have become completely deranged; the world is full of women who have not yet reached that stage.

"How awe-inspiring is the woman's act of bearing the fruit of her womb and nursing the child she has borne! It is our successors she creates, those who are to prolong the

---

* *Klikushi*—the folk name for brawling, hysterical peasant women.—*Tr.*

human race. And what is it that breaks in upon this sacred act? The very thought is horrifying! And yet they talk of emancipation, of the rights of women! It is as if cannibals who were fattening their victims for the slaughter assured them at the same time that they were concerned about their rights and freedom."

I found his ideas new and shocking.

"But what is to be done?" I said. "If what you say is true, then a man can make love to his wife only once in two years; but men—"

"Men cannot live without it," he broke in. "Again the respected priests of science have convinced everyone of this. I would like to hear what these savants would say if they were forced to carry out the functions of the women who they claim are so necessary to men. Impress upon a man that vodka, tobacco, and opium are essential to him, and they will become essential. It is as if God had created things all wrong because He did not know what was essential and did not consult the savants. As you see, things do not dovetail. The men have decided that they cannot live without satisfying their lust, but here comes childbirth and nursing to interfere with the satisfying of their lust. What is to be done? Appeal to the savants. They will arrange everything. And they do. Oh, when will the doctors and their lies be exposed? It is high time! It has reached the point at which people go mad and shoot themselves all on account of this. And how could it be otherwise? Animals seem to know that offspring are for the purpose of perpetuating their kind, and they observe laws in respect to this. Only man does not know and does not care to know. The only thing he wants is to enjoy himself as much as possible. And who is he? Man, the King of the Universe. Just think— animals copulate only when it is possible to create offspring, whereas the filthy King of the Universe copulates whenever he can, and only for pleasure. What is more, he tries to identify this with the most exalted feeling—love. And in the name of this love—that is, this vileness—he sacrifices half of the human race. For the sake of his own pleasure he makes an enemy of woman, who ought to be his helpmate in leading mankind to a recognition of goodness and truth. Tell me this: who prevents mankind from moving ahead? Woman. And why is she what she is? Only because of this. Yes, yes," he repeated over and over again as he rummaged for a cigarette, then began to smoke, evidently trying to compose himself.

XIV

"So that was the bestial sort of life I lived," he went on in the same tome. "The worst thing about it was that, living such a life, I fancied that because I did not allow myself

to be seduced by other women and remained
faithful to my wife I was a man of moral
principle, a man without fault, and that if
we quarrelled, she, or rather her character,
was to blame.

"But she was not to blame. She was no
different from all other women, at least the
majority of them. She had been brought up
in the way demanded by the position of
woman in our society, in the way all women
from the privileged classes are brought up, in
the only way it is natural for them to be
brought up. We hear much talk about the
modern education of women. Empty words.
The education of women is exactly what it
ought to be so long as our attitude to women
remains what it is (and not what we pretend
it is).

"The education of women will always
correspond with men's attitude towards them.
We all know how men look upon women.
'*Wein, Weiber und Gesang*,'—that is what the
poets sing. Take the whole of poetry, the
whole of painting and sculpture, beginning
with the appearance of love lyrics and naked
Venuses—everywhere woman is looked upon
as a means of enjoyment, at court balls as
well as on Trubnaya Square or Grachevka
Street. And not the devil's cunning: if it were
nothing but pleasure and enjoyment, we
would accept it as such—pleasure and enjoyment. Woman is a sweet morsel and nothing
else. But no, the knights were the first who

professed to worship woman as something above them (worshipped her and yet looked upon her as a means of enjoyment). Today men profess to respect her. Some men give up their chairs to her and pick up her handkerchiefs, others recognize her right to occupy any post at all—administrative, executive—any at all. That is what they profess, but their attitude towards her remains the same. She is a means of enjoyment. Her body is a means of giving pleasure. And she is aware of this. It is a form of slavery.

"Slavery is nothing but a state in which some people reap the benefit of the forced labour of others. Slavery can be abolished only when people no longer wish to reap the benefit of the forced labour of others because they consider it sinful or shameful. But what they actually do is to change the outer forms of slavery by forbidding the sale of slaves, and then they fancy (and convince themselves) that slavery has been abolished, not seeing and not wishing to see that slavery continues to exist because people go on wanting to reap the benefit of other people's labour and consider it right and just to do so. So long as this is considered right, there will be found people who, being stronger and more cunning than others, will bring about slavery.

"So it is with the emancipation of womam. The slavery of woman consists in having man consider it right and desirable to use her for his pleasure. And then they set about emancipating her—they give her the same rights as man but continue to regard her as a means of enjoyment, training her to this in childhood and teaching it by means of public opinion. And she continues to be the same debased, profligate slave, and men continue to be the same profligate slave-holders.

"They emancipate woman in colleges and courts, but go on regarding her as a means of enjoyment. As long as she is taught (as we teach her) to look upon herself in this way, she will continue to be a creature of a lower order. Either, with the aid of the dastardly doctors, she will prevent herself from conceiving, which means she will become a prostitute, one who has descended to the level not of beasts, but of things; or else she will be what she really is in most cases— miserable, hysterical, mentally unbalanced, incapable of spiritual development.

"Schools and colleges can do nothing about this. The only thing that can change it is a change in man's attitude towards woman, and of woman's attitude towards herself. It will only be changed when women come to consider a state of virginity the highest state and not the shame and disgrace it is now considered. Until such a time, the aspiration of every girl, no matter what her education, will be to attract as many men as she can so that she will have a chance to choose from among them.

"The fact that she knows mathematics or can perform on the harp will not change matters in the least. A woman is happy and has achieved her highest aim when she has captivated a man. And so her principal aim in life is to be able to captivate men. It has been so in the past, it will be so in the future. It applies to unmarried girls as well as to married women. Unmarried girls must be able to do this to insure themselves a choice; married women must do it to exert power over their husbands.

"The one thing that stops her efforts in this direction, or rather suspends them temporarily, is childbirth, and then only when she is a true mother, that is to say when she nurses her babies herself. But again the doctors step in.

"My wife, who wanted to nurse her children and did nurse five of them, was not well after the birth of her first child. The doctors, who shamefully stripped her and felt her all over (for which I was expected to thank them and pay them a fee)—these honourable doctors found that she ought not to nurse her first child, and so she was deprived of the only means of getting rid of her coquetry. A wet-nurse was found for the child, which meant that we took advantage of a strange woman's poverty and ignorance to lure her away from her own baby and give her to ours, for which we dressed her in a starched cap with braid on it. But that is aside from the point. The point is that when my wife's confinement was over and she was released from nursing her child, the coquetry that had been lying dormant in her broke out with exceptional force. And in direct proportion to her coquetry I was tortured by a jealousy that had not given me a moment's peace since the first day of my married life, a jealousy that must inevitably torture all husbands who live with their wives as I lived with mine, which is to say—immorally."

XV

"Not for a minute during the whole of my married life was I free of the pangs of jealousy. But there were periods when my sufferings became more acute. One of these periods was after the birth of our first child, when the doctors forbade my wife to nurse it. I was particularly jealous at this time, first of all, because my wife experienced the anxiety which any mother would feel on having the natural course of things interrupted without any good cause; and secondly because, on seeing the ease with which she shook off the moral obligations of a mother, I justly (if unconsciously) concluded that she might just as easily shake off her conjugal obligations, especially since she was perfectly well and, despite the prohibition of the honourable doctors, nursed her other children herself without any ill effects."

"You waste no love on the doctors," observed I, having noticed a particularly spiteful tone in his voice every time he mentioned them.

"It is not a question of loving them or not loving them. They ruined my life just as they ruin the lives of hundreds of thousands of others, and I cannot detach cause from effect. I can understand that they, like lawyers, are anxious to squeeze money out of their patients and I would gladly have given them half of my income (as would anyone else who understood the true state of affairs) if by doing so I could have kept them from having anything to do with my family life. I have not gathered statistics, but I know of dozens of instances (there are innumerable ones) when doctors killed either the baby in the womb, declaring that the mother was unable to bear children (although later she bore them very successfully), or the mother herself by subjecting her to some sort of operation. Nobody calls such deaths murder, just as in the Middle Ages the killings of the Inquisition were not called murder, because they were said to be done for the human welfare. The crimes doctors commit are countless. But all these crimes are as nothing compared with the moral corruption of the materialism they bring into the world, especially through the medium of women. Moreover, if we were to follow their advice we would seek to achieve a state of isolation one from another due to the infection to be found everywhere and in everything, instead of striving towards the unity of the human race; according to their teachings each of us should sit alone with a solution of carbolic acid in his mouth (although this, by the way, has recently been discovered to be ineffective). But that, too, is nothing. The main thing is that they corrupt people, especially women.

"Nowadays one cannot say, 'Your ways are bad, you must change them.' One cannot say this to oneself or to anyone else. If your ways are bad the cause lies in a disturbance of the nervous system or something of the sort, and you must go to the doctors and they will prescribe thirty-five kopeks' worth of medicine which you must take. You become worse, you go to more doctors and take more medicine. A splendid practice!

"But that is not the point. I only wanted to say that she successfully nursed her other children and that her pregnancies and periods of nursing were the only things that saved me from the sufferings of jealousy. If it had not been for them, what happened eventually would have happened much sooner. The children saved her and me. In eight years she had five children. And she nursed all five of them herself."

"And where are they now, your children?" I asked.

"My children?" he repeated with a frightened look.

"Forgive me; perhaps it is painful to be reminded of them?"

"No, it is nothing. My children were taken by my wife's sister and brother. They would not let me keep them. I gave them all of my wealth, but they would not let me keep the children. I'm considered insane. I have just been to see them. I spoke to them, but they will not give the children to me. You see I would bring them up to be different from their parents, and they must not be different. Ah, well, what is to be done? Naturally they will not give them to me and will not trust me. And I am not sure I would have the strength to bring them up. I am afraid I would not. I am a ruin, a wreck. But there is one thing I have. Knowledge. Yes, I know things that it will take others a long time to learn.

"My children are alive and growing up to be barbarians, like everyone else. I saw them—three times. There is nothing I can do for them. Nothing. I am on my way to the south. I have a little house and a garden there.

"Yes, it will take others a long time to find out what I know. It will not take us long to find out how much iron and other metals are contained in the sun and the stars, but to find out things exposing our own bestiality—that is hard, very hard...

"You, at least, listen to what I have to say. For that I am grateful."

XVI

"You mentioned my children. Again, what a false attitude is taken towards children! Children are a joy! Children are God's blessing! A lie. They may have been once, but they are not now. Children are a torment, and nothing else. Most mothers are fully aware of this and even say as much if they are caught off their guard. Ask any mother of the privileged classes and she will tell you that she does not want to have children for fear of their falling ill and dying, and if she happens to give birth to a child she does not want to nurse it for fear of becoming too attached to it and having to suffer. The delight taken in a child's loveliness—in its little hands and feet and body—all the delight a child affords is less than the suffering caused not only by its falling ill or dying, but by the very fear of its falling ill or dying. In weighing the advantages and disadvantages of having children, the disadvantages always outweigh the advantages, and that is why it is better not to have children. Women say this plainly, boldly, fancying that their feelings spring from a love of children—a good, commendable feeling, one of which they are proud. They fail to realize that this way of thinking is a denial of love and an assertion of selfishness. The joy they take in a child is less than the suffering it causes them, and therefore they do not want to have a child. It is not

themselves they sacrifice for the sake of the
loved one, but what might be a loved one for
the sake of themselves.

"Clearly this is not love but selfishness.
But it is hard to blame rich mothers for this
selfishness—one cannot utter a word of
protest if one recalls what the health of their
children costs women (again thanks to the
doctors) in aristocratic society. Even
today a shudder passes over me every time
I remember the life and the mental state of
my wife in those early days when there were
three or four children who took up every
minute of her time and every ounce of her
energy. She had no time for me at all. We
lived under a constant threat of danger,
of being rescued from this danger, of having
it return, of making desperate efforts to ward
it off, of being rescued again—as if we were
on a sinking ship. Sometimes it occurred to
me that this atmosphere was created on
purpose, that my wife feigned anxiety for the
children's welfare so as to insure her triumph
over me; it was a very simple, tempting means
of having all questions solved to her advantage.
Sometimes I fancied that all she did and
said was done and said hypocritically. But
I was wrong. She was really dreadfully
harassed, she was in a constant state of
anxiety about the children, their health, their
ailments. It was torture for her as well as for
me. And she could not help being tortured.
Concern for her children, the animal concern

to see that they were fed, comforted, defended, was as strong in her as it is in most women, but she had something else that animals are free of—reason and imagination. A hen does not worry about what may happen to her chick, she does not know of all the many diseases that it may fall prey to, nor does she know of all the remedies that people fancy can prevent illness and death. And so for the hen offspring are not a torment. She does for them what she must do, and does it joyfully; for her, offspring are a joy. If her chick falls ill she knows exactly what to do: she feeds it and keeps it warm. And in doing this she knows she is doing all that is necessary. If the chick dies she does not ask herself why it died and where it has gone; she clucks a bit, gets over it, and goes on living as before. But this is not enough for our unfortunate women, my wife in particular. She heard and read a countless number of the most varied and variable rules on the education and up-bringing of children, to say nothing of children's diseases and their cure. They must be fed this and that; no, not this and that, but that and this. Every week we, especially my wife, found out something new about how they should be fed, clothed, bathed, put to bed, taken for walks, given the air. As if children had begun to be born only yesterday. If one of the children fell ill it was because it had not been fed right, or bathed right, or at the proper time; in a word, my wife was to blame for the illness because she had not done what she ought to have.

"It was bad enough when the children were well, but if they fell ill, life became hell. It is assumed that diseases can be cured, that there is a certain branch of science dealing with this and there are certain people—doctors—who know how to effect these cures. Not all of them know how, but the best of them do. And so here we have a sick child, and we must find that very best of doctors, the one who knows how, and then the child will be saved; but if we do not find that particular doctor, or if we do not happen to live where he lives, the child is doomed. My wife was not the only one who believed this; all the women of our set did, and on every hand she heard nothing else: 'Yekaterina Semyonovna lost two children because she did not call in Ivan Zakharich soon enough.' 'Ivan Zakharich saved Maria Ivanovna's elder girl.' 'On the doctor's advice the Petrovs went to live in different hotels and the children were saved; if they hadn't the children would have died.' 'So-and-so's child was very frail; on the doctor's advice they moved to the South and the child was saved.' How could she help being perpetually worried and harassed when the life of her children, for whose welfare she was as concerned as any animal is, depended on finding out what Ivan Zakharich would say on a certain matter before it was too late? But nobody knew what Ivan Zakharich would say, he least of all, for he knew only too well that he knew nothing and could do nothing; he could only exert some chance influence to keep people from losing faith in him as a doctor who knew how. If she had been wholly an animal she would not have suffered these tortures; if she had been wholly a human being she would have believed in God and would have said and thought, as village woman say and think: 'God giveth, God taketh away; nothing is done but by the will of God.' She would have thought that the life and death of all people, including her own children, was within the power of God and not of man, and then she would not have been tortured by the thought that she was able to prevent the illness and death of her children and would not have attempted to. But this was how she looked at it: she was entrusted with the weakest and most delicate of creatures, creatures who might fall prey to a countless number of ills; she felt a passionate, animal love for these creatures, she was responsible for them, and yet the means of preserving them was hidden from all but a few pundits whose advice and services could be obtained only for a large sum of money, and not always, at that.

"My wife's life with her children, and consequently mine as well, was a torture rather than a joy. How could it be otherwise? She was in constant anguish. Sometimes in the calm following a jealous scene or an ordinary quarrel, I would hope to relax, I would long to read, to think, but no sooner would I set my mind on something than news would come that Vasya had vomited, or there were blood-streaks in Masha's stool, or Andrei had broken out in a rash, and there I was—all my hopes dashed to the ground. Where must I go? What doctor must I get? How were we to isolate the child? And then—medicine, thermometers, enemas, doctors... Scarcely was this siege over when another began. There was no such thing as a normal, well-regulated family life. In its stead there was, as I have said, a ceaseless rescuing of ourselves from real and imaginary dangers. That is how it is in most families. It was particularly true of my family, for my wife was extremely credulous and very fond of children.

"And so the coming of children poisoned our life instead of improving it. Furthermore, the children were a new cause of dissension. This became evident as soon as they appeared, and the older they grew, the oftener they were a means and an object of dissension. They were not only an object of dissension, they were a weapoin of struggle as well. We fought each other with our children. Each of us had his favourite child and used it as his weapon. My thrusts were usually directed against our eldest boy, Vasya; hers, against Liza. As the children grew up and their characters developed they became prospective allies, whom each of us tried to win over to his side. They, poor things, suffered dreadfully from this, but we were too much engrossed in our constant state of war to think of them. Our daughter was on my side, our eldest boy (he resembled my wife and was her favourite) was on hers, and I often found him hateful."

XVII

"And so we lived from day to day. Our relations became more and more antagonistic. In the end it was not disagreements that gave rise to antagonism, but antagonism that gave rise to disagreements. I disagreed with anything she had to say before she said it, and she did the same.

"In the fourth year both parties concluded independently that we could neither understand each other nor be in accord. We no longer tried to come to an understanding. In the most simple matters, especially if they concerned the children, each of us kept to his own unwavering opinion. As I recall it now, the opinions I defended were not so dear to me that I could not have relinquished them; but her opinions were different, and so to have given in would have meant giving in to her. This I could not do. Nor could she. Probably she considered herself to be in the right; I was certain that I was. When we were alone

together we were doomed to silence or
to carrying on conversations that were
practically on an animal level: 'What time is
it?' 'Time to get to bed.' 'What are we having
for dinner today?' 'Where shall we go?' 'What
news are in the papers?' 'We must send for
the doctor; Masha has a sore throat.' If we
diverged from these impossibly narrow
subjects of conversation by a hair's breadth,
we were sure to become exasperated. We
flared up, vituperations were called forth
by the coffee, the table-cloth, the carriage,
a move in a card-game—things that could not
possibly have held the slightest importance
either for her or for me. For myself I may say
that at times my hatred of her reached
a fantastic pitch. Sometimes as I watched her
pouring out tea, swinging her foot, lifting
a spoon to her mouth, or sipping tea I hated
her for the way she did it as much as if it were
the most heinous of crimes. At that time
I failed to notice that my periods of hate
regularly and inevitably followed the periods
of what is called love. A period of love,
a period of hate; an intense period of love,
a prolonged period of hate; a weak period
of love, a brief period of hate. We did not
then realize that this love and hate were
different aspects of one and the same animal
feeling.

"Life would have been a nightmare if we
had understood the true state of affairs, but
we did not understand, we did not see things

as they really were. In that lies a person's
salvation as well as his punishment: however
wrong a person's way of life is, he is able to
hide it from himself, to disguise the tragedy
of this situation. That is what we did. She
found distraction in strained, flustered household activities, arranging the rooms, dressing
herself and the children, looking after the
children's studies and health. I had my own
means of intoxication—the intoxication of
work, hunting, and cards. Both of us kept
busy all of the time. Both of us felt that the
busier we were, the nastier we had a right to
be to each other. 'It's all very well for you to
make those faces,' I said to her mentally,
'you kept me awake all night with that row
of yours, and now I have to attend a con-
ference.' 'It's all very well for you,' she said
not only mentally but aloud, 'but I was kept
awake all night by the baby.'

"And that is how we went on living, in a
sort of fog that kept us from seeing things
as they really were. And if what happened
later had never happened, I might have lived
to a ripe old age, thinking to the day of my
death that I had lived a good life—not particularly good, but good enough—the sort
everybody lives; I would never have realized
in what an abyss of misery and falsehood
I was floundering.

"We were like two mortal enemies put
together in the stocks, bound by a single
chain, poisoning each other's lives and refusing

to admit it. I was not yet aware that ninety-nine per cent of all husbands and wives live in the same way, and that this is inevitable. At that time I did not know this about myself or about others.

"What strange coincidences occur in life, whether one is living the right or the wrong way! When parents reach a point at which life is quite unbearable, it becomes necessary to move into town for the sake of the children's education. We, too, were confronted by this necessity."

He grew silent and twice made the sound that was like a suppressed sob. We were approaching a station.

"What time is it?" he asked.

I looked. It was two o'clock.

"Aren't you tired?" he asked.

"No, but you must be."

"I feel suffocated. I shall take a walk and have a drink of water."

And, swaying on his feet, he walked off down the corridor, I sat there alone, going over in my mind all he had said, and so lost in thought was I that I did not notice him come back through the door at the other end.

XVIII

"I cannot speak calmly," he began. "I have spent much time pondering over these things, I have come to look upon many things differently, and I want to impart my views to others.

"Well, we began to live in town. It is easier for unhappy people to live in town. In town a person can live a hundred years without realizing he has died and gone to dust long ago. There is no time to 'know thyself.' Everyone is too busy. Business affairs, social demands, health, art, the children's health, their education. Today you must entertain so-and-so; tomorrow you must call on so-and-so. You must see this and hear that. In town there is always one, or perhaps two, or even three celebrities who are not to be ignored. There is the doctor, for yourself or your children; there is the teacher, the tutor, the governess and on the whole, life is as empty as a barrel.

"That is how we lived, and the pain of our living together was assuaged. During the first months we were occupied with the fascinating task of settling ourselves in the new flat, in the new town, and making trips from town to country and from country to town.

"One winter went by, and during the next there occured what seemed to be a trifling, insignificant circumstance, but one that was directly responsible for what happened eventually. She was not well, and those rascals declared she must not have any more children and taught her how to avoid having them. I found this repulsive. I did everything I could to prevent it, but she insisted on it with frivolous obstinacy, and I gave in. The last excuse for our bestiality—children—was now removed, and life became more disgusting than ever.

"Peasants have need of children; however hard it is to feed them, they have need of them, and so their conjugal life is justified. But we of the upper classes have children without any need of them, they are only an extra care and expense, they are unwanted claimants to the legacy, they are a burden. And so we are left without any justification whatever for our bestiality. Either we use artificial means of ridding ourselves of children, or we look upon them as a misfortune, a mistake resulting from lack of caution, which is the most disgusting of all. There is no justification. But we have fallen so low that we do not even see any need of justification. The vast majority of educated people today give themselves up to profligacy without any pangs of conscience.

"And how could we suffer pangs of conscience when there is no longer any conscience, unless we can call public opinion or the Criminal Code a sort of conscience? But in this case neither the one nor the other is outraged: public opinion cannot object because *everybody* does it, even Maria Pavlovna and Ivan Zakharich. (What? Would you have us breed a lot of beggars or deprive ourselves of the opportunity of moving in society?) As for the Criminal Code—there is nothing to fear here. It is only low women and soldiers' sweethearts who throw their babies into ponds and wells; they, of course, must be put in prison, but *we* do everything in good time and antiseptically.

"For two more years we lived in this way. The rascals' methods were effective; she blossomed forth, and became more beautiful, like a flower in late summer. Aware of this, she began to pay more attention to herself. There was something challenging, something disturbing about her beauty. She was a full-blown, thirty-year-old, non-child-bearing, well-fed, spirited young woman. The sight of her caused a fluttering of the heart. When she moved among men she attracted their gaze. She was like a well-fed unexercised horse in full trappings that is suddenly given free rein. There was no rein on her at all, as there is no rein on ninety-nine per cent of our women. I realized this and was afraid."

XIX

He got up impulsively and took a seat at the window.

"I beg your pardon," he said, turning away. There he sat gazing out of the window for some three minutes. Then he gave a sigh and came back to sit beside me. His face was quite different, there was a pathetic look in his eyes and his lips were puckered into something like a smile.

'I am a bit tired, but I will go on. There is still a lot of time left—it is not yet growing light. Ye-es,'' he began, lighting a cigarette, "she grew fair and buxom when she ceased bearing children, and her illness—that incessant suffering because of the children—got better. Not that it disappeared entirely, but she was like one emerging from a drunken torpor, who suddenly sees the world about her with all its joys, a world she had forgotten about, that she had been unable to appreciate, that she had not understood. 'I must not let it slip by! Time is passing, it will never return!' That, it seems to me, is what she thought, or rather, what she felt, and she could not have thought and felt otherwise: she had been brought up to believe that there is only one thing worth living for—love. She had got married, and although she had received something from that love, it was far from being what she had expected, what she had been promised; on the contrary, it had brought her much disappointment and suffering, in addition to a quite unexpected form of torment—children. This torment had worn her out. And now, thanks to the solicitous doctors, she had discovered that one can avoid having children. She rejoiced, she enjoyed the new sensation, she was rejuvenated for the one purpose she knew in life—love. But not love with a sullied, jealous, spiteful husband. She began to dream of a different sort of love, something new and pure. At least so I fancied. And she began to look about her, as if awaiting someone. I saw this and became alarmed. Over and over again, when, as was her custom, she spoke to me through the medium of others—that is, when she spoke to others but addressed her words to me—she said boldly and with a half playful air (seeming to forget that she had expressed the opposite view an hour before) that a mother's devotion to her children was a deception, that it was not worth sacrificing one's life for one's children when one was still young and could enjoy life. So she gave her children less attention, and what she gave lacked the old desperate intensity, and she spent more and more time on herself and her appearance, although she concealed the fact, on pleasure, and even on self-improvement. Once more she took up the piano, which she had quite abandoned. And that is how everything began."

His tired eyes wandered to the window again, but he instantly drew them back and seemed to be forcing himself to go on.

"And then came that man."

He paused and made his strange sound two or three times.

I could see that it was painful for him to name the man, to recall him, to speak of him. But he forced himself to, and his voice was full of determination, as if he were tearing down barriers.

"He was a vile creature, I thought. And

not because of the role he played in my life but because he really was vile. His being vile, by the way, is proof of how irresponsible she was. If it had not been he, it would have been someone else—it was bound to happen!" Again he paused. "He was a musician, a violinist; not a professional violinist—half musician, half society man. His father was a landowner, my own father's neighbour. His father lost all his money and the children—there were three boys—were sent to boarding schools, all but the youngest, who was sent to his godmother in Paris. There he was enrolled in the conservatoire because he had a talent for music, and he finished as a violinist and played at concerts. As a man he was—" Evidently he had intended to say something beastly about him, but he restrained himself and went on quickly, "I can't say what sort of life he led there; I only know that that year he appeared in Russia and came to my house.

"Moist, almond-shaped eyes, smiling red lips, a waxed moustache, the latest style of hairdress, vulgarly good-looking, what the women call 'not bad', a weak but not ugly physique with a well-developed backside such as women have, or Hottentots, so they say. Hottentots, too, are musical I have heard. He became familiar if given the opportunity, but, being sensitive, recoiled at the slightest rebuff. He held himself with dignity, wore buttoned boots of a peculiar Parisian shade, bright neckties, and other things which foreigners pick up in Paris and which always impress the women because of their novelty and originality. He always assumed an affected, superficial gaiety, and had a manner of speaking in hints and snatches, as if everyone knew what he wanted to say and could finish it for himself.

"He and his music were the cause of everything. At the trial it was made to appear that everything happened because of jealousy. Nothing of the sort—that is, not nothing of the sort, but still—not that. At the trial it was decided that I was a wronged husband who had killed my wife in defence of my honour (that is the name they gave to it). And so I was acquitted. At the trial I attempted to get at the root of the matter, but they thought I was just trying to preserve my wife's fair name.

"Whatever her relations were with that musician, they meant nothing to me, or to her either. The only thing that meant anything was what I have already told you—my bestiality. Everything happened because there was that dreadful gulf between us; so great was the strain of our mutual hatred that the slightest provocation was enough to bring things to a head. Our quarrels had become terrible, and they were the more terrible in that they alternated with periods of intense animal passion.

"If that man had not put in an appearance,

another would. If the motivating force had
not been jealousy, it would have been something else. I contend that all men who live
as I did must either become completely
dissolute, or leave their wives, or kill themselves or their wives, as I did. Anyone who
escapes is a rare exception. Before I ended
things in the way I did, I had been many
times on the verge of suicide, and she, too,
had attempted to poison herself."

XX

"Yes, that is how things were not long
before the end. We were living under a sort
of truce that we ought to have preserved.
But then one day I remarked that a certain
dog had won a medal at a show.

"'Not a medal but a recommendation,'
she said.

"We began to argue. We jumped from one
subject to another. There were reproaches:

"'Oh, everybody knows that; it's always
like that. You said...'

"'I said nothing of the kind.'

"'In other words I'm a liar?!'

"I felt that we were on the verge of one of
those terrible quarrels that made me want
to kill her or myself. I was sure we were on
the verge of it, I dreaded it like fire, I wanted
to restrain myself, but my whole being was
consumed by fury. She was in the same or

even worse state; she intentionally distorted
what I said, gave my words the wrong
meaning. Every word she spoke was saturated
with poison; she sought out my most
vulnerable spots and was sure to make her
thrusts there. On and on. I shouted, 'Hold
your tongue!' or something of the sort. She
jumped up and rushed into the nursery. I
tried to stop her so that I could finish what
I had to say. I seized her arm. She pretended
to be hurt and cried out, 'Children! Your
father is hurting me!'

" 'Don't lie!' I shouted.

" 'It isn't the first time!' she shouted back.

"The children rushed to her side. She tried
to calm them.

" 'Don't pretend,' I said.

" 'For you everything is pretence; you
could kill a person and then accuse him of
pretending. Now I understand everything—
that's just what you want!'

" 'I'll see you dead!' I shrieked.

"Even now I can remember how horrified
I was by my own words. I had not supposed
myself capable of saying such harsh, dreadful
words, and I could not believe they had come
out of my mouth. After shrieking them I ran
into my study, sat down, and began to smoke.
I heard her go into the hall and put on her
things. I asked her where she was going. She
did not answer. 'The devil with her,' I said
to myself; and returned to my study, where
I lay down and began to smoke again.

"Through my head passed a thousand plans for taking revenge on her, for getting rid of her, for patching things up and going on as if nothing had happened. There I lay thinking and smoking, smoking, smoking. I thought of running away from her, going in hiding, leaving for America. I reached the point of imagining life without her, how marvellous it would be, how I would join my life with that of another, a wonderful woman, utterly different. I would get rid of her by having her die, or by divorcing her, and I began to scheme how to accomplish this. I realized I was thinking things I ought not to think, and I smoked to keep myself from facing this realization.

"Life in the house ran its usual course. The governess came in and asked where the mistress was and when she would be back. The footman came in and asked if he should serve tea. I went into the dining-room. The children, especially Liza, who was old enough to understand, cast looks of cold inquiry at me. We had our tea in silence. She did not come back. The evening passed and still she did not come back. Two feelings warred within me: anger with her for torturing me and the children by staying away when she knew she would only come back again, and fear that she would not come back but would lay hands on herself. I would have gone in search of her, but where was I to go? To her sister's? I would look foolish if I went and asked for her, and that was just what she wanted. The deuce with her! If she was so bent on torturing somebody, let it be herself. Otherwise the next quarrel would only be worse. But what if she were not at her sister's and intended laying hands on herself, or had already done so?

"Eleven o'clock, twelve... I did not go up to the bedroom—silly to just lie there alone and wait. I could not lie down in my study, either. I wanted to busy myself with something, to write letters, or to read, but I could do nothing. I sat alone in my study—angry, tortured by my thoughts, listening for the least sound.

"Three o'clock, four—still she did not come. Towards morning I fell asleep. I woke up. She had not come.

"Life at home went on, but everyone was perplexed and kept looking at me inquiringly and reproachfully, assuming that it was all my fault. And within me the same struggle was going on—anger with her for torturing me and anxiety about her.

"At about eleven o'clock her sister came as an emissary from her. She began in the usual way: 'She is in a dreadful state. What could have happened?'

"'Why, nothing happened,' and I added that she had an impossible character and that I had done nothing at all.

"'But things cannot remain as they are,' said her sister.

" 'That is up to her, not me,' said I. 'I refuse to take the first step. If we are to separate, we must separate.'

"My sister-in-law went away without any satisfaction. I had boldly declared that I would not take the first step, but when she was gone and I came out and saw the children looking so frightened and pathetic, I was quite ready to reconsider this. I would have been only too glad to take the first step, but I did not know how. Again I paced the floor and smoked. I drank vodka and wine for breakfast and gradually achieved what I had unconsciously been longing for: I lost sight of the baseness and stupidity of the stand I had taken.

"At about three o'clock she came home. She said nothing on seeing me. Supposing that she had repented, I began to explain that my words had been evoked by her reproaches. With the same stern and haggard face she said she had not come for explanations but to take the children, that we could not go on living together. I tried to say it was not my fault, that she had driven me to desperation. For a moment she stared at me harshly, gloatingly, then she said:

" 'Say nothing more, you'll only regret it.'

"I said I could not abide comedy. At this she shouted something unintelligible and rushed to her room. I heard the key turn in the door—she had locked herself in. I knocked, there was no answer, and I stamped wrathfully away. Half an hour later Liza came running to me in tears.

" 'What is it? Has something happened?'

" 'There's not a sound coming from mama's room.'

"We went to the room. I pulled on the door with all my might. The bolt did not hold and both halves of the door opened. I went over to the bed. She was lying unconscious, in an awkward position, in her skirts and boots. On the bed-table lay an empty bottle of opium. We brought her to. Again tears, and at last a reconciliation. But not a real reconciliation; the old animosity remained in the heart of each of us, and to it was added the resentment for the suffering this quarrel had caused us and for which each blamed the other. But we could not go on nursing our resentment for ever, and so life resumed its old course. Quarrels like this and even worse took place all the time—once a month, once a week, once a day. The same thing over and over. Once I applied for a passport to go abroad (our quarrel had lasted two days), but then there was a half explanation, a half reconciliation, and I did not go."

XXI

"This was the situation when that man put in an appearance. As soon as he arrived in Moscow (his name was Trukhachevsky)

he came to see me. It was a morning visit.
I received him. At one time he and I had been
on intimate terms, and during our talk he felt
his way, trying to restore our terms of inti-
macy, but I made it clear from the very
beginning that I did not want to, and he
adapted himself to my tone. I disliked him
the moment I set eyes on him. But oddly
enough, some strange, fatal force prevented
me from repulsing him, from sending him
away, and made me, on the contrary, en-
courage him. How easy it would have been
for me to have received him coolly and sent
him away without introducing him to my
wife! But no, I had to talk about his playing,
to say someone had told me he had dropped
the violin. He denied it and said he was
playing more than ever. He recalled that I had
once played. I said I did not play any more
but that my wife played very well.

"And an amazing thing: my relations with
him from the very first day, from the very
first hour, were such as they would have
been had I foreseen the outcome of this visit.
There was a certain tension between us;
I noted every word, every expression either
of us used, and attributed special significance
to it.

"I introduced my wife to him. The talk
immediately turned to music and he offered
to come and play with her. My wife was
handsomely and alluringly dressed (as she
always was of late) and looked disturbingly

beautiful. She seemed to like him from the first. She was also delighted with the prospect of playing piano and violin duets, for she especially enjoyed this and often hired a violinist from the theatre to play with her. Her face expressed her joy. A glimpse of my face told her how I felt about it and she instantly changed her expression, and that game of mutual deception began. I smiled graciously, pretending to be pleased. He looked at my wife in the way all lechers look at beautiful women, but pretended to be interested only in what we were talking about, although he was not at all interested in it. She tried to appear indifferent, but she could not help being disturbed by the false smile of her jealous husband (a smile she knew only too well) and the lustful glances of our visitor. I noticed a special shine in her eyes the first time she saw him, and probably it was my jealousy that caused an electric current to flow between them, making them duplicate each other's smiles, glances, and facial expressions. She blushed—he blushed; she smiled—he smiled. They talked about music, about Paris, about various trifles. He got up to leave and stood there smiling, holding his hat against his quivering thigh, glancing from her to me as if waiting to see what we would do. That moment is especially impressed on my memory because at that moment I could have refrained from inviting him back, and then nothing would have happened. But I looked at him, then at her, and said to her in my mind, 'Don't think I am jealous', and to him, 'Don't think I am afraid', and then I invited him to bring his violin some evening and play with my wife. She glanced at me in astonishment, blushed, and, as if afraid of something, protested that she played too poorly to accompany him. Her refusal to play only irritated me the more, and I insisted that he come. I remember the strange feeling with which I stared at the back of his head and noted a sliver of white neck and his black hair parted down the middle, as he walked jerkily, with a bird-like hop, out of the room. I could not but confess to myself that it was agony for me to be in his presence. 'It all depends on me,' I thought, 'whether I shall ever see him again or not.' But not to see him would mean that I was afraid of him. No, I was not afraid of him. That, I thought, would be too humiliating. And there in the hall, knowing that my wife could hear me, I insisted that he come with his violin that very evening. He promised, and went away.

"That evening he brought his violin and they played. But nothing much came of it: they did not have the right music (my wife could not play what they had without practising). I was very fond of music and helped them to the best of my ability—set up a stand for him and turned the pages. They played a few things, some songs without words and a Mozart sonata. He played beautifully, drawing the most exquisite tone from his instrument. He also displayed a refinement of taste that was not at all in keeping with his character.

"Naturally his playing was much superior to my wife's and he helped her, at the same time paying her respectful compliments. He behaved himself admirably. My wife appeared to be interested only in the music, and her manners were very simple and unaffected. I, too, pretended to be interested only in the music, but all evening I was tortured by jealousy.

"The minute their eyes met I saw that the animal crouching inside each of them, in defiance of all the rules of their social position, posed the question, 'May I?' and answered, 'Indeed you may.' I saw that he had not expected to find my wife, a Moscow woman, so charming, and was delighted with her. Not for a moment did he doubt that she would have him. The whole problem lay in getting round that insufferable husband. Had I myself been chaste I would not have understood this, but I myself, like most others, had taken the same view of women before my marriage, and so I could read his mind like a book. My tortures were increased by knowing beyond a shadow of a doubt that, outside of brief moments of sensuality, her only feeling for me was one of irritation, and that this man, because of his novelty and

his elegant appearance, but especially because
of his outstanding talent for music, because
of the closeness arising from their playing
together, and the influence wielded by music
(especially violin music) over sensitive
natures—that this man would not only make
her like him, but that without a second's
thought he would conquer her, dazzle her,
wind her round his little finger, do anything
he wanted with her. I could not help seeing
this, and it caused me untold suffering. And
in spite of this, or perhaps because of it,
some force acting against my will made me
treat him with particular consideration, made
me even gentle with him. Whether I did it
for my wife's sake, to show her that I was
not afraid of him, or for my own sake, to
deceive myself, I cannot say, but from the
very first I found it impossible to be simple
and direct with him. I countered the desire
to kill him on the spot by being gentle with
him. I treated him to expensive wines for
supper, I went in raptures over his playing,
I smiled graciously when speaking to him,
and I invited him to dine with us on the
following Sunday and play with my wife
again. I said I would also invite some of
our friends who were fond of music to hear
him.

"On that the evening ended."

In a state of great agitation Pozdnyshev
shifted his position and made his peculiar
sound.

"Strange how that man affected me," he began again with an obvious effort to compose himself. "As I entered the hall on returning from an exhibition three or four days later my heart suddenly went heavy as a stone, and I could not tell why. It was because when passing through the vestibule I had seen something reminding me of him. It was only on entering my study that I became conscious of what it was, and went back to the vestibule to make sure. No, I had not been mistaken: there hung his fashionable coat. (Without realizing it, I took particular notice of everything that was his.) I made inquiries. Yes, he was there. I went to the reception-room, not through the drawing-room, but through the children's class-room. My daughter Liza was poring over her book and the nursemaid was sitting at the table holding the little one and twirling a lid of some sort. The door into the reception-room was closed and I could hear arpeggios and his voice and hers. I listened, but could not make out anything. Evidently the piano was being played with the intent of drowning out the sound of their voices, perhaps of their kisses. Good God, what happened to me then! The very thought of the beast that dwelt within me at that moment sends shudders through me. My heart contracted, stopped, and then pounded like a sledge-hammer. The dominant feeling was pity for myself (this is always true when a person is in a frenzy). 'In front of the children! In front of the nurse!' I thought. I must have looked terrible, judging by the odd way in which Liza looked at me. 'What am I to do?' I asked myself. 'Go in? I dare not. God only knows what I am capable of.' But I could not go away either. The nurse was looking at me as if she understood my feelings. 'I must go in,' I said to myself, and I swiftly opened the door. He was sitting at the grand-piano playing arpeggios with his large white fingers. She was standing by the piano looking through the music. She was the first to see or hear me come in and she looked up. Perhaps she was frightened, but she pretended not to be, or perhaps she was nor frightened at all. At any rate, she did not start or stir; she only blushed, and that not at once.

" 'How glad I am that you've come; we can't decide what to play on Sunday,' she said in a tone she would never have used with me if we had been alone. I resented her using 'we' in respect to herself and him. I greeted him without a word. He shook my hand, and with a smile which appeared to me sheer mockery, explained that he had brought music for Sunday and that they could not come to an agreement as to what to play—a difficult classical piece (Beethoven's sonata for violin and piano) or some little pieces. He said it so simply and naturally that I could find nothing to take exception to, and yet I was certain that everything he said was false and they had come to a secret agreement to deceive me.

"A source of the greatest torture for those who are jealous (and in our form of society all are jealous) is the physical proximity of men and women sanctioned by our traditions. One would make of himself a laughing-stock if he attempted to prevent physical proximity at balls, the physical proximity of doctors and their patients, the physical proximity of those studying art, painting, and especially music. Here are two people studying music, the most noble of the arts; their study requires physical proximity and there is nothing in the least reprehensible about this physical proximity; only the most foolish and jealous of husbands could find anything to object to. And yet everyone knows that it is precisely these studies, especially music, that give rise to adultery among people of our set.

"My own disconcertment seemed to be communicated to them; for some time I was unable to utter a word. I was like an upturned bottle out of which nothing can flow because it is too full. I wanted to upbraid him, to put him out of my house, but I realized I must be courteous. And I was. I pretended to approve of everything, and because of the contrariness that made me the more gracious the more painful I found his presence, I told him that I relied completely on his judgement and advised her to do the same. He lingered for just so long as was necessary to smooth over the unpleasant impression made by my startled entry and strained silence, and then he took his leave, pretending that at last they had decided what to play on the following day. I was certain that it made not the least difference to them what they played, so absorbed were they in something quite different.

"I was particularly attentive as I saw him out (how else is one to see out the man who has come to destroy the peace and happiness of one's home!) With particular warmth I pressed his soft white hand."

XXII

"I said not a word to her the rest of the day. I could not. Her presence roused such hatred within me that I feared the consequences. At dinner she asked me in the presence of the children when I intended leaving (I had to attend a regional convention the following week). I told her. She asked me if there was anything she could get ready for me. I made no answer. I sat at the table without speaking for a while, then, still without speaking, went into my study. Of late she had ceased coming to me in my study, especially at such an hour. I lay there nursing my anger. Suddenly I heard her step. Into my mind came the dreadful, the hideous thought that, like the wife of Uriah, she was coming to me at that unusual hour to conceal her sin. 'Can she really be coming to speak to me?' I thought as I listened to her steps approaching. 'If she is, then I am right.' An unspeakable hatred for her filled my heart. The steps came nearer, nearer. Surely they would pass by the door and go into the reception-room? No, the door creaked and there she stood in the doorway—tall, beautiful, with a timid look of appeal in her eyes that she tried to hide, but which I detected and knew the meaning of. I held my breath for so long that I nearly choked. Still looking at her, I took out my cigarette-case and lighted up.

" 'Is it nice to smoke when I have come to talk to you?' she said, sitting down close to me on the sofa and leaning towards me.

"I moved away so that she should not touch me.

" 'I see you are displeased that I am going to play on Sunday,' she said.

" 'Not in the least,' I said.

" 'As if I could not see it!'

" 'I'm very glad if you do. As for me, I see nothing but that you are behaving like a bitch...'

" 'If you are going to swear like a cabby I shall go away.'

" 'Do. Only remember, if the honour of the family means nothing to you, it means much to me—it's not you I care about—you can go to the devil for all I care—it's the honour of the family!'

" 'What? What are you saying!?'

" 'Go away! For God's sake go away!'

"Feigning not to understand (or perhaps she really did not understand), she got up, hurt and angry. But instead of going out, she stood still in the middle of the room.

" 'You really have become impossible,' she began. 'Not even an angel could live with you.' Trying as usual to strike my most vulnerable spot, she reminded me of the incident with my sister (when in a fit of rage I had said all sorts of coarse things to her; it was a very painful memory and she knew it, and that was why she brought it up at this moment). 'After that, nothing you do can surprise me,' she said.

" 'You would like to insult, humiliate, and disgrace me, and then say I am to blame,' I said to myself. Suddenly I was seized by hatred such as I had never felt before, and for the first time I longed to give physical expression to my hatred. I leaped up and made for her, but I remember that just as I leaped up I became aware of what I was doing and asked myself if it was right to give way to my feelings, and answered that it was, because in that way I would frighten her. And so instead of suppressing my hatred I surrendered myself to it and rejoiced to feel it running riot within me.

" 'Get out before I kill you!' I shouted, going over to her and seizing her by the arm. I purposely stressed the tone of hatred as

I said it, and I must have looked terrible, for she was so frightened she could not move.

"'Vasya,' she said. 'What is the matter with you?'

"'Get out!' I roared louder than ever. 'You drive me to fury. I cannot answer for what I shall do.'

"Having succumbed to my fury, I exulted in it and wanted to do something extraordinary that would demonstrate the extremity of my feelings. I wanted passionately to strike, to kill her, but I knew I must not do this, and so, to give vent to my passion, I snatched up the paperweight and hurled it past her, shouting. 'Get out!' My aim was good and it went past without striking her. She went out, but halted in the doorway. And while she was still there and could see me (I did it with the express purpose of having her see me) I picked up the things on my writing-desk, the candlesticks, the ink-stand, and hurled them on the floor.

"'Get out!' I shouted. 'Get out! I cannot answer for what I shall do!'

"She went away, and I instantly calmed down.

"An hour later the nursemaid came and told me my wife was in hysterics. I went to her. She was sobbing and laughing, could say nothing, and her body was twitching all over. She was not pretending, she was really ill.

"In the morning she was better and we

enjoyed a reconciliation under the influence of the feeling called love. When, after our reconciliation, I confessed to being jealous of Trukhachevsky, she showed no embarrassment, she merely laughed the most natural laugh in the world and said it was ridiculous to suppose she would become infatuated with such a man.

" 'Could any decent woman feel anything for a man like that? Nothing but the pleasure that comes of music. If you wish, I shall refuse to see him ever again, even Sunday, although the guests are invited. Write him a note that I am unwell and that will be the end of it. The only thing I regret is that anyone, especially he himself, should fancy he is dangerous. I am too proud to admit of such a thing.'

"She was not lying; she believed what she said. She hoped by these words to make herself despise him and to build up defences against him, but she failed. Everything was against her, especially that accursed music. We said no more about it, and on Sunday our guests came and my wife and he played for them."

XXIII

"I think it is hardly necessary to say that I was a vain man; what is there to live for in our society if one is without vanity? And so I saw to it that the dinner and the evening of music were arranged so as to do us credit. I myself bought the food for dinner and invited the guests.

"At six o'clock they arrived, and he came too, in evening dress, with diamond studs, showing his bad taste. He assumed a nonchalant air and smiled readily when spoken to, as if everything one said and did was just what he expected, don't you know. I took particular pleasure in noting every mark of ill breeding in him because it served to soothe me and prove that, as she herself had said, he was too far beneath her for her to stoop to an infatuation with him. I no longer allowed myself to be jealous. In the first place, I had already suffered so much from jealousy that I was exhausted and needed a rest; in the second, I wanted to believe my wife's asseverations, and so I did. Despite the fact that I was not jealous, all during dinner and the part of the evening preceding the music I could not relax and be myself with either of them, but kept watching their movements and glances.

"The dinner was like all dinners—stiff and boring. The music began rather early. How every detail of that evening is impressed on my mind! I remember his picking up his violin, unlocking the case, removing the cover some woman had embroidered for him, taking out the instrument, and tuning it up. I remember the air of indifference my wife assumed to hide her bashfulness (a bashfulness caused primarily by her playing) and her sitting down with this false expression on her face. Then began the sounding of middle G, the plucking of strings, the setting up of sheets of music. I remember their exchanging looks, their glancing at the assembled guests, their saying something to each other, then beginning. He played the first chord. I remember the grave, strained, fine expression that came to his face, as, listening for his tone, he pressed the strings with cautious fingers. And the piano responded. They had begun."

He stopped and made that strange sound several times in succession. When he tried to speak again he could only utter a choking sound, so he waited.

"They played Beethoven's Kreutzer Sonata. Do you know that first *Presto*? Do you?" he shouted. "Ugh! A dreadful thing, that sonata. Especially that movement. And in general, music is a dreadful thing. What is it? I don't understand. Just what is music? What does it do to a person? And why does it do it? They say music has an elevating influence on the soul. Nonsense. A lie. It certainly does have an influence, and a terrible influence (I can only speak for myself), but it is not an influence that elevates the soul. It neither elevates nor abases; it merely excites. How shall I put it? Music causes me to forget myself and my true state; it transports me to another state that is not my own. Under the influence of music I fancy I feel things I really do not feel, understand things I do not understand, am capable of things I am incapable of. I explain it by the fact that music affects me like a yawn, or laughter: I am not sleepy, yet I yawn when I see another yawn; I find nothing to laugh at, yet I laugh on hearing another laugh.

"Music instantly throws me into the spiritual mood in which the composer found himself while writing it. My soul merges with his and I am taken with him from one mood to another, but why I should go through those moods I cannot say. The composer, on the other hand—let's say the composer of the Kreutzer Sonata, Beethoven—knew why he was in that particular mood. The mood led him to the performing of definite acts, and so this mood had sense for him, but it has no sense for me. Music excites to no purpose. To be sure, if a military march is played, the soldiers march off and therefore the music achieves its end; if a dance is played, I dance, and again the music achieves its end. The same thing is true if a mass is played and I take the sacrament. In other cases it merely excites, without supplying any outlet for this excitement. That is why music wields so terrible, sometimes so frightful, an influence. In China music falls under the jurisdiction of the state. And so it should. Is it permissible that any chance person should hypnotize another (or even many others) and make him do whatever he likes? The worst of it is that often the hypnotist is a person of no moral principles.

"It is a dreadful weapon for chance individuals to wield. Take this Kreutzer Sonata—the first movement. How dare anyone play this *Presto* in a drawing-room where there are women sitting about in *décolleté*?—to play it, applaud it, and then eat ices and exchange the latest gossip? Such music must be played only in very definite and meaningful circumstances, when very definite and meaningful undertakings, corresponding to the music, are to be embarked upon. Once it is played, the actions inspired by the mood must be carried out. Otherwise the unspent feelings and energies, incompatible with the place and the time, are sure to wreak havoc. On me, at least, this music had a devastating effect. It seemed to reveal to me entirely new feelings and capabilities of which I had been utterly unaware. 'This is how it is,' it seemed to say to me; 'not at all as you are used to thinking and being, but like this.' Just what this new way was I could not say, but the consciousness of the new state brought me joy. I saw all the same people, including her and him, in an entirely new light.

"After the *Presto* they played the delightful if commonplace *Andante* with its vulgar variations and weak finale. At the insistence of the guests they played a few other pieces,

an elegy by Ernst, it seems, and something
else. They were all very nice, but they did not
make one-tenth the impression on me that the
first piece did. I heard them against the
background of the impression made upon me
by the first. I was gay and light-hearted for
the rest of the evening. Never before had I
seen my wife as she was then. The shine of
her eyes, the graveness and significance of her
expression as she played, and her utter limp-
ness and her faint smile, blissful yet pathetic,
when she finished. I saw all that but the only
meaning I attached to it was that she had had
revealed to her, just as I had, new and unfamiliar emotions, evoked, as it were, from
out the depths of memory.

"The evening ended successfully and
everybody went home.

"Knowing that in two days' time I was
leaving for the convention, Trukhachevsky
said on leaving that he hoped the pleasure
he had enjoyed that evening would be repeated
the next time he came to our town. I took
this to mean that he considered it impossible
to visit at my house while I was away, and
this pleased me. Since I would not return
from the convention before he had left town,
I supposed I would not see him again.

"For the first time I shook his hand with
genuine pleasure and thanked him for the
enjoyment. He took leave of my wife, too, as
if for a long time. It seemed to me there was
nothing in their manner but what was most

natural and decorous. Everything was capital. My wife and I were both highly pleased with the evening."

XXIV

"Two days later I left for the country, taking leave of my wife with an easy heart and in the best of spirit.

"There are always no end of things to attend to in the country; it is a world of its own, with its own peculiar way of life. I attended the convention for ten hours at a stretch on each of the first two days. On the following day they brought me a letter from my wife. I read it immediately. She wrote of the children, her uncle, the nursemaid, of things she had bought, and then, in an off-hand way, as if speaking of the most ordinary thing, she mentioned that Trukhachevsky had called to bring her some music he had promised, and he had offered to play but she had refused. I did not remember his having promised her any music; I had been under the impression that he had taken final leave of her, and therefore I was unpleasantly surprised. But I was too busy to give the matter much thought until I returned to my rooms in the evening and reread her letter. It seemed to me then that, in addition to the unpleasant news of Trukhachevsky's having called in my absence, the whole tone of the letter was strained. The mad beast of jealousy roared in its den and tried to rush out, but I forced it back, so afraid was I of its brute force. 'What a low feeling jealousy is!' I said to myself. 'What could be more natural than the things she writes to me?'

"I went to bed and gave myself up to thoughts of the next day's duties. Usually I have difficulty in falling asleep in a strange bed, but that night I fell asleep very quickly. But, as sometimes happens, I woke up suddenly, as if roused by an electric shock. I woke up with thoughts of her in my mind, of my carnal love for her, and of Trukhachevsky, certain that he had had what he wanted of her. I was rigid with wrath and horror. But I began to reason with myself. 'It's all nonsense,' I told myself. 'No reason to feel this way; there is nothing and never has been anything between them. How can you lower her and yourself by supposing anything so dreadful? A sort of hired fiddler with a shady reputation, and a respectable woman, mother of a family, *your own* wife. What an incongruity!' This was one side of the argument, but the other was: 'How could there be anything but that? How could there be anything but that simple, ordinary thing, for the sake of which I married her, for the sake of which I live with her? The only thing I want of her, and the only thing that other men, including this musician, want of her. He is single and in good health (I recalled how he had ground up the gristle of a chop in his teeth, and how greedily he had sucked up a glass of wine with his red lips)—sleek, well-fed, a man who, far from being without principle, is guided by the sole principle that advantage should be taken of every opportunity that comes his way. And he and my wife are bound by bonds of music, which is the most refined means of exciting lust. What is there to restrain him? Nothing. On the contrary, there is everything to urge him on. She? Who is she? A mystery—the same mystery she has always been. I do not know her. I know only her animal nature. And an animal does not and ought not to know any restraint.'

"Only then did I recall the look on their faces that evening when, after the Kreutzer Sonata, they played a passionate little piece— I've forgotten by whom—a sensual, voluptuous thing. 'How could I have gone away?' I asked myself on recalling that look. 'Is it not clear that everything took place between them that evening? Is it not clear that on that evening there were no longer any barriers separating them, and that both of them, especially she, felt ashamed of what had taken place between them?' I remembered the faint, pathetic, blissful smile she had given me, and the way she had wiped her flushed perspiring face as I came up to the piano. Even then they had avoided each other's eyes; it was not until supper, when he poured her out a glass of water, that they glanced at each other and smiled ever so slightly. I remembered with horror having caught that glance and that fleeting smile. 'All is over,' one voice told me, while another said something quite different. 'Something has come over you,' it said. 'You are brooding over what could not possibly be true.' I could not bear to go on lying there in the darkness. I struck a match. I felt afraid in that tiny room with its yellow wall-paper. I lighted a cigarette and smoked, as I always did when I found myself running in circles around some insoluble problem. I smoked and smoked—one cigarette after another—so as to blunt my senses to the insolubility of my problem.

"I slept no more that night. At five o'clock, resolving that I could bear the strain no longer and must leave for home immediately, I got up, woke the watchman who served me, and dispatched him for horses. I sent my colleagues a note saying I had been unexpectedly summoned to Moscow on urgent business and asking them to appoint someone else in my place.

"At eight o'clock I took my seat in a tarantass and rode off."

XXV

The conductor came in. Noticing that our candle had nearly burnt out, he extinguished it without putting in a new one. It was

growing light outside. Pozdnyshev sighed
deeply but said nothing so long as the conductor was in our carriage. He resumed his
story only when he had gone out and nothing
was to be heard in the shadowy compartment
but the creaking of the windows of the
rocking train and the snoring of the shop
assistant. I could not see him at all in the faint
light of dawn. I could only hear his voice,
in which agitation and suffering became more
and more pronounced.

"I had to travel thirty-five versts by horse
and eight hours by railway. The ride in the
tarantass was delightful. It was a frosty
autumn morning with the sun shining brightly—you know the sort of morning, when the
tyres leave a sharp imprint on the moist road.
The road is smooth, the light brilliant, the air
invigorating. It was glorious, riding along. I
felt better as soon as morning came and I was
on my way. As I gazed at the horses, the
fields, the people we passed, I forgot where
I was going. At times I fancied I was simply
out for a drive, and that the circumstances
causing it were purely imaginary. I took particular joy in forgetting. Whenever I remembered
where I was going I would say to myself,
'Don't think; everything will be clear in time.'
In the middle of the journey something
happened that delayed me and distracted my
attention: the tarantass broke down and had
to be repaired. This accident had enormous
consequences; because of it I missed the

express and had to take the post train, and so I arrived in moscow not at five o'clock, as I had expected, but at twelve o'clock at night.

"A ride in a cart, repairs, the setting of accounts, lunch in a wayside inn, a talk I had with a yard porter—all of these things kept my mind occupied. By evening all was ready and I set out again, and it was even more pleasant riding in the dusk than in the daytime. There was a new moon, a slight frost, a splendid road, good horses, a jolly coachman, and I enjoyed myself to the full, hardly giving a thought to what was awaiting me; or perhaps I enjoyed myself to the full precisely because I knew what was awaiting me and therefore wished to have one last taste of the joys of life.

"But this state of composure, this ability to suppress my feelings, ended with the trip in the tarantass. The minute I entered the railway carriage I experienced something quite different. That eight-hour trip by railway was an agony I shall remember as long as I live. Perhaps it was because on entering the carriage I felt I was almost home, or because railway journeys always act on the nerves. Whatever the reason, from the moment I took my place in the carriage I was unable to control my imagination, which painted for me one picture after another to excite my jealousy, each new picture more obscene than the preceding, and all of them showing how she had been behaving in my absence,

how she had been unfaithful to me. I was
consumed by fury and indignation, and
I almost exulted in the humiliation the
contemplation of these pictures caused me.
I could not dismiss them, could not tear my
eyes from them, could not help conjuring
them up. And the longer I contemplated
these imaginary pictures, the more I believed
in their reality. The clarity with which they
presented themselves to my mind seemed
proof that my fancies were reality. Against
my will some demon was inventing and whispering in my ear the most dreadful suppositions. I remembered a talk I had had with
Trukhachevsky's brother many years before,
and with a sort of morbid ecstasy I lacerated
my heart with recollections of this talk,
applying it to the musician and my wife.

"It had taken place many years before, but
I remembered it clearly. Trukhachevsky's
brother, in reply to my question as to
whether or not he frequented brothels, had
said that no decent man would go to a place
where he might catch an infection, and where
in general it was sordid and filthy, when he
could always find a respectable woman.
And behold! his brother had found my wife.
'True, she is not as fresh as she might be, one
tooth is missing on the left side, and she
is a bit plump,' I reasoned for him, 'but it
cannot be helped; one must take what is
offered.' 'Yes, he is doing her a favour by
making her his mistress,' I said to myself.

'But then, she presents no danger of infection.'
'But what are you saying? This is unthink-
able!' I said to myself in horror. 'Nothing,
nothing of the sort has happened. You have
not the slightest grounds for supposing such
a thing. Did she herself not tell you she found
the very thought of being jealous of such
a man beneath you? Yes, but she was lying,
she was lying!' I shouted inwardly, and then
it all began again...

"There were only two other passengers in
our carriage—an old woman and her husband,
both of them very taciturn. At one of the
stations they got out and I was left alone.
I was like a caged animal: one minute I
jumped up and went to the window, the next
I staggered up and down, as if this could
accelerate the speed of the train. But the train
with its windows and benches went rocking
along at its own speed, just as ours is doing
now."

Pozdnyshev jumped up, took a turn or two,
and sat down again.

"I am afraid, dreadfully afraid to ride in
railway carriages; they always terrify me.
Yes, terrify me," he went on. "I kept saying
to myself, 'I must think of something else—
for instance, of the inn where I had lunch.'
And in my mind's eye I would see the bearded
porter and his little grandson, a boy of the
same age as my Vasya. 'My Vasya! One of
these days he will come upon the musician
kissing his mother. How the poor child will

suffer! But that is nothing to her! She is in love!..' And again the same thing. 'No, no. I will think of our inspection of the local hospital. Of how that patient complained of the doctor yesterday. The doctor had a moustache like Trukhachevsky's. With what impudence he—and she too—deceived me by saying he was going away!' And again it began. Everything, every single thing I thought of, brought me back to him. I suffered horribly. I suffered mostly because of my ignorance, my doubts, my indecision, my not knowing whether I ought to love or hate her. So great was my anguish that I remember welcoming the thought that I ought to get out of the carriage, lie down on the rails, and end it all. Then, at least, I would no longer be tortured by doubt and uncertainty. The one thing that kept me from doing this was self-pity, followed invariably by a great hatred of her. My hatred of him was mixed with an awareness of my own humiliation and his triumph; for her I felt nothing but hatred, a terrible hatred. 'I must not commit suicide and let her go free; she, too, must be made to suffer; she must be made to understand what I have gone through,' I said to myself. At every station I got out of the train to distract my thoughts. In the restaurant at one of the stations I saw some men drinking, and I ordered some vodka myself. A Jew who was standing beside me also drank. He began talking to me, and to avoid being alone in my carriage I went with him into his dirty, smoky, third-class carriage, the floor of which was strewn with the shells of sun-flower seeds. I sat down next to him and he chattered about a lot of things and told me many anecdotes. I listened but did not understand what he was saying because my mind was filled with my own thoughts. He noticed this and insisted that I be more attentive. I got up and went back to my own carriage. 'I must think it over,' I said to myself. 'I must know whether I am right in thinking what I do and whether there is any cause for me to suffer so.' I sat down to think things over calmly, but instead of thinking calmly, I began the same thing all over again. Instead of rational thoughts—pictures and fancies. 'How many times in the past have I been tortured like this!' I said to myself, recalling other fits of jealousy, 'and each time it turned out to be nothing. This time, too, I suppose—indeed, I am sure—I shall find her in bed sleeping peacefully; she will wake up and be glad to see me, and her words and looks will tell me that nothing has happened, that these are all wild fancies. Oh, how glorious it will be!' 'No; too often has it ended in that way. This time it will be different,' said the other voice, and again everything began. Yes, herein lay my punishment. Not to a hospital for syphilitics would I take young men to cure them of their lust; I would give them a glimpse into my soul, that they might see the demons rending it to pieces. The awful thing was that I claimed complete and unquestionable ownership of her body, as if it were my body, and at the same time I realized I was unable to own her body, that it was not mine, and that she could dispose of it as she wished, and she wished to dispose of it in a way I did not want her to. And there was nothing I could do either to him or to her. He, like Vanka-the-Warder in the song, would sing of her sweet kisses as he was led to the gallows. Even in death he would have the better of me. If she had not yet committed this crime, she wished to commit it, and I knew she wished to, and that made it even worse: it would be better if she had already committed it, and I knew it, and there was no longer any doubt. I could not have said what I wished. I wished her not to want what she could not help wanting. The whole thing was utter madness."

XXVI

"At the next to the last station, when the conductor came to collect our tickets, I picked up my luggage and went out on the carriage platform; the knowledge that I was almost there, that the *dénouement* was at hand, increased my excitement. I went cold and trembled so that my teeth chattered. Mechanically I followed the crowd out of the station, took a cabby, got in and rode off. As I rode I watched the few people in the streets, the yard porters, the shadow of my cab, thrown by the street lamps, now in front of me, now behind, without a thought in my head. When we had gone about half a verst I became conscious of the cold in my feet, and I remembered having taken off my woollen socks in the train and putting them in my valise. Where was my valise? Here? Here. And my basket? I had forgotten all about my luggage, but now that I remembered it and found my receipt for it, I decided it was not worth going back for and I continued on my way.

"Try as I may, I cannot remember the state I was in at that time. What did I think about? What did I want? I remember nothing except that I had a premonition of something terrible and of vast import that was about to take place. Whether this something of vast import took place because of my intentions, or because of my premonition, I do not know. Or perhaps my mind was a blank, and I just imagined afterwards that I had had such sombre thoughts.

"I drove up to the entrance. It was nearly one o'clock in the morning. Several cabbies were standing in front of the house, whose lighted windows gave them promise of passengers (the lighted windows were in our flat—the windows of the drawing-room and reception-room). Without even wondering

why there should be lights in our windows
at such a late hour, I climbed the stairs and
rang the bell, still with that premonition
of something terrible about to happen. Our
footman—kind, stupid, hardworking Yegor—
opened the door. The first thing that met my
eyes was his coat hanging in the vestibule
among other wraps. I ought to have been
astonished, but I was not; I seemed to have
expected it. 'So I was right,' I said to myself.
When I asked Yegor who was here he said
Trukhachevsky. I asked if there was anyone
else.

" 'No one, sir,' he replied.

"I remember the glad tone with which
he said this, as if anxious to disperse my fears
that there might be somebody else. 'No one.
Ah!' was what I said to myself.

" 'And the children?'

" 'All well, praise the Lord. Asleep this
long while.'

"I could scarcely breathe and could not
control the trembling of my lips. 'So this
time it is different! Those other times I
expected misfortune and did not find it;
everything turned out to be all right. This
time everything is not all right. It has come.
Here it is...'

"I almost broke down, but some demon
whispered into my ear, 'What, will you weep
and grow maudlin while they part with each
other serenely, leaving no proof of their guilt?
Do you wish to go on doubting and suffering

torment for ever?' And instantly my self-pity vanished and a new feeling took its place. You will scarcely believe it, but it was a feeling of joy that at last my sufferings were at an end, that now I could punish her, get rid of her, give vent to my fury. And I did give vent to my fury—I became a beast, a fierce and cunning beast.

" 'Wait,' I said to Yegor, who had turned to go into the drawing-room. 'Here, take this receipt and go to the station for my luggage. There is a cabby waiting at the door.'

"He went down the hall for his coat. Fearing that he might frighten them, I accompanied him to his room and waited until he put on his coat. From the reception-room that was beyond the drawing-room came the murmur of voices, the clink of knives and plates. They were eating and had not heard the door-bell. 'If only they do not come out now,' I thought. Yegor got into his coat with the astrakhan collar and went out. I saw him to the door and locked it behind him. A feeling of terror came over me when I found myself alone and knew I had to act. How, I had not yet considered. I only knew that now everything was over, that there could no longer be any question of her innocence, and that the time had come for me to punish her and put an end to my relations with her.

"Formerly I had always wavered, had said to myself, 'Perhaps it is not true, perhaps I am mistaken.' Now I felt nothing of the kind. I was perfectly convinced. Alone with him at night, in my absence! That was throwing prudence to the winds. Or even worse: this boldness, this recklessness in committing a crime, might be a boldness assumed intentionally, as proof of innocence. Everything was clear. There could be no doubt. I feared only one thing: that they might yet escape, might think of some new stratagem to rob me of proof and the opportunity of punishing them. And so, to catch them the quicker, I tiptoed to the reception-room where they were sitting, not through the drawing-room, but through the hall and the nursery.

"The boys were sleeping in the nursery. The nursemaid stirred and almost woke up, and I imagined what she would think when everything was discovered, and such a wave of self-pity swept over me that I could not restrain my tears. For fear of waking up the children I rushed on tiptoe into the hall and into my study, where I collapsed on the sofa and gave vent to my feelings.

" 'I am an honest man, the son of my parents; all my life I have dreamt of having a happy family; I, her husband, have never been unfaithful to her, and yet here she is, with five children, making love to a musician because he has red lips! She is not a human being! She is a bitch, a loathsome bitch! With her children sleeping in the next room— her children, whom she has always pretended to love so dearly! And to have written what she did to me! And to fling herself upon him so brazenly! But what do I know? Perhaps she has always done that. Perhaps she has been having children of footmen and calling them mine. Tomorrow I would have come home and she would have met me with her charming coiffure, her tantalizing waist, her graceful movements' (I saw every detail of her beautiful, hateful face), 'and the beast of jealousy would have been turned back and locked up in my heart, to gnaw it to pieces. What will the nursemaid think, and Yegor? And poor little Liza! She already has an inkling of how things are. The brazenness of it! The falseness! The animal lust that I know so well!'

"I wanted to get up but could not. My heart was pounding so hard I could not stand on my feet. I would have an apoplectic stroke. She would have killed me. That was precisely what she wanted. Oh, no; that would be too easy, I had no intention of letting her get off so easily. But there I sat while they were eating and laughing, and— Yes, he had no compunctions about taking her, even if she was not as fresh as she might be: after all, she was attractive and, what was most important, did not endanger his precious health. 'Why did I not kill her then?' I asked myself, recalling a quarrel of the previous week during which I had driven her out of my study and thrown things about. I had a vivid remembrance of the state I had been in then; more than a remembrance—I now felt the same longing to break and destroy things. I remember what an urge to action I experienced; every thought but those essential to action was driven out of my mind. I was in the state of an animal or man whose senses are quickened by threat of danger, and who, in this state, acts precisely, unhurriedly, without losing a minute, subordinating everything to a single definite purpose."

XXVII

"The first thing I did was to take off my boots and go in my stockinged feet to some weapons hanging on the wall over the sofa and take down a curved damask dagger that had never been used and was exceedingly sharp. I drew it out of its sheath. The sheath fell behind the sofa and I remember saying to myself, 'I must pick it up later or it will get lost.' Then I took off my coat, which I had kept on all this time, and went noiselessly out in my stockinged feet.

"I crept up to the door and flung it open suddenly. I remember the expression of their faces. I remember the expression of their faces because it caused me a pang of joyful torment. It was an expression of horror. That was just what I wanted. To the end of my days I shall remember the expression of

horror and despair that flashed across both
their faces in that first second of beholding
me. He, it seems, had been sitting at the table,
but on catching sight or sound of me he
leaped to his feet and stood with his back to
the bookcase. The look on his face was indu-
bitably one of horror. The look on hers was
also of horror, but horror combined with
something else. Had it been horror alone,
perhaps what happened might not have
happened. In her look there was also (or at
least it seemed so to me that first moment)
an expression of disappointment, of vexation
that her love-making and her happiness had
been interrupted. It was as if she wanted
nothing but the happiness of the moment.
But the expression on both of their faces was
fleeting. His look of horror was instantly
supplanted by one of inquiry: 'Is it possible
to lie to him or not? If it is, then I must
begin. If it is not, something is about to
happen. But what?' He looked at her inquiringly. On catching his glance her look
of disappointment and vexation changed, or
so I thought, to one of anxiety for him.

"For a moment I paused in the doorway
with the dagger behind my back. In that
moment he smiled and said in a tone so casual
as to be almost comic:

" 'We were just having a little music...'

" 'You're back so soon...' she said at the
same time, copying his tone.

"But neither he nor she were given a

chance to finish. I was possessed of the same
fury I had known the preceding week. Again
I felt the urge to smash, to destroy; I was
in a mad frenzy, and I gave myself up to my
frenzy.

"Neither of them had a chance to finish.
That was happening which he feared would
happen, that which instantly cut off what
they were saying. I threw myself upon her,
still concealing the dagger lest he prevent me
from plunging it into her left side, just below
the breast. I had chosen this spot from the
very first. The moment I threw myself upon
her he perceived my intent and seized me by
the arm, a thing I had not expected him to
do.

"'Think what you're doing! Help!' he
shouted.

"I snatched my arm away and hurled
myself at him. His eyes met mine, he suddenly
went white as a sheet to the very lips, a
peculiar shine came to his eyes, and he
ducked under the grand-piano and made for
the door, another thing I had not expected
him to do. I would have pursued him, but
some weight hung upon my left arm. It was
she. I tried to free myself. She tightened her
hold and would not let me go. This unexpected obstruction, her weight on my arm, the
repulsiveness of her touch, incensed me the
more. I felt completely mad, I knew I must
look terrible and was glad of it. I wrenched
my left arm away with all my force and in

doing so struck her face with my elbow. She let our a cry and released her hold on my arm. I wanted to dash after him, but the absurdity of chasing my wife's lover in my stockinged feet flashed across my mind; I did not want to be absurd, I wanted to be terrible. Despite the state of frenzy I was in, I was constantly aware of the impression I was making on them, and my actions were partly governed by this impression.

"I turned back to her. She had fallen upon the sofa and was staring at me, one hand over the eye I had injured. Her face expressed fear and hatred of me, her enemy. It was the expression of a rat when someone lifts up the trap in which it is caught. I, at least, could detect nothing in her face but fear and hatred. It was a fear and hatred of me that love for another was sure to inspire in her. But perhaps I would have restrained myself and not have done what I did do if she had kept silent. But suddenly she began to speak and to seize the hand that held the dagger.

" 'Think what you're doing! What is it? What has come over you? There is nothing between us, nothing, nothing, nothing! I swear to it!'

"I still might have hesitated, but those words, which meant just the opposite to me, namely, that there was something between them, called forth a response corresponding to the state I had worked myself up into and which was developing in a *crescendo* and must go on developing until it reached its highest pitch. There are laws governing even frenzy.

" 'Don't lie, you slut!' I shrieked, and caught her in my left hand, but she broke loose. Without dropping the dagger, I seized her by the throat with my left hand, threw her down on her back, and began choking her. How resistant her throat was! She seized my hand in an effort to tear it off her throat, and as if it was just this I had been waiting for, I plunged the dagger into her left side below the ribs with all my force.

"When people say they do not know what they are doing in a fit of frenzy, it is nonsense, it is untrue. I realized everything, and not for a moment did I stop realizing it. The more the steam that my fury generated, the brighter the glow of my reason, so that I could not possibly have failed to perceive everything I did. I knew what I was doing every second of the time. I cannot say I knew what I would do later, but at the moment I knew what I was doing, and I seemed even to know slightly ahead of time, for the purpose, perhaps, of being able to repent, to tell myself I might have stayed my hand. I knew I was striking her below the ribs and that the dagger would enter at that spot. I fully realized I was doing something dreadful, something the like of which I had never done before, something that would have terrible consequences. But the consciousness of this flashed through my mind like a streak of lightning, and the consciousness was instantly followed by the deed. The deed was perceived with striking clarity. I remember feeling the momentary resistance of her stays and something else, and then the passing of the blade into softness. She clutched at the dagger with her hands, cutting them, but not stopping the knife. Later when I was in jail, after the moral transformation I underwent, I brooded long over this moment, recalling it again and again and trying to plumb its meaning. I remember that for a second, a brief second before the deed, I was filled with the terrible realization that I was killing a woman, had already killed her, a defenceless woman, my wife. I remember the horror of this realization, I even remember vaguely that that was why, having plunged in the dagger, I instantly pulled it out, wishing to undo what I had done. For a second I stood motionless, waiting to see what would happen, wondering if what was done could not be undone. She leaped to her feet and shouted:

" 'Nurse! He has killed me!'

"The nurse, waked by the noise, was standing in the doorway. I went on standing there waiting and not believing. But from under her stays the blood came gushing forth. Only then did I realize that it could not be undone, and instantly decided that it ought not to be undone, that this was what I wanted and what ought to have happened. I waited until she fell and the nurse ran over to her crying. 'Dear God!' and only then did I throw down the dagger and made for the door.

" 'I mustn't get excited, I must calmly consider what I am doing,' I said to myself, refusing to look at her or the nurse. The nurse wailed and called for the maid. I went down the hall, sent the maid to her, and went into my own room. 'What must I do now?' I asked myself, and knew what I must do. Going into my study, I went straight to the wall, took down a revolver, examined it—it was loaded—and put it on the writing-desk. Then I picked up the dagger sheath that had fallen behind the sofa and sat down on the sofa.

"I sat there for a long time. I thought of nothing, remembered nothing. I heard noises in the other rooms. I heard someone drive up and enter the house. Then someone else. I heard and saw Yegor bring my luggage into the room. As if I had any need of that now!

" 'Do you know what has happened?' I said. 'Tell someone to notify the police.'

"He went out without a word. I got up, locked the door, took out a cigarette and some matches, and began to smoke. Before I had time to smoke a single cigarette I was overcome by sleep. I must have slept for two hours. I remember dreaming that she and I were on friendly terms; we had quarrelled and made it up, there was a certain tension

between us, but we were on friendly terms.
I was waked up by a knock at the door. 'The
police,' I thought on waking. 'I seem to have
killed her. But perhaps it is she and nothing
has happened.' There was another knock at
the door. I did not answer, I was too busy
trying to decide whether it had really
happened or not. Yes, it had. I remembered
the resistance of her stays and then the
sinking in of the dagger, and little chills ran
up and down my spine. 'Yes it has. Now for
myself,' I said. But even as I said it I knew
I would not kill myself. Yet I got up and
picked up the revolver. And a strange thing:
I remembered how many times before I had
contemplated suicide, as I had in the train
on that very day; it had seemed an easy
thing—easy because I knew what a punishment it would be to her. Now I could not so
much as contemplate killing myself, let alone
do it. 'Why should I?' I asked myself, and
there was no answer. Once more came the
knock at the door. 'First I must find out who
is knocking. I can do it later.' I put down the
revolver and covered it with a newspaper.
I went to the door and pushed back the bolt.
It was my wife's sister, a silly, kind-hearted
widow.

" 'Vasya! What has happened?' she said,
and the tears that were always ready, over-
flowed.

" 'What do you want?' I asked her roughly,
I saw that it was foolish and unnecessary to

be rude, but I could not help it.

"'Vasya, she is dying! Ivan Fyodorovich has said so.' Ivan Fyodorovich was the doctor, my wife's doctor, her adviser.

"'So he is here?' I asked, and again I felt my anger rising. 'Well, what of it?'

"'Vasya, go to her. Oh, how awful, how awful!' she moaned.

"'Go to her?' I repeated to myself. And I answered that of course I must go to her, that it was the thing to do, that when a man kills his wife as I had done, the thing to do is to go to her. 'If that is the case, I must go,' I said to myself. 'If I must do the other, I shall have plenty of time,' I thought, having in mind my intention to shoot myself. 'There will be words, grimaces, but they will not touch me,' I said to myself.

"'Wait,' I said to her sister. 'I will look foolish going in my stockinged feet. At least let me put on some slippers.'"

XXVIII

"And strange as it may seem, again as I went out of the room and walked through the chambers I knew so well, there arose the hope that nothing had happened. But I was struck by the horrid smell of medicines—iodoform, carbolic acid. Yes, it had happened. As I went down the hall past the children's nursery I caught sight of Liza. She looked at me with frightened eyes. I even fancied that all five of the children were there and all were staring at me. I went to the door. The maid-servant opened it to me and went out. The first thing that caught my eye was my wife's pearl-grey dress flung on a chair, covered with blood. There she lay with her knees up, on our double bed, on my side of the bed, for hers was against the wall. She lay raised very high on a mound of pillows, and the jacket she had on was unfastened. Something had been placed over the wound. The air reeked of iodoform. I was struck most of all by the bruised swelling of her cheek, part of her nose, and one eye—the result of the blow of my elbow when she had tried to stop me. There was nothing beautiful about her whatsoever, I found her even repulsive. I stopped on the threshold.

" 'Go over, go over to her,' said her sister.

" 'Perhaps she wishes to ask forgiveness,' I thought. 'Shall I forgive her? Yes, she is dying and so I can forgive her,' I thought, resolving to be generous. I went straight to her. With a great effort she raised her eyes, one of which was all swollen, and haltingly, with an effort, she said:

" 'So you got what you wanted ... you killed me.' And through her physical suffering, through her consciousness of death, glimmered the old familiar expression of cold animal hatred: 'But I won't ... give you ... the children... She (her sister) shall have them.'

"She found what I considered the main thing—her guilt, her infidelity—not worth mentioning.

" 'I hope you enjoy the sight of what you have done,' she said, and, glancing towards the door, she gave a sob. There in the doorway stood her sister and the children. 'See what you have done.'

"I looked at the children, then back at her, at her bruised and swollen face, and for the first time I forgot myself, my rights, my pride; for the first time I saw her as a human being. And so insignificant seemed my jealousy and all that had injured my pride, and so significant seemed that which I had done, that I was ready to fall on my knees and press my face against her hand and say, 'Forgive me!' But I could not.

"She grew silent and closed her eyes, apparently lacking the strength to utter another word. Then her mutilated face quivered and contracted. Weakly she pushed me away.

" 'Why did you do it? Why?'

" 'Forgive me,' I said.

" 'Forgive you? Nonsense. If only I don't die!' she cried, raising herself and fixing feverish eyes on me. 'Yes, you got what you wanted! I hate you! Ah! Oh!' she cried, evidently frightened by something in her delirium. 'Kill me! Kill me! I'm not afraid! But everyone, everyone! Him, too! He's gone, he's gone!'

"She was delirious to the end. She did not recognize any of us. She died at noon of that same day. Long before that, at eight o'clock, they took me to police headquarters and then to jail. There, during the eleven months I awaited trial, I pondered over myself and my past and came to understand it. I began to understand on the third day. On the third day they took me back there..."

He tried to go on, but, unable to suppress his sobs, he stopped. With a great effort he took himself in hand and resumed:

"I began to understand when I saw her in her coffin." He caught his breath and began to speak hurriedly. "Only when I saw her face in death did I realize what I had done. I realized that it was I, I who had killed her, that she had once been alive, warm, full of movement, and because of me she was now motionless, cold, waxen, and that this could never be undone—never, anywhere, by anyone. Only one who has lived through this can understand. Oh, oh, oh!" he cried several times, then was silent.

For a long time we sat without speaking, he whimpering and shaking with suppressed sobs.

"I'm sorry..."

He turned away and lay down, covering himself with a blanket. When, at eight o'clock in the morning, we reached the station at which I had to get off, I went over to him to say good-bye. I did not know whether he was asleep or only feigning, but he did not stir. I touched his hand. He threw back the blanket and I saw that he had not been asleep.

"Good-bye," I said, holding out my hand.

He gave me his with a faint smile that was so pathetic it moved me to tears.

"I'm sorry," he said, repeating the words with which he had concluded his story.

1889

FATHER SERGIUS

I

It occasioned much surprise in St. Petersburg, in the forties, when a handsome prince, commander of His Majesty's squadron of a regiment of Cuirassiers, for whom everyone predicted a royal adjutancy and a brilliant career under the Emperor Nicholas I, and whose marriage with a beautiful maid of honour, high in the favour of the Empress, had been set for the coming month, resigned his commission, broke off his engagement, made over to his sister his none-too-considerable estate, and left for a monastery, to become a monk. To people unacquainted with the reasons behind it, all this seemed extraordinary, inexplicable; but to Prince Stepan Kasatsky himself it was so natural a decision that he simply could not have conceived of any other.

Stepan Kasatsky's father, retired colonel of the Guards, died when Stepan was only twelve. His mother, for all her reluctance to send her son away from home, dared not disobey her husband, who had willed that, in the event of his death, she was not to keep the boy at home, but to enter him in the Cadet Corps. And so she sent him to the Corps, and herself, with her daughter Varvara, moved to St. Petersburg, to be near her son and be able to have him at home on holidays.

The boy was distinguished by marked ability and tremendous pride; and those qualities brought him to the fore both in his class-work—particularly mathematics, for which he had a special inclination—and in riding and the other military arts. He was handsome and, though unusually tall, well-built and of good carriage. In conduct, too, he would have been a model cadet, but for his hot temper. He had no taste for drink or debauchery, and he was wonderfully truthful. His only fault were the fits of rage which sometimes came over him, when he lost all self-control and was transformed into a raging beast. On one occasion he all but threw a fellow-cadet through the window for poking fun at his collection of minerals. On another, he was very near to catastrophe; for he hurled a whole platter of cutlets at the steward, rushed at an officer, and, they say, struck him, for disavowing his own words and lying brazenly. He would certainly have been degraded to the ranks, had not the Corps director hushed up the whole affair and dismissed the steward.

At the age of eighteen he received his commission, in an aristocratic regiment of the Guards. Emperor Nikolai Pavlovich, who had noticed him while he was still in the Corps, singled him out for favour in the regiment as well, and it was generally expected that he would advance to a royal adjutancy. This he greatly desired, not only because he was ambitious, but chiefly because, while still in the Corps, he had conceived a passionate—yes, that was the only word for it: passionate—love for Nikolai Pavlovich. Every time Nikolai Pavlovich visited the Corps, and he was a frequent visitor; every time he came striding briskly in, a tall, full-chested figure of a man, in military uniform, with his hooked nose, his moustache, and his short side-whiskers, greeting the cadets in that rolling voice of his, Kasatsky experienced a lover's rapture, the same rapture that he was later to feel in the presence of her he loved. Only the rapture Nikolai Pavlovich evoked was more intense. It made the boy eager to demonstrate his infinite devotion—to sacrifice anything, all of self, for the adored one. And Nikolai Pavlovich knew that he evoked this rapture, and deliberately encouraged it. He played with the cadets, gathered them around him, addressing them now with boyish simplicity, now as an elder friend, now with stately majesty. After Kasatsky's trouble with the officer Nikolai

Pavlovich made no remark, but when the boy approached waved him away theatrically and, frowning, shook a finger at him; and as he was leaving, said:

"You must understand that I know. But there are things I do not wish to know. But they lie here."

And he laid a hand on his heart.

Afterwards, however, when the graduate cadets presented themselves to him, he made no more mention of the incident, but told them, as always, that they might come directly to him in case of need; that it was their duty to serve him and the Motherland faithfully; and that he would remain always their greatest friend. As always, the cadets were touched; and Kasatsky, remembering what had gone before, wept real tears and vowed to devote his every energy to the service of his beloved Tsar.

When Kasatsky received his commission his mother and sister moved to Moscow, and later to their home in the country. Kasatsky made half of his property over to his sister. The income from the remainder served only to cover his expenses; for it was a gilded regiment in which he served.

Outwardly, Kasatsky seemed no more than a brilliant and ambitious young Guardsman of quite the usual type. Beneath the surface, however, he was engaged constantly in intricate and strenuous endeavour. It had been going on, this endeavour, since his early childhood—taking the most varied forms, but essentially always the same: the pursuit, in everything he did in life, of such attainment, such pre-eminence, as to evoke other people's praise and wonder. When it was a question of knowledge, of studies, he would get down to his books and keep at them until he was praised and held up as a model. One thing mastered, he would turn to another. It was thus that he won the first place in his classes; thus; while still in the Corps, after once experiencing a certain embarrassment in French conversation, that he achieved the same mastery of French as he had of Russian; thus, when chess attracted him, that he attained a high degree of proficiency at that game.

Aside from his general mission in life, which consisted in serving his Tsar and his country, Kasatsky had always some immediate aim before him; and however trifling this aim might be, he would throw himself entirely into its pursuit, living only for its attainment, until finally it was reached. But no sooner was it reached than some new aim would rise before him to replace it. And it was this striving for distinction, and, to attain distinction, this pursuit of one aim after another, that formed the content of his life. Thus, on receiving his commission, he determined to attain the utmost perfection in knowledge of the service; and very soon became a model officer—though, again, with the one exception of his uncontrollable temper, which now, as before, led him into conduct evil in itself and harmful in its effect on his career. Then, one day, a turn of conversation made him conscious of the shortcomings of his educational background. He determined to overcome this deficiency; surrounded himself with books, and achieved his aim. Then he felt the desire to distinguish himself in the world of society; trained himself to perfection in ballroom dancing, and soon advanced so far as to receive invitations to every society ball, and even, at times, to more narrow gatherings. This, however, did not satisfy him. He was accustomed to first place, and in society he was far from that.

High society in those days consisted—as, I suppose, it consists always and everywhere—of four categories of people: 1) people who are wealthy and of the Court; 2) people who are not wealthy, but who by birth and training belong to those of the Court; 3) people of wealth who try to ingratiate themselves with those of the Court, and 4) people neither wealthy nor of the Court, but eager to ingratiate themselves both with those of wealth and with those of the Court. Kasatsky was not of the first category. He was well received among the last two categories. When entering into society, he had set himself the goal of a liaison with some woman of society—and, more quickly than he could have hoped, had attained this goal. But he very soon perceived that the circles in which he moved were of the lower order; that there were higher circles, and that in these higher Court circles, though received, he remained an outsider. He was treated with courtesy, but in every word and action he sensed that there were those who belonged, and that he did not belong. And he wanted to belong. There were ways of achieving that. One way was a royal adjutancy—and that he was expecting. Another way was marriage with someone of this circle. And he decided to make such a marriage. He chose a beautiful girl, one of the Court; a girl who not only belonged to those circles into which he sought acceptance, but whose friendship was sought by people the most highly placed and the most securely established in those lofty circles: Countess Korotkova. It was not only ambition that made Kasatsky single out the Countess. She was most attractive, and he soon fell in love with her. At first she received him with marked coldness, but then, suddenly, all that changed. She grew softer, and her mother became particularly cordial.

Kasatsky proposed, and was accepted. He was surprised by the ease with which he had attained such felicity. There was something that seemed strange, unusual, in the manner of both mother and daughter. But he was very much in love, and therefore blind; and so he did not know what almost everyone in town was whispering of: that his betrothed, a year past, had been mistress to Nikolai Pavlovich.

II

Two weeks before the day set for the wedding, Kasatsky was visiting his betrothed at her summer retreat in Tsarskoye Selo. It was May, and very warm. They wandered up and down the garden for a while, then sat down on a bench on one of the avenues, where tall limes afforded pleasant shade. Countess Mary, that day, in her white muslin dress, was particularly charming. She looked the personification of innocence and love, as she sat there, her head bowed, looking up now and again at the handsome giant who spoke to her so tenderly, so gently—fearful lest some word or gesture offend and sully her angelic purity. Kasatsky was one of those men of the forties—there are none of them left today—who, while for themselves admitting of sexual impurity and seeing no wrong in it, of their wives demanded ideal, celestial purity; and, assuming such celestial purity in all girls of their social circle, treated these girls accordingly. There was much that was wrong in those views, much harm in the licence which men allowed themselves; but their attitude to women, so radically differing from the attitude of young men today, who look on any girl as on a female in search of a mate—that, I think, was a wholesome attitude. Finding themselves so idealized, girls tried really to be ideal, as well as they were able. Such, then, was Kasatsky's attitude towards women, such was his conception of his betrothed. More in love than ever, that day, he felt not the slightest carnal impulse towards her, but, rather, rejoiced tenderly in her inaccessibility.

He rose and stood before her, leaning with both hands on his sabre.

"It is only now I have learned what happiness life can bring," he said. "And that I owe to you."

Diffidently, he smiled at her. Looking up to her as he did in the moral sense, he was almost too afraid to talk to this angel so intimately.

"I have come to know myself, thanks to ... you, to know that I am better than I thought," he went on.

"I have known that for a long time," she answered. "It was that that made me love you."

A nightingale began to sing nearby. The fresh foliage rustled in a sudden breath of wind.

He took her hand, and kissed it. Tears rose to his eyes. She understood: he was thanking her for saying that she loved him. He paced up and down for a while, without a word, then returned and sat down at her side.

"I wanted to tell you... Ah, well, no

matter. It was a selfish aim, at first, that brought me to you. What I sought was a place in society. But then... How insignificant all that became in comparison with you, when I learned to know you. Does that anger you?"

She did not answer, but her hand touched his.

He understood. She was not angry.

"And now I hear you say..." He paused, fearing to seem too bold. "Well, that I have made you love me. But—forgive me. It is not unbelief. But there is something, too, that disturbs, disquiets you. What is it?"

Yes, she thought: it must be now or never. He would be sure to find out, in any case. But now—now he would not leave her. Ah, but she could not bear it if he left her!

Lovingly, her eyes took in his tall, stalwart, impressive figure. She loved him now, more than she had the Emperor. Were it not for the royal prerogative, she could not have preferred the Emperor to him.

"Listen, then, I cannot lie to you. I must tell you the whole truth. You ask—what is it? It is this: I have loved before."

She laid her hand on his, in timid pleading.

He did not speak.

"Shall I tell you who it was? It was he, yes. His Majesty."

"We all love His Majesty. And while you were at school, I suppose..."

"No, I was out of school. It was infatuation, but it is over now. But I must tell you..."

"Well, but what of that?"

"It wasn't simply..."

Her hands flew up, hiding her face.

"What! Do you mean you gave yourself to him?"

She did not answer.

"Do you mean you were his mistress?"

She did not answer.

He sprang to his feet and stood facing her, pale as death. His lips were quivering. Suddenly, he recalled how affectionately Nikolai Pavlovich had congratulated him on his engagement, on meeting him one day on the Nevsky.

"Dear God! What have I done!" she cried.

"Don't touch me! Don't you touch me! How could you!"

He turned and strode to the house. In the hall, he met her mother.

"Why, what's the matter, Prince? I thought..."

But, seeing the look in his face, she stopped short. He had flushed violently.

"You knew!" he shouted at her. "You meant to use me to cover it up! If you were a man..."

His great fist flew up. He turned sharply, and ran out of the house.

Had her former lover been anyone else, he would have killed him. But it was his adored sovereign.

The next day he applied for leave, and at the same time submitted his resignation. To avoid seeing anyone, he let it be understood that he was ill. Soon he left for the country.

He spent the summer on his estate, arranging his affairs. When the summer ended, instead of returning to St. Petersburg, he left for a monastery, to become a monk.

His mother wrote him there, trying to dissuade him from so final a decision. He replied to her that God's call must be set before all other considerations, and that this call had come to him. Only Varvara, his sister, proud and ambitious as he was himself, understood and sympathised.

As she saw it, he had chosen monkhood in order to set himself above those people who had wished him to understand that they stood above him. And she was right. In entering monkhood, he demonstrated his contempt for all those things that seemed to others so important—that to him also, in his army days, had seemed important; he raised himself to new heights, from which he could look down upon the people he once had envied. But it was not only by this feeling, as Varvara thought, that he was guided. Mingling with his pride, with his need always to be first, was another motive, at which Varvara did not guess—a truly religious urge. His disillusionment in Mary (his betrothed), whom he had imagined such a saint, his feeling of outrage was so cruel that he sank into despair; and despair led him—whither? To God, to the faith of his childhood, which had never lost its hold upon him.

III

Kasatsky entered the monastery on the day of Intercession.

The Superior at this monastery was a nobleman, a scholar and man of letters, and, too, a *starets*—one of a succession of monks, deriving from Walachia, distinguished by unquestioning obedience to the will of a chosen leader and teacher. The Superior was a disciple of the famed *starets* Amvrosi—disciple of Makari, disciple of the *starets* Leonid, disciple of Paisi Velichkovsky. Kasatsky acknowledged him as his own *starets*, or teacher.

Apart from the feeling of superiority over others which his entry into the monastery gave him, Kasatsky derived satisfaction here—as he had always, in everything he did—in the pursuit of the utmost perfection, inner as well as outer, in his new calling. Just as in his regiment, he had been not merely an irreproachable officer, but one who did more than was required of him, who carried duty beyond what was officially laid down—so now, as a monk, he also sought perfection, striving to be industrious, abstemious, meek, gentle, pure—not only in deed, but in thought—and obedient. This last quality, or virtue, in particular, made his life easier than it might otherwise have been. Many of the demands made upon him by the life of a monk in a much-visited monastery near the country's capital were unpleasant to him, led him into temptation; but this was cured by obedience, by the understanding: it is not for me to reason; what I must do is to carry out the duties laid upon me, whatever they may be—watching beside the sacred relics, or singing in the choir, or keeping accounts for the monastery hostel. All possibility of doubt in any sphere was eliminated, too, by this same virtue of obedience to the *starets*. Were it not for this obedience, he would have been oppressed by the length and monotony of the church services, by the restless comings and goings of visitors, by the unpleasant traits of the monastic brotherhood; but obedience made of all this not merely something to be gladly endured, but a new comfort and support in life: "I do not know why it should be needful to hear one and the same prayer several times a day; but I know that it is needful. And, knowing that it is needful, I find happiness in it." Just as material food is essential for the support of life, the *starets* told him, so is spiritual food, church prayer, essential to spiritual life. This he believed; and, in truth, the church service for which he sometimes found it so difficult to get up of a morning brought him undeniable peace and happiness. There was happiness in the feeling of submission, in the unquestioning acceptance of the things that he must do—all laid down for him by the *starets*. The point of life lay not only in an ever greater curbing of his own will, an ever greater submission and humility, but, further, in the attainment of all the Christian virtues. These, at first, seemed to him easily achieved. He had made over his entire estate to the monastery, and felt no regrets for it. He was not lazy. Humility in relations with his inferiors was not only easy, but a source of joy. Even the sins of the flesh, both greed and lust, were easily conquered. Against these sins the *starets* had warned him particularly; but Kasatsky was free of them, and rejoiced in his freedom.

Only one thing tormented him: the memory of his betrothed. And not only the memory, but the vivid realization of what might have been. Involuntarily, he would recall another of the sovereign's former loves, who had afterwards married and become a model wife and mother. Her husband had been appointed to an important post; had attained power and esteem, and with them a good and repentant wife.

In Kasatsky's better moments, these thoughts were not disturbing. Coming to mind at his better moments, they made him but rejoice in his escape from temptation. But there were other moments, when all that now filled his life seemed suddenly to dim and fade; when he lost, not exactly his faith in this new content of his life, but rather his vision of it, his ability to summon it up within him. And then he would be seized with memories and to his horror, with repentance for his adoption of the religious life.

Escape, again, lay in obedience: in the work laid down for him, and the prayers that filled every hour of the day. He would pray as always, and prostrate himself in humble obeisance. He would pray, indeed, more than always; but his prayer at such times was purely physical. There was no soul in it. This would drag on for a day, perhaps two, and then it would pass. But that day, or two days—they were a time of horror, when he felt himself in someone's power: not his own power, nor God's, but another's. And all that he could do, all that he did, at such times, was what the *starets* counselled: to hold on, undertake nothing, and wait. Altogether, throughout this period, Kasatsky's life was regulated not by his own will, but by the will of the *starets*; and this complete submission was a source of spiritual tranquillity.

Kasatsky lived in this way, at his first monastery, for seven years. At the end of the third year he was ordained as a hieromonach* and given the name of Sergius. This was an event of great moment in his inner life. Participation in the communion had always brought him great consolation and spiritual uplift; and now, on those occasions when he himself was the celebrant, the ceremony of the oblation filled his soul with throbbing

* Hieromonach—a monk who is also a priest.—*Tr.*

rapture. In time, however, this emotion began to lose its intensity; and when one day, he had to celebrate the liturgy in that state of depression which came upon him now and again, he realized that this, too, would pass. And, truly, the feeling of rapture weakened; but the habit remained.

On the whole, in the seventh year of his life at the monastery, Sergius began to feel a certain boredom. He had mastered all there was for him to learn and master here. There was nothing more to occupy him.

But, on the other hand, the state of lethargy into which he had begun to fall was growing steadily deeper. The news of his mother's death, and then of Countess Mary's marriage to another, coming in this period, did not move him. All his interest, all his faculties were concentrated on his inner life.

In the fourth year after his ordainment the bishop was particularly cordial to him, and the *starets* told him that, should he be named for some higher office, he need not refuse. And then he felt a rising ambition, that monastic ambition that was so abhorrent to him in other monks. He was appointed to a monastery situated near the capital. He would have liked to refuse, but the *starets* told him to accept. And so he accepted the appointment, took his leave of the *starets*, and left for his new monastery.

This move to the vicinity of the capital was an important development in Sergius' life. Temptation of every kind surrounded him and all his energy went into resistance.

At his first monastery Sergius had suffered little from the temptation of sex. Here, however, this temptation arose with fearful power. It even assumed definite shape. A certain lady, of unsavoury reputation, began to seek Sergius' attention. She spoke to him, and asked him to visit her. He sternly refused. But he was appalled by the sharp strength of his desire. He was so alarmed that he wrote to the *starets* about it. More, to curb himself, he called the young lay brother who attended him and, humbling his pride, confessed his weakness to him, asking that he keep watch and let him go nowhere but to services and about his monastic duties.

Another sore temptation lay in the extreme dislike that Sergius conceived for the Superior of his new monastery, a shrewd, worldly, and ambitious man. Strive as he would, he could not conquer this antipathy. He endured—but in the depths of his soul continued to condemn. And this sinful feeling broke out of control.

It happened in the second year of his stay at the new monastery. And this is how it came about. It was Intercession, and vespers were being sung in the big monastery church. There were many visitors. The Superior himself conducted the service. Father Sergius stood in his usual place, absorbed in prayer, or rather, in that state of inner struggle which always came upon him during services, particularly in the big church, when he was not officiating. The cause of this struggle lay in the irritation that the visitors caused him—the fine gentlefolk, and particularly the ladies. He tried not to notice them, not to see what went on in the church: the way a soldier ushered in the gentry, jostling the people to make way for them; the way the ladies pointed out monks to one another—and, often, it was he they pointed out, or another of the monks known for his handsome face. He tried to create blinders for himself, to keep his attention from straying; to see nothing but the gleam of the candles before the iconostasis, the icons, and the monks engaged in the service; to hear nothing but the words of prayer, sung or said; to allow himself no feeling other than that sense of duty fulfilment which came to him at every hearing and every repetition of the prayers heard so many times before.

He was standing thus, bowing down or crossing himself where the service required, engaged in his struggle between cold condemnation and a deliberately induced deadening of thought and feeling, when Father Nikodim the sacristan, came up to him. This Nikodim was another source of sore temptation to Father Sergius, who could not help but condemn his flattering, ingratiating manner towards the Superior. With a bow that bent him almost double, Father Nikodim delivered

his message: the Superior desired Father
Sergius to join him in the sanctuary. Sergius
adjusted his habit, covered his head, and
moved slowly forward, trying not to disturb
the people.

"*Lise, regardez à droit, c'est lui,*" a woman's
voice exclaimed.

"*Où, où? Il n'est pas tellement beau.*"

They were speaking of him, he knew. And,
hearing this talk, he repeated over and over to
himself, as always when his spirit was so tried,
"Lead us not into temptation." With bowed
head and lowered eyes, he passed the ambo,
skirted the surpliced precentors, who were
moving past the iconostasis, and went in at
the northern doors. Entering the sanctuary,
he crossed himself and bowed to the ground,
as the custom was, before the icon; and only
then raised his head and glanced at the
Superior and at the glittering figure beside
him, which he had already noticed out of the
corner of his eye as he came in.

The Superior stood by the wall, his short,
plump arms stretched over his fat belly, his
fingers toying with the gold embroidery of his
vestments. With a smile on his face he was
engaged in smiling conversation with a man
in the uniform of a Staff general, adorned
with gold braiding and shoulder knots which
Father Sergius' practised military eye quickly
assessed. This general had been Prince
Kasatsky's regimental commander. Now,
it seemed, he was a personage of some import-

ance; and the Superior—as Father Sergius immediately noted—knew of this, and so rejoiced in it that his fat red face, under his bald crown, simply beamed with pleasure. This offended and angered Father Sergius, the more so that, as he now learned, the Superior had sent for him for no other purpose than to satisfy the general's curiosity—his desire to have a look at a one-time colleague, as he put it.

"Very glad to see you in angelic guise," the general said, holding out his hand. "You haven't forgotten an old comrade, I hope."

The Superior's face, red and smiling in the frame of his grey beard, beaming approval, as it were, of the general's words; the general's face, so carefully groomed, his complacent smile, the odour of wine that issued from his mouth and of cigars from his whiskers—all this was too much for Father Sergius' self-control. He bowed once more before the Superior, and said:

"Your Reverence was pleased to send for me."

And, as he paused, his face—his very pose—inquired, "What for?"

"Why, yes, to see the General," the Superior said.

Father Sergius turned pale.

"Your Reverence," he said, with trembling lips, "I renounced the world in order to escape temptation. Why, then, do you subject me to temptation—here, in God's church, in the hour of prayer?"

"Go, then. Go," the Superior exclaimed, flushed and frowning.

The next day Father Sergius asked pardon of the Superior and of the brotherhood for his overweening; but nonetheless, after a night spent in prayer, decided that he must leave this monastery. Of this he wrote to the *starets*, imploring permission to return to the monastery at which the *starets* was Superior. He felt his weakness, he wrote, and his inability to fight down temptation without the help of the *starets*; and he confessed his sinful pride. The next post brought a reply from the *starets*, who wrote to him that the cause of all his trouble lay in his pride. His wrathful outburst, the *starets* explained, had come about because it was not for God that he had humbled himself, rejecting honours and advancement in the church—not for God, but to satisfy his own pride, to be able to tell himself how virtuous he was, seeking nothing for himself. That was why he had not been able to endure the Superior's conduct. Because he felt that he had given up everything for God, and now he was being put on display, like some strange beast.

"If it were for God you had given up advancement, you would have let it pass. Worldly pride is still alive in you. I have thought about you, my son, and I have prayed, and this is what God put in my mind for you: live on as before, and submit. And as

I was thinking thus, the news came to me that the saintly recluse Illarion lies dead in his hermitage, where he lived for eighteen years. The Tambino Superior inquires whether there is no brother who would wish to live there. And there lay your letter before me. Go to Father Paisi, at Tambino monastery. I will write to him. Ask to occupy Illarion's cell. Not that you can fill Illarion's place; but you are in need of seclusion to subdue your pride. May the blessing of God go with you."

Sergius obeyed the *starets*. He showed the letter to his Superior and, with his permission, having given up his cell and all his belongings to the monastery, set out for the Tambino hermitage.

The Superior there, an excellent manager, of the merchant class, received Sergius with quiet dignity and lodged him in Illarion's cell—at first with a lay brother to attend him, but later, at Sergius' wish, in complete solitude. The cell was a cave hollowed out in the rock. Illarion now lay buried here. There was an inner chamber, in which Illarion was buried, and an outer one, furnished with a small table and a shelf for books and icons and, in a niche at the side, a mattress of straw. The door to the cave could be locked. Outside it there was a shelf, on which, once a day, a monk sent from the monastery would lay a supply of food.

And Father Sergius became a hermit.

IV

At Shrovetide in the sixth year of Sergius' seclusion, a merry company of wealthy men and women, gathered in the neighbouring town for the season's pancakes and wine, called for sleighs and went out driving. Two of the company were lawyers, one a wealthy landowner, and one an officer. The other four were women: the officer's wife, the landowner's wife and unmarried sister, and, for the fourth, a divorcée, wealthy and beautiful, known for her odd ways and queer escapades, which kept the whole town gaping and gossiping.

It was a splendid evening, and the road was smooth and firm. Some ten versts out of town they drew up to confer: forward, or back?

"Where does this road go?" asked Makovkina, the divorced beauty.

"To Tambino," the lawyer who was seeking her favour replied. "That's another twelve versts."

"And from Tambino—where to?"

"Towards L., past the monastery."

"The one where Father Sergius lives?"

"That's right."

"Kasatsky? The handsome hermit?"

"That's right."

"Mesdames! Gentlemen! Let's visit this Kasatsky. We can rest and eat at Tambino."

"But we can't make it there and back tonight."

"No matter. We can stay the night with Kasatsky."

"Well—there's a hostel at the monastery, not bad at all. I lived there when I was working on the Makhin case."

"Not for me. I'll stay the night with Kasatsky."

"Umm. Even for one omnipotent as you, that's impossible."

"Impossible? Will you bet on it?"

"Well and good. If you stay the night with him—ask what you please of me!"

"*A discrétion*?"

"If the same holds for you."

"Of course. Let's be going!"

They gave the drivers wine, and for themselves got out a hamper filled with pastries, wine, and sweets. The ladies bundled up in their white fur cloaks. The drivers argued among themselves a bit as to who was to lead; and then one of them, a young fellow poised dashingly sidewise on his seat, swung his long whip and shouted at the horses. And they were off, with a jingling of bells and a squealing of runners.

The sleigh swayed and vibrated. The willing horses ran briskly and smoothly, their bound-up tails bobbing over the ornamented breeching; and the firm, even road slipped rapidly back, back and away. The dashing driver seemed to be playing with the reins. From the forward seat, the lawyer and the officer bombarded Makovkina and her neighbour with idle chatter. But Makovkina sat motionless, wrapped close in her white cloak, thinking her own thoughts: "Always the same—everything always the same, and always horrid. Shiny red faces, smelling of wine and tobacco. Always the same talk, always the same thoughts, and always the same filth behind it all. And they're all so satisfied, so convinced that that's the only way to live. And they can go on that way to the day they die. I can't. I'm sick of it all. What I need is something that would turn it all over, shake it all up. Like—well, say, like those people in Saratov, or wherever it was, that set out for somewhere, and froze to death. What would these people do? How would they behave? Contemptibly, I suppose. Every man for himself. And me, too—I'd be just as contemptible. But at least I'm good to look at. They know that. What about that monk, I wonder? Has he really lost the taste for it? No—it can't be! That's the one thing they really want. Like that cadet, last autumn. And wasn't he a silly fool!"

"Ivan Nikolayevich," she said aloud.

"At your service!"

"How old is he?"

"Who?"

"Kasatsky."

"Past forty, I should say."

"Does he receive all comers?"

"All comers, but not at all times."

"Tuck the rug in around my feet. Not that

way. How clumsy you are! There—tighter, tighter. That's right. And there's no need to squeeze my legs."

At length they reached the wood in which the cell was situated.

She got out of the sleigh, and told the others to drive on. They tried to dissuade her from her purpose, but that only angered her, and she demanded again that they drive on. Then they left, and she turned down the path alone, in her white fur cloak. The lawyer got out and stayed to watch.

V

It was the sixth year of Father Sergius' seclusion. He was forty-nine years old. And life was hard. Not in its rigours of fasting and prayer—these were not hard; but in an inner struggle such as he had never foreseen. The causes of struggle were two: doubt, and lust. And always they came together. He took them for two distinct foes; but actually, both were one. So soon as doubt was conquered, lust, too, gave way. But he thought them separate demons, and fought them separately.

"Oh, Lord, my God," his thoughts ran, "why dost Thou deny me faith? Lust that I can understand. Lust tormented St. Anthony, yes, and others, too. But faith! They had faith, whereas for me there are moments, hours, days when faith is not. Why should the world exist, with all its beauty, if it is sinful and must be renounced? What for hast Thou created this temptation? Temptation? But is it not temptation that prompts me to abandon the joys of the world, seeking to prepare a place for myself where—perhaps—there is nothing at all?"

But even as this thought passed through his mind he shrank from it in horror, in violent self-loathing.

"Beast! Beast!" he railed at himself. "And I make myself out a saint!"

And he turned to prayer. But as he began to pray he suddenly had a vivid picture of himself as he had been at the monastery, in flowing habit—a majestic figure. And he shook his head, thinking, "No. That's not real. That's sham. But—I can fool others with it, perhaps, only not myself, and not God. No, I'm not majestic. I'm ludicrous, pitiful." And he threw back the skirts of his cassock and looked down at his pitiful drawered legs. And smiled.

And then he let his cassock drop into place, and began to pray, crossing himself and bowing himself down. In his prayers came the line, "Will this bed, then, be my bier?"— and it was as though some demon whispered to him. "A lone bed is a bier in itself. Lies, lies!" And memory pictured for him the shoulders of the widow with whom he had sinned. He shook off these thoughts and continued his prayers. When he had recited the Rules, he took up his Testament and opened it at random. It opened on a passage which he knew by heart, for he had often and often repeated it: "Lord, I believe; help Thou mine unbelief." He dragged back all the doubts arising in his mind. As one sets up a body in unstable equilibrium, so he set up his faith once more on its wavering foundation— and drew back cautiously, lest he jolt and upset it. Again his blinders came into place, and he was at peace. He prayed his childhood prayer—"Lord, take, take me!"—and he was not merely eased, but filled with joyful emotion. He crossed himself, and lay down on his narrow bench, bedded with a thin straw mattress, with a light summer cassock under his head for a pillow. And he fell asleep. It was a light sleep, and through it he seemed to hear the jingle of sleigh bells whether dream or reality, he did not know. But then a knock came at his door, waking him thoroughly. He sat up, doubting his own ears. But the knock was repeated. Yes, it was here, at his door. And a woman's voice, calling.

Dear God! Could it be true, what he had read in the lives of the saints—that the Devil sometimes took the shape of a woman? Yes, it was a woman's voice. And so gentle, and timid, and charming! Avaunt!

He spat.

But no, it must have been his imagination. He went to the little lectern in the corner, and there dropped to his knees in a smooth, accustomed movement in which—in the actual physical movement—he had grown to find comfort and pleasure. He bowed down, so that his hair fell over his face, and pressed his forehead—higher now than it once had been, with advancing baldness—to the damp, cold matting. (There was a draught along the floor.)

...The psalm he was reciting was one that, old Father Pimen had told him, helped to conquer obsession. He rose, his sinewy legs easily swinging up his light, emaciated frame, and was about to continue the psalm—but instead, involuntarily, strained to hear that voice. He wanted to hear it. All was still. Nothing but the usual drip of melting snow from the roof into a tub set out to catch it. The world outdoors lay cloaked in damp, cold fog. All was still, very still. Then, suddenly, there was a rustling at the window and, clear and distinct, a voice—that same voice, gentle and timid; a voice that could belong to none but an attractive woman.

"Let me in," it said. "In Christ's name."

He felt the blood rush to his heart, and pause there in its flow. He could not catch his breath.

"May the Lord rise, and his enemies be confounded..."

"Why, I'm no evil spirit!"—and he could tell by the voice that the lips were smiling. "I'm no evil spirit. I'm just a sinful woman that has lost her way. Literally, not the other way." She laughed. "And I'm half frozen, and begging you for shelter."

He pressed his face to the window-pane. All he could see was the reflection of his icon lamp in the glass. Then he shielded his eyes with his hands, and stared out again. Foggy darkness. A tree. And—just to the right. There. A woman, in a cloak of shaggy white fur and a little hat. With such a charming, charming face, kindly, and frightened—leaning towards him, only an inch or two away. Their eyes met, and they knew one another. Not that they had ever met before—no, they had never met; but in this glance that they exchanged they felt (he, particularly) that they knew, understood one another. There could be no thought, after this glance, of evil spirits. No, she was a woman—simple, kindly, charming, timid.

"Who are you? What do you want?" he asked.

"Ah, do open up," she returned, wilfully, imperiously. "I'm half frozen. I told you I've lost my way."

"But I'm a monk. A hermit."

"Well, open up, then. Or do you want me to freeze to death outside your window, while you stand there praying?"

"But how..."

"Ah, I won't eat you. Let me in, in God's name. I'm so cold!"

Now she, in turn, was beginning to be

frightened. There was a hint of tears in her voice.

He moved away from the window, and turned to glance at the icon of Christ, in his crown of thorns. "Help me, Lord. Help me, Lord," he murmured, crossing himself and bowing down. Then he went out to the entry-way, and groped in the darkness until he found the hook fastening the outer door. He could hear footsteps outside. She was coming away from the window, towards the door. "Oh!"—she cried suddenly. She must have stepped into the puddle that had collected by the threshold. His hands were shaking, and the hook was tight. He could not undo it.

"Open up, do! Why do you keep me so? I'm wet through, and freezing. You think of nothing but your soul, and I stand here freezing."

He pulled at the door. The hook loosened, and he undid it. Throwing the door open, he pushed it harder than he had meant to, and it struck against her.

"Oh, I beg your pardon," he said, swept suddenly back into the old, accustomed courtesies.

She smiled at the sound of that "pardon". No, he was not so very formidable, after all.

"No need, no need," she returned, as she passed him in the doorway. "I'm the one that ought to be begging pardon. I'd never have had the effrontery, only—such a dreadful situation!"

"Come in," he said, moving aside to let her by.

The delicate fragrance of perfume, so long forgotten, assailed his nostrils. She passed through the entry into the room. He shut the outer door, but did not hook it; crossed the entry, and went into the room.

"Lord Jesus Christ, son of God, have mercy on me, a sinner. Lord, have mercy on me, a sinner," he kept praying, not only in his heart, but with involuntary movements of his lips.

"Make yourself comfortable," he said.

She stood, dripping, in the middle of the room, looking at him curiously, with laughter in her eyes.

"You must forgive me for breaking in on your solitude. But you see what a predicament I'm in. It all came about because, you see, we were out driving, and I wagered I'd walk back to town alone, all the way from Vorobyovka. But I lost my way, and if I hadn't stumbled on your cell here..."

She broke off. His face so disconcerted her that she could not go on lying. She had expected something very different. He was not so handsome as she had imagined him, but to her he seemed very beautiful, with his crisp, greying hair and beard, his straight, fine-cut nose, and his dark eyes—like burning coals, when he looked straight at her.

He saw that she was lying.

"Yes, I see," he said. He glanced at her,

then dropped his eyes again. "I'll leave you now. Make yourself at home."

He took down the lamp and lit a candle at it, bowed to her, and went out into the little back room. Soon, through the partition, she heard him moving something heavy.

"Blocking the door against me, probably," she thought, and smiled.

She threw off her shaggy cloak, and removed her hat—it had caught in her hair—and her knitted shawl. She had not been cold at all when she spoke to him at the window, and had only complained to make him let her in. But as she came up to the door she had stumbled into a puddle, and now her left foot was wet over the ankle, and her shoe and overshoe full of water. She sat down on his bed—a narrow bench, with nothing to cover it but a thin mattress of straw—to take off her shoes. This cell in which she found herself—she thought it charming. It was a narrowish little room, some three *arshins* by four, sparkling with cleanliness. There was no furniture but the bench on which she sat, and over it a shelf of books; yes, and a little lectern in the corner. By the door, on nails driven into the wall, hung a cassock and a fur-lined coat. Over the lectern, an icon of Christ, crowned with thorns, with an icon lamp burning before it. There was a strange odour in the room, of lamp oil, and sweat, and soil. She thought it all very pleasant. Even the smells.

Her wet feet were uncomfortable, particularly the left, and she began hastily to free them, smiling all the time with pleasure—not so much at the winning of her wager as at the disturbance which, she well knew, she had brought into the soul of this charming, striking, strange and attractive male. True, he had made no response. But what of that?

"Father Sergius! Father Sergius! That's your name, isn't it?"

"What do you wish?" came his low voice in reply.

"Do please forgive me for breaking in on your seclusion. I couldn't help myself, truly I couldn't. I'd have been taken ill. Even now, I may. I'm soaking wet, and my feet are cold as ice."

"I'm sorry," the low voice answered. "But there's nothing I can do."

"I'd never have dared disturb you, if I could have helped it. I'll only stay until the light."

He did not answer. And she could hear him whispering—praying, she supposed.

"You won't be coming out here, will you?" she asked, smiling. "Because, you see, I must undress, to dry my things."

He did not answer. His even voice came through to her, murmuring in prayer.

"Yes, he is a man, a real man," she thought, as she tugged at her water-filled overshoe.

She tugged and tugged, but the overshoe would not come off. That amused her, and she broke into a laugh, barely audible. But, knowing that he heard her laughter, and that her laughter might affect him precisely in the manner she desired, she laughed more loudly. And, truly, her laughter—merry, unforced, kindly—affected him, and precisely in the manner she desired.

"Yes," she thought, "one could love a man like that. Those eyes. And his face, so simple, noble, yes, and—mumble what prayers he will—yes, passionate! We women can't be fooled. Why, when he pressed his face to the window, and caught sight of me—he knew. He realized. It flashed then, deep in his eyes, and it made its mark. He knew love for me, and desire. Yes, and desire."

Her shoes and overshoes were off at last, and she could get at her stockings. To remove them, those long, gartered stockings, she must lift her skirts. She felt ashamed, and called:

"Don't come out."

But no answer came from the other room. The monotonous murmur continued, and there was a sound of movement.

"Prostrating himself in prayer," she thought to herself. "But it won't do him much good. He's thinking of me. Just as I am of him. Thinking, with just the same feeling of these feet of mine"—and, her wet stockings removed, she stamped her bare feet against the straw mattress, then drew them under her for warmth. She sat thus awhile, hugging her knees and staring dreamily at the wall. And her thoughts went on: "Why, we're in the wilderness. Such a hush! No one would ever know."

She got up and took her stockings to the stove, and hung them up on the damper. It was a peculiar damper, not the sort that she was used to. She fingered it idly, then turned back across the room, her bare feet treading lightly on the floor, and got up on the bench again. There was not a sound, now, in the other room. She glanced at the tiny watch that hung on a ribbon around her neck. It was two o'clock. The sleighs were to return at about three.

Only an hour left.

Was she to spend that hour all alone? Ridiculous! She would not. She would call him to her at once.

"Father Sergius! Father Sergius! Sergei Dmitrich! Prince Kasatsky!"

Not a sound in the other room.

"How can you be so cruel? I'd never call you. Never, if I weren't in need. I'm ill. I don't know what's wrong with me," she cried, her voice full of suffering. "Oh, dear! Oh, dear!"—and she threw herself down on the bench. And, strange as it might seem, she truly felt that she was ill, so ill. Her whole body ached, and she was trembling as in a fever.

"Do come and help me! I don't know what's the matter. Oh, dear! Oh, dear!"

She unhooked her dress, exposing her

bosom, and threw out her arms, bare to the elbow.

"Oh, dear! Oh, dear!"

He had been standing in the back room, all this time, praying. He had recited all the evening prayers, and now stood motionless, his eyes focused on the tip of his nose, praying inwardly—repeating in his spirit, "Lord Jesus Christ, Son of God, have mercy upon me."

But he had heard everything—had heard the rustle of silk as she lifted her dress, and the patter of her bare feet on the matting, and the sound that her hands made, rubbing her wet legs. He felt his weakness, felt that at any moment he might be lost; and therefore he prayed incessantly. He experienced something of what must have been felt by that fairy-tale hero who could attain his goal only if he advanced looking ahead, never for an instant glancing back. Like that hero, he sensed—he knew—that danger, perdition hung over and around him, and that the only escape lay in refraining from so much as a glance at it. But, all at once, he was seized with the desire to glance at it. And just at that moment she called:

"You're simply inhuman. I might be dying."

Yes, he would go to her—go as that holy father had who laid one hand on the forni-catress and thrust the other into a brazier. But he had no brazier. He looked about the room. The lamp. He held a finger over the

flame, and, frowning, set himself to endure.
For quite some time he seemed to feel
nothing at all; but suddenly—whether it hurt,
and how badly it hurt, he did not really
know—he grimaced disgustedly and jerked
his hand away. No, that he could not do.

"In God's name! Oh, come and help me!
Oh, but I'm dying!"

Must he, then, be lost? He would not. No.

"I'll be with you in a moment," he said,
opening his door; and passed through the
room, without a glance at her, into the entry.
It was here that he always chopped his firewood. Groping, he found the chopping block,
and then the hatchet, propped against the
wall.

"In a moment," he said again; and, grasping
the hatchet in his right hand, laid the index
finger of his left hand on the block. He swung
the hatchet and brought it down on his finger,
below the second joint. The finger was
severed more easily than wood of the same
thickness. It flew up, turned over in the air,
and fell, first to the edge of the block, and
then to the floor.

He heard it strike the floor. He had not yet
felt any pain. But just as he began to wonder
that there was no pain, the pain came, sharp
and burning, and on his fingers he felt the
warm trickle of blood. Quickly, he wrapped
the bleeding stump in the folds of his cassock
and pressed it against his side. Then he went
into the room and, pausing opposite the

woman, asked quietly, with lowered eyes:

"What did you wish?"

She saw his blanched face, and the tremor in his left cheek. And, suddenly, she was ashamed. She jumped up and got her cloak, and wrapped it close around her.

"Why, I was in pain... I've caught a chill... I... Father Sergius... I..."

He looked up, his eyes beaming with gentle rejoicing, and said:

"What for, dear sister, would you have doomed your immortal soul? Temptation must come into this world, but woe to those through whom temptation comes... Pray to God, that he may forgive us."

She stood listening, watching his face as he spoke. And suddenly she heard a sound of something dripping. She looked down, and saw the blood running from his hand down the folds of his cassock.

"What have you done to your hand?"

She recalled the sound she had heard. Seizing the lamp, she ran out into the entry. There, on the floor, she saw the blood-stained finger. Paler even than he, she returned, and would have spoken to him; but he slipped quietly out into the back room, and fastened the door behind him.

"Forgive me," she said. "What can I do to expiate my sin?"

"Go."

"Let me bind up your finger."

"Go."

Hastily, in silence, she dressed. When she was ready, she sat down, wrapped in her cloak, to wait. Soon the sleigh bells sounded.

"Father Sergius. Forgive me."

"Go. God will forgive."

"Father Sergius. I'll change my ways. Don't abandon me."

"Go."

"Forgive me, and give me your blessing."

"In the name of the Father, and the Son, and the Holy Ghost," came the voice from the other room. "Go."

Sobbing, she left the cell. The lawyer appeared, advancing to meet her.

"Well, I've lost, I see, worse luck! Which seat will you take?"

"It doesn't matter."

She got into the sleigh, and said not a word all through the drive to town.

———————

A year later, she took simple vows and settled down to a strict religious life at a nunnery, guided by the hermit Arseni, who wrote her letters now and again.

VI

Father Sergius lived in his hermitage seven more years.

At the beginning, he had used much of what was brought him: milk, sugar, tea, white bread, clothing, and firewood. But as time passed his way of life grew more and more austere. He gave up all habits of indulgence, reducing himself, in the end, to coarse black bread, a portion of which he accepted once a week. All else that was brought him, he gave away to the poor.

He spent his days in prayer in his cell, and in the reception of his visitors, who grew more and more numerous. He left his cell only for church—two or three times a year—or to fetch wood or water, when needed.

After five years of this life came the divorcée's nocturnal visit, and the change it brought about in her, and her retirement into a nunnery. All this became known, and Father Sergius' fame began to spread. Visitors came in ever greater numbers. Monks were settled near the cell, and a church and a hostel built. Father Sergius' fame—as always, exaggerated—spread over further. People began to flock to him from distant places. The sick and the suffering were brought to him, for it was said that he could heal them.

His first healing was performed in the eighth year of his life as a hermit. It was the healing of a boy of fourteen, whose mother brought him to the hermitage and demanded that Father Sergius lay his hand upon him. It had never occurred to Father Sergius that he might be able to heal the sick. Such a thought would have seemed to him sinful presumption. But the mother of this boy pleaded, and grovelled before him, and would not desist. He helped others, she said; why, then, would he not heal her son? In Christ's name, she implored him. To Father Sergius' explanation that only God could heal, she replied that she asked him only to lay his hand upon her son and pray. Father Sergius refused, and retired into his cell. But when he went out to fetch water next day (it was autumn, and the nights were cold) he found this same woman waiting for him, with her son, a thin, pale boy of fourteen; and again she poured forth her entreaties. Father Sergius recalled the parable of the unrighteous judge; and while until that moment he had never questioned but that he must deny the woman's plea, he now felt less certain. With this uncertainty, he began to pray, and prayed until decision took shape within him. His decision was, that he must do as the woman asked; that her faith might save her child; and that he, Father Sergius, in this case, would be no more than God's unworthy instrument.

And Father Sergius came out of his cell once more and went to the woman, and did her will. He laid his hand on the boy's head, and prayed.

They left, and a month later the boy's health returned. And the news spread far and wide of the miraculous healing power of *starets* Sergius, as people now called him.

From that time forth, not a week passed but that the sick came to Father Sergius. And, having yielded to the pleas of one, he could not refuse the pleas of others. He laid his hand upon them, and prayed; and many were healed; and his renown spread ever further.

Thus did the years pass: nine in monasteries, and thirteen in this hermitage. Father Sergius was a venerable figure now. His beard was long and grey, but his hair, though it had thinned, remained black and crisp as always.

VII

For some weeks, Father Sergius' mind had been occupied with the one persistent thought: was he doing right in submitting to this position in which he found himself, not so much by his own will as by that of the Archimandrite and the Superior? It had all begun with the healing of that fourteen-year-old boy. Since that time Sergius had felt with every passing month, week, day a gradual breaking-down of his inner life, and the growth, in its place, of a life purely external. It was as though he were being turned inside out.

He served, he realized, as a means of attracting visitors and donations to the monastery; and for that reason the monastery authorities sought so to order his way of life as to derive the greatest possible benefit from him. Thus, he was no longer permitted to labour physically. All that he might possibly need was supplied to him, and only one demand was made upon him: that he receive the people who came to him, and grant them his blessing. For his greater convenience, regular days were set for visitors. A reception-room was arranged for men, and a railed-in place where he could not be thrown from his feet by the women crowding to see him—a place from which to pronounce his blessing. He could not but submit when it was argued that people needed him; that, in obedience to Christ's law of love, he had not the right to deny them in their need of him; that it would be cruel to withhold himself from them. But as he was drawn more and more into this way of life, he felt more and more that his inner world was being transformed into a world of externals; that the source of living water within him was going dry; that all he did was done, to a greater and greater degree, for man, and not for God.

Whether exhorting, or simply blessing, whether praying for the sick, or giving counsel to seekers of a right way in life, or receiving the gratitude of those whom he had helped by healing, as they said, or by edification—he could not but be pleased, could not but be interested in the results of his efforts, in the influence that he exerted over others. The thought came to him that he was like a burning torch; and the stronger this feeling

became, the more deeply he sensed the
weakening, the dimming of God's light of
truth burning within him. To what degree
were his works done for God, and to what
degree for man?—this question tormented him
unceasingly; and never was he able not so
much to answer it, as to face the answer
squarely. In the depths of his soul he knew
that, in place of all his work for God, Satan
had substituted work for man. He knew it by
the way solitude now weighed on him, as
violation of his solitude had weighed on him
before. His visitors burdened and wearied
him; yet in his heart he was glad of them,
glad of the praises that rang around him.

There was a period when he made up his
mind to leave, to escape. He even planned
out all that he must do. He prepared peasant
clothing—shirt and trousers, hat and coat.
He needed them, he said, to give in charity.
And he kept this clothing in his cell, and
made his plans of how he would put it on,
one day, and cut his hair short, and leave. He
would go by train at first, three hundred
versts or so, and then get off and go wandering
about the countryside, from village to village.
He questioned an old invalid soldier who
came to him, asking how he got on, and how
he asked alms and shelter for the night. The
soldier told him how it was, and where it was
easiest to find alms and shelter. And Father
Sergius thought that he would do as this old
soldier did. He actually got into his peasant

clothes, one night, intending to go; but he did not know what was best: to go, or to stay. For some time he remained undecided. But then his indecision passed. He grew accustomed to his life, and submitted to Satan. And the peasant clothing remained no more than a reminder of his one-time thoughts and feelings.

With every day more and more people came to him, and less and less time remained for prayer and spiritual fortification. At times, in his better moments, the thought occurred to him that he had come to resemble a place where there once had been a spring.

"There was a spring, a gentle spring of living water, flowing softly through me and out of me. That was life in truth, when she"— Mother Agnia, now. It was always with rapture that he recalled that night, and her— "when she came to tempt me. She partook of that pure water. But now, before the water can collect, the thirsty rush to drink, crowding, jostling one another. And they have trampled out the spring, and only mud remains."

Thus did he think in his rare better moments. But his more habitual state was one of fatigue, and of self-admiration evoked by this fatigue.

———————

It was spring, the eve of the feast of Mid-Pentecost and Father Sergius was conducting vespers in his cave church. There were some twenty people present—all that the cave could hold; gentlefolk and merchants, people of wealth. Father Sergius admitted all comers, but they were filtered out by the monk in attendance on him and the assistant sent daily from the monastery. Outside, some eighty pilgrims, chiefly women, crowded around the door, waiting for Father Sergius to appear and give them his blessing.

The service went on. As, singing praise, Father Sergius approached the grave of his predecessor, he swayed suddenly, and would have fallen had he not been caught by a merchant who stood behind him and by the monk who served as deacon.

"What's the matter? Father Sergius! Dear heart!"—women's voices sounded. "The Lord preserve us! You're as pale as a sheet!"

But Father Sergius quickly recovered himself and, though very pale, brushed aside the merchant and the deacon and continued to sing. The deacon, Father Serapion, and the attendants, and Sofia Ivanovna, a lady who lived always near the hermitage and made it her business to look after Father Sergius—all begged him to break off the service.

"It's nothing, nothing," Father Sergius murmured, his lips, beneath his moustache, curving in the shadow of a smile. "Don't interrupt the service."

To himself he thought, "The saints did thus."

And, at once—

"Saint! Holy angel of God!" came Sofia

Ivanovna's voice, behind him, and the voice of the merchant who had supported him. He would hear no persuasion, but continued to sing. Crowding together, they all returned through the narrow passageway to the tiny church; and there, though he abridged it slightly, he completed the service.

Immediately after the service Father Sergius blessed all present and went out of doors, to a bench that stood in the shade of some elms by the entrance to the caves. He thought to rest there a while, in the fresh air; for he felt the need of it. But the moment he appeared the waiting people crowded about him, asking his blessing, seeking counsel and aid. There were women among these pilgrims who spent their lives in wandering from holy place to holy place, from *starets* to *starets*, touched to tears at the sight of any *starets*, of anything considered holy. Father Sergius knew this, the most common, the most irreligious type, cold-hearted, conventional. There were men among the pilgrims, discharged soldiers for the most part, who had somehow lost their place in normal life; old men, poverty-stricken and in their majority drunkards, who wandered from monastery to monastery for the alms to be got along the way. There were peasants, too, among the pilgrims, ignorant men and women, with their selfish demands for healing or for advice in the settlement of the most practical, worldly affairs: marrying off a daughter, or renting a village shop, or the purchase of land, or remission of the sin of a child overlain in sleep or begotten out of wedlock. All this was long familiar, and held no interest for Father Sergius. He knew that these people could tell him nothing new, that they could evoke no religious feeling in his heart; yet he liked to see them, as a throng which needed and treasured his presence, his word and blessing. And so, while he was irked by this throng, it was at the same time a source of pleasure. Father Serapion began to thrust the pilgrims back, declaring that Father Sergius was tired. But Father Sergius said that he would receive the people—and, as he spoke, recalled the words of the Gospel, "Suffer them (children) to come unto me"; and, recalling this passage, felt a warm glow of self-approval.

He got up and went to the railing, where they were crowding, and began to bless them and to answer their questions, in a voice so weak that he himself was deeply touched by it. But, however he might wish to, he was not able to receive them all. Again the darkness swept down over him, and he swayed, and seized at the railing for support. Again the blood rushed to his head, and his face first paled, then suddenly flushed.

"You must wait until tomorrow, I'm afraid. I can do no more today," he said, and, with one general blessing for all, turned back to his bench. The merchant took his arm again, and led him to the bench, and helped him to sit down.

"Father!" people were crying in the crowd. "Father! Father! Don't abandon us! We are lost without you!"

Having settled Father Sergius on his bench under the elms, the merchant now assumed police duties, and set energetically to work to disperse the throng. True, he kept his voice low, so that Father Sergius would not hear him. But his words were angry and determined:

"Be off, be off! He blessed you, didn't he? Well, then, what more do you want? Be off. Or I'll show you—that I will! Get along, get along! You, there, in the black foot wrappings—get along, get along, old woman! Where d'you think you're pushing to? You've been told once—no more today. Try again tomorrow. Today, he's all worn out."

"Just one look," the old woman pleaded. "Just one look at his sweet face."

"I'll teach you to look! Where d'you think you're pushing to?"

Father Sergius noticed that the merchant seemed to be going about things rather too severely, and said faintly to his attendant that the people should not be driven away. Father Sergius knew that the merchant would drive them off anyway; and he very much wanted to be alone, so that he might rest. But he sent his attendant with this message for the impression it would make.

"All right, all right," the merchant answered. "I'm not driving them away, I'm trying to teach them sense. Leave them alone, and they'd wear a man to death. They have no hearts—care for nobody but themselves. Get away, I tell you! Get away! You can come tomorrow."

And, in the end, the merchant drove them all away.

The merchant's zeal rose in part from a love of order and a love of driving people, ordering them about; but mainly from the need he had of Father Sergius' aid. He was a widower, with an only daughter who was ill and could not be married off; and he had brought his daughter here, a distance of fourteen hundred versts, for Father Sergius to heal her. He had tried several cures, in the two years of her illness. First, there had been the clinic at the gubernia centre, a university town. That had not done any good. Then he had tried a peasant healer in the Samara Gubernia. She had been a little better after that. Then he had taken her to a Moscow doctor, who charged no end of money and did no good at all. Then someone had told him of Father Sergius' cures, and he had brought her here. So that, when he had driven all the people off, the merchant came up to Father Sergius and, without preliminaries, dropped to his knees and began loudly:

"Sainted father, grant thy blessing to heal my daughter who is ailing from her pain and from her ailment. Dare I to thy holy feet bring my great plea?"

And he joined his hands in a gesture of appeal.

All this was said and done as though it were a formula clearly and unquestionably defined by law and custom; as though it were only thus, and in no other conceivable way, that one might and must request healing for one's daughter. It was done with such confidence that even to Father Sergius it almost began to seem the proper way of speech and conduct. Still, he bade the merchant get up and explain his trouble. The merchant said that his daughter, a girl of twenty-two, had been taken ill two years past, after the sudden death of her mother—had squawked, as he put it, and lost her wits. And so he had brought her here, a distance of fourteen hundred versts, and she was waiting at the hostel for Father Sergius to send for her. She went nowhere by day, being afraid of day-light, and could only come out after the sun was down.

"Is she very weak, then?" Father Sergius asked.

"No, I wouldn't call her weak, and she's got flesh enough on her, only she's nervasteenic—that's what the doctor called it. If Father Sergius would only say the word, I'd have her here in a jiffy. Sainted Father, revive a parent's heart, restore his line, let your prayers heal his daughter from her illness."

And again the merchant threw himself down on his knees, and bowed his head sidewise over his cupped hands. Father Sergius once more bade him get up; sighed heavily over the thought of how difficult his labours were, and how submissively, for all that, he pursued them—and, after a moment's silence, said:

"Very well. Bring her this evening, and I'll pray for her. But I'm tired now"—and his eyelids drooped. "I'll let you know."

The merchant left, tiptoeing across the sand—which only made his boots squeak the louder. Father Sergius remained alone.

All the days of Father Sergius' life were crowded with services and with visitors. But this had been a particularly difficult day. In the morning there had been a visiting dignitary, who talked with him endlessly. And then a lady had come, with her son. This son, a young professor, was an atheist; and his mother, a fervent believer and devoted to Father Sergius, had brought him here and begged Father Sergius to talk to him. It had been a very difficult talk. The young man, evidently reluctant to argue with a monk, had agreed with everything that Father Sergius said, as one agrees with the weak. But Father Sergius had seen clearly that the young man did not believe, and that, nonetheless, he was happy, comfortable, at ease. It was unpleasant to Father Sergius, now, to recall that conversation.

"Something to eat, Father," his attendant said.

"Yes. Bring me something."

The attendant went into the little cell that had been built a few paces from the entrance to the cave, and again Father Sergius was alone.

The time had long since passed when Father Sergius lived in solitude, and did all his work himself, and ate nothing but the communion loaf and plain black bread. Long since, it had been urged upon him that he had not the right to neglect his health; and he was served Lenten, but wholesome food. Though he ate little, it was a great deal more than formerly; and, whereas formerly he had eaten always with repulsion and consciousness of sin, he now often took great pleasure in his food. So it was today. He ate some porridge, and, with his tea, half of the white bread that was brought him.

The attendant left, and he remained alone on his bench under the elms.

It was a beautiful May evening. The leaves had only just uncurled on birch, elm, aspen, bird-cherry, and oak. The bird-cherry bushes beyond the elms were in full bloom, and the blossoms had not yet begun to fall. Nightingales were singing--one close by, and two or three in the bushes down by the river bank. A song sounded far over the river, where working folk, probably, were returning home after the day's labour. The sun, sinking beyond the woods, sent its slanted beams in a bright spray through the foliage, and all that part of the world was light green, while the rest was dark. May beetles were flying, bumping, falling.

After his supper Father Sergius prayed mentally the prayer, "Lord Jesus Christ, son of God, have mercy upon us," and then began to chant a psalm. While he was chanting, a sparrow skipped suddenly down from a bush nearby and began hopping towards him, chirping merrily—then took fright at something and flew away. Father Sergius went on to a prayer in which he spoke of his renunciation of the world. He recited it hurriedly in order the sooner to send for the merchant and his ailing daughter; for she interested him. She interested him as a diversion, as somebody new; interested him, also, because she and her father thought him a saint, one whose prayers God granted. He rebuked those who spoke of him as of a saint, but in the depths of his heart thought himself truly one.

He often wondered that he, Stepan Kasatsky, should have become so extraordinarily sainty, a veritable worker of miracles. But that he had, there could not be the slightest doubt. He could not refuse to believe in miracles he himself had witnessed, from the first sickly boy and to the last old woman who had regained her sight as a result of his prayer.

Strange as it might seem, it was true. And the merchant's daughter interested him because she was new, and because she believed in him, and, too, because he might once more, in curing her, confirm his power of healing, and his fame. "People come from thousands of versts around," he thought to himself. "The newspapers write about it. His Majesty knows of it. It's known in Europe, in atheistic Europe." But suddenly he was struck with shame at his vainglory. And again he began a prayer to God.

"Lord, King of Heaven, consoler, soul of truth, come, take up Thy abode in us, and cleanse us from all sin, and save and glorify our souls. Cleanse me from the sin of vainglory that has seized upon me," he prayed—and recalled how often he had prayed thus and how vain, as yet, had been his prayers. For others, his prayers brought miraculous healing; yet for himself he could not gain from God the liberation he sought from so mean a passion.

He recalled his prayers in the first years of his life here, when he had prayed God to grant him chastity, humility, and love; recalled how, in those years, it had seemed to him that God had needed his prayers; how he had remained chaste, and had struck off his finger. And he picked up the shrivelled finger and kissed it. It seemed to him now that he had been truly humble in those years when he so loathed himself for his sinful desires; and it seemed to him, too, that in those years he had love in his heart—for he recalled the emotion with which he had encountered an old man who came to him then, a drunken soldier who demanded money, and, yes, her. Well, and now? And he asked himself: was there anyone he loved? Did he love Sofia Ivanovna, or Father Serapion? Did he feel any love for all those people who had come to him today? For that learned young man to whom he had talked so instructively, concerned only to demonstrate his own mental powers and un-forgotten education? People's love was pleasant, was necessary to him; but he felt no answering love for them. He had no love now in his heart; had no humility, no, nor chastity.

It had pleased him that the merchant's daughter was a girl of twenty-two, and he had wanted to know whether she was pleasing to look upon. And in asking whether she was very weak, his real purpose had been to dis-cover whether or not she had the charms of femininity.

"Can I really have fallen so low," he wondered. "Lord, help me, restore me, my Lord and God." And, folding his hands, he began to pray. The nightingales were in full song. A May beetle buzzed past his ear and began crawling along the nape of his neck. He brushed it off. "But—does He exist? Am I not knocking at locked doors? Locked from without, with a lock that I might easily see? Nightingales, May beetles, Nature—are not these the lock? Suppose that young man was right?" And he began to pray aloud; and he prayed long, until all such thoughts vanished and he was calm and confident once more.

Then he tinkled his bell, and when his attendant appeared said that the merchant and his daughter might come to him now.

The merchant came, leading his daughter by the arm. He led her into the cell, and immediately left.

The daughter was a fair-haired and very fair-complexioned girl, pale and plump, and short in the extreme; with the face of a frightened child and the figure of a mature woman. Father Sergius had remained on his bench by the entrance to the cell. When the girl came past, and paused beside him, and he blessed her, he was struck with horror at the way in which his eyes probed her body. She went inside, leaving him with the feeling that something had stung him painfully. By her face, he realized that she was sensual and feeble-minded. He got up and went into the cell. She was sitting on a stool, waiting for him.

She got up when he came in.

"I want to go home," she said.

"Don't be afraid," he answered. "Tell me: what ails you?"

"Everything ails me," she said; and suddenly her face lit in a smile.

"You will be well," he told her. "Pray."

"What's the good of praying? I've prayed and prayed, and nothing comes of it." She was still smiling. "You pray, and lay your hands on me. I've dreamt about you."

"What did you dream?"

"I dreamt you laid your hand on my breast, like this"—and she took his hand and pressed it to her breast. "Just here."

He had given her his right hand.

"What's your name?" he asked, trembling from head to foot. He was vanquished, he knew. Desire had grown past all control.

"Marya. Why?"

She took his hand and kissed it, and then put her arm around him and drew him close.

"What are you doing?" he said. "Marya! You're Satan!"

"Ah, well, it's no great harm."

And, still embracing him, she sat down on the bed and pulled him down beside her.

————

At dawn, he went out to the porch.

Had it really all happened? Soon her father would come. She would tell. She was Satan. What to do, what to do? Ah! There it was—the hatchet he had struck his finger off with! He seized the hatchet and turned back to his cell.

His attendant hurried up.

"Do you need firewood? Let me have the hatchet."

He gave up the hatchet and returned to his cell. She lay there, asleep. He glanced at her in horror. Then he went to the back of the cell, took down the peasant clothing hanging there, got into it, found the scissors, and cut his hair, and went out and down by the path that led to the river. It was four years since he had been there last.

There was a road along the river bank. He took the road, and followed it until noon. At noon he turned into a field of rye, and lay down among the rye. Towards evening he approached a village. He did not enter the village, but turned off to the bluff river bank.

Early morning, perhaps half an hour before sunrise. Everything was grey and gloomy. A cold morning wind blew from the west. Yes, the thing must be ended. There was no God. How end it? A leap into the water? But he could swim. He would not drown. Hanging? Yes, by his belt. From a tree. Death seemed so easily accomplished, so very close, that horror swept over him. He wanted to pray, as always in moments of despair. But there was no one to pray to. There was no God. He lay there, his head propped on his hand. And suddenly he felt such a great need of sleep that he could no longer keep his head propped on his hand. He let his hand drop, and laid his head on his outstretched arm, and immediately fell asleep. But this sleep lasted only an instant. He woke at once, and his mind filled with memories. Or perhaps he was simply dreaming.

He recalled himself as a boy, hardly more than a child, at his mother's country home. And a carriage drove up to the house, and out of the carriage got Uncle Nikolai Sergeyevich, with his great black spade-shaped beard, and with him Pashenka—a skinny little girl, with big, meek eyes set in a timid, pitiful little face. And she was brought to the boys in the children's room, this Pashenka, and they were expected to play with her. But that was dull. She was so silly. And in the end they made a mock of her. They would not believe she could swim, insisted that she show them how she did it. She got down on the floor and showed them. And they all laughed aloud, and thought her a great fool. And she realized it, and red spots came out on her face, and she looked pitiful, so pitiful that he felt ashamed; and he was never to forget that twisted smile of hers, so gentle and submissive.

Then he recalled the times when he had seen her after that. He had seen her years later, just before he entered the monastery—a married woman, wife to some country landowner who had squandered all her fortune, and who beat her. She had had two children, a boy and a girl, but the boy had died young.

Sergius recalled her as he had seen her then, so unhappy. Later, at the monastery, he had seen her again, a widow. She had been the same as ever—not stupid, exactly, but somehow insipid, insignificant and pitiful. She had come to the monastery with her daughter and her daughter's fiancé. And they had been poor. Later still, he had heard that she lived in some small town, and that she was very poor.

Why on earth did he keep thinking of her, he wondered. But he could not stop thinking of her. Where was she now? What had become of her? Was she wretched and unhappy still, as she had been when she got down on the floor to show that she could swim? Ah, but why think of her? He was forgetting! It was time to end things.

And again fear swept over him. And again, to escape the thought of what must be, he began to think of Pashenka.

Thus he lay for some time, thinking now of the end that he must make of himself, now again of Pashenka. The thought of Pashenka seemed to carry deliverance. In the end, he fell asleep. And in his sleep he dreamed that an angel came to him and told him, "Go thou to Pashenka and learn from her what thou must do, and wherein lies thy sin, and wherein thy salvation."

Waking, he decided that this had been a vision sent by God. And he rejoiced, and decided to do as he had been bidden in this vision. He knew the town she lived in. It was three hundred versts away. And he set out for that town.

VIII

Pashenka had long since ceased to be little Pashenka. She was Praskovya Mikhailovna, now—an old woman, gaunt and wrinkled, mother-in-law to a luckless and drink addicted government clerk named Mavrikyev. She lived in the little town where her son-in-law had held his last position; and there she supported her family: daughter, and sickly, neurasthenic son-in-law, and five grandchildren. She supported them by giving music lessons to the daughters of the local merchants, at fifty kopeks an hour. Some days she had four lessons, some days five, so that she managed to earn something like sixty rubles a month. And so they lived, for the time being, until some new position for the son-in-law should be forthcoming. Praskovya Mikhailovna had written to all her relatives and acquaintances, asking their help in getting him a position. She had written, too, to Sergius. But he had left the hermitage before her letter arrived.

It was Saturday, and Praskovya Mikhailovna was preparing the dough for a batch of the sweet raisin-bread that she had learned to bake, long years ago, from the serf cook in her father's kitchen. It was to be a Sunday treat for her grandchildren.

Masha, her daughter, was busy with the baby. The eldest of the children, a boy and a girl, were at school. The son-in-law had fallen into a doze, after a sleepless night. Praskovya Mikhailovna, too, had had very little sleep. Far into the night, she had talked with Masha, trying to soothe her anger against her husband.

He was but a weak creature, Praskovya

Mikhailovna realized, incapable of changing his thoughts or his ways of life. Nor, she realized, could his wife's reproaches do any good. And she did everything in her power to smooth things over, to prevent reproaches, to prevent ill feeling. With an acuteness that was almost physical pain, she suffered from all unkindness in human relations. She saw so clearly that it could do no good, that it could only make things worse. It was not that she actually thought all this out. Simply, she suffered at the sight of malice, as at an evil odour, or a harsh sound, or a blow.

Proud of her skill, she was explaining to Lukerya how the dough must be mixed, when little Misha, her grandson, came running in—a boy of six, in a pinafore, his rickety legs cased in much-darned stockings. He looked frightened.

"Granny! There's such a dreadful old man, asking for you!"

Lukerya went to the door.

"So there is, mistress. Some sort of pilgrim."

Praskovya Mikhailovna brushed the flour from her bony elbows, wiped her hands on her apron, and was about to leave the kitchen, to fetch five kopeks for the pilgrim from her purse; but recalled that there was nothing smaller in her purse than a ten-kopek piece, and decided to give bread instead; but then, as she was turning to the cupboard, flushed suddenly at the thought that she had begrudged alms, and, telling Lukerya to cut a good slice of bread, went to get the ten kopeks as well. She would give double alms, to make up for her stinginess.

She asked the pilgrim's pardon as she offered him the bread and the coin. Proffering them, far from pride in her generosity, she felt but shame that she gave so little—so impressive was his figure.

He had begged his way, in Christ's name, over a distance of three hundred versts. He was gaunt, ragged, weather-beaten, his hair cut short. He wore rough, peasant hat and boots. Yet for all that, and for all the humility with which he bowed low in the doorway, Sergius still retained the impressive aspect that so attracted people to him. But Praskovya Mikhailovna did not recognize him. Nor could she well have recognized him, not having seen him for almost thirty years.

"Pardon, Father. You're hungry, perhaps."

He took the bread and the money. And Praskovya Mikhailovna wondered that he did not go, but stood there, looking at her.

"Pashenka. It's you I've come to. Don't turn me away."

And the beautiful dark eyes, looking intently, appealingly into hers, filmed with glistening tears. And the lips, beneath the greying moustache, trembled pitifully.

Praskovya Mikhailovna's lips parted, and her hand flew to her withered breast. Her eyes searched the pilgrim's face.

"It can't be! Stepan! Sergius! Father Sergius!"

"Yes," Sergius answered, very low. "Only—not Sergius, not Father Sergius, but the evil sinner Stepan Kasatsky, a lost and evil sinner. Help me. Don't turn me away."

"It can't be! How you have humbled yourself! Ah, come in, come in."

She held out her hand. But he did not take her hand. He followed her into the house.

But where was she to put him? They had very little space. There was one tiny room, hardly more than a closet, that had been hers at first; but then she had turned even this closet over to Masha. And there Masha sat now too, rocking the baby to sleep.

"Sit here for just a moment," Praskovya Mikhailovna said, pointing to a bench in the kitchen.

Sergius sat down at once, and removed the pack from his back, slipping the straps first from one shoulder, then from the other, with what had clearly become habitual movements.

"Dear God, dear God, that you should have humbled yourself so! Such great glory, and—all at once..."

Sergius did not answer, except by a gentle smile, as he laid his pack down on the bench.

"Do you know who that is, Masha?"

And Praskovya Mikhailovna whispered to her daughter who their visitor was. And, together, they removed Masha's bedding, and carried out the baby in its cradle, freeing the little room for Sergius.

Praskovya Mikhailovna took Sergius to his room.

"You can rest here. I'm sorry it's so small. I must go now."

"Where to?"

"It's these lessons that I give. I'm ashamed even to tell you. I teach music."

"Music? That's very good. Only—you see, Praskovya Mikhailovna, it's a serious matter that brings me to you. When could I have a talk with you?"

"It will be a great happiness to me. Will this evening be all right?"

"Of course. Only—one more thing. Don't tell people who I am. It was only to you I could trust myself. No one knows where I've gone. It's very necessary."

"Oh! And I told my daughter!"

"Then ask her not to speak of it."

Sergius pulled off his boots, lay down, and fell asleep at once, after a sleepless night and tramp of forty versts.

————

When Praskovya Mikhailovna returned, Sergius was awake, waiting for her in the little room. He had not come out to dinner, but had had some soup and porridge that Lukerya brought him.

"You're earlier than you promised,"

Sergius said. "How is that? Can we have our talk now?"

"To think that I should be granted such happiness, such a visitor! What have I done to deserve it? Well, and so I just skipped a lesson. I'll make it up afterwards... I'd been hoping and planning to visit you. I wrote to you. And now—such unexpected happiness!"

"Pashenka! What I say to you now—receive it as holy confession, made before God, in my hour of death. Pashenka! I am no holy man, no, not even a simple, ordinary man. I am a sinner, a vile, evil, benighted, presumptuous sinner. I am worse—perhaps not than all men: that I cannot say—but worse than the very worst of men."

At first Pashenka stared at him, wide-eyed. How could she believe him? Then, when she really began to believe, she touched his hand with hers and said, smiling sorrowfully:

"Perhaps you're exaggerating, Stepan."

"No, Pashenka. I'm a fornicator. I'm a murderer. I'm a blasphemer and a deceiver."

"Dear God! How can it be?" Praskovya Mikhailovna whispered.

"But life must be lived. And I, who thought I knew all there was to know, who advised others how to live their lives—I know nothing at all, and I have come to learn from you."

"What are you saying, Stepan? You're making fun of me. Why do people always make fun of me?"

"Well, say I'm making fun, if you like. Only tell me: how do you live? And how have you spent your life?"

"I? Why, I spent it in the worst and vilest way. And now God is punishing me, and rightly, and life is so bad, so bad..."

"How did your marriage come about? And how did you live when you were married?"

"It was all bad, all bad. How I married? I fell in love, the wickedest way. Father was against it. But I wouldn't hear of anything. And so I was married. And when I was married, instead of helping my husband, I tortured him by my jealousy, that I simply couldn't conquer."

"He drank, I was told."

"Yes. But I—I couldn't learn to quiet his nerves, I kept reproaching him. And, after all, it's really a disease. He couldn't help himself, and I remember still how I locked it away from him. And we had dreadful scenes."

And her beautiful eyes, turned to Kasatsky, clouded with pain at the remembrance.

Kasatsky recalled the rumours he had heard, that Pashenka's husband beat her. And, looking now at her gaunt, shrivelled neck, and the tendons standing out behind her ears, and her knot of thin hair, half brown, half grey, he seemed to see it all.

"And then I was left alone, with two children, and with absolutely no means."

"Why, but you had land."

"We sold that while Vasya was still alive, and ... well, the money all went. So that—we had to live, somehow, and there was nothing I knew how to do. Like all us daughters of the gentry. Only I was particularly bad, particularly helpless. We lived, somehow, on the last remnants. I sent the children to school, and studied a little myself, too. And then Mitya took sick, in his fourth year at school, and the Lord took him from me. Masha fell in love with Vanya—that's my son-in-law. Well, and—he's a good soul, only unhappy. He isn't well."

"Mother!" the daughter's voice broke in. "Take the youngster. I can't do everything!"

Praskovya Mikhailovna started. She went quickly out of the room, in her down-at-heel shoes, and immediately returned with a two-year-old boy in her arms. The child kept throwing itself back, and pulling at her kerchief.

"Where was I? Ah, yes. Vanya had a position here, a good position, and such a pleasant chief. But he couldn't go on any longer. He had to resign."

"What's wrong with him?"

"Neurasthenia. It's a dreadful sickness. We've consulted about it, but—he needs to go away, and we haven't the means. But I keep hoping it will pass. He has no pain in particular, only..."

"Lukerya!" came the sick man's voice, weak and querulous. "They're always sending her off somewhere, just when she's needed. Mother!"

"Coming!" Praskovya Mikhailovna called, breaking off her tale once more. "He hasn't had his dinner yet. He can't eat with all of us."

She left the room, and could be heard moving about the house. Then she returned, drying her thin, sun-browned hands.

"Well, and so we go on. Always complaining, always dissatisfied, and yet, praise be to God, the children are all good, and well, and life is really tolerable. Ah, but why talk of me?"

"What do you live on?"

"Why, I earn a little. Music always seemed so dull to me, yet how it helps me now!"

Her hand lay on the bureau beside her. A small, thin hand. She worked her slender fingers, as though playing an exercise.

"What are you paid for your lessons?"

"A ruble, or fifty kopeks. Some pay thirty. They're all so kind to me."

"Well, and do they make progress?" Kasatsky asked, with the ghost of a smile deep in his eyes.

Praskovya Mikhailovna did not believe, at first, that he was asking seriously. She looked questioningly into his eyes.

"Yes, they do. There's one very nice little girl, the butcher's daughter. A kind, good girl. Of course, if I were good for anything, I'd manage to find Vanya some position, through my father's old connections. But I'm no good, and so I've brought them all to this."

"So, so," Kasatsky murmured, bowing his head. "Well, and church life, Pashenka—do you take any part in that?"

"Ah, that's best not talked of. It's so bad, the way I've come to neglect it. We fast in Lent, and go to church. But often I don't go for months. I send the children."

"And why don't you go yourself?"

"Well, to tell you the truth"—and her face flushed—"I don't like to shame my daughter, and the children, going in my shabby clothes. And I have nothing new. And—well, I suppose I'm simply lazy."

"Do you pray at home, then?"

"Yes, but it's not real prayer—just mechanical. That's no way, I know, but I have no real feeling. Only the realization of my own vileness."

"So, so. I see, I see," Kasatsky responded, as though in approval.

The son-in-law called again.

"Coming, coming," she answered, and, patting her hair, left the room once more.

This time her absence was more lengthy. Returning finally, she found Kasatsky sitting as before, bowed forward, with his elbows on his knees. But now his pack was on his back.

When she came in, carrying a small tin lamp without a shade, he lifted his beautiful, weary eyes to hers with a deep, deep sigh.

"I haven't told them who you are," she began timidly. "I just said—a pilgrim, of the nobility, and that I'd known you once. Won't you come to the dining-room to tea?"

"No."

"Then I'll bring you some here."

"No. There's no need. God save you, Pashenka. I must be going. If you feel for me, tell no one that you've seen me. By the living God I adjure you, tell no one of it. And thank you. I would bow to the ground before you—but that would embarrass you, I know. Thank you, and forgive me, in Christ's name."

"Give me your blessing."

"God will bless you. Forgive me, in Christ's name."

And he would have gone, but she detained him, and brought him bread, and rusks, and butter. All this he took, and left.

It was dark, and he was hardly two houses away before she lost sight of him, and could only tell he was there because the archpriest's dog began to bark at him.

————

"So that was the meaning of my dream. Pashenka is precisely what I ought to have been, and what I have not been. I lived for man, pretending to live for God; but she lives for God, imagining that she lives for man. Yes, one good deed, a cup of water offered without thought of reward, is dearer than all those I have helped for the sake of man's approval. But"—he asked himself—"was there not some particle of the true wish to serve God?" And he had to answer, "Yes, but all that was defiled, overgrown by the wish for glory among men. No, there is no God for one who has lived, like me, for glory among men. But I shall go, then, and search for Him."

And he went, as he had come to Pashenka, wandering from village to village, now joining, now parting with other pilgrims, men and women; asking food and shelter in Christ's name. At times, some ill-tempered housewife might scold at him, or some peasant in his cups abuse him; but far more often he would be given food and drink, and even provision for his way. His appearance, betraying his aristocratic origin, inclined some people in his favour. Others, on the contrary, seemed well pleased to see one of the gentry reduced to beggary. But his gentle ways conquered all with whom he came in contact.

Often, finding the Gospel in some home, he would read aloud from it; and always, everywhere, people would listen, touched and amazed, as to something ever new, though long familiar.

If he had an opportunity to help people, by advice, or by writing letters or documents for the illiterate, or by conciliating wranglers, he never heard their gratitude, for he would leave before it could be tendered. And, little by little, he began to find his God.

One day he was on the road in company

with two old women and a discharged soldier. Some gentlefolk stopped them—a gentleman and lady in a gig drawn by a smart trotter, and another gentleman and lady on horseback. The riders were the husband and daughter of the lady in the gig; the other gentleman, apparently, a French visitor.

They stopped the wanderers to show their visitors *les pélérins*—men and women led by the superstition inherent in the Russian people to wander from place to place instead of working.

They spoke in French, thinking that the pilgrims could not understand them.

"*Demandez leur,*" the Frenchman said, "*s'ils sont bien sûrs de ce que leur pélérinage est agréable à dieu.*"

The question was put. The old women answered:

"As God may find it. Our feet have been to the shrine. Perhaps our hearts will be there."

The soldier was asked. He replied that he was alone in the world, and had no place to stay.

Then they asked Kasatsky who he might be.

"A servant of God."

"*Qu'est ce qu'il dit? Il ne répond pas.*"

"*Il dit qu'il est un serviteur de dieu.*"

"*Cela doit être un fils de prêtre. Il a de la race. Avez vous de la petite monnaie?*"

The Frenchman had some silver in his pocket. And he gave each of the pilgrims twenty kopeks.

"Mais dites leur que ce n'est pas pour des cierges que je leur donne, mais pour qu'ils se régalent de thé. Tea, tea"—and he smiled. *"Pour vous, mon vieux,"* he concluded, patting Kasatsky's shoulder with his gloved hand.

"Christ save you," Kasatsky responded, hat in hand, bowing his bald head.

And this encounter brought Kasatsky particular happiness, because he had been able to disregard what people thought of him, had been able to do the simplest, the easiest thing—humbly accepting twenty kopeks, and then giving it away to a comrade, a blind beggar. The less human opinion came to mean to him, the more strongly he could feel his God.

Eight months passed in this way. In the ninth month, passing through a gubernia centre, Kasatsky was questioned at a shelter where he had spent the night with other wanderers; and as he could produce no passport, he was taken to the police station for further examination. Asked his name, and what he had done with his passport, he replied that he had no passport, and that he was a servant of God. He was tried as a vagrant, convicted, and exiled to Siberia.

In Siberia he settled on a rich peasant's farm, where he lives to this day. He works in this peasant's garden, and teaches the village children, and nurses the sick.

1898

AFTER THE BALL

"So you contend a man cannot judge independently of what is good and what is bad, that it is all a matter of environment—that man is a creature of environment. But I contend it is all a matter of chance. And here is what I can say about myself..."

This is what our respected friend Ivan Vasilyevich said at the conclusion of a discussion we had been having about the necessity of changing the environment, the conditions in which men live, before there could be any talk about the improvement of the individual. As a matter of fact, no one had said it was impossible to judge independently of the good and the bad, but Ivan Vasilyevich had a habit of answering thoughts of his own stimulated by a discussion, and recounting experiences from his own life suggested by these thoughts. Often he became so absorbed in the story that he forgot his reason for telling it, especially since he always spoke with great fervour and sincerity. That is precisely what happened in the present case.

"At least I can make this claim with regard to myself. My own life has been moulded in that way and no other—not by environment, but by something quite different."

"By what?" we asked.

"That is a long story. If you are to understand, I must tell it all to you."

"Then do."

Ivan Vasilyevich considered a moment and shook his head.

"Yes," he said, "my whole life was changed by a single night, or rather, a morning."

"Why? What happened?"

"It happened that I was deeply in love. I had often been in love before, but never so deeply. It took place a long time ago—her daughters are married women by this time. Her name was B., Varenka B. She was still strikingly beautiful at fifty, but in her youth, when she was eighteen, she was a dream: tall, slender, graceful, and majestic—yes, majestic. She always held herself as erect as if she were unable to bend, with her head tipped slightly backward; this, combined with her beauty and height, even though she was so thin as to be almost bony, gave her a queenly air that would have been intimidating if it had not been for her gay, winning smile, her mouth, her glorious shining eyes, and her whole captivating, youthful being."

"Ivan Vasilyevich certainly does lay it on thick!"

"However thick I were to lay it on, I could not make you understand what she was really like. But that is beside the point. The events I shall recount took place in the 'forties.

"I was then a student at a provincial university. I don't know whether it was a good or a bad thing, but in those days there were none of your study circles, none of your theorizing, at our university; we were just young and lived in the way of young folk— studying and having a good time. I was a very gay and energetic youth, and rich in the bargain. I owned a spirited carriage horse and used to take the girls out for drives (skating had not yet become the fad); I went on drinking-parties with my fellow-students (in those days we drank nothing but champagne; if we were out of money, we drank nothing, for we never drank vodka as they do now); but most of all I enjoyed parties and balls. I was a good dancer and not exactly ugly."

"Come, don't be modest," put in one of the listeners. "We've all seen your daguerreotype. You were a very handsome youth."

"Perhaps I was, but that isn't what I wanted to tell you. When my love was at its height I attended a ball given on the last day of Shrovetide by the Marshal of Nobility, a good-natured old man, wealthy, and fond of entertaining. His wife, as amiable as he was, stood beside him to receive us. She was wearing a velvet gown and a diamond tiara in her hair, and her aging neck and shoulders, plump and white, were exposed, as in the portraits of Empress Yelizaveta Petrovna. The ball was magnificent. The ball-room was charming, in the gallery were famous serf musicians belonging to a certain landowner who was a lover of music, the food was abundant, the champagne flowed in rivers. Much as I loved champagne, I did not drink—I was drunk with love. But I danced till I dropped. I danced quadrilles, and waltzes, and polkas, and it goes without saying that I danced as many of them as I could with Varenka. She was wearing a white dress with a pink sash, white kid gloves that did not quite reach her thin, pointed elbows, and white satin slippers. A wretched engineer named Anisimov cheated me out of a mazurka with her. I have never forgiven him for that. He invited her the moment she entered the ball-room, while I had been delayed by calling at the hairdresser's, and at the haberdasher's for a new pair of gloves. And so instead of dancing the mazurka with her, I danced it with a German girl I had once had a crush on. But I am afraid I was very neglectful of her that evening; I did not talk to her or look at her, for I had eyes for no one but a tall, slender girl in a white dress with a pink sash, with radiant, flushed, dimpled cheeks and soft, gentle eyes. I was not the only one; everyone looked at her and admired her, even the women, though she outshone them all. It was impossible not to admire her.

"Formally I was not her partner for the mazurka, but as a matter of fact I did dance it with her—at least most of it. Without the least embarrassment she danced straight to me down the length of the whole room, and when I leapt up to meet her without waiting for the invitation, she smiled to thank me for guessing what she wanted. When we had been led up to her and she had not guessed my mazurka pseudonym,* she had given a little shrug of her thin shoulders as she held out her hand to another, turning upon me a little smile of regret and consolation.

"When the figures of the mazurka changed into a waltz, I waltzed with her for a long time, and she smiled breathlessly and murmured *'encore'*. And I waltzed on and on with her, quite unaware of my own body, as if it were made of air."

"Unaware of it? I'm sure you must have been very much aware of it as you put your arm about her waist—aware of not only your body, but of hers as well," said one of the guests.

Ivan Vasilyevich suddenly turned crimson

* In order to decide on partners for the mazurka the gentlemen each thought of a pseudonym for themselves; the ladies each chose one of these pseudonyms, and her partner would thus be made known to her.—*Ed.*

and almost shouted:

"That may apply to you, modern youth—all you think of is the body. In our days things were different. The more deeply I loved a girl, the more incorporeal she seemed to me. Today you are aware of legs, ankles, and other things; you disrobe the ladies with whom you are in love, but for me, as Alphonse Karr has said—and a very good writer he was—the object of my love was always clad in bronze raiment. Far from exposing, we tried to hide nakedness, as did the good son of Noah. But you cannot understand this."

"Pay no attention to him. Go on with your story," said another of the listeners.

"Well, I danced mostly with her and did not notice the passage of time. The musicians were so exhausted—you know how it always is at the end of a ball—that they kept playing the mazurka; mamás and papás were rising from the card-tables in the drawing-room in anticipation of supper; footmen were rushing about. It was going on for three o'clock. We had to take advantage of the few minutes left us. I invited her once more, and for the hundredth time we passed down the length of the room.

"'Will I be your partner for the quadrille after supper?' I asked her as I took her back to her place.

"'Oh, yes, if they do not take me home,' she said with a smile.

"'I won't let them,' I said.

" 'Give me my fan,' she said.

" 'I am sorry to give it back to you,' I said as I handed her her cheap white fan.

" 'Here, to keep you from being sorry,' she said, plucking a feather out of the fan and giving it to me.

"I took the feather, unable to express my rapture and gratitude except with a glance. I was not only gay and content—I was happy, I was blissful, I was benevolent, I was no longer myself, but some creature not of this earth, who knew no evil and could do nothing but good.

"I tucked the feather in my glove and stood riveted to the spot, unable to move away from her.

" 'Look, they are asking papa to dance,' she said, indicating a tall, stately man who was her father, a colonel, in silver epaulettes, standing in the doorway with the hostess and some other women.

" 'Varenka, come here,' called the hostess in the diamond tiara.

"Varenka made for the door and I followed her.

" 'Do talk your father into dancing with you, *ma chère*. Please do, Pyotr Vladislavich,' said the hostess to the colonel.

"Varenka's father was a tall, handsome, stately, and well-preserved old man. He had a ruddy face with a white moustache curled *à la* Nicholas I, white side whiskers that met his moustache, hair combed forward over his temples, and the same smile as his daughter's lighting up his eyes and lips. He was very well built, with a broad chest swelling out in military style and with a modest display of decorations on it, with strong shoulders and long, fine legs. He was an officer of the old type with a military bearing of the Nicholas I school.

"As we came up to the door the colonel was protesting that he had forgotten how to dance, but nevertheless he smiled, reached for his sword, drew it out of its sword-belt, handed it to a young man eager to offer his services, and, drawing a suede glove onto his right hand ('Everything according to rule,' he said with a smile), he took his daughter's hand and struck a pose in a quarter turn, waiting for the proper measure to begin.

"As soon as the mazurka phrase was introduced he stamped one foot energetically and swung out with the other, and then his tall heavy figure sailed round the ball-room. He kept striking one foot against the other, now slowly and gracefully, now quickly and energetically. The willowy form of Varenka floated beside him. Imperceptibly and always just in time, she kept lengthening or shortening the step of the little white satin feet to fit his.

"All the guests stood watching the couple's every movement. The feeling I experienced was less admiration than a sort of deep ecstasy. I was especially touched by the sight

of the colonel's boots. They were good calf-
skin boots, but they were heelless and had
blunt toes instead of fashionable pointed
ones. Obviously they had been made by the
battalion cobbler. 'He wears ordinary boots
instead of fashionable ones so that he can
dress his beloved daughter and take her into
society,' I thought to myself, and that is why
I was particularly touched by his blunt-toed
boots. Anyone could see he had once danced
beautifully, but now he was heavy and his
legs were not flexible enough to make all the
quick and pretty steps he attempted. But he
went twice round the room very well, and
everybody applauded when he quickly spread
out his feet, then snapped them together
again and fell, albeit rather heavily, on one
knee. And she smiled as she freed her caught
skirt and floated gracefully round him. When
he had struggled back to his feet, he touching-
ly put his hands over his daughter's ears and
kissed her on the forehead, then led her over
to me, who he thought had been her dancing
partner. I told him I was not.

" 'It doesn't matter: you dance with her,'
he said, smiling warmly as he slipped his
sword back into the sword-belt.

"Just as the first drop poured out of a
bottle brings a whole stream in its wake, so
my love for Varenka released all the love in
my soul. I embraced the whole world with
love. I loved the hostess with her diamond
tiara, and her husband, and her guests, and

her footmen, and even the wretched Anisimov, who was clearly angry with me. As for
her father with his blunt-toed boots and
a smile so much like hers—I felt a rapturous
affection for him.

"The mazurka came to an end and our
hosts invited us to the supper table. But
Colonel B. declined, saying that he must be
up early in the morning. I was afraid he
would take Varenka with him, but she
remained behind with her mother.

"After supper I danced the promised
quadrille with her. And while it had seemed
that my happiness could not be greater, it
went on growing and growing. We said nothing of love; I did not ask her, nor even myself, whether she loved me. It was sufficient
that I loved her. The only thing I feared was
that something might spoil my happiness.

"When I got home, undressed myself and
thought of going to bed, I realized that sleep
was out of the question. I held in my hand
the feather from her fan and one of her
gloves, which she had given to me when I put
her and her mother into their carriage. As
I gazed at these keepsakes I saw her again at
the moment when, choosing one of two
partners, she had guessed my pseudonym and
said in a sweet voice, *'Too proud*? Is that it?'
then joyfully held out her hand to me; or
when, sipping champagne at the supper table,
she had gazed at me over her glass with
loving eyes. But I saw her best as she danced

with her father, floating gracefully beside him, looking at the admiring spectators with joy and pride for his sake as well as her own. And involuntarily the two of them became merged in my mind and enveloped in one deep and tender feeling.

"At that time my late brother and I lived alone. My brother had no use for society and never went to balls. He was getting ready to take his examinations for a master's degree and was leading the most exemplary of lives. He was asleep. I felt sorry for him as I looked at his head buried in the pillow, half covered by the blanket—sorry because he did not know and did not share the happiness which was mine. Petrusha, our serf valet, met me with a candle and would have helped me undress, but I dismissed him. I was touched by the sight of the man's sleepy face and dishevelled hair. Trying to make no noise, I tiptoed to my own room and sat down on the bed. I was too happy. I could not sleep. I found it hot in the room, and so without taking off my uniform I went quietly out into the hall, put on my greatcoat, opened the entrance door, and went out.

"It had been almost five o'clock when I left the ball; about two hours had passed since, so that it was already light when I went out. It was typical Shrovetide weather—misty, with wet snow melting on the roads and water dripping from all the roofs. At that time the B.'s lived on the outskirts of town,

at the edge of an open field with a girls'
school at one end and a space used for pro-
menading at the other. I went down our quiet
little by-street and came out upon the main
street, where I met passers-by and carters with
firewood loaded on sledges whose runners cut
through the snow to the very pavement. And
everything—the horses bobbing their heads
rhythmically under their shiny yokes, and the
carters with bast matting on their shoulders
plodding in their enormous boots through the
slush beside their sledges, and the houses on
either side of the street standing tall in the
mist—everything seemed particularly dear
and significant.

"When I reached the field where their
house stood I saw something big and black
at the promenade end of it, and I heard the
sounds of a fife and drum. My heart had been
singing all this time, and occasionally the
strains of the mazurka had come to my mind.
But this was different music, harsh and
sinister.

" 'What could it be?' I wondered, and made
my way in the direction of the sounds, down
the slippery waggon road that cut across the
field. When I had gone about a hundred paces
I began to distinguish in the mist a crowd of
people. They were evidently soldiers. 'Drilling,'
I thought, and drew closer, following a blacksmith in an oil-stained apron and short sheepskin coat who was carrying a large bundle.
A double row of soldiers in black coats were

standing facing each other motionless, their guns at their sides. Behind them stood a fifer and a drummer-boy who kept playing that shrill tune over and over.

" 'What are they doing?' I asked the blacksmith who was standing next to me.

" 'Driving a Tatar down the line for having tried to run away,' replied the blacksmith brusquely, glaring at the far end of the double row.

"I looked in the same direction and saw something horrible coming towards me between the rows. It was a soldier bare to the waist and tied to the rifles of the two soldiers who were leading him. Beside him walked a tall officer in a greatcoat and forage cap whose figure seemed familiar to me. The punished soldier, his whole body twitching, his feet squashing through the melting snow, advanced through the blows raining down on him from either side, now cringing back, at which the soldiers holding the rifles would pull him forward, now lunging forward, at which the soldiers would jerk him back to keep him from falling. And next to him, walking firmly, never lagging behind, came the tall officer. It was her father, with his ruddy face and white moustache and side whiskers.

"At every blow the punished man turned his pain-distorted face to the side from which the blow had come, as if in surprise, and kept repeating something over and over through bared white teeth. I could not make out the words until he came closer to me. He was sobbing rather than speaking them. 'Have mercy, brothers; have mercy, brothers.' But the brothers had no mercy, and when the procession was directly opposite me I saw one of the soldiers step resolutely forward and bring his lash down so hard on the Tatar's back that it whistled through the air. The Tatar fell forward, but the soldiers jerked him up, and then another blow fell from the opposite side and again from this, and again from that... The colonel marched beside him, now glancing down at his feet, now up at the soldier being punished, drawing in deep breaths of air, blowing out his cheeks, slowly letting the air out between pursed lips. When the procession passed the spot where I was standing I got a glimpse of the punished man's back through the row of soldiers. It was something indescribable: striped, wet, crimson, unnatural. I could not believe it was part of a human body.

"'God in heaven!' murmured the blacksmith standing next to me.

"The procession moved on. The blows kept falling from both sides on the cringing, floundering creature, the drum kept beating, the fife shrilling, and the tall, stately colonel walking firmly beside his victim. Suddenly the colonel stopped and went quickly over to one of the soldiers.

"'Missed? I'll show you!' I heard him say in a wrathful voice. 'Here, take this! And this!' And I saw his strong hand in its suede

glove strike the small weak soldier in the face
because the man's lash had not come down hard
enough on the crimson back of the Tatar.

" 'Bring fresh whips!' shouted the colonel.
As he spoke he turned round and caught
sight of me. Pretending not to recognize me,
he gave a vicious, threatening scowl and
turned quickly away. I felt so ashamed that
I did not know where to look, as if I had been
caught doing something disgraceful. With my
eyes fixed on the ground I hurried home.
All the way I kept hearing the rolling of the
drum, the shrilling of the fife, the words,
'Have mercy, brothers,' and the wrathful,
self-confident voice of the colonel shouting,
'Here, take this! And this!' And the aching of
my heart was so intense as to be almost
physical, making me feel nauseated, so that
I had to stop several times. I felt I must throw
up all the horror that this sight had filled me
with. I do not remember how I reached home
and got into bed, but the moment I began
to doze off I saw and heard everything all
over again. I jumped up.

" 'There must be something he knows that
I do not know,' I said to myself, thinking of the
colonel. 'If I knew what he knows, I would
understand, and what I saw would not cause
me such anguish.' But rack my brains as I might,
I could not understand what it was the colonel
knew, and I could not fall asleep until evening,
and then only after having gone to see a friend
and drinking myself into forgetfulness.

"Do you suppose I concluded that what I had seen was bad? Nothing of the sort. 'If what I saw was done with such assurance and was accepted by everyone as being necessary, it means they know something I do not know,' was the conclusion I came to, and I tried to find out what it was. But I never did. And not having found out, I could not enter military service, as it had been my intention to do, and not only military service, but any service at all, and so I turned out to be the good-for-nothing, that you see."

"We know very well what a 'good-for-nothing' you turned out to be," said one of the guests. "It would be more to the point to say how many people would have turned out to be good-for-nothing had it not been for you."

"Now that's a foolish thing to say," said Ivan Vasilyevich with real vexation.

"Well, and what about your love?" we asked.

"My love? From that day on my love languished. Whenever we went out walking and she smiled that pensive smile of hers, I could not help recalling the colonel out in the field, and this made me feel uncomfortable and unhappy, and I gradually stopped going to see her. My love petered out.

"So that is what sometimes happens, and it is incidents like this that change and give direction to a man's whole life. And you talk about environment," he said.

1903

REQUEST TO READERS

Raduga Publishers would be glad to have your opinion of this book, its translation and design and any suggestions you may have for future publications.

Please send all your comments to 17, Zubovsky Boulevard, Moscow, USSR.